DARK SAVIOR OF THE DRAGONS

ELYSIUM'S FALL – BOOK TWO

NIKKI McCORMACK

ISBN: 978-0-9983765-8-5
First Edition 2019

Published by
Elysium Books
Seattle, WA

Copyright © 2019 Nikki McCormack

All rights reserved. No part of this publication may be copied or reproduced in any format, by any means, electronic or otherwise, without prior consent from the copyright owner and publisher of this book.

This is a work of fiction. All characters, names, places and events are the product of the author's imagination or are used fictitiously.

Written by Nikki McCormack (https://nikkimccormack.com/)
Cover Design by Robert Crescenzio (https://robertcrescenzio.artstation.com/)
Typesetting and Design by Brian C. Short

I dedicate this book to my readers.
My books are a labor of love.
Thank you for letting me share them with you.

CHAPTER ONE

Raine prodded a large black beetle with the toe of one supple deer hide boot. The irritated insect flared its wings but stayed stubbornly put. She stared at the creature and shifted her seat on the stump outside of the small deserted cabin she and Siniva had claimed as their hideaway after fleeing the cave. The cabin did not have much to offer. It leaned a bit toward the west because of several rotted timbers at the base of that side and rain leaked through the roof in no less than seven different places. Still, no one had been living there, and it was within several hours hard ride of the village of Ithkan, not that she had dared to go near there yet. The mere thought of being around that many people all at once was terrifying.

She prodded the beetle again, and it moved a few steps this time, flaring its wings twice. It was remarkable that a creature the size of her thumb should be so stubborn it would ignore the possible threat from something so much larger than it. Was that courage or ignorance?

A small cloud passed over, casting a shadow on them for a moment. Shifting onto her heel, Raine lifted her boot toe up over the beetle, throwing it into even deeper shade. This time the beetle inched forward until its head was out from under the shadow of the offending boot.

Hydra, the magnificent white stallion with his black mane and tail, that had belonged to her father, Dephithus, was grazing nearby. Now he threw his head up and perked his ears. Raine looked in the direction he was staring and held her breath to listen. Seconds later, pounding hoof beats of a fast-moving horse reached her. She watched with a deepening scowl as Siniva galloped into view, heading her direction at high speed. When he drew near, bouncing haphazardly on the back of the tolerant animal, she could make out the angry glower that set his red-bronze eyes aflame. The beetle was forgotten before the unnerving anticipation of an approaching confrontation.

For some reason, the prospect of an argument with Siniva left her more nervous than facing her captors in the cave ever had. Like Theruses at that time, Siniva was a dragon bound in human form, but Theruses had been more intimidating to look upon. Siniva looked somewhat more human, where Theruses had been more beast. Still, she had grown up around Theruses. She barely knew Siniva, and that made his anger more alarming. Before Theruses killed him, her father had left her in Siniva's care out of desperation to help her escape. Once they were free of the cave, the man-shaped dragon brought her here and left her.

She stood up, determined to appear more confident than she felt. A crunching sound accompanied the crack and squish under her foot. The sensation seemed to pass through the thin deer hide and shoot up her leg, coming to rest as a twinge of nausea in her stomach. Perhaps that answered the question of courage versus ignorance.

Lifting the boot, she grimaced down at grisly remains of the once beetle, a twinge of guilt tightening her chest. If the creature insisted on being so stubborn, then perhaps it deserved its fate, but she could think of no way in which her boot had earned this slime. Diligently, she rubbed the bottom of her boot on the grass, vibrant green with recent rains, while Siniva pulled his mount to a stuttering stop, the animal tossing its head in protest of the uneven pressure on the bit. He swung off before the horse was fully stopped and stumbled forward a few steps, forgetting again that he was not at all skilled in the arts of horsemanship. After a quick recovery, he turned his burning gaze on her and growled.

She could not stop herself from flinching. His unkempt bronze-red hair was in wild disarray. That combined with the similarly colored scaling that highlighted his cheekbones and temples and the burn of anger in his catlike eyes made him look even less human than normal.

It made no sense that his appearance increased her unease. She also had slit pupils and areas of scaling, all of which were a strangely metallic brassy black like her hair. Then again, unlike him, she was not actually a dragon, she had merely been imbued with enough of their power at her conception to have acquired some unusual physical traits.

"What kind of half-wit are you?" Siniva roared.

Now that she faced his anger head on, it occurred to her that being a human with a few dragon traits was a lot different than being an actual dragon trapped in human shape. The latter had to be torturous. To be a magnificent beast with the ability to fly trapped in this awkward, ungainly form. A swell of pity made her hold her silence since he obviously had much to say, but her own anger simmered under the surface, ready to come to her defense.

"Someone came into town last night claiming they had seen a strange girl out this way dancing with daemons. When I left, a mob of villagers was ready to come out here and drive away the daemon-girl. Do you think it's going to be easy to find another place to stay? Do you?"

"I was bored," she defended, trying to ignore the growing warmth in her cheeks. "There's nothing to do out here."

Siniva started to say something else while his mount wandered off toward where Hydra was grazing. After a few seconds, he shut his mouth, glancing after the animal. He drew in a deep breath and exhaled, then he turned back and gave her a long piercing look. His brow furrowed up toward his thick red hair. "How can you look older already?"

"The moon has come and gone twenty-nine times since the day you rode to town to get supplies. I counted," she snapped.

"Most people don't age noticeably in a month."

She hugged herself, rubbing her arms, and shrugged. She was not normal. She knew that, but being here alone had let her ignore it for a while. His comment forced her to acknowledge that uncomfortable truth again.

He glanced away, taking a sudden interest in the listing cabin. The musty smell of moldering wood wafted to them on a light breeze.

"You weren't going to come back. What changed your mind?"

"Of course, I was going to come back," he muttered, avoiding her gaze.

Irritation flared like an annoying rash. "Why did you come back?"

"I can't connect to the dragon web, and I can't find the dragons without it."

"What does that have to do with me? Tell me," she growled. "You owe me that much."

He looked at her now. One eyelid began to twitch. "I was worried about you."

She gave him a hard look.

Siniva shifted his feet and stared hard over her shoulder at the forest now.

"If I learned anything from my time as a prisoner in the cave it was how to recognize when I'm being lied to," she pressed.

Siniva's chest rose and fell with a heavy sigh. The breeze picked up his hair, exposing more of the red-bronze scaling at his temple and along the edge of his strong jaw. "The dragons had to link you to the web to tie their freedom to you. I thought you might be able to access that link to help me find them."

Behind him, Hydra snorted and nipped at the other horse, driving the gelding away from the lush patch of grass he had claimed. A lock of brassy black hair fell into Raine's face. She brushed it away with a curt swipe.

"The dragons *used* my father and I to free themselves. Theruses *used* me to thwart them for a time. Now it's your turn. You were going to abandon me until you realized you could *use* me too." She felt the sting of tears in her eyes and clenched her teeth, determined to fight it.

Siniva nodded. "I can't say you're wrong. Though using you again isn't my first choice." He frowned at his human hands. "If only Vanuthan were still part of the web. She would find me and bring the dragons together."

"My grandmother?"

His quick mystified glance told her she had surprised him.

"Yes. I know Vanuthan. She's the Mother Dragon. She made my father and I what we are... were," she amended, reminding herself that, no matter how vivid his memories were in her mind, Dephithus was dead now. "I think I can find her."

"How?"

"I'm connected to her through the power she placed in me and the power she placed in my father that passed to me. With that connection and my parents' memories of the region to guide us, I believe I can find her."

Siniva took a step back from her, and her throat tightened. Was that fear in his eyes? What did she dread more, his judgment or the possibility that he might leave her again? Both equally perhaps.

"I remember things," she offered as a hasty explanation. "Things that happened to him. Things that happened to my mother. I remember them like I lived them, but the memories come in fragments. The bad ones are always stronger."

Siniva muttered something under his breath. She only caught enough to know that it was comprised of a few vulgarities. He finally shook his head at her. "You have ancestral memories too?"

Her chest opened. Suddenly she could breathe more freely. He knew what this was. That meant it was normal, not just another way in which she could be considered an aberration. "Yes! That's what it is."

"What have we made?" He stared at her now like a daemon had sprouted out of her forehead.

The brief relief vanished, and pressure wrapped around her chest again. "What's wrong?"

"Human children don't inherent memories from their parents. That's another trait of the dragons you apparently acquired through our meddling, just like your accelerated growth. You were supposed to be a child with enough power stored in you to free us. A human child. Not this."

The way he gestured at her then, with a look that was somewhere between dread and disgust, made Raine back away a few steps. She could feel the weight of this strange world pressing down on her shoulders, trying to drive her down. To crush her will as it had crushed her mother's. She knew nothing about this world beyond what she gleaned through her parents' memories. This man—this dragon—before her was not in those memories. She was alone here, and it terrified her. Was this the feeling of despair that had driven her mother to suicide?

Siniva looked at her, and something changed in his regard then. His expression softened. He started to reach out to her, then his hand stopped and sank back to his side. "I apologize. We aren't all that different. The council of dragons used me too. Now I'm trapped in this form, and the atrocity I committed to get here will haunt me forever. We're both alone, you and I."

She watched him warily. He shifted his feet like a child caught doing something wrong, and she found herself wondering exactly how old he was. Dragons reached physical maturity very quickly after all.

He lifted his shoulders then and stood tall, meeting her eyes steadily now. "I shouldn't have left you, Raine. That was wrong. But maybe we can help each other. If you can lead me to Vanuthan, I believe she might be able to help both of us. She's the Mother Dragon, after all, and a dear friend."

"She's my grandmother," Raine persisted.

"In a sense," Siniva granted. "What say you? We can't stay here?"

Raine shrugged. What else was she going to do?

Siniva grinned then. He was roguishly handsome when he grinned like that, though he also looked less trustworthy. For all that she wanted to accept the comradery he was offering, she could not bring herself to smile back.

"I'll get my things and saddle Hydra."

Siniva's grin faltered. He glanced over at the warhorse. "Dephithus stole Hydra from King Allondis. It might be a mistake to go galivanting around the region on a stolen horse."

Defensive anger swelled. She remembered Dephithus going to see the new stallion his mother had given him for his sixteenth birthday. Remembered the excitement he had felt. A joyful anticipation drawing him out to see his new horse at the end of a wonderful birthday. She also remembered what had happened to him that night. The cruel gift Amahna and Rakas had forced upon him. How it had changed everything.

Daenox began to seep up from the ground beneath her, the violet tendrils of daemon power rising to her anger.

"Hydra was not stolen. He was a birthday gift for my father."

Siniva backed up and held out a placating hand, fear rising in his eyes again. "All right. Keep him for now. We'll figure it out when we get closer to Imperious."

Raine gave a sharp nod. The daenox dropped away, sinking back into the ground. "I'll get my things."

She ran inside and grabbed her scant belongings. The ratty clothes she had been wearing when she escaped the caves that she could not bring herself to throw away though they were already too small, a little moldering straw-stuffed doll that she imagined had belonged to a child who once lived in the cabin, and a dagger that Siniva had left with her. She stuffed these things into her father's saddle packs that still held the clothes he had been carrying and some of his other travel provisions. While she packed, tears stung her eyes again.

Trapped in the cave for the first five years of her life, she spent a lot of time perusing the memories of her parents. Their childhood together had been happy, and she imagined it would be magnificent to experience the world they lived in. To be free and learn of all the wonders life could hold. But there was no wonder to behold in this place for a child who looked like a teenager and had the unusual dragonkin traits she had. They were traits her father also shared, but things had changed dramatically since the peaceful times of his childhood. There was only fear and persecution here.

The light of day still felt foreign to her. Even the grey,

rainy days that had come often since that first sunny day when she escaped the cave left her feeling exposed and vulnerable. There was none of the comforting closeness of the solid rock walls she had grown up with.

Dark nights put her more at ease, but even then, she could feel the endless space around her. No rock walls. No prison bars. She was exposed to everything. Her only comfort came from charming daemons as she had done to entertain herself during her years in the cave. She tried to keep hidden, only going on the very darkest nights when she was sure no one would be wandering the woods. It felt so good to be surrounded by their twisted forms, to have them swarm around her, creating a buffer between her and all that open space, that she sometimes stole away on nights when the cover of dark was not so complete. Nights like last night.

Hydra perked up when she walked out with the saddlebags, his fine ears so erect the tips almost touched. A small circle of warmth opened within her, like that she had begun to feel for the young woman, Kara, who cared for her in the cave. Kara who, like her father, had died trying to help her get free.

Hydra appreciated her in some way. The day she emerged from the caves into the blinding sunlight, the stallion had been attracted to something in her. Did he sense some aspect of Dephithus in her or was it something else? Something related to the dragon power in her perhaps. Regardless, she felt a connection to the horse that was somehow stronger than that she had felt even with Kara. The stallion did not judge her, and he had attacked Theruses in his dragon form to protect her. That was a lot to ask of any creature. She would not discard him out of fear of who might recognize him, and she would fight anyone who tried to take him away.

When she went to saddle him, the stallion started to

prance in place. She popped his reins lightly once, correcting him without being harsh. He stopped prancing and nudged her with his nose almost hard enough to knock her over.

Raine laughed and pushed his soft nose away. "Patience. These things are heavy."

When she turned to pick up the saddle, Siniva was already there. He popped the heavy thing up on Hydra's back like it weighed a feather and started to tighten it for her.

"In a hurry?" she snapped.

He stepped back from the partly tightened cinch, throwing his hands up before turning to stalk over to his mount. "I was only trying to help."

"I can manage on my own."

She heaved on the cinch, knowing she could not tighten it as much as Siniva could. It did not matter. She had a natural balance that made it unnecessary to overtighten like he did out of fear of sliding off, and she had used some of the month he was gone to get used to working with the stallion. Then again, she could not short Siniva for not being able to ride well. He had spent the part of his life that he was not imprisoned in stone with the ability to fly. Why would you learn to ride a horse when you could fly?

She fastened on the saddlebags and checked the cinch one more time. Hydra tensed as a hatchet flew past her head, hitting the wall of the cabin.

"There she is!"

For someone who looked rather like he was having a seizure whenever he got on a horse, Siniva managed to spring up with stunning speed, his seat touching down in the saddle before the thrown hatchet hit the ground alongside the cabin. Over Hydra's back, Raine saw villagers storming through the trees carrying anything that might pass as a weapon—hatchets, pitchforks, the odd sword, kitchen knives. They were here to kill the evil that had invaded their area. They were here to kill her. This was the world outside the cave and, so far, it was not that charming.

Hydra tossed his head and struck the ground with one hoof, ready to move. Heeding his warning, she swung up on his back and corrected him quickly when he started to turn toward the approaching mob.

"No fighting today, my friend."

She urged him after Siniva who was already kicking his mount up to a run. Hydra lunged after the other animal with so much power she had to grab the front of the saddle to keep from being left behind. She had been practicing with him a lot, but she had only been on a horse for the first time a little over a month ago when she took the big war-horse from outside the cave. Fortunately, now that Hydra was focused on pursuing the other horse, she could straighten herself out and get her balance.

An arrow whistled past her head and sank into the side of Siniva's saddlebag. At least one of them had a bow. Behind them, she heard people shouting to burn down the cabin. There was little point in that since she suspected they would not be coming back, but perhaps it would give the villagers a sense of satisfaction if they got to destroy something. She did not care much so long as that something was not her. A few more arrows flew past, missing their marks, and shouted threats flew after them, hitting a little closer than the arrows. She was a freak of nature, an abomination, a daemon creature that deserved to die. Their hatred and fear drove into her with stinging accuracy. This was the world she had to find a place in.

She almost missed her prison in the cave.

*

Since their pursuers were on foot, they did not have to keep up the reckless gallop for long. Siniva eased them down to an extended trot after a time, making it a little easier to spot low hanging branches before getting struck across the head. Spider webs were another matter. He was taller than her and riding in the lead, but somehow, she still got a fair number of the nearly invisible webs and a couple of resident spiders on her face.

She was placing one of those spiders on the back of her saddle now. It seemed cruel to throw the poor little creatures to the ground, so she figured they could ride along and relocate themselves when they finally stopped.

"Why wasn't my father's birth enough to free the dragons?"

Siniva was silent for several strides, then he slowed his mount to a walk and let her move up beside him. Hydra laid his ears back and bared his teeth in warning at the other horse. He did not like the other animal for some reason. Maybe it was a stallion thing.

"You have to understand a little more about dragons to understand that. When dragons are free in the world, the dragon web that connects us all generates power through our interactions within the world. Every time a dragon kills to feed, some of the power of that animal's death is absorbed by the web. Every time a dragon sleeps in the spring grass, some of the power of the life growing around it is absorbed by the web. Power is accumulated in small amounts through every dragon. That power adds up quickly when we are free. Because we were imprisoned in stone for all those years, the web could only absorb a reduced amount of power from the environment immediately around our statues.

"It took twenty years for the dragon web to accumulate the power Vanuthan placed in Dephithus at the moment of his conception, but it was not a strong enough connection to the outside world for us to use it to break free. For the next almost seventeen years, we waited while more power slowly accumulated in the web. When Dephithus conceived a child, some of the dragon power in him would be passed down. If we also placed the power we had gathered in that child, the resulting pool of power would be enough."

Raine gritted her teeth. One of the most vivid memories she had of her parents' lives was one of the last. It was an awkward memory because it was the memory of her conception. A moment she felt should remain only between her parents. It was a powerful memory, however, because there was so much emotion in it, and it refused to stay dormant. For her mother, Myara, there was so much love and hope. Hope that their coupling in a loving way meant Dephithus could be brought back from the darkness that was overtaking him. For Dephithus, it was love, pain, and despair. His extraordinary love for Myara had given him the strength to fight the daemon-seed within him for a short time. But he had known as he was joining with her, as he battled the pain and the hatred boiling over inside him, that it might push him over the brink. Still, he had loved her too much not to try, and he had indeed succumbed to the daemon-seed after that. She knew that because the next time Myara saw him, there had been madness in his eyes, and he had murdered a friend of hers in front of her.

Siniva continued, oblivious to her inner struggle. "Through that child—you—the dragon web would have a substantial connection to the world outside our prisons. We hoped that connection would be strong enough to free us once you were born into the world."

"Why Dephithus?"

"I wish I could tell you there was some great purpose in his choosing. The truth is, his proximity to Vanuthan's prison played a large role. The Mother Dragon has the most natural power in the realms of birth and nurturing. Having her place the power in the child meant that it would be more potent. Dephithus was also conceived when we were ready to move forward with our plan, and he was born to a family that had the means to protect him and teach him to protect himself. He would have advantages that many other children might not have."

It was a little disconcerting to think that her fate was decided largely by chance. "How did it work though? The freeing of the dragons. And why did Theruses go free when I was freed, but you and Vanuthan did not? Didn't he break from the web long before the two of you did?"

Siniva gave her a sideways glance. "You're full of questions today."

She answered his look with a glower. "You left me alone for a month. I couldn't spend all that time worrying over how I was going to survive without you. What did you expect? I think you owe me a few answers."

"I suppose I do." He faced forward again and looked around them for a few minutes in silence, gazing at the changing leaves getting ready to fall around the narrow forest track they were following. "Like I said, the power placed in you is linked to the dragon web. In Dephithus, we simply couldn't put enough power in him for his birth alone to overwhelm the power that kept us imprisoned. He was too weak a link to the outside world. The power we were able to put in you, combined with the power you inherited from him, was enough to truly open the web to the outside world once you were free, and that let us overwhelm the power keeping us imprisoned.

"Theruses broke from the web long before the dragons were imprisoned, but he didn't break away completely. He maintained a small connection to the web, and because of that, even though he was imprisoned with the daenox, his freedom was still tied to the dragons. Vanuthan and I broke from the web during our imprisonment. Because the web had become, in a sense, part of that imprisonment, we had to sever the link completely to free ourselves. With the severing of that link, our freedom is no longer tied to the web or the other dragons. We are in prisons now of our own making."

A shadow fell over his features then. The handsome man with his burning eyes took on a brooding look, so she thought it best not to press the subject. She had enough worries of her own without digging into his.

"Do you think…" She swallowed against a swell of panic. The question had haunted her through most of her years in the cave. "Do you think the daemon-seed in my father…"

It was her father's memories that pummeled her now. The fear, the pain, the hatred. The overwhelming shame.

I was going to see Hydra that night. It happened because of him.

Her hands tightened on the reins. The stallion tossed his head. So much confusion. So much anger. Her breath came faster, panic and the need to flee making her heart pound in her chest. Blood thumped in her ears so she could no longer hear the soft sounds of the forest.

"Raine. Are you all right?"

Someone touched her arm, and she cried out, jerking away so hard she almost unseated herself. She stared at the stranger next to her, breath coming in gasps. She shook herself hard, fighting back memories.

"Siniva?"

His brow furrowed. They had stopped moving at some point. "What happened?"

"Memories," she breathed. Her pulse was still running wild.

Siniva paled and seemed to shrink before her. His haunted look told her he had guessed what memories tormented her. "We underestimated the reach and power of Theruses's followers. We had no idea they could or would do such a thing. But no, I don't think the daemon-seed in your father passed anything to you."

When he looked at her his eyelid was twitching again. Did he even know he had such an obvious tell?

She decided to let it go this time.

He faced forward and urged his mount to a walk again.

She let Hydra follow.

"You grew up immersed in the daenox," Siniva continued. "I don't think that needs to be a bad thing. You can manipulate it with great skill, like that remarkable barrier you made to deflect Theruses. You can manipulate the daemons as well. Let that be a strength, not a weakness."

Raine suspected his words were as much for his comfort as for her own. She nodded and glanced down at her hands. Hands that had done nothing good in the world. Hands that played with daenox to entertain daemons. Hands that belonged to a creature raised in a lair of cruelty and hatred.

She had their memories. She knew her mother had been a good person to the end of her days, as tragic as that end was. She knew Dephithus had been a good person before the daemon-seed changed him. What was she but a child that had grown up in darkness?

She reached out and grabbed a leaf off one of the trees. It cracked and fell apart when she started to crush it into a ball like her parents had done in some of her favorite of their memories. She stared at the bits of brown leaf as they fell onto her legs and the saddle and slowly blew away.

The younger the leaf, the better the ammunition.

"That's right," she murmured, and grabbed a leaf that had not yet turned off the next tree. This one crushed down better. She tucked the resulting ball alongside her leg then went for a second one.

"You get to choose, Raine."

She glanced at the dragon beside her, trapped, possibly forever, in an almost human form. Trapped because everything his kind had tried to do to free themselves had gone wrong and he was chosen to pay the price.

"It's not up to the dragons and the daenox anymore. You get to choose who you are now."

Raine suddenly wanted to reach out and hug him. Maybe it was true. Maybe her past meant nothing now. Or maybe it was not true. Maybe she was broken because of the daemon-seed in her father and her years living in the daenox-saturated cave. Either way, she appreciated his words.

She collected three more leaves that she crumpled

into balls while Siniva rode alongside her, glancing over curiously at her growing collection.

"What are those for?" He finally asked while peeling another spiderweb from his face.

Raine grinned and started pummeling him with leaf bombs.

Darkin dug a heel into his mount, moving the animal's hindquarters around to block the daemon-wolf charging up behind him. The gelding was trained in combat and aware enough that he struck out with his hind legs, catching the daemon-wolf with a skull-cracking blow to the head while Darkin focused on the warrior in front of him. He feinted to one side, dodging his opponent's blade, and followed with a powerful thrust that sunk through the warrior's worn leather armor and into his abdomen. He twisted the blade before ripping it free. In the back of his mind, he thanked Dephithus yet again for those mounted combat lessons. They were paying off frequently in this tumultuous new age.

The opposing warrior dropped his blade and curled forward, bringing a face covered with festering sores much closer than Darkin would have liked. Slipping a foot out of his stirrup, he brought his leg up and kicked the other man's horse, making it lunge forward and away, so the mortally wounded warrior fell between the two mounts instead of on Darkin.

He spun his mount again and found himself staring down the dangerous end of Suva's crossbow. She pulled the trigger, either planning to kill him or trusting him to duck, which he did. He felt the bolt's passage disrupt his hair then there was a thud and a choking sound.

Glancing over his shoulder, he watched another warrior go down with a bolt in his throat. She was getting quite good with the weapon, but he made a mental note to talk to her later about the risks she took with her timing, especially when he was involved.

Another couple of daemon-wolves and one more warrior lay dead or dying on the ground around them. It had been a small group. Perhaps scouts or some stragglers who had wandered off from the main army. It was lucky, really, since only he and Suva had come out here.

He glanced back toward the trees in the distance. Kovial and two other soldiers waited there. Kovial and one other were injured too badly to continue fighting, so they were set to turn back toward Imperious, but this was where most sightings of the main force of the daemon army came from. It looked like the army might have moved on, but there was a chance they had left some clues behind as to where they were going. He and the others had decided it was worth having a look.

"Darkin."

Suva had dismounted and was taking a closer look at some dead Legion soldiers they had found before the daemon-wolves and warriors came over the rise and attacked them. Darkin stared in the direction they had come from. He would have sworn there was no one for miles in that direction when they rode out here.

"Darkin."

After adjusting the cloth he had over his nose and mouth to block out some of the stench, he moved his mount over beside Suva who was kneeling now next to an overripe body.

She looked up at him, a hint of distress in her blue-grey eyes. "This is Lady Avaline."

"She and her troop were declared dead years ago. There wouldn't be anything left but bones if she were laying out here that whole time."

"I know. It doesn't make any sense, but it is her."

He took a good long look at the woman soldier lying there. Death had not been kind to her, but it rarely was. Strangely, it looked as though the bodies here had not been fed upon by scavengers. Some decay was certainly starting to do its work, but even if he had not recognized the somewhat distorted features, the insignias on her armor would have confirmed her identity.

"Unfortunately, I think you're right."

"Ugh," Suva grunted. "We can't take them all, but I suppose we should try to take her back with us."

"I'd really rather you didn't," another voice said.

They both started, Suva jumping so violently she almost fell on top of the late Lady of Imperious. Behind them, a man about their age had appeared, sitting comfortably on his mount. His dusty blond hair blended well with his simple tan garments. He might have been any young man from any village, but there was something in his blue eyes that chilled Darkin. To his left, a much younger boy with similar features sat his mount with the same unnerving calm. To his right, a hideous abomination of something that might once have been a man, but now appeared to be more of a skinless, partially rotten animated corpse, sat on a horse that was no less offensive to eyes and nose. The undead man-thing clicked his teeth together several times, moist muscle and sinew working over the bones of his jaw.

Darkin swallowed hard, placing one hand on his sword hilt, and gestured with the other in the vague direction of Avaline's corpse. "She's—"

"I know very well who she was. I've been preserving her and her troop here for some time. Legion soldiers come following rumors of daemons and undead. I find seeing her there demoralizes and disorients them." His expression turned thoughtful as he looked down at the dead Lady of Imperious. "Perhaps it would be even more effective if I raised her."

Bastard.

Whoever this man was, Darkin already disliked him. "Where did you come from?"

The man chuckled and spread his arms wide. "I've been watching you for a little while. We all have."

The air behind him rippled like a mirage for several seconds, then, gradually, it dissolved like sand, and they could see the army. Thousands of warriors and daemon beasts stretched as far as he could see on the flats beyond the man and his two companions. He could hear them now too. The noises of leather, hoofbeats on dry ground, warriors talking, and beasts fighting over scraps of carrion. There was a smell too. An even stronger stench of sickness and decay wafting toward them on the warm air. It was all he could do not to retch.

Darkin eased his mount back from Avaline's body and motioned Suva to do the same. She did as directed, though she lifted her jaw in subtle defiance. She never did like to give quarter to anyone.

"Why send only a few to fight us when you could have easily killed us?"

"I didn't feel like killing you. This was a good bit of entertainment. You handled yourselves well."

Darkin said nothing and Suva chose to follow his example.

The young man smiled. It was unnervingly friendly. "I'm Kyouin, High Priest of the daenox and leader of this army."

"Pleasure's all yours," Suva answered, lifting her lip in a snarl of disgust.

Kyouin laughed.

A muscle in Darkin's shoulder started to twitch with every click of the undead rider's teeth. "What now?"

Kyouin's gaze moved to Suva, perhaps drawn by her

attitude. "You will agree to leave these corpses here, and I will offer you the opportunity to join my army. You fight well. It never hurts to be on the winning side."

Darkin saw the flicker of interest in Suva's eyes. He felt it too. It was best to be on the winning side, and this man with his motley army was likely to win if nothing changed soon. But he had seen some of Kyouin's human warriors up close. Most of them looked sickly. Some were so bad they had boils and sores on their skin like the last one he had killed. Another he fought before had reddish pus running from his bloodshot eyes. He suspected it was some reaction to all the daemons and the daenox surrounding them or perhaps the many corpses, animate and otherwise, they were interacting with. No matter the reason, that was not a look he coveted for himself or his companions.

He glanced at Suva. She looked up at him, meeting his eyes. She took another step back. Whatever she saw in his face was adequate warning, and they had fought together enough to have built up a bond of trust.

"We'll consider your offer. We would be fools not to, but now is not the time."

Kyouin gave a nod that said he had expected as much. "Sensible enough. Timing is everything." He chuckled to himself, but the humor vanished a second later. "I will allow you and your soldiers back in the trees to leave here unharmed. You will take no dead with you, but you will take a message. You see, I've grown bored of our quaint village near here, and to be honest, it isn't adequate to meet the needs of my army. It should take you around fourteen days to get back to Imperious. Tell your little King Allondis that I will give him one month and fourteen days, starting the moment you leave here. At the end of that time, I will arrive at the gates of Elysium, and he will give me his crown. If he does not, I will take it from him."

Darkin forced himself not to look at the undead warrior on his undead horse. He forced himself not to look at the malformed daemon-dogs that had come up and were now milling about around and under Kyouin's horse or any of the beasts and sickly men farther in the distance. For the moment, he would not allow himself to see what was coming. It would not do to allow this man to see how much it unnerved him.

What he did see that he found rather curious was the hilt of the serpent dagger Dephithus used to carry poking up from a sheath at Kyouin's waist. He did not let his eyes linger on it. However the other man had come by the dagger, it seemed wise not to risk lengthening the encounter in case Kyouin changed his mind about killing them.

He inclined his head slightly to Kyouin. "Your message will be delivered."

"Good. And Darkin," he said, making it clear he had been close enough to hear them talking after their fight, "if your king does as I ask, I will make you an officer in my army."

Darkin merely gave another nod and turned away, not looking at Avaline's body. It was only a body after all. The Lady Avaline was long gone from this place with the many others who had died here. Suva mounted up. They rode away, keeping to an easy lope. He did not stop feeling like something was going to attack him from behind until they were well away into the trees and had slowed their pace to avoid injuring their mounts.

"What did you think of his offer?" Suva asked under her breath, aware that they were getting close to where the other three waited.

"What would you have done if I hadn't ducked under your shot fast enough?"

She jerked her shoulders in a quick shrug that shifted her lengthening blond hair. "I would've mourned you."

"I'm serious."

She glanced over at him, her cold eyes narrowing. "So am I."

"You saw those warriors. Most of them look ghastly ill. I think his offer was a fine idea as a last resort, but I'd be more likely to desert Imperious and make a run for the Illtide Coast," Darkin answered, being more frank than usual. He had considered the idea several times before this and would be surprised if she had not as well.

Suva nodded. "I saw the recognition in your eyes. I knew you would move out of the way."

"I might have hesitated," he countered.

"It was a risk, but I need risks to know I'm alive."

"I think I have more than enough risk in my life. I don't need to spend time worrying about whether I'm going to die at the hands of my enemies or my friends."

Her shrug was slower this time, more thoughtful. "Fair enough. I'll try to be more careful."

"Swear?"

She glanced over at him again, her lips curving in a wicked little smirk. "Don't push your luck."

The smirk vanished a few minutes later when they rode back into the rough little camp. Her brother, Kovial, lay moaning, sweat beaded on his brow. His arm, mangled by a blow from a heavy mace, was wrapped in bloody bandages. The other injured soldier, the Lance Knight who led their troop, lay unnaturally still. The uninjured soldier they had left behind to keep an eye on their injured companions was in the process of closing the Lance Knight's eyes. They exchanged a glance while Suva hurried over to her brother. The Lance Knight's death promoted Darkin to leader of their sad little troop.

Darkin dismounted. "Let's get him tied onto his horse. I don't want to leave any more bodies for those bastards to use."

There was much grunting, cursing, and sweating involved in getting the Lance Knight up over the saddle. He had been a solid man. Six feet of powerful muscle. Darkin felt a bit sorry for his horse, but he refused to give Kyouin another Legion body for his army. For all that the strange young priest had let them go, Darkin found himself developing a more personal hatred for the man with every second that passed. He could not quite say why, but he wanted to see the daenox priest suffer. Perhaps it was just the man's arrogance. Perhaps it was the fact that he could have killed the two of them so easily and chose not to, letting them ride away perfectly aware of how vulnerable and inadequate they were in that moment.

He left the other soldier to secure the dead man and walked over to join Suva. Her teeth were gritted, and her lips pulled back in a fierce grimace. She was fighting tears, at least he was willing to bet that was what that expression meant. For all that she was tough as iron, she did have a weakness, and her brother was it.

"Kove," she murmured, brushing his sweat-dampened hair out of his face. "We have to go now."

"I can't," he gasped, crying out when he tried to sit up despite his words.

"You have to," Darkin stated. He reached out to grab Kovial's good arm. Suva gave his hand a solid smack. He drew back, glaring at her. "We have to move."

"I've got it under control."

Darkin backed away. He watched for a few minutes while Suva helped her brother into a sitting position amidst many cries of pain and grunts. Then he went and got Kovial's horse ready, bringing it over. Suva let him help her get Kovial the rest of the way to his feet and up on his mount. Darkin dug a rope out of one of the packs.

"Kovial?" He waited until the other man met his eyes. "The movement of the horse is going to jar that wound, and it's going to hurt. We need to tie you to your saddle in case you pass out."

Kovial nodded, already wavering slightly in the saddle, and managed a weak smile for Suva. "Remember when you used to threaten to tie me to a horse in my sleep and send it running toward the horizon?"

Suva nodded and swallowed hard. When they were done tying Kovial so he would not topple off, they started toward their own mounts.

"Looks like you've got a little something in your eye," Darkin remarked. "If you need a moment to take care of that, we can wait."

Suva nodded and turned away, wiping roughly at her eyes.

Raine stared up at the stars. Night was better. More than a month of exposure to the daylight, even on the days it was overcast, had not gotten her used to how bright it was outside the cave. She felt like the whole world could see her in the daylight. There was no privacy. No place to hide. On the sunnier days, the light made her eyes hurt a bit still. Nighttime felt more like being in a cave again, if a rather enormous one. On clear nights, she liked to stare up at the moon and stars. They lit the sky, but not with the same offensive intensity as the sun. The night was cooler too, like in the cave.

Daytime always left her feeling emotionally drained and weary. When night fell, however, she found it hard to stay asleep. She wanted to be a part of it. She wanted to watch the stars and listen to the sounds. Nocturnal insects, bats, and owls created a haunting chorus. The ground critters that came out at night added their own voices on occasion. She could sometimes hear them swishing and crackling through the brush. Even the steady sound of Siniva breathing in his sleep was a pleasant addition to the music of the night.

His breathing was not always steady though. Something tormented him. A memory perhaps that made him moan and thrash in his sleep at times. When his sleep was restless like that, she could see tears streaming from his closed eyes. After their second night at the cabin, she had tried asking him about it. He had grown angry, denying the restless slumber, and turned to brooding. The next day he left, saying only that he was going for supplies. She knew when he rode away that day that he did not mean to come back. Then he found he had a use for her, so he came back after all.

At least I'm useful. What would I have done if he hadn't changed his mind?

She scowled at the stars and got up from her bedroll. Drawing on daenox that ran deep in the ground, she wove it around her feet, muffling her footsteps with that power, and crept away from the camp. She wandered out to the slow-moving creek they had gotten water from before bedding down for the night. Crouching at the edge of the water, she began to draw on more daenox, pulling it up and into the water. She gave it the color it had always had in her mind at first, a deep purple, then made it begin to glow. The glow lit the water. She made it brighter, giving some of it a soft blue light and weaving that in with the purple, letting the color twist and eddy with the currents of the stream.

Adding more color, she held her hands out over the water, drawing the daenox up to her fingers and winding it around them. Turning her hands over, so the palms faced up, she began to shoot sprays of daenox infused water into the air above the creek, creating bright bursts of color that reflected in the eyes of the creatures that had come to watch. Her audience was varied—raccoons, a jorycat, a few squirrels and rabbits, even an owl. Among them were some that were so deformed by the daenox it was hard to tell what they had once been. All of them had the grey eyes of daenox infected beasts. Since coming into the world, she found that animals not already infected seemed to be repelled by her displays.

The creatures drew near and settled, resting to-gether to watch her show. Predator and prey lounging side-by-side, their natural conflict forgotten before their shared affliction and the calm her displays seemed to bring them. Raine smiled and made the patterns more elaborate, adding in additional colors. Her shows were much brighter now than they had been in the cave. She had seen more colors with her own eyes. Her father had given her the gift of that color when he helped set her free. He had also left her his stallion, which was why she tried to keep these shows away from the camp. She would never forgive herself if Hydra became daemon in-fected.

A daemon-wolf came and joined the others, rest-ing its head on folded paws to watch, entranced. The other creatures were so enthralled they did not notice the newcomer.

She expanded her display, weaving the colors higher and wider, watching them reflect in the grey eyes of her spectators.

"Raine!"

Siniva's frantic call warned her, but not soon enough. He burst through the bushes as she stopped the show. A large quantity of ordinary water fell back into the creek, the resulting spray cold wherever it hit her exposed skin, making her flinch. The creatures who had gathered made varied sounds of distress and sprinted or flew off deeper into the woods.

"What is wrong with you? Are you trying to get us killed?"

She touched the water, watching as a one last glow-ing violet tendril of daemon power reabsorbed in the creek bed. "Of course not. There's no one here to see."

Siniva's eyes glowed eerily. The tips of his mussed red hair created a halo around his head in the moon-light. "Let's pretend for a moment that we could be absolutely sure there's no one else in this part of these woods. That doesn't change the fact that you are drawing daemons in close to our camp. Daemons that could attack us while we sleep or infect the horses."

He was right, but she could not bring herself to admit that. Anger and disappointment at having to stop her display so suddenly made it hard to be sensible. She got to her feet. "Most daemon forms can't infect an animal the size of a horse."

"Given how much effort you're putting into not looking at me, I'd say you already know that's a pathetic defense."

She had been ready to dart around him, but now she stopped and made herself face him. "What am I supposed to do? This is the only thing that makes me feel at ease in this world. It chases away the bad memories and lets me sleep without nightmares."

"Why should you be so privileged?" He snapped.

"Whatever haunts you has nothing to do with me, so don't try to guilt me with it."

Siniva drew in a breath that somehow made him appear bigger than normal and she was reminded again how little she knew about him.

"It has everything to do with you. I gave up everything for you. To make sure you made it out of that cave alive."

Something ignited in her chest. She wanted to hurt him. Daenox pulsed through the ground beneath her, strong and vibrant and ready to do as she bid. "You gave up everything for the dragons," she snarled. "Not for me. It was never for me."

She did storm past him then. If she stayed, she might do something she would regret. Better to walk away before that happened. As it was, she could feel the daenox in the ground rising to meet each footfall as she stomped through the trees. Back at the camp she threw herself down on her bedroll and closed her eyes, but sleep did not come for a long time. At some point, she heard Siniva return. She pretended to be asleep, though she thought he would probably be able to tell by her breathing that she was still awake. That her heart was still racing. He said nothing. He walked up to the edge of the camp, and his footsteps stopped there. For a long time, he stood still, and it was all she could do not to squirm with unease at the desire to know what he was thinking. Eventually, he went back to his own bedroll. At some point after that, sleep took her.

When morning came, they ate a meager meal in silence, breaking off some bread and sharing dried meat and nuts. Part of her wanted to talk about what had happened last night. A larger part did not want to talk about it ever again. He had been right about the riskiness of her behavior, but he was subdued now. That was enough to tell her she was right as well. It had never been about her, and it still was not. Whatever he had given up to free her had ultimately been done to free the dragons. Now it was about finding a way to free himself.

When they finished eating, they stood up in silent accord and packed their things back on the horses. When he was done, Siniva stood staring into one saddle-bag. His horse shifted its weight from one back foot to the other. Raine thought the animal might fall asleep there before Siniva got around to saying what was on his mind.

"Hm." He fished around in the bag with one hand and stuck his face down closer to the opening as if he hoped to find some hidden secret inside.

"We need supplies." She moved around Hydra, tightening the straps that held her sleeping roll in place on the back of his saddle.

"Ah. Well..."

"Don't hedge. Neither of us is a great hunter, and we didn't have that much to start with," she stated.

Siniva's head snapped up, his fire-colored eyes flaring to life. "I am an excellent hunter."

Raine rolled her eyes. "I'm sure you are, Great Dragon, but not in this form."

He shook his head at her. "You have no compassion." He let the flap of the saddlebag fall shut and fastened it closed. "But you're right. We need some supplies, and I'm virtually useless in this pitiful shell."

"Honestly, Siniva. It could be worse. You could be a five-year-old in a teenage body who's lived her entire life in a cave."

Siniva scowled at her, but he did not say anything this time.

She turned to scratch Hydra's head under his forelock. The big horse pushed into her hand, relishing the attention. "We should stop at the next town."

"We?"

"Last time you went to town without me, you almost didn't come back."

"But I did come back," he said, checking the tightness on his girth.

"Only after you decided I might be of some use to you." She came up on her toes to glare at him over Hydra's back now, but he was facing the other direction.

"Exactly. I know now that we need each other, so you have nothing to worry about."

Raine gathered the stallion's reins in her hand and swung up in the saddle. Hydra's muscles bunched with the excitement of doing something, so she turned him in a circle to get control of his head and remind him who was in charge, though she was not entirely convinced herself.

"Why should you go without me. It isn't like you don't look strange enough to draw unwanted attention."

He glanced up at her, his gaze touching quickly on her strange eyes and hair and the scaling at her temples. Pointing out everything that made her stand out without having to say a word. "That is precisely why you shouldn't come. One apparent dragonkin throwback is enough to make people uneasy. Two of us might incite panic."

"There's a hooded cloak in my pack. I could wear that. It was my father's, so it..."

Siniva was staring at her now, a strange look in his eyes. "That's perfect. If it fit your father, it should fit me reasonably well. It might be a little small, but—"

"I meant for me. It belonged to my father. Why would I give it to you?"

Siniva's face darkened, and he opened his mouth to speak. Then he glanced up at the bright blue sky. "It may not matter. If the weather is this nice when we reach the next village, either of us would draw as much attention wearing a full cloak as we would without. Let me think about it. The next village is probably a few days ride still from here."

He looked at her for a long moment then. Long enough that it started to make her uneasy. There was something in his regard, like he was seeing her differently, or perhaps just really seeing her for the first time.

"Have you ever slept in a bed?"

What an odd question. "No."

"Hm." He turned to finish his preparations.

A little blue butterfly fluttered down and landed on Hydra's mane. Its wings were outlined in precise black lines that enhanced the bright blue color. She held a finger out next to its legs. The delicate creature climbed up on her fingertip, its tiny footsteps tickling on her skin. She brought it up close to her face and watched its minuscule antennae flitting about. It was beautiful. So simple and perfect. It belonged here, in this forest.

"Do you think I'll ever find a place I belong?"

Siniva swung up in the saddle. His horse threw a back leg out wide to balance against the clumsy maneuver. "We should get going," he said once he was situated in the saddle.

Raine blew on the butterfly, sending it flying off. "That was a definite no."

Siniva exhaled frustration. "I don't know, Raine. I can't know that. But right now, we have more than enough obstacles in front of us that I think we should perhaps try taking them on one at a time."

Memories flashed through her mind. Dephithus in the Mother Tree with Myara. Dephithus earning the praise of the Legion Commander. Dephithus playing through the halls of the palace as a child. Dephithus dancing with so many potential suitors at his Dawning Day. He had the dragonkin traits too, but he had been loved and accepted until the daemon-seed ruined everything. Now it seemed she would never get the chance to know that kind of belonging. All because the dragons and Theruses chose to use him for their own ends. She could easily hate them for that, and yet, none of it would have happened if humankind had not imprisoned the dragons and the daenox in the first place. Perhaps they were the ones who deserved her hatred. Perhaps they all did.

A dark sensation seeped through her. It was sinister and unclean, and she did not like how it felt. Her throat tightened. She clenched her teeth against the sting of tears as Siniva led them back onto the narrow track through the woods.

K ovial was pale as a fish's belly with perhaps a tinge of green mixed in. He had passed out a few times along the way. Darkin was sick with the sound of his friend's agonized moans. He knew it must be tearing Suva apart. She looked almost as pale as her wounded brother. If they did not get him medical care soon, he was unlikely to survive this injury. Corbent Calid might have someone qualified to amputate the shattered limb, but Kovial had vehemently refused that option when he was still coherent enough to have an opinion. Now that he was largely incapable of expressing his opinion on the matter, Suva continued to defend his wishes. Even if they got him back to Imperious, Darkin suspected there was little chance of the limb being saved. They were just delaying the inevitable and increasing the risk that the injury would infect and kill him.

The original plan had been to ride past Corbent Calid. They were almost past the city now when Kovial bent over his horse's neck and retched. He passed out before he was through and started to fall back. He snapped back to awareness almost instantly, coughing violently. Darkin and Suva were off their horses and at his side in seconds, both pushing him forward so that anything still in his mouth could run clear and Darkin smacked him hard on the back. Kovial made a hideous noise in his throat and vomited again. When he finished, his face was wet with perspiration and tears of pain.

Darkin hopped back up on his horse and moved the animal up alongside Kovial's mount on the side away from the injury. Supporting his friend with one arm, he helped him drink from his waterskin so he could rinse his mouth. After a few rinses, Kovial sagged in the saddle, the ropes keeping him from falling out pulling taught.

Darkin gave Suva a hard look. "We're stopping here. He needs help."

Suva shook her head. "We can't. We need to get him back to Imperious."

The other soldier, Karik, who had kept mostly silent on the matter, moved closer then. "I don't believe he was asking."

Suva glared at Karik who shrugged it off and gave Darkin a nod that said he, at least, intended to follow his superior's orders.

Suva's glare snapped to Darkin. "You're not bringing rank into this. He's my brother."

"He's not going to make it to Imperious. I'll use my rank if you force me to."

"You're a daemon-spawn," she hissed.

He let her rage slide off him. She was hurting and afraid for her brother. She never had been any good at dealing with her emotions. "There's an inn at the end of town. Let's see if we can get a bed to let him rest a little and talk this out. He at least needs a break from the constant pain of riding."

The wild look in her eyes was such that he would not have been surprised if she grabbed Kovial's reins and tried to run away with him.

"Please, Suva."

They all turned to Kovial then. He looked ready to pass out again.

His voice was a raspy whisper. "Let me rest."

Suva turned away, though not before Darkin saw the tears welling in her eyes. Without speaking, she mounted up and started toward the inn at the end of town. They followed. Outside the stable, they were greeted by a young boy. Darkin swung down and handed the youth his reins.

"Give them some food and loosen the girths a little. We may not be here long."

The boy nodded and held a hand out. Darkin grudgingly handed him a coin and let him take his mount before going to help Suva get Kovial untied from his saddle. Karik held his horse steady while they helped him down, being careful of his injuries. Kovial was hot to the touch when Darkin ducked under his good arm to help him stagger to the door of the inn. The worn sign above the door depicted a worried looking man holding a frayed piece of rope as he fell down the side of a cliff. Large faded red letters introduced the building as The Drop Right Inn.

Inside a lonely musician with a lute and a pleasant voice sung a solemn travel song. Much of the conversation coming from several occupied tables stopped when they entered. Darkin was not surprised. Kovial looked like death. The skin on either end of the bloody bandages around his arm was swollen and black with bruising. A slim gentleman who had been reclining on a stool behind the bar was on his feet, coming toward them before anyone else had finished gawping. One of the serving women put her pitcher down and hurried over as well, drying her hands on the towel hanging at her waist.

"We need a room where he can rest," Darkin stated as they approached.

The man nodded and turned to the serving woman. "Get the room by the stairs ready and make sure the linens are clean."

She nodded and turned to her task.

The man turned back to them. "I'm Random, and this is my inn. It's an honor to serve the Legion. Can I get you some food and refreshment once he's settled?"

Darkin had not planned on it, but now that the innkeeper mentioned it, the smells of cooked food were making his mouth water and his stomach growl. He could also use a stiff drink.

"Please. Nothing fancy though. We're only soldiers."

Random chuckled. "We don't get fancy visitors here."

The serving woman was already returning. She gave Random a nod that he returned. "Thank you. Could you start some food and drink for our guests?"

She nodded again and cast a sad look at Kovial before disappearing through a doorway behind the bar.

Random turned back to them. "I'll show you the room."

It was odd that the innkeeper would go to such trouble himself, but Darkin was more concerned with getting Kovial's sagging weight off his shoulder right now. They followed him back to a room past the staircase leading up to the second floor. There were six cots in the room. It looked as if it were designed to cater to a party of travelers. A selection of clean bandages and other minimal medical supplies sitting on some of the side tables suggested it had been used for tending injuries on more than one occasion.

It took some time to get Kovial settled. When they were done, Darkin dismissed Karik to go eat and left Suva by the bedside. He walked over to Random who had stood watching from next to the doorway, a troubled look furrowing his brow. Darkin gestured down the dark hall with a jerk of his head, and they moved several doors down.

"You've something on your mind?" Darkin prompted, keeping his voice low so as not to be overheard by Suva.

Random shifted his feet and glanced around as though afraid the walls might be listening. "He looks bad, Sir."

"He is. Is there a decent surgeon in the city? I think that arm needs to come off."

Random glanced around again, his eyes lingering a few seconds longer on a door at the end of the hall. "There's a man here. He's been here for a while now. He doesn't talk much, but he has some… skills."

Darkin felt his chest tighten and his hand itched to reach for his sword. "Daenox."

Random grimaced. "I know it's what you're fighting, but I don't think he's out to hurt anyone. He's helped with some injured horses and a few badly wounded folks, discreetly. I can't promise anything, but I think he might be able to help your companion."

Suddenly a hooded man was standing in the shadows next to Random and Darkin started so hard he bit his own lip. He also had his blade out so fast he nearly cut off the hand Random had put up to stay him. Random jerked his hand back in surprise. The stranger, whose face was mostly hidden in shadow, did not react to the weapon now pointed at him.

"This was explicitly excluded from our deal," the man said under his breath.

Darkin could feel the stranger's gaze on him, measuring him. Disdaining him.

Random turned to the hooded man. "I know you said no soldiers, but—"

"But you've got a heart twice the size of your head. When it gets you killed, I don't want to be an incidental casualty."

Darkin found himself liking Random a bit more, suddenly. "I don't care who you are or how you do it. If you can help him, I'll see that you're well compensated."

The stranger drew back his hood then. He had refined features, long black hair, and eyes that were just as black in the dark hallway. He gave Darkin a dubious look as he gestured to the bared blade between them.

Darkin sheathed the blade.

The stranger grimaced and exhaled heavily. "Show me. I'll see if there's anything I can do."

Random put a hand on the man's shoulder. "Thank you, my friend."

The stranger shrugged the hand off irritably and started down the hall. Darkin followed him into the room and up to the bed where Kovial lay.

Suva, who had been sitting on the far side of the bed, stood and placed her hand on the hilt of one of the many daggers she wore. Her eyes narrowed. "Who's this?"

Her lip lifted in a silent snarl and the stranger mirrored the expression.

Darkin almost chuckled at that, but a groan from Kovial kept him on task. "He might be able to help."

"You cut off his arm, I'll cut off your head," Suva warned.

The stranger glanced at him.

Darkin smirked. "It wasn't a bad greeting, given the source and the situation. He's her brother."

The stranger held a hand out to Suva. "Give me one of those daggers. I need to remove these bandages so I can see what we're dealing with."

Suva stared at his hand like she had never seen such a thing in her life. For a few seconds, she looked conflicted. Then, when Darkin was ready to offer up his own dagger, she handed him one. The stranger began to cut carefully at the bandages. His fingers were light and quick, but careful. Even so, Kovial moaned and gasped. Suva sat back down on the bed and took his other hand, letting him squeeze hers. Given the way she clenched her teeth, his grip was still plenty strong on that side.

Darkin moved over and sat on the next bed where he could watch the stranger work. When the bandages were off, the stranger sucked in a breath. The flesh where the mace had struck was mangled. Around it, the arm was black with bruising and swollen. There were signs of a developing infection as well, which Darkin had suspected from Kovial's temperature.

The stranger looked at Kovial, meeting his glazed eyes. Kovial's eyelids drifted shut and then he was breathing, slow and deep as if in normal sleep. His hand relaxed around Suva's. He had not slept normally in days with the severity of his pain. This was not like the several times he passed out. This was calm and peaceful.

Suva snapped to her feet, drawing another dagger. "What did you do?"

The stranger did not look at her. He started moving the cut bandages off the bed to get them out of the way. "I need to be able to feel the injury. I put him to sleep so he wouldn't have to deal with that pain."

"Daemon," she hissed.

"Go get something to eat," Darkin said firmly, making it an order.

"It's a sad world where you're the best we can do for a ranking officer."

He let the insult go. She was not necessarily wrong anyhow. "If you managed your temper better it would be you, and this decision would be yours to make."

"You're all right with this?" She gestured to the stranger with the point of her dagger.

Darkin met her challenging stare. "I'm all right with anything that might help Kovial. Are you?"

Suva's expression twisted. The hand holding the dagger shook. "Don't you dare hurt him."

"Go get something to eat. I'll watch out for Kovial."

The hatred in her gaze said she understood it for the order it was. Sheathing her dagger, she strode from the room. There was a stink to the exposed wound that made Darkin wish he was also leaving. Instead, he sat patient, watching as the stranger felt the arm and examined the injury. It was some time before he finished his inspection.

"The bone's shattered. I might be able to fix it at some point, but I can't do anything right now with the swelling and infection. I would need a few days to draw out the infection and bring the swelling down, then I could give you a better answer."

Darkin ground his teeth. That was not what he wanted to hear. It did make sense though. "We haven't got a few days. We need to get back to Imperious."

"He can't travel that far like this. It will kill him." The stranger examined the injury for a few minutes more then turned to Darkin. "With two or three days, I could get him in good enough shape to travel safely and figure out if the arm can be saved. Or you can try to take him to Imperious with you now and watch him die along the way."

Suva would hate leaving him. Darkin could leave her behind with him, but he needed her. He needed her because she could help him try to convince the king of the danger they faced. He needed her because she had always been by his side and he was not ready to go on without her. Besides, she had a responsibility as a soldier that she needed to follow through on. She could do nothing for Kovial. He could do nothing for Kovial. This man could help him and perhaps even save his arm.

"I will make sure he survives. I can promise that much, but only if you let me have him for a few days to work on this."

He met the stranger's eyes. There was something about him, a sorrow and aloneness that hurt to look at.

There was more there as well. A compelling need to do this for them. Perhaps as an atonement for something.

He offered a hand. "I'm Darkin."

The stranger took the hand. His hand was slender, but his grip was firm. "Rakas."

"I'm going to trust him to you. We will return for him as soon as we can, though you may have a hard time keeping him here when he starts improving. In fact, I hope he does so well you can't stop him from heading home. For now, I'll leave you to it. I need to go fight this out with his sister."

Rakas nodded and turned his attention back to his patient.

Dreading the coming encounter with Suva, Darkin left the room. Perhaps he would have a bite to eat before he confronted her. That might ease the shake in his hands. Suva mad was his least favorite thing to deal with, down on a level with fighting enemies covered in festering sores.

ark fell. Tonight, it did nothing to calm Raine's nerves. Hydra was prancing in place. Responding to the storm of her anxiety. There was even a small tempest brewing in the daenox well beneath her feet. While they watched from a distance, the city had gone from bustling to comparatively quiet, though there were still plenty of people wandering about this early in the evening. Numerous torches along the streets had been lit, joining their light with that coming from the windows of many buildings.

IIt did not look as terrifying at night, but the confidence she had built up over the last few days fizzled the moment she considered facing the myriad strangers.

"Why don't you wear the cloak."

She glanced at Siniva, trying to be annoyed that he would change his mind yet again. The familiar and somehow pleasant smell of him brought comfort and safety, especially when facing the prospect of entering her first human town of any size. Her mouth was dry.

"Why me?"

He glanced back at her. "Because I'm more intimidating. People are less likely to start something with me. Also, red hair is more normal than whatever that color is." He gestured vaguely toward her head with one hand.

"Thanks."

He watched the town in silence for a few more minutes.

She tried to swallow. Her throat was dry too. "I'm thirsty."

"You're just nervous. We're only going to the inn on the outskirts of town there. You'll be fine." He stood up from the rock he had been sitting on. "Put on the cloak."

Raine drew the cloak out of her bags and threw it around her shoulders. It smelled like Dephithus. Odd that she should remember what he smelled like, given that she had only met him the once and it had been a rather high-stress situation. She also remembered loving him, but that was not her memory. That was her mother, and it was not the kind of love a daughter should have for her father, so she tried to push away the emotion.

"Are you coming?"

Siniva was staring down at her from the back of his mount. Had he actually gotten on that gracefully or had she been too invested in her own thoughts to notice his usual awkwardness? She did not suppose it mattered in the end.

She fastened the cloak and mounted up. Once settled in the saddle, she pulled the big hood up, so it hid her face in shadow.

Siniva nodded approval and started toward the inn. She yearned to hold Hydra back. To turn and run the other way even. This was what she had asked for, however. She wanted to go into town with him. Partly to make sure he did not desert her again, but also because she wanted to see a city with her own eyes, not just with her parents' eyes in memories.

The closer they got to the inn, the more her nerves danced. A few people in the area glanced their way. One did not seem to really see them. The other let his gaze linger a moment longer before he shook his head and hurried away. Siniva was a lot more intimidating than she was. He was a big man. Not inhumanly so like Theruses had been, but still tall and muscular. He had even picked up a battle ax off a dead, half-eaten warrior they had come upon in the woods. The belt he had the handle shoved through was a bit small on him, but it worked well enough for now.

When they stopped in front of the inn, a young boy appeared in the doorway of the adjacent stable. He stood there, staring at Siniva, and made no move to come any closer. Siniva dismounted and started toward him. The boy turned and vanished into the stable.

"Nice start," Raine muttered.

Siniva gave her a sharp look. "That isn't helpful."

Raine dismounted and led Hydra closer to the stable, eager to get out of the street. When she was almost to the door, an older gentleman walked out of the deeper shadows. He looked at Siniva, then his gaze moved to her and came to rest on Hydra. The man smiled and walked up to the stallion, offering up a hand for him to investigate.

"You came back to us."

Raine was disconcerted, watching Hydra lip the man's palm in search of some treat. "He was my father's horse," she stated, feeling a need to say something.

The man looked at her now, his eyes straining to see into her hood in the dark. "I see. Did he tell you that I helped care for his horse when it was injured?"

"No. He died before he could tell me much."

"I'm sorry." The man's eyes narrowed. "You seem a bit old to be his child."

Siniva stepped close behind her. "It's a long story."

The man shifted back slightly at Siniva's approach. "I can take your mounts. There are rooms at the inn and few questions asked."

The man reached for Hydra's reins, and Raine pulled them away. Siniva put a hand on her arm. "He'll be fine. It's this man's job to care for the horses of the inn's guests."

The man nodded and kept his hand out.

"I know." Her voice sounded small and frightened even to her. She hated it. Hydra was her companion. Her one constant since leaving the cave.

She breathed, smelling her father on the cloak, and tried to calm her nerves. Daenox danced in the ground beneath her feet. She turned to Hydra and stroked his neck. Had this man really cared for him before? Did Hydra remember him?

She pressed her face against the stallion's neck through the cloak then turned and handed the reins to the strange man. His fingers touched hers, and she flinched away as if he had bitten her. The man gave her a curious look then. She felt her cheeks burn, thankful for the cover of the hood. Siniva's hands came to rest on her shoulders, and he steered her away. The man led the two horses into the stable and Siniva guided her to the inn.

She was shaking now. Could Siniva feel that? Did he think poorly of her for it? She dug in her heels in front of the door. Siniva reached around her, pushing the door open. In sheer strength alone, she was no match for him. For a second, she started to draw on daenox, pulling it into herself to push back against him. Then she stopped herself, realizing that the daenox rising around her feet would be visible with the purple color she had always given it. If someone saw that?

She let it fall away and stumbled into the inn. The people who looked their way saw Siniva walk in behind her and their eyes widened. Some turned away again quickly as though afraid to be caught looking. Some continued to stare.

A hooded figured disappeared down a hallway in the back. The man behind the bar turned to face them. His smile faltered for a few seconds when he looked

Siniva over, then it came back strong, and he nodded to one of the women moving about the room. She nodded in return and walked over to them, the nervousness in her eyes belying her smile.

"Welcome. How can I help ye?"

Raine was still watching the man behind the bar. He had a pleasant smile. She liked it. It was simple and open.

"A room, please. Two beds if possible, though I can sleep on the floor if not."

The woman glanced at Raine, trying to peer into the hood and she shrank back, bumping into Siniva's chest. The woman gave up and mustered another smile.

"If ye've got the coin, I can get ye the room. Food as well?"

Siniva kept one strong hand resting on her shoulder. Whether to keep her from fleeing in panic or to comfort her, she could not be sure, but it worked for both.

He drew out a coin pouch he had lifted off the body in the woods along with the ax. "Yes. We'll dine in our room."

The woman nodded. "Follow me."

Siniva propelled Raine along after the woman. She was barely paying attention now. Somewhere very near someone was drawing on daenox. She could feel it. In a strange way, it felt like someone was stealing from her. The daenox was not hers by any means. Growing up with it and using it so much had developed a certain sense of ownership in her. It was not someone in the common room. She was sure of that. In fact, following the woman was bringing them closer.

When they passed by the stairs into a long dark hallway, she could tell they were very close to it. She could not say anything now. The incident outside of Ithkan had made it clear that most people did not appreciate the use of daenox in their presence. Which meant that most people must not be able to feel what she felt now, or they would know someone was using it right here in their midst.

The woman led them a few doors down, near the middle of the hall. The sensation got stronger the further they went until she was almost certain it was coming from one of the rooms at the end. She let Siniva turn her into the room the woman opened. He shoved her gently inside but did not follow. The woman entered and lit a few candles around the room.

When she left, Siniva turned to follow her back out. "Settle yourself. I'll get our saddle bags and some food and be right back."

Raine wanted to go in search of whoever was using daenox, but she did not want to go back out alone. Not now when people were awake and apt to see her wandering. Not when someone might speak to her and try to peer into her hood again. Here, at least, there was no one else. There were two beds, rough made, but real beds. There was a single table against one wall with a couple of drawers in it and another smaller table between the two beds.

Having Siniva out of her sight made her uneasy. Would he leave her here?

Her nerves crackled. She struggled not to draw on the daenox for comfort, especially now that whoever else was drawing on it down the hall had stopped. It was too likely that they would be able to sense her as she had sensed them. She walked around the small room once. Twice. Three times. Then she sat on one of the beds and sank a bit. She stood up quickly, alarmed, and poked at it. It was soft and squishy. She walked to the other bed and poked it. It was the same. Perhaps that was how they were supposed to be.

She sat down on the first bed again. It was kind of nice in a way. Slowly, she lay back, letting her body sink ever-so-slightly into the softness. It was strange, but sort of pleasant. She closed her eyes for a second and felt like she might sink even deeper. Her eyes snapped open, and she sat up. Leaning over, she looked underneath the bed. It was dark, but there did not appear to be anything there.

Siniva came back about the time she had mustered the courage to lie back again. She sat up immediately, her stomach rumbling with the savory aromas that entered with him. He set a couple of trenchers on the long table and dropped their saddlebags on the floor. The woman followed him in, setting two mugs on the table as well before leaving them alone again.

"These are strange," she commented, patting the bed.

"Those are very normal, I assure you." His grin told her he found her comment amusing. "You can take off the cloak now. We shouldn't be disturbed."

With some reluctance, she discarded the cloak and accepted the trencher he offered her. She stared at the substance on it for several minutes, aware that Siniva had started eating. He stopped after perhaps another minute had passed and looked at her.

"It's stew."

"Uh huh."

"Don't act like you knew. Just eat it." Siniva chuckled and returned to his meal.

The meal was savory and fragrant, though the meat was a bit tough. All around, it was better than most meals she had in her life up to that point. After eating, she followed Siniva's example and lay back on the soft bed again. When she commented on the softness, he laughed again and told her these beds were not soft. Her cheeks burned with her own naivete. She descended into silence, trying to fall asleep in the bed that was so much different than anything she had ever slept on.

Some time later, the draw of daenox from down the hall resumed. Siniva was breathing evenly, deep asleep. Raine got up and donned the cloak. She walked to the door and counted to ten, listening to Siniva's breathing to see if her movement had disturbed him. Then she opened the door and peeked out. The hall was quiet. She darted out, easing the door shut behind her, and followed the pull of the daenox to the last door on the right at the end of the shadowed hallway. When she tried to open the door, the handle did not turn, so she drew on a tiny tendril of daenox—small enough that whoever was using it inside would be unlikely to notice amidst their own draw—and used it to unlock the door.

Taking a deep breath, she opened the door and stepped into a candlelit room much like the one Siniva had steered her into. Only this room looked very lived in. There were clothes, books, and other belongings on many of the flat surfaces. The near bed looked like it had been slept in. A man sat in a chair next to the far bed leaning over another man who lay there still as if asleep. There were clean bandages on a table next to the bed along with a pile of discarded bloodied bandages. She could smell the metallic scent of blood, old and new, from the bandages and the wound they had been covering.

She took a few more steps into the room and drew back her hood to look around without the fabric obscuring her vision. The draw of daenox stopped then. The man lying in the bed opened his eyes and turned, looking directly at her.

"Who's she?"

The man sitting next to the bed turned abruptly, knocking over the chair when he hastened to his feet. He was already drawing on daenox again, and Raine did the same, preparing to defend herself. He looked at her and she at him.

She knew this man.

Memories flooded her. Pain. Humiliation. Confusion. Shame. Fear. She staggered a few steps, stumbling and grabbing her head in her hands. She lost her hold on the daenox, and it fell away. A small cry rang out in her own voice. She grabbed a corner post of the bed to steady herself, fighting the torrent of emotion that came with the memories. She made herself look at him again, cringing with the power of the memories still assailing her. Tears flowed down her cheeks.

"I know what you did to my father."

His eyes widened. He lost his hold on the daenox then, and she felt it fall away.

You're her," Rakas breathed. "You're the dragon-child. Dephithus's daughter."

"What's going on?" The man in the bed rasped.

There was a quick manipulation of daenox, and the man dropped into sleep.

"Rakas," Raine tasted the name. It was like bile across her tongue.

He took a few steps closer, and she reclaimed the daenox she had lost, drawing it up through her. He stopped.

"I didn't want to do it. I tried to refuse, but Amahna wouldn't allow it."

He spoke in front of her, but his voice also spoke in her head, rising from memory.

"Then I refuse. I won't do this to him."

And Amahna's answer, her voice a blade that cut through Raine's very being.

"That's adorable. And I just took away your ability to refuse. Do what we came here to do."

She squeezed her eyes shut and pressed her hands to her ears, trying to block out the voices. Trying to block out the fear and the hatred and that tiny glimmer of hope that had come to her father with Rakas's words. Trying to block out the awfulness that followed Amahna's words. It came from within, and she could do nothing to stop it.

She was not sure how much time passed. All she knew was that she was lying in a bed when she came back from that awful place in her father's memories. It was not the bed she had been in before. Siniva was not the one lying in the next bed, but a normal man with his arm wrapped in heavy bandages. On the other side of him, in the back corner of the room, Rakas sat watching her. He looked as hideous as she felt. There was some satisfaction in that. He deserved to feel awful.

The man between them moaned in his sleep. She sat up on the edge of the bed, refusing to think about who must have put her there.

"Who is he?"

Rakas's expression eased some, perhaps relieved that she had not immediately brought up her father again. "His name's Kovial. His arm was shattered with a mace. I've been clearing the infection and trying to bring down the swelling so I can attempt to heal the bone."

Curiosity got the better of her. "Can you do that? With daenox?"

"I can do some healing using daenox. I've been practicing for a while now. I've never tried anything this complex before."

"Why did you do it?"

"Why did I heal him?" He looked at her then. Shadows fell across his features again as he realized what she meant. "I don't know. I followed Theruses loyally for years. So long that, even after I stopped caring if he ever went free, I didn't have the courage to walk away. To defy him. Until that night. I went with Amahna to plant the daemon-seed in Dephithus, but I did not really think what it meant to do so. Dephithus was an obstacle to overcome to keep from falling too far in my master's favor. Then I met Dephithus. He was alive and beautiful and charismatic. I realized there was nothing I wanted less than to hurt him. Not for Theruses. Not for anyone. Not even to save my own life. I wanted to love him.

"It was too late for that. Amahna would not allow me to fail Theruses. Not when it was that important to him. She used daenox to compel me until the deed was done. Then she left me weeping on the floor of that shed while she took Dephithus, broken and beaten by what I had done to him, back to his room. I wanted to die, but, once again, I lacked the courage."

"You should have died," she stated. Then her gaze drifted to the sleeping man. "Though, perhaps it is good that you didn't. For his sake and that of anyone else you've helped since."

"I healed your father's horse and led him to the cave so he could free you," Rakas muttered, staring at the floor now.

"That's good, I suppose." Was it? What good had it done? It had gotten Dephithus killed. It had freed her and the dragons. Now she was stuck, an outcast in this world. And where were the dragons? What good had freeing them done? "At least for Hydra."

They both sat in their silence for a time, then she looked at Kovial again. He seemed quite peaceful in his slumber, though she was not sure if the sleep was natural at this point or still the daenox induced sleep Rakas had forced on him.

"How's he doing?"

"Well. I might be able to try healing the bone by tomorrow. He wants to get back to Imperious and his sister as soon as he can. It's been hard convincing him to stay put."

"Hm." She stood up from the bed. "I should get back before Siniva knows I'm gone. I don't think he'd like that."

Rakas looked like he wanted to say more, but he only nodded.

"Goodnight."

"Goodnight… What's your name?"

"Raine."

"It suits you. Goodnight, Raine."

She slipped from the room and started down the hall. When she got close, she could see that the door to the room she shared with Siniva was standing open. She rushed to it, her heart pounding, and peered inside. Siniva's covers were thrown back, and he was gone. Pulling up the hood of her cloak, she hurried toward the common room. Had he found her gone and taken the opportunity to leave her? Would he be so cruel? She had not looked to see if his saddlebags were still on the floor.

She was almost to the end of the hall when she heard low, intense voices coming from just around the corner.

"I can't go stomping into the rooms of all my guests in the middle of the night looking for the girl."

"She can't have gone far." That was Siniva. "We have to find her now. If she's not here—"

"I'm sure she's fine. I—"

Raine hurried out into the common room and the other man, the one who had been lounging behind the bar when they arrived, raised a hand to point in her direction.

Siniva turned. Rage and relief warred across his features. He rushed over to her, doom in his angry strides. At the last second, when she thought perhaps she should run, the rage dissolved from his features and relief took control. He grabbed her and pulled her to his chest. She could feel him trembling.

Was this sincere? Was it some show he was putting on for their audience? If so, it was a convincing one.

Before she could reconcile this sudden display of concern, he pushed her away, holding her at arm's length with his hands gripping her shoulders. The rage resurfaced, though not as fierce as it had been a moment ago.

"Where were you? I was sure something awful had happened. Could you not sleep? Are the beds too soft?"

She almost burst out in inappropriate laughter at the last question, but she had a feeling he would not see the humor right then. Why was he so worried? When, in the last few days, had he decided to start caring about what happened to her?

She glanced at the other man who stood watching them. With him there, she could not tell Siniva why she had left the room or what had happened.

Siniva caught on quickly and turned her around to guide her back to the room, saying nothing to the man they left behind in the common room. When they were in their room again, he shut the door and locked it.

"Where did you go?"

His tone was angrier now and still somewhat worried. Almost paternal. How peculiar.

"When did you start caring?"

"Daemon's blood, Raine! I care what happens to you. I care because you were right. It was never about what was good for you or for your father. You were both pawns in a bigger game. You never mattered beyond what could be gained from placing the dragon power in you." His eyes flared to life again as if tiny fires burned within them. He swiped one of the emptied trenchers from the table with one big hand and sent it slamming into the far wall.

She sat on the bed, deeming it wise to hold her silence and wondered passingly if there was someone on the other side of that wall trying to sleep.

Siniva sank down on the edge of the other bed and rested his arms across his thick thighs, his shoulders slumping. "I realized, after thinking about what you said, that we are much the same. Like you, the dragons deemed me expendable. We were both acceptable losses. But…"

He stopped speaking then and hung his head. Raine tried to be patient, waiting until he was ready to continue. The silence lengthened until she worried that he might have fallen asleep that way, though his eyes were still open.

"But what?"

He drew a deep breath and looked at her. She did not like the pity she saw in his eyes.

"But, if I can become a dragon again, I would be free. I could rejoin the other dragons. Return home, in a sense. You don't even have that. Right now, I am the closest thing to family you have. It was vile and selfish of me to leave you before. I'm sorry."

Raine shifted in her seat on the bed. She had a powerful urge to duck out and find a quiet place to hide. That was not the right way to respond to his sudden compassion for her plight or his apology. Of that she was sure. It was a tempting idea, nonetheless.

"Perhaps we both need to try harder," she offered. That sounded like a reasonable comment, though she could not be sure if it was the right one.

Siniva brightened a little. "Yes. I think that's a grand idea. A good start might be if you stopped wandering off without warning in the night. I feared you might have gone to play with the daemons again. I had visions of you being stabbed to death by an angry mob of townsfolk."

"I wouldn't do that here." *No matter how much I want to.* "Someone in the inn was using daenox, so I went to investigate."

The stone-faced silence that met this announcement told her this had not been the right thing to do.

"I won't do it again. I promise."

"What did you find?"

"Amahna's former companion, Rakas, is in the room at the end of the hall."

One second Siniva was sitting on the bed. The next the flame in his eyes swelled to an inferno, and he rushed toward the door, grabbing the ax as he stormed past. Raine scrambled over the bed and ran after him, grabbing his arm when he reached for the door. He was so strong. She threw her whole body back against the strength in that arm. Still, he reached up as if a mere cobweb tried to hold him back and unlocked the door.

"If I can't play with daemons in town, you can't go killing other guests at the inn," she declared, grunting with the effort of trying to pull him back.

His hand rested on the door lever, but he did not move it. "Do you know what he did to Dephithus?" His voice was a low growl.

"Yes. Better than you." She cringed inwardly, fighting to keep those memories from swarming back in again. "I remember it happening."

Siniva's hand fell away from the door. The ax hit the floor with a hollow thud. He turned to her, and for the second time that night, he pulled her to his chest. This time he drew her in close to him and folded her in his arms, keeping her there.

For a few seconds, she resisted, trying to push away. Then the weight of those memories crashed down. Every agonizing second her father had suffered sweeping through her like she had lived it herself. She crumpled against him. He lifted her, carrying her back to one of the beds. There he sat and held her while she wept herself to sleep in his firm, protective embrace.

Raine woke curled against Siniva with her head pillowed on his shoulder. What had seemed paternal and caring in the night felt awkward and inappropriate now. She attempted to extract herself without waking him, moving slow and careful. Shifting one leg a few inches. Lifting one hand slowly, finger by finger. Pausing if he moved or his breathing changed. For a few seconds, it seemed like it might work, then he stiffened and made a small choking sound. They sprang up on either side of the bed at the same time, neither meeting the other's eyes.

"How are you feeling this morning? Better?" The words spilled over his lips with uncomfortable haste as he wandered over to pick up the ax up off the floor. He stood there frowning at the door for a long moment, noting, she suspected, that he had left it unlocked.

"Yes." That was all she could think to say. Everything else that came to mind would probably increase the sense of discomfort in the room. She picked up her cloak that had also ended up on the floor somehow.

"Those clothes don't fit you very well anymore, do they."

Not at all.

She shrugged, noticing how tight the shirt pulled across her growing chest even with such a small movement.

Right now, she wanted nothing more than to put the cloak on and hide her changing body in its folds. Doing so felt like it would draw more attention to the things she wanted to cover, however, so she just folded it into her arms.

"It's a shame we don't have more time and more coin. There's certain to be a tailor in this town who could fit some clothes for you."

Oh, to have clothing that actually fit. To not have to worry about the seat of her pants ripping out when she bent over or to have the legs reach her ankles. To have a shirt with sleeves that reached her wrists. The idea appealed more than she could put words to. She went and dug into her saddlebags, pulling out a coin pouch she had found in there. It must have belonged to Dephithus, and it had a good heft to it. She held it up. "We could use this. I think it was my father's. Would that be enough?"

Siniva held his hands out, and she tossed it to him. He caught it, loosened the ties, and looked inside. A grin curved his lips. "This would be more than enough. Still," he pulled the ties tight again, "even if we bought some things to have altered, it would take a day or two to get it done."

"Perfect."

He gave her a puzzled look, finally meeting her eyes. "How so?"

"Rakas," his expression darkened before the name finished crossing her lips, so she pushed ahead in a rush, "is trying to heal a soldier from Imperious. In a day or two, he might be ready to ride back to the capital. If we ride into Imperious as the escort to an injured Legion soldier, it might lend us some credibility."

His brow went up. He cocked his head to one side, regarding her with a look of mild surprise. "It's easy to forget sometimes that you aren't nearly as old as you look."

"Is that good or bad?"

A hint of flush touched his cheeks, and he glanced away. "It can be either depending on the moment. In this case, I think you might be on to something. I'd rather not linger in the city, especially with Rakas here, but it might be worth it, and it would give us an opportunity to get clothes that fit us. Fitted clothes and a noble purpose would also improve the impression we give others."

"I'll go talk to Rakas." She started toward the door, unfolding the cloak as she went.

"Stop right there."

She stopped and turned, puzzled.

"I don't want you anywhere near him alone."

Raine heaved an exasperated sigh, making sure he could hear it, and threw the cloak around her shoulders. She liked the way it flourished when she spun it. It was dramatic and added nice emphasis to the sigh.

Siniva gave her a wearying look and shoved the handle of the ax into his belt. He gestured for her to proceed and followed her down the hall to the last door on the right. When she grabbed the handle, he grabbed her arm, holding on until she let go of the handle. He shook his head at her and reached up to knock on the door.

Oh. Perhaps she should have done that last night too. "Who is it?"

She recognized Kovial's weak, rasping voice.

"It's Raine. I came by last night," she called back.

"Rakas isn't here."

It would be better if she did not ask the injured man to try to come open the door, so she drew upon a tendril of daenox and unlocked it again. When it clicked, she quickly grabbed the handle and pushed it open, darting in before Siniva could stop her a second time.

"Raine," he growled under his breath, following behind her.

She ignored him and walked over to Kovial's bedside. He was propped up with some pillows today, so it was a little easier to look him in the eyes. There was a hint of more color in his face as well. Rakas's treatments must be working. She drew her hood back and sat in the chair there.

"We weren't properly introduced. I'm Raine, and that scary looking man is Siniva."

His eyes widened a little as he looked from her to Siniva—who stood staring at Raine in annoyance—and back again. She realized her error quickly. They did not look like Kovial. They did not look like any normal humans. The young soldier did not appear afraid though, only surprised and perhaps a bit intrigued.

He looked Raine over for a few more seconds before speaking. "You look like someone I knew. I mean, not exactly. He was a man, and you're obviously not, but the eyes and the scales…"

A smile curved her lips. "You knew my father."

Now Kovial looked a touch confused. "Your father? No. I don't think that's possible. The man I speak of was Dephithus de NuTraven, former heir to the throne of Imperious."

Maybe she should let it go. It was too confusing to explain. But Dephithus *was* her father, and this man had known him. If she let it go, she would be giving up that connection. "No. Dephithus was my father. I…" His dubious look made her hesitate. Siniva's hand rested on her shoulder. Comfort, encouragement, or warning? "I can't explain it, but I really am his and Myara's daughter. There's power involved that changed how quickly I age."

Though Kovial still looked dubious, there was something in the way he studied her then that told her he wanted to believe her. He stared long at her face. She stared back, unsure what else to say or do. He brought up his good hand and brushed a lock of blond hair out of his eyes. A hesitant smile curved his lips. "You know, you have some of her facial features, and until now, he was the only person I'd ever met with the cat eyes and the scaling." He glanced up at Siniva, frowned, and turned quickly back to her.

She could not blame him if the red dragon made him uncomfortable. He was rather imposing standing there with his muscular arms now crossed over his chest and his disapproving scowl.

"Maybe you are his daughter. It wouldn't be the craziest thing that's happened in the last few years."

"No, it wouldn't."

They all turned to look at Rakas as he entered. He flinched noticeably when Siniva's gaze fell on him and turned his attention to Kovial.

"I see you're wearing out my patient."

"It's all right," Kovial defended. "I'm feeling more like I might live today."

Rakas shut the door and walked around to the far side of the bed. "Exactly, let's not do anything to reverse that."

Raine stood and faced Rakas now. He looked tired like he had not slept in days. Perhaps he had not, given the care his patient needed. She could not bring herself to feel sorry for him, however. Not with her father's memories threatening at the edge of her awareness every time she looked at him.

"Siniva and I will be here a couple more days. I thought we might offer to escort Kovial home when we leave, if he's ready."

"I'm ready now," Kovial stated, giving Rakas a sullen scowl.

Rakas ignored the look, he was staring hard at Siniva. "The Fire Dragon. You travel in interesting company, Raine."

Siniva growled low in his throat, and Raine forced a small laugh. It sounded uncomfortable even to her ears. She was going to have to work more on her diplomatic skills.

"Why are you staying in Corbent Calid?" Rakas gave them both a critical look. "I assume it isn't to mingle with the locals."

Siniva was silent. Perhaps he did not want to demean himself by speaking to the other man. That was fine. The fastest way to learn how to interact in the outside world was by doing so.

"We thought there might be a tailor here who could…" She trailed off, puzzled by the mocking sneer Rakas gave her then.

"Who do you think would consider working for someone who looks like you in these troubled times?" Rakas shook his head at them. "I wouldn't get my hopes up."

"He's not worth your time," Siniva grumbled, putting a hand on one arm to draw her away.

Raine's temper flared. She jerked her arm out of Siniva's grasp. Daenox rose through the floorboards. Rakas looked up at her, his eyes going wide. He stood and held his hands out in a placating gesture. His hands shook.

"Wait!"

Raine stopped drawing on the daemon power, though she did not release what she had already drawn.

"Perhaps I put it too indelicately, but it's still true. It's unlikely that you will find a tailor in this town or any other who is willing to work with you. You look like dragonkin, and the last throwback to the dragonkin anyone heard anything about was Dephithus. The things he did after the daemon-seed changed him aren't going to inspire people to trust you."

Raine let daenox spread through her, calming her and pushing back the surge of her parents' memories that threatened to bury her again.

"There is a tailor not that far from here. Random can give you better directions. I don't go out much." He walked to the table by the wall and lifted a black cloak off it. "Take this. It will fit you better. Siniva can wear that one. You'll at least have less trouble getting to the tailor. Once you're there, it's up to you to get them to work with you."

She stared at the cloak he was offering her. In her head, her father's memories crashed into the wall of daenox she had constructed, threatening to bash their way through. She started to shake her head when Siniva reached around her and grabbed the cloak.

"Come along. Let's get this taken care of. The sooner we get ourselves outfitted, the sooner we can leave this place, and him, behind."

With a nod, she turned to follow the Fire Dragon from the room.

Rakas called after her.

She turned, not far enough to actually look at him, but far enough to show that she had heard and was listening.

"Let go of it. There are those who will notice."

"Let go of..." Siniva started.

She turned in time to see his fierce glower as he realized what they were talking about. Grudgingly, she released the daenox, letting it sink through the floorboards and down into the ground beneath. To her immense humiliation, Siniva looked to Rakas then, waiting for the other man's nod before turning to lead her from the room.

Wearing the cloak was a special kind of torture for Raine. A voice, sometimes her father's, sometimes her own, screamed and wailed in the back of her mind from the moment the fabric touched her shoulders. Memories crept in, lurking in the background then surging up unexpectedly as they walked through the streets of Corbent Calid. She had already bumped into two people walking along, both of whom cursed her, one loudly and the other under her breath, but no less harshly. Neither took the time to stop and engage her or try to see into the hood she kept pulled far forward.

Siniva took to keeping one hand firmly around her upper arm, correcting her course when memories from a life that was not hers—memories she wished she could get rid of—made it hard to focus on their surroundings.

Even without the memories, the city was hard to deal with. There were too many people. Young and old. Male and female. From the well-dressed to the shabbily attired like themselves. From the pungent to the fragrant. Smells were coming from street vendors and shops as well. And so many sounds. People walking, their shoes crunching on the dry ground and grit. People talking amongst themselves and vendors shouting for people to come to their stalls and shops. Dogs barking.

Horses nickering, their hooves loud on the roadways. The clanging of a blacksmith's hammer.

She thought she would be excited to see all the glorious wares. Cloth and food and flowers and pottery and colors and sounds and smells and...

Something hit her legs from behind, and she was falling. Her arm jerked free of Siniva's grasp. The ground came up to meet her, hard enough to scrape her palms, and the boy who had run into her fell across her legs. Her hood fell away. The boy looked at her, let out a shriek of fright, and scrambled away, landing a solid kick to her gut in his frantic effort to escape. Raine grabbed her abdomen and glanced up, looking for Siniva. A nearby woman looked down and recoiled with a cry, running into the man behind her who turned to see what had happened. When he saw Raine, his eyes went wide.

"Daemon," he shouted.

"Idiot," Siniva snarled, pushing another man out of his way. "Daemons have grey eyes."

The man shrank away, staring wide-eyed into Siniva's hood. The damage had been done. Hands were reaching for weapons or anything that could pass as one. Those who had nothing were backing away, some pushing their children behind them. Raine grabbed Siniva's hand, trying to pull her hood back up with her free hand as he lifted her to her feet. Ignoring the stinging in her palms and the ache in her gut.

"Look at this pretty mess." A woman's voice rose above the din of spreading panic. "I told them not to go into town made up like that, didn't I, Cadovan?"

The woman was weaving her way through to them on a slim black horse that looked as if it had been through a war or two and come out on the losing side. There were jagged lines and splotches along its chest, legs, and shoulders where hair had grown in white over scars and one ear was chopped about an inch shorter than the other. The woman had a wide swatch of pink in the front of her lank blond hair and looked far too slight for the volume she was projecting. The hard, unyielding lines of her face and the many daggers sheathed upon her person marked her as someone to be wary of upsetting.

"That you did, Nakia. That you did." The man on foot walking along next to her cracked a wide grin at them. The jovial expression did not seem to go with the dark tattoos on his bald head and down his scarred arms. There were scars on his muscular bare chest as well that made it look like he had been in the same fight as the horse. He did not have eyebrows, but the mustache and precisely trimmed beard that highlighted his strong jaw somehow made up for that oddity.

Confusion and curiosity subdued the crowd some and Siniva jumped on the offered opportunity. "Sorry, Nakia," he addressed the mounted woman as though he knew her. "I thought we would be inconspicuous enough with the cloaks."

Raine caught on then. It was a bit of a ruse, and whatever the reason for it, these two rough looking individuals had probably saved them from injury and perhaps death at the hands of a frightened mob.

The woman, Nakia, scratched her head and smirked at Siniva. "You never did have much sense about these things."

Siniva's face darkened. Raine hoped he would have the prudence to keep his somehow fitting, if unfortunately fiery, temper at bay. She stepped closer to him, setting a hand on his forearm. "You know how he can be."

Nakia and Cadovan both grinned at her then. The sudden attention of the two strangers made her want to step back and hide behind Siniva, but that would draw the wrong kind of attention if they were going to convince the crowd that they knew each other. It appeared to be working. Some people had already relaxed their hands away from their weapons, and a few children were peeking out from behind their parents.

"Don't I just," Nakia agreed with a long-suffering shake of her head. Then she looked around at the staring faces. There was still fear in many of the eyes watching them. "Move on folks. Spectacle's over for now. If you want to find out what this is all about, come see Fools Errant perform in the old town square tomorrow night for a show you won't forget."

Her words seem to satisfy most of the crowd. Expressions of relief altered the mood of the onlookers, taking away the sense of pressing threat. While Nakia and Cadovan closed the remaining distance, people began to move along again. Some stared as they passed, but the crisis had been averted.

"Just so you know, this wasn't Raine's idea," Siniva stated when they were closer, maintaining the ruse while people were still apt to be listening.

Raine realized he was dropping her name so they could use it without drawing suspicion by having to ask. She could not think of a quick and clever way to drop his name without sounding awkward, so she said nothing for now, letting those who knew more of the outside world guide the moment.

"I didn't think it was," Nakia replied.

She shifted her seat on her horse, and Raine noticed that she was riding without a saddle. A thick woven blanket was all that rested between her legs and the horse's back. Her bridle also did not have a bit in it. A chunk of his lip was missing on the near side where the bit would normally rest that had scarred over, leaving a small perpetual peephole into his mouth. Raine could see his pink tongue moving within.

"Why don't we return to camp where we can have a little private talk about the risks you keep taking." Nakia gestured back the direction they had come.

Siniva glanced in the opposite direction toward where the tailor's shop waited. After a few seconds, he nodded and put a hand on Raine's arm to turn her back toward the inn at the edge of town.

Cadovan smiled at Raine then. There was something in his expression and the shine in his hazel eyes that made her cheeks grow warm. No one said anything more as they walked past the inn and stable at the end of the street. Their new companions veered off the main road toward a grove of trees. Siniva stopped, pulling Raine to a stop as well.

"I thank you for your intervention, but we would be fools to follow you out there without knowing anything about you. If there is something we can do to repay you, I would prefer to discuss it here."

Nakia gave Siniva a measuring look. "From what I've seen so far, I'm not convinced you aren't fools. You must have known you would run into trouble if anyone got a good look at you."

Siniva growled at her. "Then why did you help us. Given the burn scars on this one," he gestured with a jerk of his head to Cadovan, "you two are no strangers to getting into trouble yourselves."

Cadovan and Nakia both laughed then, and Raine felt her brow furrowing.

What about that was humorous?

"I'm a fire dancer," Cadovan stated, lifting his wrists in front of his face to show off the flame tattoos running up his arms. "I dance with fire. I've gotten a few burns practicing my craft and pushing my limits to keep the audience entertained."

A memory had been tickling at the back of her mind since they encountered the strangers. Now it came clear. Dancing and acrobatics and music. Someone breathing out great gouts of fire. It was one of those confusing memories that came from both Dephithus and Myara at the same time. It was a happy memory at least, one in which they were enjoying a troop of performers who had come to entertain at the palace.

"Are you really a performance troop?"

"Yes. We are." Nakia stated and urged her mount toward the trees again. "Fools Errant is not just a clever cover story."

Siniva let out an irritable huff and followed them, so Raine did too.

"I think we could help each other..." Nakia trailed off with a meaningful glance at the Fire Dragon.

"Siniva," Raine filled in.

Nakia gave her a quick nod of appreciation. "You two are unusual. As I'm sure you noticed, people don't like unusual things, especially during dark times like this. They might have been more inclined to accept you back before the heir to the throne turned bad, but not now."

Raine opened her mouth to speak in her father's defense and Siniva squeezed her arm. Hard. When she looked questioningly at him, he only shook his head.

Nakia was still talking. "Audiences at our performances, however, like unusual things. Especially when they think those things are controlled. So long as the people here believe you are part of our troop and your appearance is something we manufactured, you should be able to roam the town in reasonable safety."

"So that's how you could help us," Siniva concluded. "What do you expect to get in return? We obviously haven't much coin."

She glanced at them and smirked. "Obviously." She stopped at the edge of the trees and hopped off the horse. "I'm guessing you two aren't completely useless. With your looks, you wouldn't have to do much to please a crowd, but I'd be happier if you told me you have some skill that would add value to our troop for a few performances."

Siniva scoffed. "You want us to perform with you?"

"Yes. One of our acrobats died in a daemon attack a few nights ago. His husband refuses to perform without him. I'm sure he'll start up again when he's had some time to mourn, but right now, we are short a popular act. I could use a little extra something to fill in."

Her steady gaze made it clear even to Raine that she was serious.

Siniva shook his head. "I don't have much to offer. You already have a firebreather."

Cadovan's grin faded while Nakia's blossomed. It was almost as if someone had trimmed the edges off Cadovan's smile and given them to Nakia to broaden hers. "I can't have gotten lucky enough to stumble upon another fire performer."

"I'm not a performer, I just have some skill with fire."

"Good enough. We'll see what you can do." Nakia's enterprising gaze moved to Raine. "What about you, my fascinating young temptress. What skills do you have?"

Temptress?

Siniva reached out to squeeze her arm again, and Raine shook him off. She took a step closer to Nakia, meeting the woman's eyes. They were about the same height. The woman was not very tall now that she had come down from her horse, though Raine remained poignantly aware of the many daggers she wore.

"I can make colorful light shows using daenox."

Nakia's expression turned thoughtful, but Cadovan was shaking his head slightly. Neither recoiled or rejected her outright, which was a far better reaction than Raine had expected. She hated hiding that part of herself though, and it was something she was good at. For all that Siniva wanted her not to use her skills, she yearned to do so, and this might give her a way to do so while also helping their situation.

"We'll find a secluded spot later where you can show me what you can do. Then we can decide if it might be useful."

The dark look Siniva gave Raine then said he had his own opinions on the subject, but he chose not to bring them up just then.

Nakia gestured Cadovan to go ahead of them, and he obliged. "Come, we might have some better clothes you can use in one of our packs. We tend to accumulate outfits."

"We were on our way to take care of the clothing problem when you found us," Siniva grumbled.

"Such gratitude." Nakia started walking after Cadovan. "Marisa can tailor some clothes for you, and she'll charge a sight less than any of the tailors in town. Come on. I'll introduce you to the troop."

She pushed a branch out of the way, letting go of it as soon as Siniva started to follow. The branch smacked him in the shoulder, and Raine snorted a small laugh behind him.

Raine chewed at a bit of tough meat she had been given and pretended great interest in watching Marisa, a shapely woman with luxurious long black curly hair and beautiful dark skin, while she dug through a pile of clothing that the troop had assembled. She occasionally stood straight and held whatever garment she had brought with her up to Siniva, twisting her full lips into an expression of great consternation when she decided the chosen article was not right. Then she would drop it to one side and go rummaging again.

Raine did find this process entertaining, but while her eyes stayed forward, her focus was on her periphery where some of the other players sat also watching and eating. Most notably, she tried to keep aware of Florin, the acrobat whose husband had recently died and who was watching them with no little suspicion, and Myrza, the slender, androgynous individual Nakia had introduced as their contortionist. The latter she maintained an awareness of simply because those wide dark eyes never stopped watching her from the moment they first entered the camp. Myrza's grip was firm and lingering when they were introduced. Her hair was black and straight with three tight braids woven along the left side above her ear. Her features were refined and delicate, just like her build. Her skin was a warm bronze that fell evenly between dark

Marisa and pale Nakia. Mryza was disturbingly enchanting in a way that Raine was not sure how to respond to.

Marisa finally found some clothes she approved of and sent Siniva into the trees to try them on. As he walked away, she motioned Raine to come to her. Raine set down the remains of her food. As she stood, a sweet, soft whistling rose into the air from over by Myrza. Glancing that direction, she saw the musician Nakia had introduced as Kelcy playing a flute. Nakia began playing along on a rebec she pulled up from behind the log she was sitting on. A little disconcerted by the haunting music they made, Raine walked around the small fire over to where Marisa waited.

Marisa began to hold up articles of clothing she had set aside while digging through the pile for Siniva, eyeing them critically. Raine barely noticed. Myrza had started to dance to the music, weaving a haunting spell with her flexible, elegant form. The flickering firelight in the shadows of the forest canopy added mystery and seduction to the dance.

Raine stared, letting the music pull her in and watching every sinuous movement. Myrza was like a tendril of daenox weaving patterns in the air. Her movements were snakelike and eerily beautiful. The music wove around her now, like a transparent cloak, beholden to her shape. Raine could imagine a weave of daemon power around Myrza, music given color and shape. It would twist up out of the ground, twining around her ankles, swirling up her legs—

A slender hand with an iron grip closed on Raine's wrist, snapping her from her reverie.

"Come with me, Pip," Nakia snapped under her breath, pulling Raine toward the edge of the camp.

Marisa made a small squeak of dismay, looking after them with a few articles of clothing hanging loose in her hands.

Raine only now noticed that the music from the rebec had stopped at some point, leaving the flute to weave Myrza's music alone.

"I'll bring her back in a minute," Nakia called over her shoulder.

"You have strong hands," Raine remarked, stepping hastily over a rotting log as she was dragged out of sight of the camp.

Nakia glanced down at her hand and loosened her grip. "Sorry, but you were about to cause an incident."

"An incident?"

Nakia continued pulling her along, not stopping to explain until they could barely hear the music from the camp. The woods were thicker here. Darker. The sounds of other life—birdsong and the chirping of rodents—took the place of the crackle of the campfire.

"I saw the movement of the daenox at Myrza's feet. I've seen that kind of thing before."

"Oh." Puzzled, Raine rubbed at her wrist. "I was only thinking about how I could use daenox to add to the performance. I didn't realize I was drawing on it though. I didn't mean any harm by it."

"Of course, you didn't," Nakia allowed, "but we had a daenox priestess with our group for a time. She could do some brilliant tricks with daemon power. Unfortunately, we didn't realize at the time that using daenox tends to lure in daemons. One night, she was practicing a routine and Florin's husband, Allic, wandered off to take a piss. The daemons her power had drawn near the camp attacked and killed him. We heard his screams and came running, but they tore him apart in less than a minute. Florin isn't going to like having another priestess in the troop."

"I'm not a priestess."

Nakia shrugged. "Whatever you are, you can control daenox, and he won't see the difference."

"Using daenox doesn't have to draw in daemons," Raine countered. "I can control how far out the lure reaches. If I keep it close enough, then no daemons should notice."

Nakia raised one brow and smirked. "You can do that?"

"Mm-hm." There were daemons nearby now. Raine could feel them. Their presence caused ripples in the daenox flowing beneath the ground and under her skin. Around Corbent Calid, there were countless ripples.

Nakia scanned the forest floor around them, looking for something. Then she walked over and retrieved two sticks, breaking them down until they were of a relatively uniform size. These she held up to Raine who made no move to take them. "I saw the colors you were drawing up out of the ground at Myrza's feet. Can you make it look like those colors are coming out of something? The end of these sticks, for example."

Raine took the two sticks, understanding Nakia's intentions now. They would disguise what she was doing by using the sticks as props. "Certainly. I just have to draw it up through myself."

Nakia's brow furrowed under her swatch of pink hair. "Is that safe?"

Raine shrugged. If it was not safe, it was much too late for her to worry about it now. She had been using her own body to focus daenox almost since the day of her birth. She pulled on the daenox in the ground beneath them and drew it in through her feet, up her legs and torso, then down through her arms, and out the end of the sticks. Bright violet sparks of daenox erupted from the ends of the sticks. First in smaller spurts, then in jets and whorls. She gave it more color. First green and blue, then red and gold, and myriad others.

Nakia's eyes lit with the colors, and her smile glowed with appreciation. "Perfect. I'll have Myrza show you some moves so you can make a full show of it. Nothing too complicated," she reassured when Raine's eyes widened with alarm.

The daenox slipped away, rushing out into the ground again. "Myrza? She's a woman, right?"

Nakia's expression was firm but indulgent. "Yes, she is. Her androgynous beauty is part of her allure. It makes the audience both aroused and uncomfortable because they aren't entirely sure what they're attracted to."

Raine shook her head, not sure she understood.

"People think they know what they want sexually. It's part of how they identify themselves. They get uneasy when that is put to the test, but it also turns them on in a way."

"Why does it matter?"

Nakia's smile was patient and a little amused. "You're perhaps too young to understand the nuances of sexuality. You'll learn the ways in which it matters eventually."

What ways were those? Raine stared hard, looking for more clarity, not from Nakia, but from the memories she carried. She gave up quickly though. The freshest, strongest memories were all from her father's Dawning Day and the tormented months that followed as the daemon seed slowly broke him. Those memories held too much pain. If her parents had anything to offer on this matter, it would stay buried under those things Raine did not want to face. This was something she was going to have to build her own reference for.

"Are people like Myrza common?"

"Not extremely so, but not as rare as all that either." Nakia gave her a once over, curiosity giving a twist to her smile. "Where are you from?"

"I grew up in a cave in the Dunues Mountains."

Nakia's lips stretched into a tight, disapproving line.

Was that the wrong thing to tell her? Raine glanced around, suddenly missing Siniva. He was supposed to be there to guide her through these interactions. She was a child in years after all. Even with her parents' memories, she could not be expected to navigate these things alone.

As if on cue, his voice cut through the trees, calling her. He sounded on the verge of panic.

Nakia's expression darkened a fraction, then she called out in response, letting him know where they were. When he came into view, he was wearing an off-white, lace-up shirt and a light brown suede jacket with suede pants of a similar color. The pants had lacing up the side, so they had fitted them to his muscular legs. The jacket looked like it could use a little trimming and Marisa was following behind Siniva, brandishing a bone needle and an annoyed scowl.

"If you don't stand still, I'm going to stab you with this," Marisa threatened.

Siniva growled over one shoulder at her. His growl was authentically animal enough that Marisa stopped. She stood and watched from there as he stalked the rest of the way over to them.

"What are you doing out here?"

"I was talking to her," Nakia snapped.

Siniva stepped close, glowering down at the woman.

To her credit, Nakia shifted in closer still and glared back up at him. "What's this about her being raised in a cave?"

Siniva glanced at Raine, and she shrugged. "She asked where I was from."

His aggressive stance eased a fraction. "I didn't put her there. I did help get her out."

Nakia glanced over at Raine. "Is that true?"

Raine nodded, remembering her father, the only time she would ever see him in the flesh. He had died that day, for her, she supposed, though he had been trying to save her mother as well. Now, all she really knew of either of them was from their memories of each other.

"You two aren't related, are you?" Marisa had come closer and was looking from one to the other.

Raine hesitated, not sure if it would be better for her to lie about it, but Siniva gave a small, abrupt shake of his head.

"I'm not here to share life stories," Siniva stated. "You helped us. We'll help you in return. That doesn't mean we have to know one another beyond names."

For a few seconds, it looked like Nakia meant to attack him. Her hands curled into fists, and her muscles tightened. Then her expression relaxed in a way that made Raine particularly uneasy. "I suppose that's true. So long as Raine trusts you and doesn't feel mistreated by you, we don't need to know more." She waited for a nod from Raine before continuing. "Why don't you show me what you can do with fire."

Siniva started to remove his jacket and Marisa leaped in.

"Wait! Give me one minute." Without waiting for an answer, she began to walk around Siniva, drawing spots in on the jacket to improve the fit and pinning them in place with bone pins that she pulled from some hidden stash on her person. When she finished, he handed her the jacket, and she hurried back toward camp.

Siniva removed the shirt as well, the reddish-bronze of his scaling now showing down the length of his spine and slightly over the curve of his strong shoulders. He picked up a small stick up off the ground and broke it in half. Then he held up one in each hand. There was a moment of expectant silence, then the ends of both pieces burst into flames, making Raine and Nakia start. The fire burned quickly down the dry wood until it reached his fingertips. The sticks burned to ash in seconds, crumbling to the ground. Now flame danced over the ends of his fingertips. The flame traveled down his fingers and pooled into his palms. From there, it grew bigger and brighter and started to create a trail of fire running up his arms toward his shoulders. Fire still burned in his palms as well. He brought one hand up close to his mouth and blew upon the flame. A massive plume of fire shot out from his hand barely missing the nearest trees. The fire reflected brightly in his catlike eyes. His expression was one of ecstasy. For a few more seconds, the flame grew, engulfing more of his form, then he let go of it, leaving trailing brightness behind that remained etched in her field of vision for several seconds.

Nakia's expression wavered between concern and delight. "You use daenox too?"

Siniva shook his head, his hair was slicked down with sweat, and a gloss of sweat covered his chiseled torso. "It's a different kind of power. It won't draw daemons if that's your concern."

He gave Raine a vaguely accusing look. She fought the urge to stick her tongue out at him in response. She needed to try and act the age she looked, after all.

There was something in the air in town the next evening. It crackled like the energy before a storm. Up until a short time ago, about the time the music started, Raine thought performing with the troop was going to be fun. She and Siniva had practiced with Fools Errant at their camp most of yesterday and today, returning to the inn only to sleep. She had even told Rakas and Kovial about the upcoming performance and invited them to attend in case there was not much of an audience. Kovial, who Rakas said would be ready to ride soon, expressed interest. Rakas expressed nothing.

Now she felt a little foolish for even considering that they might not draw a crowd. Alongside the stage assembled in the town square, the musicians in the group—Nakia and Kelcy on the rebec and flute again with Idrin and Florin playing drums—were drawing out lively tunes that had already lured in a sizeable crowd. Now they switched to something more exotic. Marisa and Myrza took to the stage to dance, their sensual movements enthralling the existing crowd and drawing in even more townsfolk.

Raine started to chew at her fingernails, and Siniva raised a brow at her.

He looked good in the fitted clothes Marisa had altered for him. Good enough to belong with this vivid group of performers. He looked comfortable too, though how he could be comfortable under the scrutiny of all these people she could not begin to fathom. It was bad enough that she was expected to go up and perform in front of this crowd, but she was also wearing the very precisely fitted clothes Marisa had altered for her. Clothes that emphasized all the blossoming curvature of a maturing teenage body she did not feel at all ready to acknowledge.

She leaned close to Siniva, stealing some comfort from his strength and calm. "How can you be so relaxed? Can't you feel the air? How… nervous it is?"

Siniva chuckled. "It's the excitement and anticipation of the audience that you're feeling."

She withdrew from the laughter in his eyes. "Hmph. It feels nervous."

His expression softened, and he leaned into the space she had moved out of. She could smell the odd musk of him. Like a man, but different somehow. Darker. Stronger. Forged in the fire of the dragon he was supposed to be.

"It feels hostile because you're resisting it. Close your eyes."

Raine shook her head emphatically.

"You'll be safe." He stepped around in front of her and placed his hands on her shoulders. "I'll be right here."

She looked into his red-bronze eyes, eyes that burned to life with the reflection of torches being lit around the square to ward against the falling dark. Once she had seen resentment in those eyes. A desire to be free of her. That was gone now. There was something else there. Something new and protective.

She closed her eyes.

"Good. Now just feel." His voice took on a depth and cadence that was complimented by the music from the players. "Feel the music washing over you. Let it inside. Let it move you. Feel each drumbeat. Each rise and fall of the flute. Each strum of the rebec. Isolate the sound of each instrument until you can tell them distinctly apart, then let them merge within you."

He was silent for a time. She did as he instructed, finding and isolating each of the sounds until she could feel them in her chest, then she let them blend, hearing and feeling them all at once. It felt like daenox moving within her. It felt like power, molded and made beautiful by the musicians. She let her body move with the sounds, just a little.

"Good." Siniva's voice was a deep purr now, melodious in its own way. "Keep feeling the music. Let it become your center. Then reach out from that center and feel the crowd. Let the energy of their excitement lift you. Let it bolster you and feed you. Feel how the energy of the crowd gives to the performers and how they give back to the crowd with their performance. Feel the exchange of that energy as it gains momentum. Let that guide you when your time comes to perform. Become part of that cycle."

She could feel it now. The energy feeding from the crowd to the performers and back to the crowd, creating an ever-increasing loop that could sustain them all as it gained power. Siniva's hands left her shoulders, and she opened her eyes. He had moved aside. Before her, the dancers in their beautiful outfits swirled and swayed. Myrza especially had become something otherworldly. Her contortionist's muscles moved in an unusual way, making her seem like a different kind of being. Something more than the rest of them.

Torches were burning all around the square now. The crowd had doubled in the short time since she closed her eyes, and for a few seconds, alarm started to creep back in, but Raine held on to what Siniva had said.

She watched the dancers. Watched Myrza. She let herself feel the music and the energy, allowing it to move in her chest along with the woman's movements.

One of the drums dropped away, and Idrin walked up to the stage with hands full of long curved daggers. Myrza and Marisa danced off while he set most of the weapons on a table and began to toss the two he kept, spinning, into the air. He wore fingerless leather gloves so thin that it was clear they were for costuming, not protection.

Myrza came to stand next to Raine who felt a sudden need to run her fingers through her hair to make sure it was not disarrayed. Her heartbeat sped up. She could smell the salty-sweet tang of sweat from the woman.

Raine swallowed against her nerves and said, "You dance beautifully."

It sounded lame to her ears, but Myrza's eyes came alive with pleasure.

"You enjoyed it then?"

Her voice was soft and silvery, like a girl's or a young boy's. Her tone sounded genuinely inquisitive. Raine glanced over at her, wondering if her opinion should really matter all that much. She found herself looking into eyes that were deep and dark and full of mystery, like the night sky she loved so much. She swallowed again.

"Very much."

Myrza smiled, a hint of a blush darkening her cheeks in the flickering torchlight. "I hoped you would."

There was a synchronized gasp of surprise from the audience members. Raine took advantage of the distracting sound to free herself from Myrza's gaze and look back at the stage. The music had gotten more dramatic, and Idrin was doing his own kind of martial looking dance, now juggling five spinning blades. The audience was enraptured and, if she was not mistaken, had grown some more.

A few minutes later, Idrin had all seven blades swirling through the air and was stepping through a complex array of moves that could have passed for either dance or combat. There were people in the audience chewing their nails by the time he caught the seven blades and bowed. Before he finished his bow amid considerable applause, Siniva and Cadovan were stepping onto the stage, each holding a staff that burned on both ends.

Whether Siniva could dance or fight under other circumstances did not matter. With fire involved, he could do anything. They had figured this out quickly in practice. When he tried practicing different moves, at Nakia's request, without a live flame, he had appeared hopelessly awkward and unable to follow her instruction. She had almost given up but decided to try a few simple things with a live flame to see if they looked good enough to at least justify his presence in the troop. It was then that they discovered fire brought him to life. It gave him power and grace, turning movements that had been clumsy and inelegant into a beautiful, powerful dance. Fire was the blood that ran through his veins. It was his daenox.

At least that was how she thought of it. Daenox gave her confidence and made her something more than what she was without it. Even now, she yearned to draw upon it, but she knew she needed to be selective about how she used it, here among all these people especially. Until it was her turn to perform, she would draw upon the energy Siniva had helped her find that swirled ever-stronger between the performers and their audience.

The two fire dancers were using their staffs in a mock battle that had some degree of true rivalry in it. Cadovan did not like having someone step in to share his role. It was evident in the force of his strikes and the grimace he wore. The man's aggression seemed to amuse Siniva, however, and he had no fear of the weapon or the fire on it, so it gave the audience some authenticity to add to the excitement of the show.

Suddenly, Siniva's staff split in the center, and he dropped to his knees, holding up the two halves as though to defend himself. Then Cadovan split his staff in two. Siniva surged to his feet and they continued to battle, using the split staves like dual swords now. The fire on the ends, which should have been dwindling by now, was still burning strong. Raine had no doubt that Siniva was responsible for that. Then they tossed the flaming staff ends off the back of the stage where Marisa quickly used a wet towel to douse them.

The two men moved to the sides of the stage and knelt there on one knee, their heads bowed, their muscles glistening with sweat in the light of the torches. Applause burst from the crowd. Raine's breath caught in her throat. She felt her body wanting to freeze in place. She fought it, knowing she would embarrass them all and ruin the show if she did not follow through. Remembering what Siniva told her, she let the music move through her and the energy of the rapt audience fed into her. She drew on daenox, careful about how much and how fast she pulled it into herself, and grabbed the two short "wands" Marisa had fashioned for her. They had small, shiny beads woven around them, designed to glint enticingly in the flickering light of the torches. At the ends, they branched out crookedly in several places, creating multiple points where she could draw the daenox out.

Every tiny hair on her skin felt as if it were vibrating at incredible speed and her mouth had gone dry, but she remembered the moves Marisa and Myrza had shown her. She remembered that Myrza was watching her. She took the starting pose Myrza had chosen for her, facing slightly to the side with her far arm stretched across in front of her, holding up that wand as if to shield herself from the crowd, and the arm nearer the front pulled in so that wand was close in front of her face. She paused there, counting heartbeats, until the music changed, the other instruments dropping back so the flute could send its voice up into the night alone.

She counted five more beats, then she drew daenox up through one of the branch tips on the shielding wand, making it emit a tiny swirl of gleaming orange. The audience murmured in surprise and curiosity. She turned to the wand, giving it a look of surprise as if she had not expected this, and drew out small swirls of bright blue and bright orange from two different tips. She smiled at the colors and began to move, counting her heartbeats and letting the music guide her speed. Drawing colored daenox from both wands now, small bursts and swirling tendrils dancing out of the many different branch tips, she stepped through a straight-forward series of moves Marisa and Myrza had choreographed for her. The sequence of steps repeated numerous times, but the changes in the color and complexity of the light show coming from the wands distracted from the repetition.

The crowd was once again rapt, but this time she was the one keeping them mesmerized. She fed off their energy, weaving it into the flow of daenox, letting the powers merge. Her confidence grew. She let herself go, adding energy and emotion to the movements. The lights became brighter and lifted higher from the tips of the wands, creating occasional shapes now, vibrant flowers and stars rising in the darkness.

At either end of the stage, Cadovan and Siniva had been handed burning blades, preparing for the next act. They were starting to rise very slowly. Her moment was almost over.

Then everything went still. Everyone in the audience stopped moving, freezing in the middle of whatever motion they were making, their expressions locked into place. Everyone in the troop froze as well, the music stopping and the two men on the stage stalling halfway up. Even the energy stopped in its cycle, deserting her. Everything was still except the fire of the torches and the burning blades, which flared up as if someone had fed the flames. The daenox she was weaving crashed into a much greater weaving of the same power.

A solitary figure moved through the frozen crowd now. A familiar young man with blue eyes, dusty-blond hair, and a crooked smirk. A man she had met once before when she was still a prisoner in the Dunues Mountain cave. His presence overflowed with daenox, almost as if he had been constructed of it. He wove his way through the stationary audience to the foot of the stage, and she narrowed her eyes at him, clinging to the daenox for courage.

The young man smiled up at her. "Raine," he greeted.

Kyouin.

She did not speak his name. She did not feel like being that courteous. Besides, her throat had gone uncomfortably dry, and her heart was beating so hard she thought he might hear it pounding if she opened her mouth.

hat a quaint little display," Kyouin nodded to the wands. "So delicate. So controlled."

He was close enough now that Raine could smell the death on him from the many undead creatures he had in his army. It made her stomach do several flips.

"It isn't for the likes of you," she growled, somewhat pleased to find that the growl sounded convincingly animalistic. A flurry of memories flashed through her mind. Her father, Dephithus, discovering his dragonkin growl as a child. His mother, Avaline, her grandmother, chiding him for frightening the other children with it. The gleam of delight in the eyes of her mother, Myara, when Dephithus would growl for her. She slammed a door on the memories. It was hard enough to keep herself together in front of him without the bombardment of memories that did not belong to her.

"That's not nice," Kyouin pushed out his lip in a mock pout. "Besides, whether it was for me or not, I could feel you practicing it from miles away. How could I resist such enticement?"

Her glower faltered, and her skin crawled. She had taken such pains to keep from broadcasting her use. How could he have felt it?

Kyouin smirked. "Oh dear," he put his fingers to his

lips, somehow knowing exactly how to mock her at that moment. "And you were being so careful too."

She could feel herself starting to tremble. He was a natural with the daenox, so much so that he could have been made from it, and he had a lot more life experience than she did. Where now was the courage she had faced him with in the cave? Had that been a false display made possible only by the protection of the bars between them? Was she nothing more than a coward after all?

"I came to give you a gift."

The torches flared higher. In the periphery of her vision, she could see the flames on the blades flaring up as well, licking toward the two men holding them. She did not think the fire would hurt Siniva, given his nature, but there was no point taking chances. With a quick redirection of daenox she had pulled in for the performance, she created an invisible barrier of power to block the flames.

Kyouin nodded as if in approval. As if she needed approval from him.

"Nicely done." He reached up to the chain around his neck and took it off. Then he held it out to her. The ring that had been Avaline's dangled from it in the space between them. "You said once that you were going to come and take this from me. You seemed to feel quite strongly about it at the time, so I thought it might make a nice peace offering."

Raine held his gaze, making no move to take the ring. The world hung in stasis around them, only the flames moving. Inside, she shook with terror, her gut turning to mush. She had said she would take it from him, but she was far from ready to confront him. Not yet. Not alone.

"Why would you want to make a peace offering?"

He let go of the chain, using daenox to keep the

ring suspended in the air front of her. "At some point, our paths will cross again, Ele Arithe. We are conduits of daenox, you and I. If we were to fight one another, our combined powers would bring destruction to this land the likes of which no one has seen before. I offer you this ring, whatever it means to you, to symbolize a possible alternative. While you hold it close, perhaps you will consider what we could accomplish if we were to work together instead."

A movement in the frozen crowd caught her eye. She glanced over, spotting Rakas watching them between two frozen women. The saturation of daenox in him apparently rendered him immune to Kyouin's working. Kyouin followed her gaze and gave a slight nod as though acknowledging a fellow craftsman. Then he turned back to her, not waiting to see if Rakas returned the gesture. It comforted her that he did not.

She turned her attention back to Kyouin, refusing to look at the ring that hung between them. She was not about to give him the satisfaction of reaching for it. Instead, she drew it from the air using the same power that held it there and slid it into her pocket without setting a finger upon it. Kyouin offered her a slight bow and walked away with a confidence that left her even more disconcerted. He had come here alone and entirely without fear.

She and Rakas watched him go. As he was stepping past the last few members of the audience, Rakas called out to her.

"Get ready."

It took only a few seconds for her to understand what he meant. She drew more daenox back up through the wands and resumed her dance as the audience and the troop reanimated, continuing their activities as if nothing out of the ordinary had occurred. From somewhere in the crowd, she could feel Rakas watching her, the daenox in him strong and awake after Kyouin's visit.

When her performance was over, she retreated from the stage, amazed that she did not fall off given how rattled her nerves were. The show continued with an elaborate flaming sword fight around and over Myrza as she danced and twisted into unnatural poses between the two men, appearing to narrowly dodge the blades. The music built a glorious tension that Raine might have appreciated more under different circumstances. It ended with Myrza folded on the stage in a way that no body was meant to fold. The two men breathed great bursts of fire into the air above Myrza and then above the crowd, the heat of the flame so intense it made Raine's skin tighten.

The applause was deafening. The crowd's appreciation electrifying the air like a storm cloud.

Inside, Raine still trembled. Kyouin had found her already, and so effortlessly. Would Theruses find her next? Where was he? Was his wing healed from the damage Hydra had inflicted on it defending her outside the cave?

Her father's enemies were made hers through no choice of her own. They were, supposedly, the enemies of the dragons as well. But where were those dragon's now? The mighty beasts that her freedom had released from their stone prisons. Why weren't they fighting the daemon army and bringing the world into balance again?

At least she did not have to fear Amahna coming after her. They had found her body outside the cave the day Dephithus came for her and Siniva had rather unceremoniously shoved it down one of the pits near the entrance.

Her gaze wandered to where Rakas had been in the crowd. He was not there now, and glancing around, she spotted him walking back toward the inn with Kovial.

Was Rakas not one of her father's enemies as well? Should she not hate him?

"You were magnificent!"

A pair of slender hands squeezed her shoulders. Myrza leaned in to kiss her on one cheek that felt like it was suddenly on fire. When Myrza drew back, her face filled Raine's vision, and the sounds around them became muffled somehow. Voices and images in her periphery blurred. Raine's breath caught in her throat. Her gaze got stuck on Myrza's lips. Thin, but full enough for her slender features. Soft.

Those lips curved in a pleased little smile, and Raine's face burned hotter.

"I told you that you could do it," Siniva rumbled as he stepped in and, in one abrupt motion, extricated her from Myrza to pull her up into a hug.

Raine was not sure if the gesture was a show of genuine affection or if he merely wanted to interrupt whatever had been going on between her and Myrza, but she appreciated it almost as much as she resented it.

Marisa, Kelcy, and Idrin were working through the gradually dispersing crowd with hats or sacks in hand, accepting what generosity the bedazzled folk of Corbent Calid were willing to part with. Judging by the gleaming coins that were Nakia's eyes, they were having a good run. Nakia glanced their way, and the coins of her eyes sparkled even brighter as she walked over.

"I don't suppose you two are heading in the direction of Imperious?"

Siniva started to open his mouth, his expression of enthusiasm flipping to one of instant false regret.

Raine could see the lie in his expression and headed him off. "Actually, we are traveling that way."

Siniva's mouth shut, his expression as stony as the statue he had once been imprisoned in.

"Marvelous," Nakia exclaimed. "We can travel together. You can perform with us in the towns, and you won't have to worry so much about people questioning your appearance."

Siniva's expression softened ever-so-slightly at that. Even he could not argue with the value in being part of a performing troop where eccentricity and strange appearances were expected. The less they had to defend themselves from suspicion for their looks the easier and safer their journey would be. She already had the attention of the leader of the daemon army. She could do without any more unwanted attention.

"We'll have an injured Imperious soldier traveling with us as well," Raine added, ignoring Siniva's eye roll.

Nakia shrugged. "As long as he's well enough to travel, he's welcome. We'll be heading out early tomorrow. You're welcome to stay in the camp tonight or join us in the morning."

Raine glanced up at Siniva in time to see his gaze wander over to Myrza who had gone to help clean up their props.

He grimaced slightly. "We have the room at the inn for another night. We'll join you in the morning."

"Suit yourself, though there will be some celebrating in the camp tonight. It's a shame you'll miss it. You earned a bit of celebration as much as the rest of us."

"Raine could use the rest," he stated.

Raine looked up at him, confused. "I'm not that tired." Besides, a lively celebration might keep her from thinking about Kyouin for a while. Siniva did not know about that. Should she tell him? Perhaps not, given his newly developed protectiveness.

Unfortunately, Nakia chose that moment to defer to Siniva. She glanced at Raine, her expression unreadable, then gave him a long look. "You'll have to let her grow up eventually," she commented enigmatically before turning away to go assist with the cleanup.

Siniva watched her go and muttered under his breath, "Maybe when she's at least seven." Then he put and hand on Raine's shoulder and started to steer her away.

"Shouldn't we stay and help?"

"Not tonight. I'm sure we'll have plenty of opportunities to prove our worth on the way to Imperious."

Raine glanced back as they walked away, trying not to let her gaze linger too long on Myrza since those interactions seemed to cause Siniva some consternation. There would be time to show their worth, and time for lingering gazes, on the road to Imperious. Tonight, she would also defer to Siniva, at least in going back to the inn. She needed to talk to Rakas.

As soon as they reached their rooms, she dismissed herself, leaving Siniva staring after her in frustration when she insisted on going down to check on Kovial's readiness to travel. She had barely stepped into the room down the hall when Rakas ushered her back out and led her to a door at the back of the inn. They stepped outside into a small yard between the inn and a storage building. The uniform black of his eyes was unnerving in the moonlight, refusing to impart any insight into his mood.

He glanced around as if to ensure they weren't being watched and leaned in close. "You draw the most disagreeable attention. What did he give you?"

She reached into her pocket and touched the ring. She could feel Kyouin's influence on it. It would take some time for that to wear off. She drew it out and slid it off the chain, dropping the latter in the dirt. No need to keep more of his influence on her person than necessary. The ring had a large green gemstone set in it and delicate vines carved around the perimeter of the silver band. It was simple and beautiful. She eyed the size and slid it on the ring finger of her right hand.

"Are you sure you want to wear that?" Rakas asked, eying the object dubiously. "I can sense him on it."

"It was Avaline's ring. It carries traces of her life in it. He'll fade from it soon enough."

Rakas nodded, his expression softening.

"What did he call me? Ele Arithe?"

"It's an old word in the language of the dragons. It's like a kindred spirit. Fated to be together in a non-romantic sense."

Raine shuddered and shook her head in rejection of the name.

There was a hint of pity in his face before he drew a sheathed sword out from under the cloak he wore and held it out to her. "This was supposed to be a Dawning Day gift for your mother. Dephithus was bringing it to her. I think it should be yours."

Raine took a step back. "I…" she stared at the weapon he held out to her. The ring on her finger felt heavier. The past closed in on her. Not her past, but that of her parents. She shook her head. "What would I do with a sword?"

Rakas frowned. "It is not mine to keep, and I would do no more with it. Do what you want with the weapon. It's yours." He held it out more forcefully now.

She lifted her gaze, staring into those blackened over eyes. "You could have sold it."

"It was not mine to sell. I've done enough wrong in my life. I made a choice to change that when I left the service of Theruses. Sell it if you wish, but it is yours by right."

She stared at him for several more seconds in silence. He had done a great deal of wrong. His actions, willing or otherwise, had brought about the freeing of the daemons into the world again. He had changed her father's life. Destroyed it.

She grabbed the offered hilt. "You're right. This shouldn't be in your hands."

He flinched as if she had struck him and swallowed, bolstering himself for whatever he intended to say next. "I want to come with you if you would allow it. Kovial could use additional healing, and you could use someone else to help watch your back."

"Siniva would rather stab you in the back than have you watching mine."

Rakas stood a little taller then, as though finding some bastion of defiance in himself. "I'm not asking Siniva."

She suspected he was playing off her own defiant streak, appealing to that part of her that wanted to make her own decisions. He was asking her permission, not anyone else's. She held the sword close, absently noticing the strange boost of confidence the weapon gave her, even if she did not have the faintest idea how to wield it properly.

"You may join us but know that, at the first sign of any ill intent, I won't stop Siniva from ending you."

"I would expect no different."

She gave a firm nod. Then, not quite sure how to follow it up, she turned to go inside, calling back over her shoulder, "We leave early tomorrow."

The Elysium Palace loomed over Darkin and Suva. The elegant flowing waves of stone around the entrance had lost their power to enchant and encourage visitors walking between them. At least Darkin felt as though they had. Perhaps it was due to the newly acquired film of dirt upon the stone or the way so many blooms wilted prematurely in the gardens leading up to the entrance no matter how hard the gardeners worked to keep them healthy. It could also have something to do with the solemn mood of everyone there. There was a pervasive sense of despair filling the air like overpowering perfume, chipping away at any vestiges of hope they had for stopping the tide of daemons plaguing the region.

For Darkin, it was all those things to some degree, but a significant portion of it was because of the new king himself. He would have said once that he did not notice or care much about the goings-on so far above his station, but he recognized now how much those goings-on could affect the people. Allondis was not an unfair king. Nor was he a cruel king. Mostly, he was an absent king. He was rarely seen. He did nothing to rally the people and give them hope. He never came out among his troops and rarely granted anyone ranked below the area or lance commander an audience.

"I suppose I should feel honored," Darkin muttered under his breath.

"What?" Suva quickened her pace to move up beside him.

"Nothing." He strode up to the guards in front of the closed entry to the palace. As someone who never sought favor among the nobility, knowing he had every right to be here did not make coming here feel any less peculiar. It felt stranger still if he thought about how, not that many years ago, this entrance had stood open to all.

The guards stood rigid, their hands on their weapons, no welcome in their eyes.

"What business do you have here?" The guard on his right demanded.

"I have an audience with King Allondis, and frankly, I'd like to get it over with. These clothes are so dirty they itch. I'd like to get out of them as soon as possible."

The guard looked him up and down, his lip curling in a grimace. "The way you smell, I don't think the palace hounds would grant you an audience. Clear out of here."

Darkin sneered and took a step closer, letting his hand shift toward his sword and trusting his ruthless fighting reputation to intimidate the man. "Perhaps you've forgotten that we're all on the same side. I understand how that could be a problem. I'm struggling to remember it myself right now."

The guard lifted his chin a bit more, though a bead of sweat showed on his brow. "I don't have permission to let you in."

"Horse farts," Darkin snapped. Suva choked back a laugh, resulting in a very indelicate snorting sound. "Lance Commander Jayik has never liked me, but she has enough sense to know that this isn't the time for indulging petty feuds. We all have a common enemy right now, and my troop had a run-in with the leader of that enemy. Commander Jayik told me to come up here and talk to the king. Now!" He barked the last word, making the guard jump.

"Your troop?"

Darkin heaved a sigh. He could almost feel Suva behind him itching to hit the guard, but she held her ground, making some effort to respect his rank, at least in front of their current audience. "Don't play dumb. You know how many officers we've lost out there. They're being picked off like flowers for a table setting."

"I guess anyone can advance ranks these days."

This was the other guard, and Suva started toward him. Darkin threw up a hand. She stopped in response, which surprised him a little. He made a mental note to thank her for her remarkable restraint later.

He gave the other guard a withering look before turning back to the one he had been dealing with. "Soldiers of the Imperious Legion are dying off fast enough out there. Do you really think we should be wasting our precious energy fighting amongst ourselves?"

The silence stretched between them. Most people knew Darkin and his group had started spending time with Dephithus around the time the former heir to the throne began acting strangely and bad things started to happen in Imperious and the surrounding areas. Few people seemed willing to forget it. The new lance commander was one of the few who did not seem to care or was at least willing to overlook those things in favor of his combat skills. For his part, he did not feel like he had much of a hand in Dephithus's deterioration. That started before he entered the picture. Mostly, he had just taken advantage of the situation to blackmail his way into some mounted combat training from one of the best students in the Legion. What was a little blackmail compared to some of the terrible things Dephithus had done?

Of course, he had helped Dephithus sneak onto the palace grounds long after he was wanted for murder to collect some of his things, including Hydra, but no one knew about that except for Suva and Kovial. Dephithus needed supplies for his journey to try and save Myara and their child. That seemed as noble a reason as any for a bit of subterfuge. Darkin sometimes wondered what had become of them. Maybe Dephithus had found them and they had gone off together somewhere to live out their lives in peace. He liked to think that was what had happened, even if it probably was the least likely outcome.

The silence had drawn on long enough.

"Let me clarify the situation. I," he pointed a finger at himself, "have a message from the leader of the daemon army. A message that Lance Commander Jayik ordered me to take directly to King Allondis. You," he pointed at both guards, "are currently the only thing standing in the way of my completing those orders. If you like, I can go get the lance commander, and she can explain the situation, or you can stop behaving like a horse's ass and let me through. I'm sure she won't mind the hassle any more than the king will mind you delaying important, time-sensitive information."

"Why didn't you say that from the start." He looked at the other guard, missing Darkin's glower. "Stop mucking around over there and escort these two to the audience chambers!"

The other guard narrowed his eyes, but he held his tongue and moved to open the door. Darkin gave the first guard a nod as he passed. It was more courtesy than the man deserved, but it might make him think twice about his opinion of them if they were forced to interact again. There was a time for conflict and a time for diplomacy. The tricky part was keeping the two straight when dealing with stubborn fools, and Allondis seemed to have an affinity for keeping such men close. They were always men too. It was a curious thing. Allondis had no women soldiers among his personal guard, nor had he taken any lovers of any gender, not even in secret. It would have been common knowledge if he had because everything the king did was common knowledge whether he wanted it to be or not. Did the king have some sort of dislike for women? More importantly, did he have an affinity for dumb men?

Darkin smirked to himself and followed the guard down the halls with Suva flanking him. Leaving Kovial behind had subdued her fierce spirit enough that she almost seemed a part of these hopeless, dim hallways.

Since the rise of the daemons and the new saturation of the power they called daenox, many people were falling ill. The king's new sage—a role that had only recently been reintroduced to the palace—said that a significant number of people reacted poorly to daenox and that it could leave them weak and susceptible to illness. The evidence supported his words. The palace staff was drastically diminished by illness, and the population of the city was also afflicted. At least half the residents of Imperious showed some signs of illness ranging from slight lethargy to the worst who were completely bedridden and appeared to be wasting away, wracked with seizures, severe fevers, and an inability to keep food down.

Suva's father had died from it. That was one of the few good things that had come from the rise of daenox here. No one would argue that truth.

There was also a shortage of food in many places now. Daenox saturation caused some crops to wither and livestock to sicken. Many farmers were also losing livestock to daemon attacks. If things did not change soon, the outlook was bleak.

The guard led them to a smaller audience chamber with one of the king's many ornate thrones sitting on a low dais at the head. There were no chairs for those seeking an audience. No one sat while seeing the king. Fortunately, there were a few chairs for palace advisors and dignitaries along the sides of the room. Darkin and Suva were directed to two of these chairs and told to wait for King Allondis.

They waited. For a long time. They waited without speaking, perhaps both afraid that these walls might have ears. Suva picked at her fingernails with the point of her dagger, wiping the dirt on her grimy pants. Darkin tapped out several tavern tunes on the floor with his boots, wondering if the chairs would be cleaned after they left, or just burned. The latter thought made him smile to himself, for a while anyway. After perhaps an hour had passed, he stood up to go see if they had been forgotten. The door behind the throne opened then, and a tired-looking gentleman in palace livery stepped up beside the throne.

"All rise for the Lord High Commander of Imperious, King Allondis Verathian."

His booming voice bounced off the walls, and Suva almost dropped her dagger in surprise. She quickly hopped to her feet and sheathed the weapon, giving the man a sour look. Darkin smirked at her then schooled his expression as the king entered the room in the company of four guards.

Where his predecessor, Dephithus's den-father, King Mythan, had often dressed as a noble but rarely as royalty outside of special occasions, Allondis looked like he was heading for a royal fete every time Darkin had seen him. Today was no exception. He was dressed in dark blue pants and matching jacket over a white silk shirt, all of the finest materials with elegant gold trimmings. He wore a bejeweled crown upon his pale brow, a symbol of his office that had seen little use under Mythan's rule. His dark eyes constantly shifted, untrusting, beneath those sparkling gems. His face was so young. He barely looked old enough to have had his Dawning Day yet.

Darkin and Suva both knelt and bowed their heads, waiting for the king to settle.

"Rise and explain yourselves."

Darkin's temper took a quick jump. At the very least, they deserved proper acknowledgment as soldiers in his army who put their lives on the line almost daily for the kingdom. He had little choice other than to swallow his irritation for the moment.

"Your Highness, our troop had a run in with the leader of the daemon army—"

The king interrupted with a scoff. "Army. There is no army. Just a lot of roving bands causing mischief."

Mischief?

How many soldiers had to die before the king acknowledged that they were facing something far more significant than a bunch of roving bands? Darkin drew a deep breath. He noticed the tremble in the king's hands resting on the arms of the throne.

"With all respect, your Highness, there were several thousand gathered not far from Corbent Calid. Human and daemon alike gathered under a single leader. If not an army, then still an organized force large enough to be a significant threat."

Allondis glanced at Suva and quickly looked back at Darkin, his pale skin reddening a little. "If you saw this, how are you still alive?"

"Most of my troop is not. We got lucky. The man leading them decided he needed someone to deliver a message for him, so he let us go."

The king's gaze drifted to Suva. She smiled like a jorycat might smile before finishing off its prey. Allondis gripped the throne and turned back to Darkin again.

"What message?"

"He said he would be at the gates of Elysium one month and fourteen days after we left him. At that time, he expects you to give him Imperious, or he will take it from you. His words, not mine," Darkin added when the king's expression soured.

"I'm not giving Imperious to some self-important madman," Allondis snapped, a small tremble in his voice.

Darkin could not help wondering if Suva had as much trouble as he did not saying that Imperious already was in the hands of a self-important madman. Though, to be fair, he suspected Allondis was mostly underprepared for the role he had taken on. He had not been groomed to it from birth the way Dephithus had been. Stepping in as king unexpectedly when the previous heir was renounced and the prior king descended into madness would be a hard adjustment for anyone. Darkin tried to keep that in mind.

"I can only tell you what he told us. It is, of course, up to you how to respond to that information," Darkin stated, hoping he sounded more deferential than he felt. Mostly, he just wanted the audience to be over.

"How much of that time remains?"

"A month, give or take a day or two."

Allondis stared through them, his eyes narrowing. His lips moved for several seconds, speaking without making a sound. Darkin made out the word troops and commander and perhaps betrayal, though he hoped he was wrong about the last one.

Eventually, he focused on Darkin again.

"I need to consider this. Meet with the lance and area commanders and tell them everything you can remember about this army. I expect you to be in Elysium when your new friend arrives. You may go."

"Our new..." Darkin bit his tongue and bowed. "Yes, your Highness."

Suva also bowed, muttering something under her breath that could have been a "your Highness" at least if you were far away and perhaps a bit deaf.

Darkin rose and made a quick exit with Suva on his heels, hoping Allondis had not heard what she actually said.

Kyouin felt the concentration of daenox approaching almost ten minutes before he heard the swoop of great wings cutting through the air. It was a dark night, but the light of a sliver moon still glinted on the gold scales of the massive dragon as it descended, throwing muscular legs before it to catch itself. Despite the beast's magnificence, he found himself focusing on the scar that marred the membrane of one wing and caused a slight wobble in the dragon's descent.

The part of his attention that was not tuned to his unannounced visitor was busy warning back his army. Mostly that took the form of manipulating the control he had over the undead officers. The reanimated dead were easiest to control with the daenox, even more so than the simpler creatures, so Kyouin had put them in charge of most of his troops. It made it possible to issue synchronized commands across the army.

For some reason, Ryche was not as easy to control as the others. With Ryche, it was more like passing along strong suggestions and hoping they would be followed through. In some ways, it made him uncomfortable, but it was also why he had made the monster his Area Commander. The undead warrior brought some skill at strategy back from the grave with him. Ryche could direct the army for him when he was otherwise occupied. No one questioned the undead commander on his partially decayed mount.

Kyouin suspected his army could take down the dragon, though not without some losses. He was curious, however, what made Theruses so bold as to approach him amid that army, so he kept them back, giving the dragon plenty of room to land.

Around his feet, buffeted by the wind created by the dragon's wings, several daemon-dogs slunk. Their tails were tucked, and they whined uncomfortably. The dragon created confusion in them. Dragons and daenox were, by nature, contradicting forces. Not quite enemies, they were tied together in a delicate balancing act that did often put them in opposition. Yet here was a creature that was both a dragon and a vessel for daenox. The daemons could sense both about him, and it confused them.

As the dragon settled, looming over them, another whine caught Kyouin's attention. His little brother, Vaneye, reached up and took his hand. It was a bit jarring, feeling how strong the saturation of daenox had become in the boy. That much daemon power in the child should have made him stronger, but he had only grown more insecure and needier. He was not more robust, braver, or more confident than Kyouin had been at his age. He was weak. Weak and vulnerable and reminded Kyouin far too much of his younger self, the pathetic, angry child he left behind when the daemon power welcomed him.

He twisted his hand free of the smaller one and took a step closer to the settling dragon.

"Theruses, what brings you to me?"

The dragon narrowed his black eyes at Kyouin and brought his head down, filling his field of vision with a massive jaw full of long, tapered teeth.

"You've taken many of my followers," Theruses accused, though he did not sound all that upset.

"You turned into a dragon and disappeared," Kyouin countered. Then he held his hands out to indicate the army around them. "What could I do but welcome them into the fold."

Theruses lifted his head, scanning the landscape of warriors, daemons, and undead that surrounded them. He stretched his great wings. When the scar in the one wing pulled taught his lip lifted in a silent snarl that gave a clearer view of those deadly teeth. After perhaps a minute of silence he folded his wings and lowered his head again.

"You mean to take Imperious."

Kyouin felt a twist of unease in his chest. "Why do you assume such?"

The dragon chuckled, a rumbling sound deep in his chest. "I've been watching you. You've been moving your army that direction in indirect increments. I presume a full-on attack is imminent."

How could Theruses have been watching his army? The dragon was rather conspicuous. Even in his more human form, he would stand out in any crowd. Aside from that, the concentration of daenox within him was enough to give Kyouin substantial warning of his approach. There was no way he could have gotten close enough to spy on the army without Kyouin noticing.

Unless there was a traitor in their midst. Or perhaps the dragon was using some of his daemons against him.

It was all Kyouin could do not to shift his feet or clench his fists. Those were childish shows of temper though. He was not a child anymore, and no self-important dragon was going to make him act like one.

"Perhaps I am marching on Imperious. How does that concern you? Shouldn't you be going to join the other dragons in whatever hole they've crawled into now?"

Theruses flexed and contracted his claws, digging runnels in the hard stone under his feet. A not-so-subtle display of strength. "To say that I am unwelcome among my kind would be a gross understatement. I thought that, perhaps, you and I might arrange an alliance of some kind."

Kyouin caught himself reaching down in search of Vaneye's hand and jerked his own hand back to his side. "What could you possibly have to offer me?"

"The power of a dragon. I can wreak havoc on the enemy at a greater rate than any three of your troops combined." There was a strange glint in his black eye then as he turned his head and cocked it to the side to look down on Kyouin. "I can also help you deal with the greatest single threat to your army."

Kyouin found himself going for the bait. "Which is?"

"Raine."

Kyouin barked a laugh to hide the chill that swept through him. Raine's brassy-black eyes stared into him in his mind. For a heartbeat, he was back in Corbent Calid, looking at her there up on the stage. Her fear of him and her defiance acting like a potent aphrodisiac, but not nearly so potent as the daenox that swept through her, yielding to her will. "She's only a child. She's no threat."

Theruses lashed his tail, barely missing a daemon-dog that had dared get close to sniff at him. The army stirred around them. Ryche circled the hillock they were conversing on at a controlled trot, the clacking of his undead horse's hooves on rock filling the gap in conversation.

"She carries within her the power of the dragons and the daenox both. If she figures out how to tap into the potential of that combined power, she could unravel what you have built. I alone share those two powers. I alone can understand both of those forces well enough to counter her."

"If she was such a danger, why did you let her go?" Kyouin demanded.

His tail lashed harder. "She was taken from me."

"Bah!" Kyouin rolled his eyes at the dragon, insulting and dismissive. "You let her go because you wanted to go free. Now you're merely jealous that I've already begun to woo her to my side. She fears me, and she will follow me in time. I don't fear her."

"You covet what you do not understand." Theruses rumbled. "The more you try to drive fear into her, the more she will rebel against it. I held her for most of her young life. She is something new. An abomination created by the dragons and daenox." Muscles in his powerful forelegs rippled beneath his scaled flesh, reminders of the sheer physical power of a dragon. "She needs to die before she realizes what she is."

Doubt was creeping in, like some vile parasite, worming its way into Kyouin's brain, bringing back foul memories.

Kyouin faced his father over a wobbly little foal born too soon. The small animal had a coat as black as midnight and a white blaze down its forehead. It had fallen, again and again, unable to hold itself up on weak legs.

"I can raise it," he protested, tears running down his cheeks.

"You have chores you're already too blasted lazy to keep up with. The animal won't survive on its own, and mark my words, you won't survive if I catch you wasting time trying to keep it alive."

"I don't care! I'm going to keep it. You can't stop me."

His father's eyes darkened, turning black in his memory, though he knew that had not truly happened. Suddenly, he was staring up at the roof of the stable from where he landed on his back, his shirt soaking in moisture from the warm manure he had been shoveling out. His ears were ringing, and his head spun, his jaw shooting with pain.

His father moved into his vision, standing over him with hands on his hips. "When I come out here next time, that animal had best be dead, or you will be."

His father left him there. Weeping like a babe, he took a hammer from the wall and smashed the foal's head. It took several strikes, and he was crying so hard he could not see when it was finally over. He hid the hammer under his bed. One year later, on the very day the foal died, he used it to do the same thing to his father. It had been harder. His father's skull did not give as quickly as the foal's had, but he was determined. He did not cry this time.

"I can handle Raine," Kyouin growled under his breath. "Begone from here. My army doesn't need you."

Those deadly jaws hovered in his vision for a time, the lips curving into a snarl or a smile, he was not sure which. Was the beast playing with him?

Theruses rose up tall, stretching his wings again. "With pleasure. Your army reeks of death. I've had enough of the stench."

Kyouin sneered. "I thought you were the Death Dragon."

Theruses matched his expression. "I *bring* death. I do not wallow in it." The dragon jumped into the air, buffeting them with the wind from his massive wings. "Raine will destroy you, and you will remember this moment quite clearly when she does."

The dragon rose up fast then and left Kyouin standing coated in the dust his departure had roused. He stared after Theruses until the glints of gold in the moonlight could no longer be seen.

Theruses was wrong. Raine was the perfection of the two powers combined. When she joined him, they would be unstoppable. Her power was too much for her now. Eventually, her uncertainty and the attraction of the daemon power would bring her to his side. It would be an unforgivable waste to destroy the girl merely because she could be dangerous. If he nurtured her properly when she finally came into his fold, she would be the power that secured his throne and helped him rebuild this world.

And yet…

His gaze went to the rock, scarred by the talons of the Death Dragon. Theruses had spoken with such certainty.

Kyouin summoned his top officers to him, though with Ryche it was more of an invitation than a summons. It only took a few minutes for his officers to gather, a motley assembly of partly decayed warriors. Some were fresh enough that they could still speak, unlike Ryche who could only make those hideous clicking sounds. His new favorite, the former Lady Avaline of Imperious, was the first to arrive. He remembered the moment her spine cracked across the pommel of his saddle with sweet nostalgia. It eased some of the distress of uncertainty.

"My lord," her voice had deteriorated to a rasp now, her pale skin discolored and marred by the ravages of decay.

The other undead gathered there with her, eager to serve. Ryche's teeth clicked together softly as he rode up behind them. Kyouin liked to pretend those clicks were expressions of respect and deference, though he suspected they were no such thing.

"I need you to send out your scouts. Find me Priestess Jadean. I require her foresight." Sending someone for Jadean was not entirely necessary, since she would already know he needed her. She did drag her feet about coming to him sometimes, however, so sending someone ensured a faster response.

There were expressions of obedience all around,

excepting the non-committal clicking from Ryche. Kyouin watched them there for a minute, letting them wait while he considered. A small hand took hold of his, and he glanced down at Vaneye. Matte grey eyes stared back up at him. He grimaced and twisted his hand free again.

"We'll continue toward Imperious. Bring her to me there." He made a dismissive gesture.

They started to move away.

"And..." The officers all stopped and turned back to him. "If the dragon comes back, feel free to kill it."

He let them go then. Raine was not his greatest threat. She was his greatest potential. She was his *Ele Arithe*. They were meant to be together. Two creatures in whom daenox flowed like blood. Two beings who suffered no ill effects from that saturation of daemon power. He could understand why Theruses would not want to acknowledge that. After all, he was the one who had her and let her get away.

"Kyouin?" Vaneye's voice had changed. It was a little ragged now. A little more desperate sounding.

"Leave me alone. I need to think."

A tear ran down from one grey eye, then the boy's face lit up, and he hurried past Kyouin. Curious, Kyouin turned to see his little brother take hold of Avaline's rotting hand. She turned away and led him down the hill.

Curious.

Another chill of unease swept through him.

There was a crispness to the morning. It was a hint colder than previous mornings since they left Corbent Calid. Threatening dark clouds gathered overhead. They were four days outside the last village where they had performed and replenished their stores. Raine glanced up at the sky, already done with her preparations for another day of travel. She woke up earlier now that she was not spending her nights sneaking off to entertain daemons. Traveling with the larger group made it more difficult to get away with such nocturnal adventures.

She scratched under Hydra's forelock, enjoying the way he pushed his head into her hand even though it nearly knocked her over sometimes. What she loved the most about the stallion was the lack of that glimmer of hidden intent in his eyes. In the caves, she thought that glimmer was a hostile thing that only existed because the people there were her captors. Her enemies. Now she realized that most everyone she met had something hiding behind their eyes, secrets they kept that influenced the way they interreacted with the people around them.

Glancing around the group, she caught Myrza looking her way. She met those lovely eyes for a moment, forcing herself not to look away despite the flush rising in her cheeks. It was there too, that glimmer.

Myrza started to smile. She had a beautiful smile, but Raine did not feel like reciprocating this time. Mostly, she felt a strange, pervasive disappointment that made it impossible to respond in kind. Myrza's smile faltered, and she turned back to adjusting her saddlebags.

Raine turned to watch Nakia saddling her black gelding. The animal was a patchwork of scars, the jagged lines showing bright white against his blackness. The gelding had little interest in the other horses and not a lot more interest in food. The one thing he seemed to have endless interest in was the woman currently cinching up his girth. His ears, one whole and one half missing, twitched to attention whenever Nakia murmured to him. He always watched her and nuzzled her whenever she was in reach. In the mornings, he would nicker softly at her the moment she got up from her bedroll.

"Are you ready?"

She glanced at Siniva and gave a quick nod. "Yes."

Nakia was finished now and stood looking over at them while she scratched at a spot under the gelding's mane. The animal pressed his neck into her fingernails, his upper lip stretched and quivering with pleasure.

Raine pointed at the horse. "What happened to him?"

Nakia glanced around, noting as Raine had that only a few of the others were ready to go. She smiled at the horse and patted his shoulder firmly. "Thorn found me several years ago. I was out poaching on some lord or another's land." She smirked at the memory. "I was following a game trail along near the bottom of a small cliff when I heard a racket up top, and suddenly this black horse comes skidding off the edge and plunges down into some wicked brambles at the base. I'm not sure what was chasing him, but the claw marks on his shoulders and the snarl from above made me think it was probably a mountain cat. He was wearing a bridle and a saddle that had flipped down under his belly. Anyhow, he got tangled up good in those brambles. Fought them with every bone in his body, thrashing about like a crazed thing. But the second I cut through the first vine to make my way in to him, he stopped moving and stood still, watching me, blood streaming from hundreds of wounds.

"I was only going in there because I thought it would be too cruel to let him bleed out slowly. I was going to put an end to his suffering. I figured he would be in too bad a condition to do much else after that fall and his tussle with the thorns. But when he stopped struggling, I took another long look at him. Those big brown eyes focused on me, and I was hooked. He trusted me. He believed I was going to fix things. I figured he would start to thrash again when I got close enough to start cutting brambles off him, but he stood still as a stone. He was trembling and obviously in a lot of pain, but patient and trusting to the last thorn I pulled from his hide."

She gazed into his big brown eye now like one might gaze into the eyes of a beloved friend. "It was a miracle he didn't break anything in the fall. His saddle and bridle were destroyed, but he just lost part of that ear and gained some nasty scars. I took him with me and patched him up. I never knew what became of the owner."

"Because you never looked?" Siniva ventured, a hint of accusation in his tone.

Nakia shrugged and moved in front of Thorn. "You're where you want to be, aren't you?" She kissed the horse on his fuzzy nose.

Siniva shook his head and walked back over to his mount.

A short distance away, Kovial was attempting to use his one good arm to position his mount next to a stump. Rakas had managed to knit the bone back together, but the injured arm still had a lot of healing to do, and swinging up from the ground was too painful for him. He got the horse into position, but as soon as he started to step up on the stump, the animal sidestepped away. This happened three times before Kovial closed his eyes, his teeth clenching with frustration. His hand tightened to a fist on the reins.

Rakas was watching from a few feet away, his mount ready beside him, making no move to assist. His lips were pressed together in a tight line of disapproval. The two seemed to have had some sort of falling out, but Raine was not about to watch Kovial reinjure himself. She dropped Hydra's reins, knowing the animal would stay there, and walked over.

"Need a little help?"

"Oh no," Rakas interjected abruptly, "Kovial doesn't need anyone's help. He can handle it on his own."

She flashed Rakas a glare then gave Kovial a hard look. "Are we honestly having one of those moments?"

Not that she had ever experienced one of those moments, but she remembered her mother saying the same thing to Dephithus when he had been too stubborn about admitting an injured ankle needed more rest before returning to Legion practice. She could see him trying to limp to the practice ring through her mother's disapproving gaze.

Like her father in the memory, Kovial had the decency to flush at her words, recognizing some of his own folly.

"You know," she took the reins out of his hand, "needing help sometimes doesn't mean you're weak. Having the sense to ask for it when you need it means you're smart." She scratched the horse's forehead, then shifted the animal back into place by the stump and positioned herself so she could discourage it from moving away again.

Kovial did not move. He stood staring hard at nothing. Rakas gave a small derisive snort behind her.

She glanced over her shoulder at the other man. "You aren't helping," she chastised.

Rakas started to glare back at her, but the expression faltered, and he heaved a sigh. "You're right. I apologize."

She turned back to Kovial. "Right now, you have a chance to heal. You need to heal well, because once you get back to the Legion in Imperious, you're going to have more chances than you could possibly want to prove how tough you are. If you don't take care of yourself now and let people help you, you're going to end up dead because of it. Is that what you want?"

Kovial gave the smallest possible shake of his head. "It's just… It's just that I hate how weak I am right now. I'm useless."

Raine stepped closer, moving around the horse's head. "You're not useless. You're healing, and when you're done, you'll be more useful than most of the rest of us combined. For now, you need to let me help you get on your horse."

Kovial looked at her. His blue eyes were bloodshot. The arm still hurt enough to interfere with his sleep. Given how restless he was when he did sleep, she could not help wondering if he relived the moment of the injury in his dreams.

He finally nodded. "I know you're right. I'm mostly worried about my sister. I should have been with her to make sure she made it back to Imperious safely."

Her father's memories of Kovial's sister swept through her mind, some of them more graphic than she liked. The fierce blond woman from those memories did not strike Raine as someone who needed much protecting.

"I'm sure Suva's fine and is back at Imperious mad with worry over you, so let's get you back to her."

Kovial gave her a puzzled look then. "How did you know her name?"

Cold swept through Raine. She did her best to shrug it off. "I'm sure I overheard you talking to Rakas about her."

Kovial did not look satisfied with the answer, but he turned and stepped up on the stump. Raine poked the horse in the ribs to shift him a little closer, and Kovial climbed painfully up. When she saw that he was situated and had control of the animal, she turned away to find that most of the others were watching them. Not staring precisely, but those who were not looking at them directly were turned slightly their way and had paused in whatever they had been doing. Siniva was the only one outright staring. She could not quite tell if what he had seen pleased him or worried him. If anything, he looked uncertain himself.

No matter how anyone else felt about it, Raine had apparently gained something in Kovial's regard. The young soldier rode by her side the entire day, telling her tales of the battles he had fought and adventures he had. His companions, Suva and Darkin, were in all those stories. Their other two companions, whose deaths Kovial blamed on a daemon attack, appeared in many an early tale of mischief.

Raine enjoyed the tales. They made the day go by much faster. Whenever he started to go quiet, grimacing with the increasing pain of travel, she would use a small touch of daenox to ease his hurting, and he would perk up again, going into some new story. She most enjoyed hearing him tell about when Darkin and Dephithus were training together. It was interesting to hear how his account of things, as an outside observer, differed from her father's memories of those encounters. Of course, her father had been blackmailed into those lessons by Darkin, who knew Larina's death at the joust had not really been an accident. That colored his emotions in those memories quite a bit.

Her father's memories of Kovial were mostly positive. Out of the group of Darkin's followers, Kovial was the one that triggered the greatest sense of trust in Dephithus. He was part of Darkin's band mostly because he would go where his sister went. At least that was her father's feeling on it. But Kovial also respected Darkin. That much was clear from his stories of their exploits. Certainly, Darkin had gotten his group into trouble now and then, and he disrespected authority on a regular basis, but Kovial's stories painted a picture of a clever man who was fiercely protective of and loyal to the people closest to him.

Suva was different. Kovial obviously loved his sister intensely, but even painted by his affection, she came across as an individual full of resentment. A woman who had been mistreated by enough people that she genuinely trusted no one and hid her hurt behind a hostile exterior. She came across as broken.

Like me.

Raine looked forward to meeting them.

When they stopped for the night, she helped Kovial with his equipment. It was a task Rakas had been managing. Rakas, however, did not seem to mind letting her take over that duty. In fact, the man looked distant, his gaze wandering off into the distance back the way they had come. Raine wanted to ask him what was wrong, but her first chance did not come until after they had eaten and most of the troop was conversing around the campfire. Rakas had wandered off into the shadows well out of reach of the firelight.

Raine followed, moving into the shadows of night with him and standing there in silence.

He did not look at her, but said softly, "Do you feel them?"

She did not answer. Instead, she reached to the daenox flowing under their feet and let it help her feel the night and the forest. It only took a few seconds for her to find what he was talking about. Prowling perhaps twenty feet further out in the darkness she touched upon the presence of about seven daemons.

"What are they doing?"

"They've been out there since it started to get dark," Rakas answered in a low voice. "I thought maybe they were attracted to us by your little draws of daenox throughout the day to ease Kovial's pain."

Raine felt her cheeks grow warm, appreciating the dark that hid it from him. "You felt that."

"Yes, but I lived in the caves for a long time. There is a lot of daenox in me. However, I don't think that's why they're gathered here. They aren't responding to my efforts to send them off. I think they were sent."

Raine shivered and wrapped her arms around herself, suddenly cold. "You don't think…"

He finally glanced at her, his expression grim. "Kyouin?" He nodded. "I do."

"But how? He was back in Corbent Calid."

"Well, either he is coming this way, or he's had them tailing us since we left, though this is the first time I've felt them."

Raine shivered again. She did not want to believe that Kyouin was anywhere near them. It made more sense than the latter option though since neither she nor Rakas had noticed the beasts before this. "We should warn the others."

Rakas grimaced. "They will blame us. We are the daenox users in the party."

True. "We have—"

Before she could finish, the daemons surged toward the camp. They swarmed past her and Rakas as if they were not there—daemon-wolves, mutated hounds, and something that looked like a twisted cross between a bear and an elk with cloven hooves in the back and massive hooked claws on its front paws. Raine could not take her eyes off the last beast. Powerful muscles rippled under its flanks and she could only imagine how much damage a single swipe of those paws would do.

She pulled on the daenox at her feet and thrust a blast of power at the beast. It hit him hard in the rear. The other six daemons kept going, but the beast in the back turned around and let out a massive roar, showing her its very large mouthful of sharp teeth. If the camp was not aware of the danger before, they were now.

Shouts rang out from the camp, but the massive daemon was no longer interested. Its grey eyes were riveted on Raine. Short, horselike hair covered its body over a thick, muscular front end that resembled an unusually large bear, narrowing down to a slimmer back end with a short tail more like an elk. If she had not already seen how fast it could move, she would expect the mismatched proportions to make it rather clumsy.

"I'm not sure that was your best idea ever," Rakas called, taking a few slow steps back.

Was he hoping to sneak away while the creature was focused on her?

For a second, she thought that might be his plan, but then he stopped moving, and she could feel him starting to draw on more daenox.

"Don't hurt it," she hissed, drawing daenox from the ground up into the beast.

Rakas made a small noise in his throat. She could see him shaking his head at the edge of her vision. He did not share her desire to save the creature.

The thing started to charge then, heading straight for her as she swept daenox through its body, searching for whatever might be compelling it. She found the source quickly enough, but the beast was not giving her much time to investigate. There was a chaotic knot of daenox woven into its brain. A knot so complex she could not make heads or tails of it. If she could only find a way to unravel it.

The beast roared again, snapping her back to herself and the realization that she was about to be rammed by a twisted monstrosity as big as a horse. Her heart leaped into her throat, and panic surged through her. Then the roar choked off, and the beast fell hard, sliding to a stop with its big, bearlike snout touching the toe of one boot. Blood gushed in great gouts from a ragged wound on the side of its neck.

When she looked to Rakas, torn between anger and gratitude, he was already running back toward the camp. She should join him. There were still shouts of alarm coming from that direction. They probably needed help.

Not that I'm much help.

She looked down at the massive thing at her feet. For a few seconds, she could only stare at the beast. At the moist black nose pressed against her boot toe. At the already slowing river of blood coming from the wound. It looked like something had torn its way out from inside the creature's neck. Her stomach turned. Then the beast twitched, one massive paw jerking violently. Raine let out a cry of surprise and ran after Rakas.

As she ran, four daemon-wolves ran past her, heading back the way they had come. The fur over one's shoulder was burned away, the scalded flesh smoking. When she burst back into the camp, she saw two more daemons lying dead. One lay at Kovial's feet, a sword driven into its chest. Kovial himself sat rocking slightly on a stump now, grimacing and holding the injured arm. Myrza was on the ground next to him, holding her hands up. Her palms were skinned and bleeding, and one sleeve was torn most of the way off.

The other dead beast had a crossbow bolt between its eyes. Over near the horses, Nakia was fastening her crossbow back to her saddle, her lips pressed into a tight line.

Marisa and Kelcy were walking over to help Myrza up. Florin was also on the ground, gripping his forearm above a bloody bite and glaring death at Raine while Idrin knelt next to him to look at the wound. Rakas walked over to Kovial and crouched next to him, laying a gentle hand on the arm, his focus turning inward.

She looked over at Siniva whose eyes appeared to be actively on fire. He gestured away from the camp with a jerk of his head and started walking in that direction, his sharp, angry strides making her chest tighten with dread. She followed.

When they were out of earshot of the camp, he spoke.

"Were you playing with daemons again?"

She bristled at the accusation in his tone. "No."

"Then what drew so many of them to us?"

She started to say it was not her but hesitated. No, she had not been playing with the daenox, but that did not mean she had nothing to do with why they came. Rather than answer, she turned toward where they left the big daemon and gestured for him to follow.

Siniva silently obliged. He drew in a sharp breath when he saw the enormous, twisted beast lying dead amidst the trees.

"Rakas killed it," she stated.

While he looked the beast over, she knelt next to its head and reached in with daenox. The knot of daemon-power was gone, unraveled with its death. She would learn nothing there.

"What's this?"

She stood and walked over to the back end of the beast. A dagger hilt protruded from one hip. Siniva pulled it free and held it up to examine the weapon. The grip was smoothed wood stained glossy black. Below the grip two gold snakes wrapped around either side of the silver crossguard, each with emerald eyes and a tail that dropped a half-inch down the blade on either side. Above the wooden grip, an emerald stone was embedded in each side of the gold pommel. It looked familiar somehow.

"This is no ordinary weapon." Siniva kept his voice low, almost as though afraid of waking the dead beast.

"It belonged to Amahna," Rakas said, his sudden appearance making Raine start. "She gave it to your father after his birthday… to torment him."

Raine shivered, staring at the weapon. She remembered it all too well now, though the memories belonged to Dephithus, not to her. "How did it end up here?"

"One of the last times I saw Amahna alive, she was with Kyouin. I can only assume he got it from her, though I'm not sure when she got it back from your father."

"When she kidnapped my mother," Raine answered with unnerving certainty. She could see Dephithus wielding the dagger through her mother's eyes. It was the last time Myara had seen him. He had been mad with senseless rage fed by the daemon-seed. Reduced to little more than a rabid animal.

Raine took the weapon from Siniva. She could sense Kyouin on it as clearly as she could sense him on Avaline's ring. "It was a message for me."

She glanced up at Rakas then.

He nodded, his gaze solemn. "He's trying to intimidate you."

"He's doing a good job," she tossed the dagger aside like it were some venomous thing likely to bite her.

Siniva slid an arm around her shoulders and drew her close.

Rakas retrieved the dagger. "The daemon must have traveled a long way with this embedded in its flesh. That's some powerful compulsion."

A ball of black hatred formed in Raine's chest. The poor beast suffered that pain merely so Kyouin could try to mess with her head. "There was a knot of daenox in its brain. It was either very complexly woven or a complete chaotic mess."

Rakas narrowed his eyes at her. "You didn't freeze up back there, did you? You were trying to override the compulsion."

She nodded. Rakas cursed under his breath, and she caught something about sentimental fools.

"Why you?" Siniva asked then. "When I was still trapped in stone in the graveyard outside of Kithin I saw Kyouin heading to the caves, to speak with Theruses, I imagine. Did something happen then?"

She gave a small shrug. "I met him. He seemed… fascinated by me somehow. I threatened him."

Siniva glanced down at her, his brow furrowing.

Rakas chuckled. "Well, perhaps you need to remember how you felt when you faced him then."

Raine responded with a shaky smile. For all that she wanted to remember how she felt then, the sensation eluded her. He had shown her tonight that he could turn the daemons against her. He had also shown her that she was a danger to the people around her. Neither of those things made her feel strong or defiant.

"Mind if I join you." Nakia's tone made it clear this was not really a question. She strode out to them and stared down at the dead beast for a few seconds. "Well, I'm glad that one didn't make it to camp."

"You're welcome," Rakas muttered.

"Nice shot with the crossbow," Siniva praised.

Nakia gave him a quick, dismissive glance. "Maybe I should take this moment to emphasize that Florin's husband, one of our performers, died in a daemon attack. Those daemons were drawn to us because another former member used the daemon power carelessly. Since you two," she pinned Rakas and then Raine with her cold gaze, "are my only daenox users, I'd like you to explain what just happened."

Raine stepped forward, pulling free of Siniva's arm. "It wasn't daenox use that brought them. They were sent by Kyouin."

Nakia's eyes narrowed. "The leader of the daemon army. Do I have to explain why that doesn't make me any happier?"

"I threatened him once. He apparently hasn't forgotten." It was an oversimplification, but it was too hard to explain the whole mess. She hoped Nakia would accept that.

Nakia smirked at her. "As much as I don't like the implications of that, it does make me like you more. You, however," she turned on Siniva now. "Would you care to explain the way you draw fire out of nowhere. You say that isn't daenox. Then what is it?"

Raine stepped back now. This was Siniva's problem. She had enough of her own that she did not need to be taking his on.

Siniva glanced down at the dead beast at their feet. He grimaced then nodded to himself. "You know how the dragons went free not so long ago."

"Yes, and subsequently flew off to who-knows-where," Nakia added rather curtly.

At least she was willing to accept that fact. Those who had not seen them in the flesh, flying above as they took off to some unknown destination, were often skeptical that the dragons had come back at all.

"Dragons have the power to take on a human form, and I am one of them. I am Siniva, the Fire Dragon."

Nakia started to chuckle. She looked from Rakas to Raine. They both offered solemn nods. Her laugh died.

"It's true," Rakas said, showing more interest in the dagger he had picked up than in their current conversation.

Nakia looked at Raine. "Does that mean you're also a dragon?"

"No. I'm..." *A freak. Something that never should have existed in the first place.*

Siniva placed a hand on her shoulder, somehow sensing that she needed the support right then. "She's a throwback to the dragonkin. Not a dragon."

A safe if not entirely accurate answer.

"And you just happen to be traveling together?"

"It is more complicated than that," Siniva replied. He glanced down at Raine, giving her shoulder a gentle squeeze. "It's a long story."

Nakia's smile was not entirely friendly now. They had all become suspect and were going to have to earn their way back into her trust. "Lucky for you we have some time before we reach Imperious for the sharing of long stories. For now, I will go take care of my troop and talk Florin down from his murderous rage."

That was not what Raine had expected to hear. "You're going to let us keep traveling with you?"

Her smile was a little more welcoming this time. "I told you, I like *you*. You've got audacity I can't help appreciating. I'm still skeptical of the company you keep, but you also draw in a good crowd at our performances. I can't say I'm interested in more surprise attacks, and yet, I feel like turning you away at this point would be kind of like leaving Thorn in those brambles."

She kicked the haunches of the dead beast with one boot, shaking her head at the creature, then turned away, heading back for the camp.

They watched her go. When she was out of earshot, Siniva said, "I can't decide if she's really likable or really irritating."

Rakas made a small noise of assent.

"I like her."

Siniva shook his head at Raine. "You would."

*

Several days later, their wounds still healing, Fools Errant danced into Imperious under a warm sun, singing and playing a lively tune. Raine and Siniva, neither of whom excelled in any of those three arts, rode along behind them, just ahead of Rakas and Kovial who were leading the rest of the horses. Their appearance created something of an attraction everywhere they went without them having to put out any real effort. Here, in the great city of Imperious, where Dephithus had spent much of his youth, they were met with many a wary gaze and even more suspicious scowls than usual.

It was strange for Raine, riding into Imperious. Almost everywhere she looked, something she saw triggered a memory from either Myara or Dephithus. It was like riding home to a place she had never been, yet somehow knew almost better than she knew herself. The disconcerting feeling of coming home as a stranger to this place combined with the many unwelcoming looks made her yearn to flee back into the woods.

At least Hydra didn't draw attention. Siniva had cleverly suggested to Nakia that the unusually flashy stallion might draw the attention of thieves. Nakia had agreed, and they fashioned full caparisons for their two horses that would make them part of the attraction. Hydra's was black with a bronze trimming and bronze dragons on the lower hanging portions over his legs. Siniva's horse wore a red caparison with similar bronze trimmings and dragons upon it. It let them be part of the attraction without performing and completely hid most of Hydra's most distinguishable traits from view.

The dragons on the caparisons were Nakia's idea. Dragons were a touchy subject, since they had only recently gone from just being statues in graveyards to living, breathing beasts. However, as Nakia liked to point out, being part of a band of troubadours often involved stretching the limits of what was comfortable and acceptable in society. In such a troop, you could be acceptably unacceptable.

The city was big. Bigger than Corbent Calid, but more structured somehow. The vendor wagons had their place in nice, neat rows along certain sections of the street between shops. No one shouted to draw people to their wares. It had been that way in her parents' memories as well. Something about laws limiting noise pollution in the city. Performers had certain exemptions. At least they had when her parents were young, and since none of the soldiers watching the streets made any move to stop them, it appeared to be the same now.

They rode to a large tavern, Nakia and the others promising a spectacular first performance tomorrow night to the people who gathered around as they passed. Once the troop had settled in for a drink and a meal, Nakia pointedly asked Siniva to help her find a place to camp outside of the city proper. The troop never stayed in the towns. Nakia said it spared them funds and a great deal of unnecessary conflict.

Siniva turned to Raine.

"I'll be fine," she answered before he could voice his concerns.

Nakia took Siniva by the arm and started to draw him after her. He continued to look back at Raine until they were almost to the door. Then he finally turned and followed Nakia out.

"I'm going to escort Kovial to the Elysium gates," Rakas announced then.

Raine, who had only just sat down in anticipation of a meal she did not have to help make or clean up after, stood up so fast the serving woman almost ran into her.

"I'll come with you."

Rakas glanced toward the door, not having to voice his opinion on what Siniva would think of that.

She glanced at Marisa and Cadovan, who seemed to run the troop in Nakia's absence. Both shrugged.

Rakas mirrored the gesture. "Come along then."

CHAPTER SEVENTEEN

It was a beautiful day. Sunny and warmer than it had been in a few weeks. The sunlight was pleasant on Darkin's face, and he liked the way it made the darker parts of his uniform grow hot if he stood in it for long enough. He could almost enjoy the moment if he were not waiting, counting down the days until an army of daemons and barbaric warriors arrived at the gates of Elysium on the heels of a powerful mad man.

Yes, that pretty well ruins it.

"Gate duty is sooooooo boring." Suva leaned heavily back against one cold stone wall, staring up at the arch above her.

Darkin chuckled inwardly, though he made a point not to let her see his amusement. In a stern tone, he said, "You would rather be out fighting daemons."

She gave him a wry look, not impressed by his superior rank today, and pushed away from the wall with a peculiar backward thrust of shoulders and hips. "I'm not all that excited about waiting for them to come to us. All our precious little king has done is increase the gate watches during the night. A fat lot of good that is going to do us."

Fair enough.

"Besides," she gazed out toward Imperious, her distant look telling him she saw beyond what was there,

"Kovial is still out there. What if he was heading back and got attacked again? Or what if that daenox wielding bastard did something to him?"

This was a daily conversation at this point. The longing to go out and find her brother was something he could commiserate with. He yearned to check on Kovial too. They had orders to stay in Imperious, however, so he had to trust in that Rakas fellow they had left their companion with. "He suffered a serious injury. We're lucky we found someone who could keep him from losing the arm. Rakas said he would send him back when it was safe for him to travel. He'll be here when he's well enough."

Suva turned to him. "Will he? Are you so sure we can trust that man?"

"What choice did we..." Darkin trailed off as Suva's features clouded over. It was the wrong answer, and it was unnecessary anyhow. Three riders were coming over the rise behind her, two of whom he recognized immediately.

Kovial spotted them as well, sitting up straighter in the saddle, a silly grin splitting his features.

Darkin could not help returning the grin. Suva spun around. She sucked in a sharp breath. Darkin walked up to her and put a hand on her arm, hoping to remind her they were here in an official capacity and stop her from running toward the approaching horses and potentially startling them. The last thing Kovial needed right now was to be thrown by a spooked horse and break something else.

Kovial urged his mount to trot, wincing a bit with the harder impacts of the horse's gait. He pulled the animal to a stop with his good arm not far from the gate. His grimace and the awkward dismount told Darkin what he needed to know about the state of his friend's injury. There was still healing to be done.

Once he was on the ground, there was no holding Suva back. She sprinted out to her brother. Kovial lifted his arms out of the way, and she threw hers around his chest. The impact of her embrace made him grimace again in obvious pain, but he quickly returned the hug with his uninjured arm and closed his eyes, giving her head a kiss as he held her close.

The other two riders stopped behind them. Rakas watched the scene with little expression, but it was not his expression that interested Darkin. Next to him, on a mount adorned in an elaborate caparison, was a young woman with long black hair that shone with a strange bronze sheen. Her eyes were the same color, and scaling showed at her temples, tapering off along her cheekbones. Her outfit, a mix of leather and black cloth, was nicely fitted in a manner that enhanced womanly curves, but there was something in her bearing and the sweet smile that she wore while watching the reunion in front of her that made her seem much younger. She wore a sword on one hip, but it hung awkwardly there as if it were a show piece rather than a weapon.

Behind the distraction of her intense, exotic beauty, there was something that struck him as familiar about her. Darkin walked out to join them, and her eyes shifted from Suva and Kovial to him, her expression turning thoughtful.

"I'm Darkin," he introduced.

"I know."

He stared at her, not sure what to say to that.

"She's Dephithus's daughter."

Darkin turned to look at Kovial. He stood next to Suva now, holding her hand and gazing fondly at the mysterious young woman on the caparisoned horse.

"Horse farts," Darkin answered, the exclamation bursting from his lips before he could catch himself.

The young woman giggled, a sound like soft bells chiming that caused a strange twisting sensation in his chest.

Kovial grinned crookedly. "It's true. Raine, meet my sister, Suva, and our fearless leader, Darkin."

Darkin turned. The young woman, Raine, was coming down off her mount, a horse that seemed familiar somehow.

Rakas, who had not shown interest in any of the rest of them, was watching her with a keen fascination.

Raine walked up to Darkin. Now that she was closer, he could see the catlike slit pupils in her dark eyes. She was a fair bit shorter than he was, but something about the way she regarded him made him feel small and naked.

"Not so fearless," she murmured, soft enough that none of the others would hear, but she did not seem to care if he heard. Perhaps she even wanted him to.

Her bold regard left him feeling challenged, and he realized his hand was now resting on his sword hilt. "You ever used that blade?" He let his gaze drop to the weapon at her hip then swing back up to meet those remarkable eyes.

She flushed slightly, her initial show of confidence faltering. "No. It's not mine."

He remembered the night he had helped Dephithus steal Hydra. His gaze jumped to the horse she was riding. The animal's bearing and the little bit of his body that showed under the caparison confirmed his suspicion. She rode here on Hydra, which explained why she would have him wearing such attire. That night, Dephithus had also been carrying a sword that was meant for Myara when he left.

"It's your mother's sword?"

She gave a slight nod.

"Then they're…" he trailed off when she flinched slightly.

"Dead," she finished.

Suva, who had walked over to them, reached out to Raine then, but the young woman seemed aware of her presence before she made contact. She turned from him and faced Suva. The departure of her intense gaze was both a relief and a disappointment.

"Kovial says you helped him a great deal. I can't thank you enough."

Raine flushed slightly again and shrugged her words off. "It was nothing."

"It was everything," Suva argued, the shine of tears in her eyes. "We knew your father."

Raine nodded. "I know. I have my parents' memories. I remember you."

Suva paled then, and Darkin wondered, not for the first time, what had happened between her and Dephithus that he had not been privy to.

Suva reached out and took Raine by the shoulders, pulling her into an embrace. She hugged the young woman more tightly than she had held her brother. Raine melted into her arms.

"I'm so sorry," Suva murmured.

Tears squeezed from Raine's closed eyes and she slid her arms slowly around the lean woman Darkin thought he knew so well. He was starting to question that. Whatever memory the two shared, assuming Raine's outlandish claim was true, it created an instant bond between them in that moment that he would always be outside of, and he was somewhat disconcerted by how jealous it made him. Not only was he captivated by Raine, but he had known Suva most of her life and was not sure they had ever shared such an obviously intimate connection.

Hydra stepped up to him then and nosed his arm as if to say he felt left out too. Darkin smirked and looked past the two women. Kovial, who had also been watching the strange phenomenon, glanced up at the same time and met his eyes. He shrugged and matched Darkin's smirk. Leaving the two women to their moment, Darkin walked around them and gave his friend a careful embrace.

"It's good to have you back." He stepped back then and looked up at Rakas. "You have our gratitude."

Rakas gave a slight nod, he was still more interested in the other two.

Darkin leaned a little closer to Kovial. "Do you believe she is who she says she is?" he inquired in a low voice.

"I know it seems impossible, but I do."

Darkin nodded and considered the way Suva held Raine. He had only ever seen her show that kind of affection for one person. Her brother. Whatever or whoever Raine was, she had already somehow earned herself a place with Suva and Kovial. He was not going to be the one to turn her away. If they accepted her, she was family.

Suva and Raine drew back from one another then. Suva smiled at Raine. A smile that Darkin was not sure he had ever seen before. She wiped a few lingering tears gently from Raine's cheeks with hands that were usually trying to kill something.

"You all right?"

Raine nodded.

A flash of light caught his attention when Raine moved, and he glanced down at her leg. Sheathed in her boot was the familiar serpent dagger that had once belonged to Dephithus. A chill raced through him.

She had the horse and dagger that had belonged to Dephithus, a dagger that had recently been in Kyouin's possession, and she had Myara's sword. Whoever she was, she was worth learning more about.

"Are you staying in town?" Darkin asked, deeming it an acceptable moment to speak.

"We're traveling with a band of troubadours," Rakas answered. "They're looking for a place outside of town to camp, but they will be performing tomorrow night."

Darkin nodded. At least they were not leaving immediately, and the troubadours explained the trappings on Raine's horse, though he expected it was a convenient excuse to hide the animal. "Unfortunately, we can't offer you an escort back to town right now, but we would love to come see you perform."

"I don't perform," Rakas grumbled.

Raine was smiling now though, which was all Darkin really cared about.

"The troop would love to have you," she said. "We've been practicing some new acts."

"We'll definitely be there," Suva declared.

The two women clasped hands for a moment. Raine flashed her a warm, but shy smile that said she had been more vulnerable before Suva than she intended to be, but she did not entirely regret it. Darkin felt another twist of jealousy. That was not like him. He did not get jealous, mostly because he had never been fixated enough on anyone for it to become an issue.

You don't even know this girl.

Raine smiled warmly to Kovial then.

"See you tomorrow," he said, reciprocating with a fond smile for her.

Raine turned a measuring gaze on Darkin then. "You're his officer. See that he doesn't overdo it."

"I will do the best I can," he answered lamely.

She nodded. "I know."

Again, he had the strange experience of feeling as if he had been stripped bare before her. If she truly had her parents' memories, what in them could possibly make her feel like she knew him so well.

She walked back to Hydra then, and he scrambled for something to say that would delay her departure.

"Be careful," he blurted.

She stopped with one foot in the stirrup and looked over her shoulder at him.

He rushed ahead. "I may not be the only one who would recognize that horse, despite the elaborate costuming."

Her hand tightened on the reins. Her eyes narrowed. Hydra stomped the ground with one hoof, reacting instantly to his rider's change of mood. Darkin suddenly felt like a horse's ass.

"They won't take him."

She punctuated her sentence with a growl that reminded him very much of her father, assuming Dephithus really was her father, which he was starting to believe was possible somehow.

"If they try, they'll have to come through us," Suva declared with her usual unstoppable defiance. She tossed her head as she said it, throwing her blond hair back out of her eyes.

Why didn't I say that first?

Raine cast Suva a look of gratitude, but there was doubt in her eyes. She appreciated the sentiment, even if she did not entirely believe it. She swung up in the saddle and gave a slight nod to no one in particular.

"See you all tomorrow," she stated abruptly. With that, she turned Hydra and started trotting away.

"Be careful with that arm," Rakas cautioned Kovial before he turned and trotted after Raine.

Darkin watched them go. He felt as if he had lost a battle he did not even know was being fought. He was not about to admit defeat that easily, however. Tomorrow night he would see if he could come out a little better.

Raine turned Hydra deeper into the woods. Siniva followed in silence. He was still angry with her for riding to the Elysium gate the day before with Rakas and Kovial while he was out helping Nakia and Cadovan find a place for them to camp. He said it had been reckless and dangerous. Given that Darkin recognized Hydra, he was probably right. She was not about to tell him about that though. Given how few words he and Rakas exchanged, it seemed unlikely that he would find out about that from there.

The woods here smelled vibrant and alive. Leaves were starting to fall, and the smell of organic decay competed with the fresh scent of a recent rain. The underbrush was dense in this part of the woods. If she needed to navigate by sight, she was not sure she could make it through. Fortunately, all she needed was to follow the draw of Vanuthan's presence, like a fishing line hooked to her sternum, reeling her in. The one drawback was that the draw had no sense of impassable obstacles in the terrain. They had to work their way around nests of thorny brambles twice and a small ravine once.

Hydra was willing to force his way through most anything she asked of him, so she was careful not to risk hurting him. The caparison she had rolled up and tied on the back of his saddle some time ago to avoid catching it on things. He seemed happier without it, prancing along with a livelier step even on the more challenging terrain.

"Are we getting close?" Siniva growled the question behind her.

"Oh. Are you talking to me again?"

"Only as much as necessary," Siniva grumbled.

"We're very close now." She could feel the Mother Dragon quite clearly now. Sometimes her presence was so crisp that it was hard to tell if the heart Raine felt beating in her chest was hers or the Mother Dragon's. One thing she could tell for certain was that the great dragon was very weak. "I don't think she's eaten in some time."

Siniva drove his horse up through the brush next to Hydra. "What do you feel?" All anger was gone from his voice now. Fear and worry took its place.

"Just that she is weak. Her heartbeat is slow. Slower than it should be. And she feels... foggy." It was the best word she could come up with for the sensations she was getting from Vanuthan.

"She must be in hibernation sleep. She probably hasn't been able to leave wherever she is now, which means she would not be able to hunt."

"Maybe we should bring her something."

Siniva gave a snort. "With our hunting skills, we'd be out here for weeks trying to catch enough to do any good. Let's get to her and see what we're dealing with first."

Raine said nothing. She had seen what Rakas did with the daenox to kill the bearlike daemon that charged her. She thought she could duplicate it, though she did not really want to. To help Vanuthan, she would do what was necessary.

Hydra stepped up on a slight rise. The clack of his hoof on stone caught her attention. Woven over by the growth of the forest was a long, flat path of carved stone several horses wide that stretched off slightly to their left, going deeper into the woods to a massive, white stone structure obscured by an overgrowth of trees and vines. The entrance was a cavernous maw with long vines hanging down over it. The remains of a huge set of hinges lay rusting on the ground to either side of the doorway, partially buried in growth.

"Big enough for a dragon to enter," Raine observed as they rode up to the entrance, the horses' hooves clacking on the cracked stone walkway.

"Made for a dragon," Siniva corrected. He dismounted and pushed aside some of the growth, revealing a small section of weathered white stone. Despite the weathering, she could still make out the shapes of dragons carved into it. "It's an old temple sanctuary for the dragons. Our kind were welcomed and worshipped, to an extent, by the ones who built these temples."

Raine dismounted and pushed her way through the hanging vines into the central part of the temple, the white, sculpted roof towering high above. There was wear and breakage in here as well as the encroachment of the forest. More interesting was the fact that part of the ceiling and a corner of the back wall simply looked incomplete, as though the structure had been abandoned before it was finished.

Another large doorway opened to the other side of the temple. Through this opening, she could see the great shape of the red dragon curled in unnatural slumber, her form gaunt, the scaled hide laying loose over her bones.

Siniva let out a cry and ran past her, falling to his knees before the head of the dragon.

"Vanuthan! No!"

Despite the volume of his despairing cry, the dragon barely twitched in her sleep, her shallow breathing catching for only a second.

"Don't wake her," Raine murmured, walking a little closer to the hulking form. "If we don't have something for her to eat when she wakes, the energy expended simply waking up could be the death of her."

There were tears on Siniva's cheeks as he nodded. "How are we going to get enough to feed her? We're dreadful hunters."

"Give me a minute."

Raine was reaching down now, through the cracked floor of the temple. Down into the ground beneath. She tried to get hold of the daenox that flowed below, but something here interfered with that power.

"I'll be right back."

Without waiting for his response, she walked out of the temple and stepped off the walkway onto the bare ground of the forest. Now she could feel the daenox strong and clear again. Uninterrupted. She took hold of it and used it to reach through the forest in search of life. Not daemon life this time, but natural life. A group of deer. Some rabbits. An elk. She found them all and drew them to her. In moments, Vanuthan's first waking meal was emerging, trancelike, from the surrounding trees. Walking to their death.

Four deer, their soft brown eyes wide with fear, stepped toward her on delicate little hooves. Two rabbits, their big ears upright and alert. The poor creatures were barely more than an appetizer, but every bit counted for Vanuthan right now. Lastly, a great bull elk stepped forward, his majestic rack of horns hanging low as he struggled to fight the lure.

Tears began to flow down Raine's cheeks. With strands of daenox, she reached deeper into them. All of them at once, so that she could get it over with as quickly as possible. She felt for the flow of blood, the pulsing beat of a heart. Fast and fierce in the rabbits, a little slower in the deer, and strong and vibrant in the elk.

I'm so sorry. I need your lives to save another.

But who was she to decide whose life was of more value? What gave her the right to determine the part they should play and how they should end?

She clenched her teeth and followed the blood pulsing from those heartbeats. Their lives pounded through her veins, changing the rhythm of her own heartbeat. She followed that precious blood to the throat of each beast where it ran healthy and vital.

I'm so sorry.

She gave the daenox a razor's edge and thrust out through the flesh, not bursting out as Rakas had done with the other beast, but making a clean slice, no less lethal than the single wound he had inflicted. The animals fell at her feet, blood gushing from their opened throats, spreading fast enough that she had to take several panicked steps back to keep it from touching her. So much blood.

"What have you done?" Siniva breathed behind her.

Raine turned, and he took a quick step back when her gaze struck upon him. There was fear in his eyes. Genuine fear. It tore her apart. She stared it down, hiding the anguish kicking inside her.

"Will this be enough to save her?" Her voice shook. Her whole body was trembling like a fall leaf clinging to its branch in the wind.

Siniva looked at the dead animals. He gave a slow nod but only stood there, continuing to stare.

She wanted to scream at him.

Isn't this what you want? Don't you want to save her?

A deep, rasping growl sounded somewhere behind them. Siniva snapped from his stunned silence. "The stench of blood must have roused her. Quick, help me move the elk to her. That will buy us time to move the rest."

*

Vanuthan was sleeping again now. Not the forced hibernation sleep this time, but a revitalizing sleep that let her body digest the first meal she had eaten in a long time. The Mother dragon had been mad with hunger. When they had taken the elk to her, Siniva would not let Raine go into the room. He shoved the elk the last several feet on his own and sprang back out of the way. Even weak from hunger and groggy from her long sleep, Vanuthan grabbed the beast so fast she nearly made Siniva part of her meal. While she tore that more substantial meal apart, they hastily brought the rest of the dead animals and pushed them within her reach, so she could focus her energy on eating.

She had not spoken. She had not even really looked at them in the time that she was awake.

Now, while they waited, reclined in the main room of the temple, Siniva avoided looking at Raine. Here she sat, with the one individual whose presence made her feel a little less freakish, and she felt like more of an aberration than ever.

"It was the fastest way to help her," she said softly into the silence, wary of disturbing the sleeping dragon.

"We can speak of this later."

Her ire sparked to life. "Which basically means you'll do your best to avoid it until I give up."

His eyes flashed with anger when he glanced her way, but he was not willing to be baited by her this time. He held to his silence, and Vanuthan's steady breathing became the loudest sound again.

Time passed. Raine did her best to keep herself occupied. She made bombs out of crumpled grass that she did not dare throw at Siniva right then. A surprising amount of time got lost to following a busy trail of bright green ants on their meandering course through the main room of the temple. Now and then she would place obstacles in their path just to watch how quickly and efficiently they rerouted the trail around things. She tried listening more carefully, in case they had some language for communicating their plans down the line, but she never heard anything.

When the ants finally lost her interest, she took to pulling up the vines and other plant life that had grown over the floor, gradually uncovering the extensive mosaic of different colored stones that had been created there. A silver circle encompassed most of the floor, and within it, a spiderweb of thinner silver lines had been woven. Amidst those lines, hundreds of stylized dragons of various colors and shapes had been painstakingly laid out in beautiful colored stones. There were cracks in the floor, but it was still possible to see the entirety of the design if she stood near the entrance.

"It represents the dragon web," Siniva said, walking up beside her now.

"Why was this place never finished?"

There was the sound of movement from the adjacent chamber, and Vanuthan's head appeared through the opening. She took a few shaky steps then slumped down, resting her gaunt form in the doorway.

"The daenox had its worshippers," the big dragon said, her voice rough with disuse. "So did the dragons. There were many temples built to honor the dragons. This would have been a grand one, but the dragons and the daenox were imprisoned before its completion. I suppose they did not see a point to finishing it then, or perhaps they were ordered to abandon it."

"Vanuthan." Siniva's voice carried awe and relief.

"My friend," she gave a weak nod in his direction, but her eyes were on Raine. "I felt you coming. It was like a fever dream. Sometimes you were Dephithus, but I knew he was dead. I'm not sure if I should thank you, child. I was nearing death. Now the two of you have prolonged my life, but I still cannot leave this place."

Raine did not speak. *You are welcome* seemed an inappropriate response. What she had done to help Vanuthan, the lives she had taken, still weighed heavily on her. It stung to have that sacrifice met with so little gratitude.

Siniva spoke into the silence. "Is there no way we can free you from this place?"

Vanuthan shook her head. "If I could reconnect to the dragon web, I could go free."

"As could I," Siniva remarked, his face darkening with the sorrow of their fates.

Raine looked at the elaborate floor. The web that connected all the dragons, riddled through with cracks from age. Something stirred in her while she stared at that image, unsure what to make of this moment. There was something deeper to it. Something she wanted to understand, but it moved just beyond her reach. It was not a memory from her parents, but it felt similar somehow. The harder she tried to focus on it, the further it slipped away.

Someone touched her shoulder, and she startled, turning to see Siniva standing next to her now. Vanuthan's eyes, a bronzed red so like the color of his eyes, watched from behind him. Even as weak and thin as she was, the red Mother Dragon was magnificent to look upon. The only dragon Raine had seen in the flesh other than Theruses, the gold Death Dragon, when he attacked her outside the Dunues Mountain cave.

"Are you well?" Siniva asked. "You didn't respond when I called your name."

She nodded. "Just a little tired."

Siniva's expression darkened a little. Remembering perhaps the energy she had expended using daenox to summon and kill the animals for Vanuthan's meal. "We have a performance tonight, perhaps we should get you back for a quick rest before then."

Vanuthan nodded weakly. "That would be well. I also need to rest more. There is much we need to discuss," Her gaze went to Siniva. "If you returned in the morning, perhaps with something more to eat, I might have the energy for conversation."

Raine stared at them both, struggling with the loss of place she felt. She had been certain Vanuthan would welcome her with love and warmth as befitting a grandmother to their deceased son's only child. Vanuthan barely acknowledged her at all. She did not belong here, with the great Mother Dragon, any more than she belonged anywhere else. There was no place she belonged. Perhaps Siniva had been right to abandon her.

"Come along, Raine."

Siniva turned her with his hand on her shoulder, and she was reminded of the first night she performed with the troop when he had helped her find the courage to go out in front of the crowd. She closed her eyes for a second and breathed deep, fighting back the sting of tears. After a few seconds, she opened her eyes and nodded, following him from the temple in silence.

The evening streets of Imperious were livelier than they had been in a while. People did not wander in the streets much after dusk these days, not with the roaming daemons growing bolder after dark. Tonight, enticing music was drawing a growing crowd around a stage in the Winter Square, a large space near the center of town that was usually reserved for festivals. The stage had been set up at the foot of The Founders, a statue with three armed women on horseback who were said to be the first to venture into this part of the country and discover the beautiful fields and forests that would become Imperious and the grounds of Elysium.

Two performers were dancing on the stage, capturing the attention of the gathered audience with their serpentine movements. Behind them, off to one side of the musicians standing next to a very intimidating red-headed man with similar dragonkin features, was Raine. She looked right somehow, standing under the watchful eyes of The Founders. Three strong women standing over a fourth, who was both strong and vulnerable, as yet largely unmolded into what she might become. Her gaze was turned inward, focused on some process within her own mind that the rest of the world would never be privy to.

Darkin turned his attention to helping Suva move

Kovial through the crowd with care, trying to avoid jarring his healing arm. They were still in uniform, which helped get them through the audience without too much hassle. The respect the people held for Legion soldiers had only grown since the daemons increased the need for them and shortened their general life expectancy by a significant amount. He was not sure the tradeoff was the best, but it was helpful at the moment.

Part of him wanted Raine to notice them. Wanted her to see them and blush or smile or wave. To him in particular, if he were to be honest. She had infected his mind since their first somewhat awkward meeting. Every other thought was of her. So many of those thoughts were juvenile fantasies of how he would show her he was better than the memories her parents had of him, assuming she really did have her parents' memories. Assuming she really was their child. A couple of significant assumptions he was not quite sure he could make. Still, his doubts did not stop his fanciful brain from running wild.

"This is good."

Suva's hand on his arm surprised him. He jumped a bit, bumping into another gentleman as a result, and quickly apologized to the stranger. The man responded with some polite muttering and offered his spot to Darkin. The man had a great view of the goings on beyond the stage, so Darkin accepted with little guilt.

Back in the deepest shadows under the statue, where the torchlight did not quite reach, Rakas stood, also watching Raine. There was a fascination in the man's eyes that Darkin suspected matched his own. It made him uncomfortable to think that he might have that same intensity in his eyes when he looked at her. At the same time, there was something validating in knowing that she was interesting enough to merit the attention of a daenox priest, validating and concerning.

The troop was talented. The dancers gave way to a man juggling long blades whose performance got Darkin to stop watching Raine for a time. As he was finishing, Darkin glanced over to see Raine looking at them. For a moment, their eyes met, and she smiled. He could not smile back. His physical body disappeared, and he could only gaze dumbly into her eyes, stuck there. Then, the juggler finished and swapped places with two others, cutting off their connection for a second and returning control of his flesh to him. A belated smile curved his lips, he could not stop it. When the obstruction was gone, he was smiling at her, and she blushed. His heart kicked in his chest.

What is wrong with me? I'm acting like a muleheaded idiot.

Darkin wrenched his gaze away and leaned close to Suva. "I'll be right back."

She nodded absently, her attention captured by the two men who were beginning a battle with staffs that burned on both ends. He turned and made his way out of the crowd. That was no small feat since people were too caught up in the performance to notice he was a soldier now, so he got no extra consideration. When he finally got out of the crowd, he walked to a nearby building where several people were standing on the upstairs balcony to watch and made his way up to claim a dark corner of the balcony.

He could still see the performance and Raine, but he was far enough away now that he did not feel as susceptible to the odd power she had over him. She was watching the two men deep in their fire battle now. One was the dragonkin man who had been standing beside her. Even from this distance, Darkin could see the sweat creating a sheen over his muscular torso. He was a fierce-looking and handsome individual, and Raine observed him attentively.

Darkin felt that same sour sting of jealousy he had experienced when she hugged Suva. It was absurd.

The music changed now, and the two men knelt at the sides of the stage. Raine stepped up on to the stage with two odd little branches in her hands. She struck a pose and waited there, one wand held before her as if to shield her face and the other held out to one side. Firelight flickered, dancing light over her beautiful shape. After a few suspenseful seconds, she began to move. Colored lights came out of the ends of the sticks, their shapes and patterns becoming more complex and captivating as she moved. It was not the lights that captured his attention though. It was the way she moved. The dance was not complicated, but it was precise and elegant, and it looked, to his trained eyes, like Suva going through forms with her daggers, only a touch more refined and less lethal. It was beautiful and full of potential.

She carried her father's dagger. Perhaps she would be interested in lessons.

And why would I be the one teaching her when Suva could do a much better job?

Suva was far more skilled with dagger fighting than he was. It was a foolish fancy. One of so many. Even quickly debunked, his mind ran with it. He could see himself reaching around her to show her how to hold the dagger, breathing in the smell of her.

Frustrated, he stepped back into the shadows a bit more and watched from a forcibly detached distance. When the performance ended, Raine helped with some of the cleanup, smiling at her companions, except for the dragonkin man, who she seemed to be avoiding to some degree. Eventually, she walked over to where Suva and Kovial were waiting. They spoke for a short time. Raine glanced around as though looking for someone, and Suva shrugged. He squashed the bitter hope that it was him she was looking for.

The crowds gradually dispersed. Suva and Kovial headed back toward the Elysium gates, glancing around as they left in search of their missing companion. Raine and the troop went the opposite direction, heading out toward the woods on the other side of town. Darkin descended and followed from a distance, keeping to the shadows. He followed all the way to the camp and watched and listened. It was late, so things quieted down quickly, and he sat there in the trees, wondering what he meant to do now. He listened to the quiet camp, to the horses shifting and the low fire crackling. Then he got up to leave, but someone else was moving away from the camp, almost invisible in the dark.

Darkin followed. When they were out of range of the camp, a pale violet orb appeared, illuminating Raine's face in the darkness. The light stayed a short distance ahead of her as she made her way deeper into the forest. Darkin kept after her, trying to maintain the distance between them and move as quietly as possible without the advantage of light.

They walked for a long time. Long enough that he could question his own sanity. Was his fixation on her so great that he was following an illusion into the woods where he would become lost or devoured by daemons? It seemed possible. He was tired. He was stressed. Maybe he was losing his mind. That would explain his strange reaction to the girl, would it not? Which was better? That he had gone mad and was chasing ghosts in the woods, or that he had become so obsessed with a girl he met one time that he was now stalking her through the forest?

"Who's there?" Raine had stopped and was peering around into the darkness. The light in front of her swept out, doing a wide circle. Darkin ducked quickly behind the trunk of a big tree, his heart pounding.

What am I doing?

The light returned to her after a few more passes, and she started moving again. Darkin considered turning back, but he was committed now. Besides, if he left her here alone, what might happen to her? Better to follow and at least be there to help if she were attacked.

They had been trudging through the dark woods for some time when her dim light fell upon the white stone of a pathway partially covered by bushes and vines. She followed this to a big, white building, also heavily overgrown. A building he had never seen in a lifetime of hunting these woods. He stopped and watched her go inside, then slunk carefully to the entrance and stopped again just outside when he heard voices coming from an adjacent chamber.

"Raine." This voice was rasping and deep, though it struck him as feminine. "Did you bring food?"

"I..." Raine's tone fell. Disappointment. "No. I'm afraid I didn't."

For a few seconds, the only sound was raspy breathing.

"I feel something amiss, but I'm still weak. I can't focus on it."

Me perhaps.

"I'll be right back."

Darkin darted back out of the temple, ducking down beside some bushes near the doorway. Raine walked out of the entrance and continued until she stepped off the side of the stone pathway. She stood there in silence, staring into the dark woods. Darkin cautiously moved closer, keeping in the cover of the bushes. He watched and waited. From his angle now, he could see her face. She swallowed hard, her focus on the dark quite intent now.

Tears started to run down her cheeks, and there was twisting in his chest. He yearned to go to her, but a rustling in the brush held him back. Two deer, a doe and a young buck, came out of the woods, moving toward her. They moved as if compelled, their legs stiff, their steps choppy.

"I'm so sorry," Raine choked out.

Then the two deer dropped where they stood, blood gushing from the slashes that had appeared in their throats. Darkin sucked in a breath and stared at her then, seeing her as something new. This girl did not need him to teach her how to use a dagger. This girl did not need him at all. She was more than capable of taking care of herself.

Or was she?

She sunk to her knees then and cupped her face in her hands. Soft sobs shook her shoulders, and he realized that she did need someone after all. She needed someone quite badly. He stood and started walking toward her. One foot cracked a small branch. Raine startled, stumbling and falling on her backside in her rush to get back up.

Darkin stopped instantly and held out both hands in a gesture meant to show her that he intended no harm.

"It's me. Darkin. I didn't mean to surprise you."

"I know who you are," she hissed. "What are you doing out here?"

"I…" he stared at her. The words stuck in his throat. There was nothing he could say that would not sound bad.

"You followed me," she accused, wiping at her damp cheeks.

He could not deny it. He had no other excuse for being out here in the middle of the woods in the dark like this. "I'm sorry."

She started to get her feet up under her, and he stepped closer, offering a hand. "Please, let me help."

For a few seconds, she stared at the hand. Then she reached out and took it, and he felt a joyful swelling in his chest.

Stop it!

Forcing himself to ignore the feeling, he pulled her up. "What are you doing out here? Who's in that temple?"

"You should go. This isn't something you need to be involved in," she quickly pulled her hand out of his. Her gaze went back to the two dead deer. She brushed at a fresh tear that ran down one cheek.

"You..." he hesitated, not sure it was such a good idea to point out what she had done.

She nodded. "I killed them." Her voice caught when she said it. More tears ran down her cheeks. "You should go," she repeated.

"What will you do with them? Do you need to take them to whoever's in the temple?"

She stared at him, the sorrow in her eyes cutting into him like a well-honed blade.

He softened his voice and took a step closer to her, looking down into those brassy-black eyes shining with more unshed tears in the dim violet light. "Let me help you, Raine."

She stared back up at him. Another tear slipped free, and she let it fall. "Why?"

"Because I want to. Do you need a better reason than that?"

Little lines of concentration wrinkled her smooth forehead. Her gaze turned distant. After several minutes ticked away in silence, minutes in which he began to feel like he was standing there alone, she focused on him again.

"You never did my father any favors."

He smirked. "I suppose he never got to tell you about how I helped him steal Hydra from Allondis and escape Elysium to go looking for you and your mother?"

She cocked her head to one side in an adorable way that made him want to kiss her so badly it hurt and eyed him dubiously. "Did you really?"

Darkin nodded, hoping his sincerity came through in his expression.

"You should still go."

He gestured to the deer. "Do you need to move those?"

Her gaze dropped from his then. She looked ashamed as she gave a tiny nod.

"You're going to have a hard time doing it alone."

She stared at his chest, her gaze turning inward and her expression changing with some inner struggle. Finally, she spoke in a small voice that forced him to lean closer.

"I don't want to do it alone."

Something released in his chest, some deep agonizing fear of her rejection. He placed a hand on her arm. When she looked up at him again, something else locked into place inside him, something he would probably regret.

"Then don't do it alone."

Darkin insisted on carrying the deer alone, one at a time. Raine did not argue. She did not want to touch them. If she touched them, she might feel the warmth of their recent life ebbing away as she had with the ones she killed before. He lifted the first one and followed her back to the temple. They walked inside, and she stopped him before the entrance to the room Vanuthan was in.

"Don't panic when you get in there. I don't think she'll hurt you."

His expression tightened with concern. He tossed his head to try and get an unruly lock of black hair out of his face. "Who?"

"It's probably easier if I just show you." She gestured with a jerk of her head toward the doorway and started walking again. His footsteps followed after a few seconds, heavy with the weight of his burden.

Vanuthan lifted her long head, nostrils flaring with the scent of fresh blood. Her eyes narrowed when Darkin entered, but her gaze quickly refocused on the deer he carried. For his part, Darkin froze in place, mouth hanging open, deer hanging limp in his arms. Vanuthan's nostrils flared again, and she reached forward, taking hold of the dead animal with surprising delicacy and pulling it out of Darkin's arms. Raine turned away, not wanting to watch her eat it, and took hold of his arm, drawing him from the room with her.

"Let's get the other one," she suggested as they walked away.

The noises of the nighttime forest met them when they stepped back outside: the hoot of an owl, chitters and chirps of nocturnal rodents in the brush, the rustle of something moving out in the trees. A bat danced in and out of the edges of her light a few times. They were almost to the second deer before he spoke.

"You're feeding a dragon?"

She looked at him. His sunbaked skin was paler than it had been earlier in her daenox light. He looked more than a little stunned. It was endearing in a way, to see him vulnerable. She managed a slight smile.

"Yes. It's probably best if you don't mention it to anyone else."

He picked up the second deer carefully, trying to avoid getting blood on his clothing. "I could have guessed that. But how—"

She placed a finger to his lips to stop his question. His eyes met hers. The look of shock vanished, replaced by something very different. Her pulse quickened in the same way it did when Myrza looked at her. She snatched her hand back away from his lips. Her heart beat in her chest, hard and fast. Suddenly she was very aware of how alone they were. Could she trust him? Vanuthan could do nothing to help her here. She was truly on her own, and the way he was looking at her...

Her cheeks grew warm. Here Darkin was offering to help her, and all she could do was question her safety with him. No matter what his expression said, he made no move to cause her any harm. Of course, he had followed her out here, which brought his original intentions into question. How did people navigate these things?

"It's a long story. Come along," she spun and started back toward the temple.

While Vanuthan ate the rest of her meal, Raine created a brighter light and showed Darkin the mosaic on the floor of the main temple. Something stirred in her again while she stared at it with him. There was something here that she felt she should know, but it eluded her, lingering on the edges of her consciousness. She chewed at a fingernail and examined the images. There had to be an answer here. If she looked long and hard enough, she was bound to find it.

"What's wrong?"

She glanced up at Darkin and quickly took her fingernail out of her mouth. "Do you feel anything when you look at this?"

"Awe," he answered.

His answer brought a brief smile. "I mean... something else."

"It represents the dragon web," Vanuthan said.

They both startled. Darkin hastened to the other side of the room. The Mother Dragon had managed, somehow, to enter the main chamber without alerting them despite her considerable size. She looked after Darkin with a hint of amusement in her eyes.

Raine turned back to the mosaic. "I know what it represents, but I feel like there is something more to it. Something I know that I've forgotten or haven't remembered yet."

Vanuthan settled there, resting her substantial form between them and the doorway, and folded her wings in against her body. "You are connected to the dragon web, Raine. You have been since the moment of your conception. Perhaps it is the web itself that speaks to you. This place is a temple to the dragons, the web is given strength here, though I can no longer feel it." There was considerable remorse in those last words.

"Is that why I can't reach the daenox in here?"

Vanuthan grimaced. "Yes. I imagine so."

"If I'm connected to the dragon web, why can't I feel it?"

Vanuthan growled low in her throat. "Perhaps because you are always feeling for daenox."

Raine flushed. The daenox. Here Vanuthan was a magnificent dragon. A creature born to balance the daemon power, but that power had caused her so much suffering. Now Raine was here, the child who freed the dragons, using daenox to the point that she could not even sense the dragon web. What an insult that must be.

"Is he trustworthy?"

Raine looked up at Darkin who was keeping to the far side of the room, watching them. She shrugged. "I'm not sure yet."

"Then why did you bring him here?"

"I didn't. He followed me."

Vanuthan gazed down at her. "Perhaps it is you who is not trustworthy then."

Raine's cheeks burned hot this time. She looked away from the dragon, too ashamed to meet her eyes.

"I suppose I could eat him."

Darkin's hands came up. "Hold on. I—"

Vanuthan chuckled, a rumbling sound deep in her chest. "I have no desire to eat you, boy. Not so long as you treat Raine well."

"It is my only wish to treat her well," Darkin answered immediately.

Raine looked at him, searching his expression for some clue as to what those words meant to him, but she did not have the practice for reading people, especially given how guarded his expression had become.

"Hm." Vanuthan looked thoughtful. She eyed Darkin for a long moment, her silence full of judgment. After a few long seconds, she got wearily to her feet. "See that Raine gets safely back to Siniva." She turned and started to go back into the adjacent room.

"Wait. Grandmother! I have questions," Raine blurted, panicked at the thought of leaving here again with no answers and no guidance.

"I will answer your questions once I have spoken to Siniva." The Mother Dragon said as she continued through the doorway.

When Raine walked over and peered in, the dragon had lain down again, and her back was blocking the doorway. Tears stung her eyes. Still, the welcome and belonging she so longed for here eluded her. Vanuthan did not want her here. She wanted Siniva. Siniva was her kin. Raine was an abomination. A creature that did not belong in the world of dragons or the world of men.

A hand rested on her shoulder. "I'll walk back with you."

Raine shook off the hand and hurried outside. She wanted to get away from the dragon. She wanted to get away from all of them. All she ever was to them was a way to get what they wanted. She did not matter now, not to any of them.

She started to run. Darkin's footsteps sounded on the stone path behind her. Tears blurred her vision as she ran faster. She would leave him here, lost in the dark, as alone as she felt. She would make him feel just a little of her pain. As soon as she was off the stone of the temple path, she reached for the daenox and started to draw on it, putting out her light and deepening the darkness so that Darkin would not see where she had gone.

"Raine?" He was not far behind her. "I can't see anything. Are you all right? Raine?" There was a touch of panic making his voice rise.

Good. Let him feel her abandonment. She plunged forward into the darkness.

Something growled in the dark behind her. She

stopped. The growl sounded again, closer to where she had last heard Darkin's voice. There was thud and a cry of pain. She brought the light back quickly, casting away the unnatural dark. Something that looked like a giant, hairless cat, but with two tails and grotesquely overdeveloped muscles in its shoulders had pounced on Darkin. It had his right arm pinned under its claws. The other arm was in its mouth, blocking its teeth just a few inches above his throat.

She reached into the beast with a swirl of daenox and drove at it, pushing it back, filling it with her fear. The daemon-cat let go and lunged away, sprinting off into the woods as though its life were in desperate danger. Raine ran to Darkin and helped him sit up. His arm was punctured and torn, gushing streams of dark blood in the violet light. She took hold of the arm, and he groaned.

"Help me find something to wrap it," he said, pain tightening his voice now. "We need to slow the bleeding."

"Hold still," she snapped.

She drew on more daenox then, using it to create a wrap of light around the wound, holding it tight. With that to stop the bleeding, she took the serpent dagger and cut his other sleeve from his shirt. With his guidance she used the sleeve to create a bandage and wrapped the wound, letting the physical wrap obscure the daenox wrap that had stopped the bleeding.

"Can you walk?"

"Yes," he snapped. "It's my stupid arm the beast bit, not my leg."

Raine let his temper wash over her. He was hurt, and it was her fault. She was not about to get upset at him for a little show of temper. She helped him to his feet and took hold of his hand, guiding him along behind her through the dark. The light was tuned to Siniva now, just as it had been tuned to Vanuthan before, and would lead them back to the camp.

He stumbled, his breath catching with a sharp gasp. "This thing hurts worse than when I busted my ankle."

"Come on. Rakas can help."

Darkin said nothing. He followed along, his hand tightening on hers every now and then when he stumbled was his only complaint of pain for a time. Then, after they had been walking for a while, he stopped.

"Can we rest for a minute?" He was sinking down on a fallen log before she could answer. "My head is spinning."

Raine stood next to him. She wanted to drag him onward. If he could not continue, what could she do about it? She did not want to leave him here alone, but she certainly could not carry him back.

"I'm so sorry."

"For what?" His eyes seemed to have trouble focusing on her when he looked up.

"It's my fault the daemon came. I was using daenox to try and lose you. It was stupid and…" She trailed off when he shook his head.

"You were hurting. I could see that. We all make mistakes when we hurt. If you really are that young, you haven't had much opportunity to learn that."

His eyes were focused now, holding hers. There was no anger or judgment in them. In the memories in her head, neither Dephithus nor Myara saw Darkin this way. Had he changed, or had he simply hidden this part of himself from them?

There was something else in his eyes, that look again that often left her breathless with Myrza. It was wanting, she realized. And what left her breathless was the feeling of being wanted, in any way.

Raine leaned in and touched her lips to his in a soft kiss. He did nothing. His uninjured arm stayed still by his side. His eyes searched hers when she pulled away, the pain in them slightly muted by surprise.

"Why did you do that?"

"It was what you wanted."

His expression soured. "But did you want it?"

That was harder to answer. "I don't know yet. What I do know is that it feels good to be wanted and treated with kindness. You followed me when you shouldn't have, but you also helped me, and you didn't ask for anything back. You also wanted me but didn't pressure me for anything. You forgave me for hurting you and tried to understand my pain. I wanted to thank you for all of that. A kiss seemed like a meaningful way to say thank you."

"You're welcome," he murmured, his gaze moving to her lips for an instant and away again, staring out into the darkness. "We should go. I think I can walk again."

Raine nodded and took his hand. They did not speak again outside of occasional checks to make sure he was all right still. He stumbled a few times and cursed the pain under his breath. His good hand in hers was gentle, never squeezing too tight or pulling too hard.

Back at the camp, she left Darkin at the edge and tried to wake Rakas quietly. By the time she had him up and out of bed, Nakia was sitting up watching them, and Siniva was stirring in his sleep. Rakas did not know about Vanuthan, so she told him she had heard something near the camp and gone to investigate. When she did, she found Darkin being attacked by a daemon-cat. Rakas made a comment about the wound looking like it had happened as much as an hour ago. He said nothing else about it after that beyond complementing her daenox bandage and focused on healing. She watched him work, her attention on feeling what he was doing with the daenox.

"Could you teach me how to heal like that?" She asked when he was done and wrapping the arm with a clean bandage.

"Maybe, when we have more time." He gave Darkin a stern look. "Come back out tomorrow evening before the performance, and I can do some more healing. For now, that should help the pain and stop the bleeding. Be careful with it though. The wounds aren't fully closed. You could tear open the healing tissues if you're rough with it."

Darkin nodded, his eyes moved up to meet Raine's. "Thank you."

Rakas said nothing. He got up and left them, going back to his bedroll. Nakia was still awake, watching. Raine led Darkin a little further out, past the reach of the firelight.

"You shouldn't hunt for Vanuthan," Darkin took her hand in his good one as he spoke. "I can see how it hurts you. Let me do the hunting for you."

Gratitude spread through her chest and it hurt. It hurt because it felt good, and she did not think the good she had found here would last. It hurt because she had to turn it down, and she did not want to. Siniva would never allow him to get any more involved than he was. It was probably better if Siniva never knew he was this involved, though Raine suspected Vanuthan would tell him. The Mother Dragon seemed unlikely to keep secrets from him.

"Thank you, but I—"

"Get out of here." Siniva snarled as only a true dragon could.

Darkin jerked his hand away from Raine. He opened his mouth as if to say something, in his defense or perhaps in hers. She shook her head and mouthed "go." Darkin nodded and turned, hurrying back toward town alone.

She's a creature of the daenox," Siniva shouted. "What am I supposed to do with her?"

Raine wrapped her hands around her knees and pulled them in close. She sat outside a crack in the wall of the temple where their voices came through. Siniva thought she had stayed behind, but a little daenox was enough to mask her presence when she followed him. Now, however, she rather wished she had not followed him. She had hoped to learn something useful, but Siniva and Vanuthan spent very little time catching up before he started in on what to do with her. He told Vanuthan how she had lured and killed the animals with the daenox. Vanuthan had expressed some concern, though she seemed less troubled by it than he was.

"She is a child, Siniva. A child with access to two great powers. What she does with those powers will depend significantly on how she is treated and guided by those around her. I wronged her last night by sending her away when I did. You wrong her now by deciding what she will be before she has a chance to figure it out herself."

"You said it yourself," Siniva countered. "She is blind to the dragon web because she is always reaching for the daenox. She grew up in it. It's what she knows."

"She knows much more than that, she's just afraid

to let go. She can learn much from her parents' memories, if she will only let herself."

"You can't blame her. Some of those memories are appalling."

Vanuthan sighed, and her voice softened. "They are."

There was a long silence. Raine rested her head on her knees. Rakas was supposed to be keeping an eye on her per Siniva's orders, but he did not feel she needed watching, so he had gone to town to get some supplies shortly after Siniva left. That was all the freedom she needed to go sprinting off after the Fire Dragon.

Siniva's right. I am a creature of the daenox. And I'm not trustworthy.

"Where are the dragons?" It was Siniva who asked.

"Without the dragon web, I cannot know, my friend."

Several long seconds of silence again, then Siniva spoke. "What do we do now? I can't leave you here to die."

"I don't know that there is another option," Vanuthan answered, her voice heavy with defeat. "Without the web, I can't leave this place. I chose my prison."

Without the web.

Those words lit Raine's nerves on fire. She opened herself to the area. Reaching deep, she found the daenox with ease, though she was too close to the temple to draw on more of it. The force that interfered with the daemon power had to be the dragon web, which meant if she changed her focus, then maybe she could connect to it.

Raine closed her eyes, putting all her attention and energy into feeling for something different. There was something more there. It ran beneath the surface like the daenox, but here it ran shallow, barely beneath the ground. It was strong, pulsing like the heart of a healthy dragon. So intense she wondered that she had not noticed it before. She plunged into it, taking hold as it took hold of her, surging through her like cold fire.

Raine gasped. Unease spread along the web. The other dragons knew she was there. They could feel her, and she could feel them. The presence of the different dragons began to wink out almost instantly, one after the other. They were blocking her out from their presence, but not from the web itself. That still ran strong through her. It writhed in her grasp, as hard to hold on to as a bucking horse, which Raine only knew because of a memory from her father's early years when some of the other Legion hopefuls played a prank on him with an untrained stallion. Hydra liked her too much to buck her like that. She held on to the power of the web and pulled, drawing as much as she could into herself. Then, when she felt like she might burst, she searched for Vanuthan, for the glow of life—weakened and frail, but still stronger than any human's—that was the Mother Dragon.

When she drew them close to each other, that feeble glow of life and the power of the web, they reached for each other like lovers long separated. They surged together, and energy pulsed out from within the temple with such force that it knocked Raine's head against her knees, bloodying her lip. A great roar sounded from within the temple.

"What? What happened?" Siniva sounded frightened.

Raine ran around into the temple. The Mother Dragon was on her feet, her eyes wide and inward focused.

Siniva turned to Raine. He looked confused. "What are you doing here?"

"You did it," Vanuthan breathed. Suddenly, her face was down in Raine's face, a gleaming tear falling from one eye.

"What's happening?" Siniva demanded.

"She found the web. She reconnected me to it." Vanuthan smiled a beautiful dragon smile. "Raine is no child of the daenox."

"You?" Siniva stepped closer to her, his eyes brimming over with joy and gratitude. "You did this?"

Raine nodded. The joy that swept through her at the fondness in their eyes felt fleeting. They loved what she had done, not who she was, and there would be a price to her success.

"Can you do the same for Siniva?"

And there it was. She looked at Siniva. He was staring at her, hope burning like a bonfire in his eyes. He did not see her. He did not see the girl he had abandoned. He did not see the girl he had held so close that night in the inn. He did not see the girl he had talked through her performance fear. He saw the key to his freedom. At that moment, she was nothing else to him. Was love so transient, or was she a fool to think that his affections amounted to anything near love.

She closed her eyes and took a deep breath, trying not to wonder if they would abandon her when they were both free, and dove back into the dragon web. It still ran strong and fierce, pounding through her when she drew it in. With the web ready to burst out of her, she searched for him. What she found was a dim light, glowing so faint that she almost did not feel it at all. When she reached for it, the web recoiled, and the dim light did the same. She tried again with the same result.

The power of the web was demanding, sapping her strength with its force. Her muscles trembled already, burning with fatigue, but she tried once more. The web and the dim glow recoiled from one another yet again. Raine let go. She simply could not hold on to the power any longer. Her body shook, and she opened her eyes, the damp of tears on her cheeks.

Siniva looked at her, and the hope guttered out in his eyes.

She shook her head. "I'm sorry. I can't. Something's wrong."

Vanuthan looked after him as he turned away, walking into the center of the main room. "How did you break from the web, my friend?" she asked gently. "Perhaps there is some clue in that."

"I don't wish to speak of it," he answered, his voice hoarse.

"I tried," Raine said in a small voice.

Vanuthan moved close to her, her foreleg pressing against Raine. "You tried. You saved my life when I did not believe it could be saved. In time, perhaps, we will figure out how to do the same for him. For now, at least we can all leave this place, and I can hunt again for myself."

Raine nodded.

"Come," Vanuthan invited. "I would like to step outside."

Raine took a step toward Siniva.

"No," Vanuthan said softly. "Let him be. He will join us when he's ready."

Raine nodded and walked with Vanuthan to the entrance. The great dragon's steps were shaky, but she strode from the temple with her head high. Outside, she stretched her wings to their full extent and extended her neck high, her eyes closed to the sunlight. Her expression was blissful. A bliss Raine wished she could share.

Siniva stepped out of the temple behind them. He looked like he wished the same.

Letting the dragon appreciate her moment, she walked over and stepped off the pathway…

…and almost fell over. The daenox was a tempest of power and life. Daemon power swarmed the area almost like an invasion of some kind. She let it surge through her, feeling the hundreds of daemons converging to the west of them. It was exactly like an invasion.

"Kyouin's here with his army!"

Siniva's eyes went wide. To his credit, he did not question how she knew. "We have to get out of Imperious. They'll be focused on Elysium. We should be able to sneak away."

They would be focused on Elysium, where Kovial, Darkin, and Suva were. She had very few people she might consider friends, she was not going to let Kyouin take these ones from her. "Kovial and the others are there."

She turned and sprinted to Hydra.

"They're soldiers," Siniva called after her. "They can look after themselves."

She leaped up on the stallion and kicked him to a gallop, charging into the dense forest.

"Raine!"

*

Kyouin sat his mount in unseen silence and watched for a time, allowing Suva and another young soldier to enjoy the game of dice they were playing in the shadows of the gate. The soldier, a young man, was favoring one arm. There was no apparent injury now, but he appeared to be recovering from one. Darkin was alternating between watching the two and scanning the horizon for anyone approaching. As their ranking officer, he should probably be insisting on their attentive duty, but the way they all interacted, seeming to anticipate one another's wants without the need for words, made it clear that the three had some bond that went beyond an officer and his soldiers. That was encouraging. It made them more vulnerable.

When he felt he had seen enough, he made himself visible. Darkin snapped to attention, his hand going to his sword hilt. The two at the table jumped to their feet. Suva stepped up, putting herself between Kyouin and the injured third soldier. Good. That helped him make an important decision.

"Is it that time already?" Darkin asked. His tone was calm, flippant even. His eyes had taken on the hard look of a soldier who had faced death before and intended to do so again after today.

"Funny how fast time goes by when you're not looking forward to something," Suva added. She had the same grim determination about her. Death had come for her, and she was not going to go down without a fight.

Kyouin was starting to like these two.

"I might be a few days early. I do lose track sometimes." He smiled. "Now that I'm here, I would appreciate an escort to meet dear King Allondis."

Darkin gave a brusque nod. "I'll send for an escort." He started to turn away.

"That won't be necessary." Kyouin's smile faded. He waited for Darkin to turn back around, watching Suva's fingers twitch closer to her daggers. He also observed with the daenox as several of his daemons moved in around them. Ryche moved in closer to where Darkin now stood, staring up at Kyouin with narrowed eyes.

"You just said you wanted an escort."

"Oh, I do. I also don't want anyone alerting the king to my arrival. He's had enough time to prepare. You and Suva will do fine."

Darkin scoffed. "We can't abandon our post."

"Your friend there can stay and watch over things." He gestured to the third, and Suva shifted protectively closer.

"He's recovering from an injury. He's not even on active duty. If we abandon our station—"

"It might look like you're acting in my interests?"

Kyouin grinned. "I wouldn't worry about that. There's about to be a change of leadership here. You would be wise to put yourselves on the winning side as soon as possible."

"I'm not leaving Kovial here alone." Suva's hand closed on a dagger hilt now.

Kyouin shook his head at her. "Perhaps you need a more compelling argument."

He let the two daemon-wolves and the undead warrior that had moved behind Kovial become visible. The warrior was reasonably fresh, the flesh of his cheek, torn by the ravages of some scavenger, hung down on one side, giving a small glimpse of discolored teeth. He held a crossbow trained on Kovial, a guaranteed bolt to the neck at close range. Before they could react, Kyouin also revealed two daemon-dogs slinking closer to Suva and then Ryche who sat patient on his mount only a few strides from Darkin. As a last touch, in case anyone was still inclined to argue, he revealed two of the human warriors flanking his horse with their bows drawn and ready.

"What do you say? Kovial stays here with my soldiers to encourage your cooperation. You two, future officers of my army, will escort me to see your soon-to-be former king."

Darkin glanced around at his companions, assessing the situation. "No harm will come to him," he demanded when he faced Kyouin again.

Suva started to shake her head until Kovial touched her arm, giving her a small nod when she looked at him.

"Swear it," Darkin insisted.

Loyalty to one's troops was not a bad thing to have in a good officer. Someone like Darkin could lead part of his force into battle without needing his guidance, if he could be trusted. If not, he would become another undead officer, but Kyouin needed living officers he could trust to make complicated decisions about strategy without him there. The undead, with a few notable exceptions, did not have the capacity for complex thought, making it necessary to manage their tactics himself to a considerable degree. They were also terrible conversationalists.

"Only if you agree to stand by my side as my warriors before the king."

It was an unfair request. If he failed to take Elysium, they would be marked traitors and likely put to death for their actions. Of course, he would not fail.

Darkin turned to his companions. He and Suva locked eyes, and Kyouin had the irritating feeling that he was being left out of something. After several seconds, during which time itself seemed frozen, Darkin turned back to him and nodded.

"We escort you as your warriors."

"Then I swear your companion will come to no harm."

Darkin and Suva nodded their acceptance, and Kyouin made his warriors and daemons go unseen again. It would help to maintain the element of surprise and make it look as though the two had abandoned their post. They were smart enough to recognize that it was one more thing that would make it harder for them to turn back from this point.

The two each clasped hands silently with Kovial before they went to retrieve their horses. They mounted up and took flanking positions to Kyouin as they started toward the center of Elysium where King Allondis waited in his palace. Behind them, hundreds of Kyouin's warriors and daemons followed after them, unseen and unheard.

CHAPTER TWENTY TWO

Darkin kept his gaze straight ahead and his expression neutral. Anything he did that called noticeable attention to them could be considered an act of betrayal. He would not be that careless with Kovial's life on the line. There were more subtle options, however.

He adjusted his belt with one hand and discreetly flipped out a small black diamond-shaped pendant that hung on a short chain attached inside the pocket. It dangled there, barely out of the top of the pocket. He silently hoped someone of adequate rank would spot it as they passed by the stables, training grounds, and barracks. Flipping out the pendant was a painful process, given the wound hidden under his sleeve where the daemon-cat had bitten him. Hopefully, it would be worth it.

There was nothing particularly odd about two soldiers escorting someone to the palace, and few who might see them were likely to know that he and Suva were supposed to be out on the main gate. Several soldiers gave nods or waves of acknowledgment. A few even offered slight bows to his rank. If anyone of sufficient rank saw the pendant, they made no outward acknowledgment of it, but that was how it should be. It was a warning, a dire and desperate warning of something very wrong. His discretion should give them some indication that, whatever was wrong, the man between him and Suva had something to do with it.

When they reached the palace courtyard and dismounted, he was relieved to see that he significantly outranked the two door guards. Somehow, the idea of a confrontation inside the palace appealed to him. Maybe it was folly, but however many hidden minions Kyouin had with him, he could only bring so many into the building without something giving them away. At least, that seemed logical. Although, little about the daemon army and its leader had proven out to be especially logical.

When they made it to the throne room entrance, the guards there blocked their passage, crossing their halberds in front of the double doors.

Kyouin stepped forward. "King Allondis is expecting me. I'm the leader of the daemon army, and I come to negotiate a peaceful solution to our conflict."

Lying bastard.

The guard glanced at Darkin. He nodded, not allowing himself to hesitate while Kyouin was watching. This was a dangerous game, and he meant to play it well. "It's as he says. Please summon the king."

The guard hesitated, his gaze lingering on Darkin's insignias of rank. "Perhaps I should summon the area commander."

"Don't be a fool," Darkin snapped. "This could be the most important moment of the war. It could be the turning point we have all been waiting for. Don't be the one who denied King Allondis the opportunity to bring peace back to our lands by forcing this man to wait."

The tiniest hint of a smirk curved Kyouin's lips and Darkin yearned to punch him in that soft, boyish mouth.

The guard looked more thoughtful now. If there was anything that they all knew it was that Allondis was the most important thing to Allondis. If he had an opportunity to look like a savior, no one better stand in the way of that. Darkin also had enough rank now to make the guard hesitant to question him. The two things together were apparently persuasive enough. The guard nodded, and they drew back the halberds.

"I will have someone summon the king and his personal guard, of course. I'm sure you understand the precautions, my lord." He said the last to Kyouin, his lip curling with distaste as he addressed the leader of their foe.

Kyouin only smiled. "I expected nothing less."

They were led into the throne room to wait. Darkin and Suva remained on either side of Kyouin.

"Why are you doing all of this?" Suva asked under her breath.

"Maybe for the fun of it," Kyouin answered. "Maybe because no one thought the bastard son of a blacksmith's daughter would ever amount to anything. Sometimes, even I'm not sure why. I only know the dae-nox came to me. I would hate to seem ungrateful for the gift it gave me."

There was an edge to his voice that told Darkin the second part was at least some of the answer. The bastard son of a blacksmith's daughter. Probably looked down upon by everyone his whole life. Then one day he discovered that he had the skill to wield this new power. Perhaps that was all there was to it. A downtrodden young man gone mad with this new power at his disposal. He hoped Suva would accept the answer. The more they spoke, the more likely they would say something to cast doubts upon their willingness to serve him.

Several minutes passed in tense silence, the light of the sconces flickering around them. Darkin noticed that the room smelled of sweat and some exotic spice or incense. He tried to focus on that. The man next to him smelled of rotting things.

"I don't suppose either of you has run across a young dragonkin girl traveling with a band of troubadours?" Kyouin asked, breaking the silence. "I know they were heading toward Imperious."

Darkin's chest tightened. There was only one person Kyouin could be referring to. He could feel the light touch of her lips on his all over again, warmth moving through him in a wave just as it had at that moment. For a few seconds, he felt a bit too lightheaded to think of an answer.

What did this hideous bastard want with Raine?

He yearned for some way to communicate with Suva. Some way to tell her not to say anything about Raine.

"We haven't been out of Elysium in weeks," Suva answered with convincing disinterest. "Who has time for such things these days?"

Thank you.

Kyouin nodded as if he had expected as much. "I'll have you help me find her when we're done here."

Neither of them responded to that. To Darkin's relief, a door opened to the right of the throne then, precluding any need for further conversation. Several soldiers walked in, all men, and arranged themselves in two groups of five to either side of and slightly in front of the throne. They all wore the distinctive insignia of the king's private guard, a falcon with a fish in its claws. Darkin always assumed Allondis was the fish.

The same tired gentleman who had announced the king on their previous visit entered the room then. He looked at Kyouin with open distaste. "All rise for the Lord High Commander of Imperious, King Allondis Verathian."

Allondis entered the room, his expensive clothes, all vibrant greens and browns trimmed with gold, hung on him like they were made for someone else. Either his tailors had departed and left him to his own resources, or he had lost noticeable weight in less than a month. His dark hair was braided back under a crown that looked too big for a face that was noticeably thinner than before.

He had lost weight.

His darting eyes looked more than ever like the eyes of a frightened rodent. He did try to look confident, holding his chin so high it was a wonder he could see where he was walking. When he got to the front of his throne, Allondis sank into it with an attempt at grace that looked more like withering exhaustion.

Kyouin grinned boldly and took several quick steps forward. Allondis tensed and pressed back into the chair. All his soldiers put hands to their weapons and shifted into defensive stances. Darkin and Suva stood their ground. Any minute now, there was going to be an important decision to make. For Darkin, there was little question how it would go, and he suspected Suva felt the same. There was one person in danger right now who they would both lay down their lives for, and it was not their king.

Kyouin stopped, holding his hands up to ward off the defensive reaction. "It's a pleasure to meet you, King Allondis. I believe my companions brought you my terms." He waved a hand in the direction of Darkin and Suva. The king's eyes narrowed at them. "Have you made your decision? Will you hand over Elysium, or do we have to be uncivilized about this?"

"How dare you." Allondis leaned forward some, his outrage giving him momentary courage. "This is my throne."

Kyouin smiled and reached for the dagger at his belt.

The soldiers surged to life, drawing their weapons and springing for Kyouin, but he vanished from the spot. They faltered, glancing around in confusion until he appeared again a few moments later behind Darkin and Suva. Four of his own warriors appeared to either side of him. The odds were not the best. Seven to ten, if one did not count Allondis and his advisors, which Darkin did not. They did have a daenox priest on their side, or what passed for their side right now, so he was willing to bet his own blood on the winner.

Darkin drew his sword, his wounded arm screaming protest. One of the king's soldiers lunged at him, but the man went down with a dagger in his throat before he made contact. That confirmed Suva's position on the subject.

Allondis sprang up from his throne and ran for the door. Darkin ducked a swinging sword and came up, thrusting his own blade deep into the belly of his attacker, feeling the deep punctures in his arm tear open with the stress. Beyond the fatally wounded man now crumpling over his sword, Darkin could see the king struggling with the door they had come in through that apparently would not open now. The man who had announced him was trying as well, his face white with fear. Kyouin, who had gone invisible again, now reappeared next to the door.

Darkin jerked his blade free, warm blood soaking into the arm of his shirt from the freshly opened wounds. He shoved the wounded man aside and engaged another guard. They danced a few steps, then Darkin dodged an attack and twisted around the man, bringing his blade up at the perfect angle to cut in under his helm. Somehow, Suva had two more guards down around her and finished off a third with a risky leap up under the man's strike to embed another dagger in his throat.

Kyouin's warriors had managed to dispatch the remaining four guards, though not without cost. One of the four was down on one knee, both hands over a gushing abdominal would that was bleeding out on the floor. Near the door to the right of the throne, some blackened husk with a vaguely humanoid shape lay smoking on the floor. Kyouin was prodding Allondis toward them with the point of his dagger.

Darkin ground his teeth against the pain in his arm and faced Kyouin. "What now?"

Kyouin pushed Allondis back down in his throne and grinned at them. "I knew you two would be excellent recruits." He turned to Allondis, pointing at him with his dagger. The king winced away. "Now it's time to convert the Imperious Legion."

"How?"

Kyouin turned back to Darkin again. "I'll show them they can't win. Anyone who survives that demonstration will be given the option to join my army."

As much as Darkin wanted to believe the man's claim was mad, he had the uneasy feeling it was entirely truthful. Still insane, but within the realm of possibility. "And what should we do?"

"You two will stay here with my warriors and keep an eye on the king. When I'm done, you can rejoin your friend at the gate and tell him how brilliant you were to side with me. I'm sure he'll be useful when he's healed."

Darkin gave a nod of acceptance that Suva mirrored.

"You might dress that wound while you're waiting." Kyouin pointed at the bloody arm, then he bowed mockingly toward Allondis and swept from the room with a delighted grin.

Darkin watched him go.

"Traitors. You'll pay for this," Allondis hissed at them.

"You didn't get hit in that fight," Suva stated. Ignoring the king, she walked over and grabbed Darkin's arm, jerking back the fabric of his shirt.

"Ouch." He wrenched the arm away and pulled the sleeve back over the wounds. "Take it easy."

"When did that happen?"

He walked toward the far corner of the room, aware that Allondis and Kyouin's three remaining warriors were watching. Suva followed him.

He stopped and faced her. "I'll explain that later."

He turned slightly, putting his right hip toward her. Her eyes lit upon the pendant hanging out of his pocket and went wide. "What have you done?" she mouthed.

He stepped closer, pulling up the sleeve as if to let her look at his wound. "Be ready to take down those three. We're getting out of here."

"But Kovial," she whispered, leaning in even more and moving his arm as if to get a better look.

"Don't worry. We'll get him on the way out, and we'll have help."

"Are you sure?"

He shrugged slightly. "Am I ever sure of anything?"

She met his eyes then. They had been together for a long time. At times their relationship had been full of conflict. At other times, full of deep physical intimacy. What they shared now was something different. They were more than siblings. More than friends or lovers. They would lay down their lives for one another, but not for love. For the belonging and the purpose and the balance they gave one another. In her cold eyes, he could see that the bond they shared was as strong as ever. She would trust him, even with the life of her brother, and he would do anything in his power not to let her down.

CHAPTER TWENTY THREE

Hydra was an exceptional mount in many ways, and he proved that now. The thick forest was full of obstacles, from clutching vines to fallen trees, and Raine had turned them away from the original path, driving them through unknown territory to shorten the distance to the Elysium gates. The big stallion stumbled a few times, caught up in thick brambles or surprised by unseen drops, but he always righted himself. Raine gave him a general direction then let him choose the immediate path while she clung tight to the saddle, awed and alarmed by the power of the animal beneath her. He wove through the trees, maintaining a gallop except in the most difficult of places.

Siniva's calls had long been left behind. He did not have the horsemanship skills or a good enough horse to navigate the woods as fast as Raine and Hydra were. When the trees finally opened ahead, she could see the side of the outer wall across the cleared area of buffer between the wall and the forest. She was too far up the eastern side of the wall, but it would not take long to get around to the front once they were out of the woods.

They were sprinting through the tall grass, almost in sight of the main gate, when the jarring gong of alarm bells started ringing from within Elysium. First one, then another, and another, until it grew to a cacophony of noise. The racket caused a twisting of fear in her gut and set her nerves on fire. Hydra only dug in harder, stretching to a faster run toward the gates. The warhorse was a lot more eager to dive into the fray than she was, but she had to see if she could help her friends.

Are they really my friends?

She did barely know them, at least, beyond her parents' memories of them, and those were not exactly complimentary. They knew her even less. She was a dragonkin child who claimed to be the daughter of a prior companion. It was debatable if they could even have been considered her father's friends, given the nature of their relationship. Dephithus had spent a lot of time around them though, finding some relief from the torment of the daemon-seed in their presence. If Darkin had helped him escape Imperious, he must have been a friend to some degree.

Kovial had become something of a friend when they traveled together. He genuinely seemed to enjoy her help and her company. She also remembered quite vividly how Suva had hugged her. Whatever the reason for it, the embrace felt sincere. Darkin had helped her bring food to Vanuthan and offered to hunt for her to spare her the pain of doing it herself. He had also been understanding and forgiving of the way she treated him when she was hurting. Perhaps they were not friends, but they had the potential to be, and they were a connection to her father. That was good enough.

Raine expected to see many daemons at the gate, even though she could feel that the massive swelling of daenox was already within the walls. Instead, the area around the gates was mostly empty. Somehow, Kyouin and his army had gotten inside without the alarm being sounded until now.

There were some daemons—mostly hounds and wolves—along with a few warriors by the gate who were dressed in patchwork, grimy armor. Obviously not Imperious Legion soldiers. Though there was one Legion soldier in their midst, a man she recognized instantly as Kovial.

The three warriors readied their weapons at her approach, one raising his crossbow at her. Raine seized hold of the daenox running beneath them and dove into the daemons with it. They were under Kyouin's influence, but it was a fragile hold, not meant to control them over great distance like that woven into the beasts that had attacked the troubadour camp. With little effort, she broke his hold on the creatures. They responded with a moment of confusion as they adjusted to the sudden change in influence, then she sent them after the warriors. They leaped to the attack, pleased to have direction.

The sudden assault from daemons behind them caught the warriors off guard. They went down screaming and flailing, daemon-dogs and daemon-wolves tearing through their patchwork armor to the vulnerable flesh beneath. The crossbow let fly as its wielder went down, the bolt passing perhaps a foot away from her head.

Raine put the near miss from her mind and kept Hydra moving past the fallen men and their attackers. Kovial was already making a run for his own mount in the paddock inside the gates. Raine followed him through and stopped Hydra.

"Where are the others?"

"That bastard made them escort him to the palace." He swung awkwardly up in the saddle. "We need to be careful. He can make his troops invisible. There were several nasty undead at the gate for a time, but they vanished. I don't know where they are now." He scanned the area." They could still be here, watching us."

That explained how Kyouin got his army into Elysium. There was no one visible between this wall and the inner wall a short distance up the gradual hill. A much less peaceful scene waited within the inner wall. Even if she could not hear the shouts and cries and clash of steel in the distance, she could feel the saturation of daenox beyond the wall. They would have to be mad to go in there.

How many creatures could she turn, the way she did the ones at the first gate, before Kyouin noticed something and took a personal interest?

She used daenox to draw the seven daemons from the first gate to her, trying not to see the blood on their jowls.

"Raine, watch out!" Kovial grabbed for his weapon when the daemons rushed up around her.

She held up a hand quickly to stop him. "These ones are on our side. Let's go find Darkin and Suva."

She did not give him time to question the situation. Ignoring the glimmer of unease in his eyes when he looked at her then, she urged Hydra toward the next gate and the sounds of battle. The stallion was all too happy to oblige her. The daemons followed Hydra, and after a few tense seconds, she heard Kovial's horse coming along after them.

She did not know the layout beyond the second gate, at least not firsthand, but her parents had grown up here. Unless there had been drastic changes in the last few years, their memories would serve as an adequate guide, so long as she could keep the unwanted ones out of the way.

The noise of fighting got louder as they galloped up the hill. Raine's stomach shriveled into a cold ball of fear, and her heart climbed up into her throat. Kovial rode next to her now, his mount galloping along on the far side of two daemon-wolves. The gate in the inner wall stood open and unguarded. Strong evidence that Kyouin really could make his troops invisible. The sheer power and control necessary to manage something like that with the daenox chilled her to the bone. She would never be able to fight him if he decided to get serious about challenging her.

And yet, here she was, charging into the midst of his army to try to save two people she barely knew. If Kyouin caught wind of her presence, it could only go badly.

The daemon-wolves stayed beside her, forcing Kovial to drop back as they passed through the gate into chaos. With the barracks and the various training grounds, there were plenty of Legion soldiers and Legion hopefuls about, though many would have been training with practice weapons and unprepared for the sudden onslaught from within the walls. They were still putting up a fierce fight from what she had time to observe.

By the closest arena, a horde of daemons and warriors were being held back by a small but determined group of mounted soldiers. Not far from there, another group of soldiers, near one of the stables, was being mowed down by some larger daemons and undead warriors, who would soon be free to reinforce the ones by the arena. Shrieks of rage and unnatural howls from the daemons rose up above the din of clashing steel. One soldier staggered their direction screaming, half of his face torn away by a twisted daemon that resembled no animal she had ever seen. Her stomach turned, and she faced forward.

To her right, a daemon-dog appeared as if forming out of the air and lunged at them. One of her turned daemons jumped to meet it. The two fell to the ground, locked in combat. She did not have time to help with that fight. Not far up the main road, a group of riders was coming their direction at a hard gallop, weapons drawn against attackers coming from both sides. She recognized Suva near the front. Darkin was a few horses behind her.

Raine glanced at Kovial and saw that he had recognized them as well. They pulled up their mounts, and she sent three of the remaining six daemons after warriors who were between them and the approaching party. The nearest daemons she began to turn a couple at a time, pulling them out of Kyouin's control and sending them against his troops to help clear a path for the fleeing group.

Suva saw what was happening ahead of them. Her brow furrowed, but she accepted their good fortune, shouting something back to the others before leaning low over her mount's neck and kicking the animal to run faster. The rest of the group followed her example. The rider to Darkin's left went down when another daemon appeared out of nowhere beside them. The beast ignored the fallen soldier and continued the chase. Raine turned it before it could lunge at Darkin and set it to guarding his now exposed flank.

Darkin glanced at the beast, but when it did not attack, he peered ahead of them. His eyes met hers for a second. His nod was one of gratitude, then he mouthed "run" at them and pointed with his sword to the gate.

Kovial circled in front of her. "He's right. They'll be here in seconds. We need to get out."

She hesitated. If she turned her back on them, she could no longer target daemons that attacked them. Then again, the fleeing party had drawn the attention of the band near the stable, and the daemons and undead there were heading their way. She was not sure she could turn that many. What she had done already was leaving her feeling drained and corrupted somehow. Perhaps because these daemons had already been turned to Kyouin's purposes and she had to manipulate daenox with his influence on it to claim them. This was far more complicated than making light shows for entertainment or luring unsuspecting animals to their deaths.

She sent one more of the daemons from the first gate out to help protect the group of riders. Then she spun Hydra, and with two daemons left to help protect them, they kicked the horses to a gallop back toward the gate.

They made it through the inner gate without trouble. Halfway down the hill to the outer gate, trouble arrived. It appeared in the form of an undead warrior on his undead horse and seven human warriors. She and Kovial skidded their mounts to a halt. The daemon-wolves she had turned moved close to Hydra, snarling at their opposition as if they had never been allied to that side.

The mounted undead warrior held a staff with a wickedly curved blade on one end. A flap of decaying flesh hung loosely from the back of the hand that held the weapon. She found herself staring at it, her stomach churning. This monstrosity was a product of Kyouin's use of the daenox. Perhaps it could be turned like the daemons.

She reached into the undead warrior with a surge of daemon power and instantly recoiled. It was as if death ran rotting fingers through her brain, leaving trails of putrefaction behind like snail slime. She did throw up then, having the presence of mind to at least lean away so she did not do so on herself or Hydra.

"Raine?"

Kovial's voice barely penetrated the residual pulse of corruption that contact left inside her before another sound caught her attention. It was the sound of horses' hooves pounding the ground behind them. Darkin and Suva's group was coming down the hill.

She spat the taste of vomit from her mouth as a rider came flying through the lower gate and charged up the hill toward them. It was Siniva, somehow keeping his seat with his ax held aloft. The warriors between them shifted, some looking past her and Kovial at the approaching group while a few others turned to glance down the hill at Siniva. Depending on how many of the group behind them had made it through the gates, this line of warriors was probably significantly out-numbered, especially if enough of her turned daemons had survived. Something about the undead warrior in the middle made her feel as though, even with greater numbers, they would not get past without considerable losses.

A roar shook the air. Vanuthan swept in, diving at the line of warriors. Raine stared, stunned that the ema-ciated dragon could even fly. As she passed through, her claws raked over the two warriors at the start of the line, sending them flying, one in a different direction than his head. The warriors on the opposite end broke rank and began to run. The Mother Dragon was slow to rise though, and the undead warrior struck out, slicing deep into one foot as she struggled to get out of reach. Her blood rained down on him. She let out a different roar this time. One of pain.

Get away!

The riders behind them were closing now, and they were not slowing. They meant to charge straight through. Raine sent the rest of the daemons she had turned after the undead warrior and his few remaining companions. Then she and Kovial kicked their mounts to a run and broke around the warriors who were now occupied fighting daemons that had been their allies a short time ago. Above them, Vanuthan made a labori-ous circle, preparing to come back for another attack if needed. Raine silently begged for her to flee.

Siniva, seeing the direction of the tide, spun his mount to join them. They were a short distance past the second gate when another dragon appeared, a mas-sive gold beast Raine recognized all too well, swooping in from the direction of the city. Siniva stopped so fast that several of the riders behind him almost plowed into his horse, swerving to continue their escape. Raine pulled up as well. They both looked back in time to see the gold dragon slam into Vanuthan. The force of the impact sent both dragons careening toward the ground inside the inner wall. Raine's heart fell with them.

She's only here because of me.

Vanuthan's eerie screams rent the air, drowned out a moment later by the deafening roar of Theruses.

"There's nothing you can do!"

Darkin's shout sounded muffled and distant after the high screams of the Mother Dragon. Raine turned to him, the movement felt sluggish and detached. Then she glanced in the direction he was pointing and saw the undead warrior, joined now by quite a few other warriors from Kyouin's army, rushing their direction.

"There's nothing you can do," Darkin repeated.

Siniva turned and kicked his horse after the others. Raine followed, pushing away the daenox as they fled and reaching into the dragon web. About the time they made it into the cover of the woods, Vanuthan's presence in the web disappeared.

CHAPTER TWENTY FOUR

You got me this bag of bones, but where is my pet king?" Kyouin snarled, pointing to the red dragon who lay upon the remains of one training arena.

Theruses, now in his hulking, semi-human form, lashed his tail in irritation. "The Mother Dragon was helping them escape. I brought her down. It was not my intention to go down with her."

"Yes. But she got hold of your wing. I know." He kicked one of the red dragon's feet. "You're lucky you changed form when you did, or I'd have two dragons littering my grounds." It still irked Kyouin that his army had not gone after Theruses, but he had explicitly told them to kill the dragon if it came back. When Theruses changed form, daenox oozing out of his very presence, they hesitated to attack him. That their confusion was understandable did not make the outcome any less irritating.

He scowled at the red dragon again then turned to Theruses. "What about Raine? I know I felt her here. What happened to her?"

"I believe she got away with your pet king," Theruses rumbled. Even in this form, he sounded like a dragon. "She was my intended target before Vanuthan made her appearance."

Cold filled Kyouin at the word *target*. "You meant to kill her?"

"That was my intent. It would be yours too if you had any sense. I felt her in the dragon web. Now that she knows how to connect to it, she is even more of a threat."

Kyouin shrugged. "You control the daenox and the dragon web. Doesn't that make you as much of a threat?"

Theruses scowled at Vanuthan. His tail lashed violently around the clawed feet at the bottom of his very muscular, mostly human looking legs. Kyouin watched that lashing tail for a second and giddiness bubbled in his chest.

"You can't control the web anymore," he stated with certainty, barely holding back a laugh. "Your fate was bound to it, but you can't control it. No wonder you're so prickly about Raine."

Those black eyes glared down at him. "My concern is not a matter of jealousy—"

"Maybe not only," Kyouin interrupted, bubbling over with glee at the Death Dragon's predicament.

Theruses growled deep in his throat, and several nearby daemons bristled, growling in response and looking around for the threat. Their response snuffed Kyouin's amusement. They were reacting to Theruses as if he were one of them. That made him a danger to Kyouin's control of that aspect of his army. For a time, he believed that was why a small number of daemons had turned on his army in the battle. He thought he sensed Raine nearby, but she feared him. Her fear when he saw her in Corbent Calid had been intoxicating. He found it almost impossible to believe she would have intentionally come to where he was. Now he knew she had been here. Perhaps the dagger had convinced her.

He smiled to himself.

"At least I'll get control of this army after she kills you."

That caught Kyouin's attention. "This is my army," he stated. "Any part that might have been yours was lost when you took to the sky and fled."

Theruses turned, his tail lashing again. "Raine is a child in human years, but she is growing and learning at the pace of a dragon. Like you, the daenox doesn't appear to have any ill effect on her. She will learn to use those powers for more than entertainment soon enough. You would be wise to end her before that happens."

"Or recruit her," Kyouin countered.

Theruses's smile was cruel. He gestured to the Mother Dragon. "Vanuthan was family to her. Do you think she'll join you now?"

Kyouin narrowed his eyes. "You killed her."

"Do you think Raine will differentiate between us? I came to the aid of your army. She will hold you responsible."

Without waiting for a response, he took several lunging strides, changing form as he moved, and leaped into the sky. There was a raw wound near the base of one wing that slowed his ascent, but he was still out of reach in a few agonizing wingbeats. Kyouin stared after the gold dragon, then glanced over at the great red beast lying crumpled on the ground. The Mother Dragon. One of the few living creatures Raine could claim some familial connection to. Very possibly the reason she had come here to Imperious. Theruses had killer her, but he had done it in Kyouin's battle, connecting her death to him. Theruses was right, she would blame them both for this.

Rage swelled in him. He shouted after the departing dragon. "What have you done?"

There was a tightening in his chest. It was panic. He had not felt this kind of panic since the day his sister walked in on him, after he killed their father with the hammer. He had solved that by stabbing her with a metal hay hook from the barn, and holding her down until she bled out. Then he pulled her a short distance from their father's body, making it look like she had dragged herself until she got too weak. He left her there with the bloody hammer in one hand and tore her dress in a few suggestive ways to make it look as if their father had attacked her. The hook he placed by their father. Their father was given to violent outbursts so often that their mother never questioned the truth. She eventually found a new man and gave birth to Vaneye.

Kyouin took a deep breath.

He had solved that problem. He would find a way to solve this one. The Mother Dragon was not the only family tie Raine had in this area.

"My lord."

He faced the warrior sinking to one knee next to him. One of many faces he could not put a name to. Living warriors were so much less interesting than the dead.

"What is it?"

"Priestess Jadean has arrived."

"Excellent. Send her to the audience chamber. Find Avaline and send her there as well." He turned to Ryche who still had dragon blood spattered over his already grisly visage from the gash he had cut in Vanuthan's foot. It was a shame he had not done something similar to Theruses. "See to it that our surrendered Legion soldiers clean up their own dead. Let them get a good look at the wounds that felled their allies. But leave this thing here. I might have a use for her."

He stood there a moment, considering the battle. He had used daenox to taste the mind of a turned daemon as it was dying. He would not admit it to Theruses, but the Death Dragon was right about Raine. She was learning to do more than play with daenox. She, not Theruses, had stolen some of his daemons from him and turned them against his army. As much as that knowledge kindled dread in him, when he tasted her power in his daemon, there had been something intensely erotic about the sense of violation. He yearned to taste that power again, to bury himself in it, just preferably not while it was being used against him.

Ryche clicked his teeth and started to turn his mount away. Kyouin nodded to him, clinging to the illusion the undead warrior had waited to be dismissed, before he mounted his horse to ride back to the palace. His palace now. Somewhere in that palace, Dephithus's den-father still lived. A bit out of his mind, if the rumors were accurate, but very much alive. There were people here with connections to Raine. He would find as many as it took to win her or break her.

He steered around humans and daemons littering the area. Some still lived, making hideous sounds as they bled out on the churned ground. By the time he reached the palace entrance, his spirits were good. The victory here was swift and decisive. Now he had the leverage he needed to bring Raine to heel. It would only take time and a little help from someone with the right skills. Jadean was that someone. Her uncanny foresight and ability to know things that were hidden from most people would help him find Raine.

He almost started skipping on his way to the audience chamber in *his* palace.

This is going to be so very fun.

Outside the audience chamber, he turned to one of King Allondis's former guards, most of whom had changed sides rather quickly.

"Lord Mythan is here, is he not?"

The man's nod was hesitant. "He isn't in his right mind anymore."

"Who among us truly is?" Kyouin laughed. The guard's brow furrowed, so he dismissed the comment with a wave of one hand. "Bring him to me."

"Yes, sir. My l… your majesty." The man's eyes grew wider as he fumbled for the proper title.

"Majesty is weighted down with jewels and responsibility. My lord is sufficient."

"My lord." The guard bowed and hurried off.

When Priestess Jadean entered the room, Kyouin sat reclined on the throne, one leg hooked over an arm. Avaline stood to one side in pungent silence, Vaneye holding her hand. Kyouin did his best to ignore the way his little brother stared at him with those matte grey eyes. The daenox that infected him should have made him fierce. Instead, the boy had become needier and somewhat incoherent. So much for that experiment. At least there was a good chance the infection would kill him in time.

Jadean wore a drab brown dress that differed little from what she was wearing the last time he saw her, though this one had split skirts for riding. The rope tied around her waist appeared to hang a bit looser as well. Her straw-colored hair fell around her shoulders in thick waves, and striking emerald eyes shone with the power of her knowing. As a daenox priestess, her eyes and hair should have begun darkening by now, but perhaps the limitations of her ability subjected her to less daemon power.

She approached with cautious steps, and he wondered if her knowing had given her insight into this moment. He would not ask, however. That would lead down an endless spiral of questions. He had a job for her.

"It's good to see you well, Jadean."

She inclined her head, not quite far enough that she took her eyes off him. "And you, my lord. I see you have been busy." Her gaze on him remained intense, but one hand absently moved to her belly, resting there for a few seconds. "Your little brother will die soon from the daenox you infected him with." She glanced at the two figures off to the side of the throne.

Kyouin sat up and leaned forward. He was more interested in the gesture she had made than in his brother's fate. "Are you with child?"

She lifted her chin, proud and defiant. "I carry the dragonkin's child."

"The dragonkin?" He stared at her a moment. "You mean Dephithus?"

"We met on the road when he was seeking Myara and his daughter."

Something wonderful bubbled up in Kyouin's chest for the second time today. He laughed. "You seduced him. You delightfully wicked woman."

"We comforted one another," she countered, her words cutting off with defensive irritation.

Kyouin did not care what she called it. He had Raine's unborn sibling. Raine would be more inclined to trust Jadean with this connection between them. He let out a whoop of glee that made the guards by the door flinch.

"The child is mine."

Kyouin smiled. "You know that's not true, Jade. You knew it when you coupled with him, and you know it now."

She covered her belly with both hands. "This child is not like Raine. It has no power."

"I think it might have a lot of power. Even now, resting in your lovely belly."

The doors opened. Lord Mythan shuffled through the door. A woman entered with him, wearing an odd boot on her right foot and leaning on a crutch. Mythan's brown hair was streaked with grey, but he was well-groomed and finely dressed, though his hazel eyes had no luster.

The woman next to Mythan stared hatred at Kyouin.

Her long dark hair was tied up in the warrior's knot many of the female Legion soldiers wore, though her injury made it clear she was not doing much fighting these days.

Kyouin looked at the guard walking behind them. "Who is this? I asked only for the late king."

"I'm Lord Mythan's guard," the woman stated.

Kyouin chuckled. "That must be a boring duty."

The woman's expression hardened more if that were possible.

"So serious," Kyouin shrugged off a flash of irritation. He opened his mouth to order her killed, then paused. "Do you have any connection to Dephithus or Myara?"

The woman brightened, taking a step closer with the aid of her crutch. "Do you have news of them?"

Kyouin stared at her, silently waiting.

Her expression darkened a touch, but she relented. "I'm Kayd, Myara's aunt."

Kyouin gave a little bounce in his seat. This day kept getting better. Now he did not need to send all his assets out into the world. He could keep Mythan here as insurance against betrayal.

"What of Myara's parents and Dephithus's blood father?"

"Myara's parents are in the city. I don't know where Lornin is."

Kyouin nodded thoughtfully. "Dephithus had two half-sisters."

Kayd shook her head. "They left Elysium with their fathers after Avaline died. I don't know where they are now."

Kyouin shrugged. "I've been told Myara and Dephithus are both dead," he did not give her time to give voice to the despair that contorted her features, "but their daughter lives."

"Daughter?" She shook her head.

"Yes. They had a daughter. Her name's Raine." A tear ran down Kayd's cheek at that. Perhaps Myara had mentioned the name for a future child. That was good. It gave this woman a connection to Raine. "I want you and my dear friend Jade to go find her and invite her back here. I would like to talk to her. To see if we can come to an accord."

Through the sorrow in Kayd's eyes, something else sparked to life. He could almost see the ideas forming in her mind. She was a plotter, this one. He could not trust her, but he did not need to. Her troubled glance at Mythan was enough to confirm that.

"I'm willing to go find her, but I would take Lord Mythan with me."

Kyouin shook his head. "He stays here. He doesn't look up to an adventure."

The old king took several steps forward then, looking toward the corner where Avaline and Vaneye stood.

"Avaline?" His voice rasped with disuse.

Kayd looked at the undead creature next to the throne and sucked in a breath. "What have you done to her?"

"You needn't worry about her. She's been dead for some time." He delighted in Kayd's look of horror almost as much as he did in the mix of confusion, disgust, and anguish that twisted Mythan's features.

"You're disgusting," Kayd declared. "I will not leave Lord Mythan with you."

Kyouin gestured to one of the guards. "Find Myara's parents and bring them here. They can keep Lord Mythan company. Start a search for Lornin as well." When the man headed off to do as ordered, he turned back to Kayd. "You *will* leave him here. And when you find Raine, you will get her to come back here, because they will be waiting for her to decide their fates." He summoned another guard. "Help these two get whatever supplies they need for their journey and get them going. They mustn't fall too far behind."

Kayd hesitated when the guard came to escort her out. "What do you want with a child?"

Kyouin smiled. "You'll see."

As he watched them walking out, a small choking sound from the near corner caught his attention. Something wet and brownish ran from one of Avaline's eyes. It almost looked like a tear. Probably some bit of rotten flesh had split open and was oozing. Still, something about it made him uneasy.

Siniva kept to the edges of camp. He spoke to no one. Raine, he would not even look at. She knew why, and she shared his loathing for herself. If she had not gone galloping into the middle of the battle, Vanuthan would be alive now. This was her fault.

She glanced over to where Suva and Darkin were helping an injured soldier wrap a deep wound and wondered if it had been a good trade. Vanuthan had died so they could live. A few mere human lives traded for that of a dragon. Not any dragon either. One of the eldest dragons of the web. The Mother Dragon. Vanuthan had placed the dragon power in Dephithus and Raine that enabled the dragons to go free from their stone prisons. She had shaped their lives in a significant way. That made her Raine's grandmother and her mother, in a sense.

Little light emanated from the camp. They made only the smallest of fires to warm food and boil water to use for tending injuries. Huddled near the fire, in clothes much too fine for such an environment, sat the king of Imperious, Allondis. He was young. She had not realized how young he was, but a brief dive into her father's memories told her he was a little younger than Dephithus. Barely old enough to have reached his Dawning Day when he assumed the throne.

His dark eyes stared into the small fire. Bejeweled fingers tightly clutched the luxurious cloak that hung around his thin shoulders. He was pale and gaunt. He almost looked like one of Kyouin's fresher undead warriors. Whatever thoughts passed behind his staring eyes, it was easy enough to see that he was not taking this turn of events well. When a Legion soldier offered him food, he did not respond. The soldier looked to Darkin who shook his head and shrugged.

That was not the first time she had seen the other soldiers turn to Darkin for guidance. Somehow, leadership of this group of Legion soldiers appeared to have been foisted upon him. He shouldered the burden silently, addressing the concerns of those that he could and checking in on each soldier to make sure injuries and other needs were seen to as best they could be under the circumstances. Suva and Kovial helped as well, though Kovial remained limited by his own healing injury.

All told, seventeen soldiers had escaped with Darkin's group and the king. Adding herself and Siniva, they numbered twenty-three in all. Somewhere out there, Nakia's troop had made good their own escape from Imperious. At least she hoped they had. When they passed through the area near the troubadours' camp in their flight, the camp had been abandoned.

Raine got up from the spot she had found under a tree and walked away from the camp, past the line of horses shifting in the dark. Since leaving the city, she had maintained her connection to the dragon web, but Vanuthan's presence there was still missing. It felt like a raw wound, ripping through the center of her. A gash into which salt was being continuously rubbed.

"Are you all right?" Suva's voice was gentle. Cautious.

For a moment, Raine thought back on the hug Suva had given her when they met. If she turned to her now, the woman would be willing to hold her like that again. She could not though. Suva, Darkin, and Kovial were her mistake. They were the wrong choice she had made. It hurt to have to acknowledge that. They might have escaped without her help. They might not have. The only certainty was that Vanuthan would not have fallen if she had not gone to help them. She could not turn to them for comfort. Not now. Not while her own sorrow drowned beneath the waves of grief rolling off Siniva in his silence. Even here, on the opposite side of the camp from him, she could feel that grief swelling like a river in flood.

"I'm well enough. See to the others."

Suva did not leave right away. Raine could feel her lingering there. When a minute or two had passed in silence, she finally heard the woman's footsteps retreating back to camp.

Alone again, Raine listened to the night. She listened with her ears for danger. She reluctantly dropped her hold on the dragon web and reached out along the flows of daenox, searching for friend or foe. There were many animals in the dark. Many daemons too. She was not sure whether the latter should be called friend or foe. Daenox made them aggressive, but they were not evil or cruel, they were merely what their nature forced them to be. She had seen the way the daemons watched her light shows. The innocent wonder that all creatures were capable of also existed in them. They were pawns of the power that drove them as much as she and her father had been pawns of the dragons and the daenox. The daemons she turned helped them escape Elysium. Even with that, she was confident she was the only one there who would hesitate to kill a daemon on sight.

Raine released the daenox, denying herself the comfort it offered. With a bit of struggle, she reconnected to the less familiar dragon web. Vanuthan's presence was still absent. That could only mean one thing. She swallowed hard against the tightness in her throat and the unshed tears that burned her eyes. Reaching through the web, she sought out the other dragons. Their presence was there, concentrations of power that were shut off from her. She could feel them, but she could not reach them.

"Can you feel her?"

Siniva's voice made her start. He had walked up next to her while her attention was on the dragon web.

"No." She kept her answer short, afraid her voice might crack otherwise.

He was silent for several minutes. It started to rain, and a few fat drops made it through the forest canopy, landing cold on her head.

"And the others?"

"They won't let me in."

Siniva growled softly. "Can you tell where they are?"

Raine focused on the web, on the many dragons that lie beyond her reach. The harder she concentrated on those centers of power, the more she started to get a sense of direction and place. She closed her eyes, letting the web take her to where they were. Soon she tasted salt upon her lips. A cool, damp wind buffeted her. The sharp squawks of sea birds reached her ears along with the whoosh of water and the rumble of waves crashing upon rocks.

"Someplace coastal. That direction." She opened her eyes to see where she was pointing.

Siniva nodded in that direction. "The Illtide Coast. The mountains there once held many sanctuaries for my kind that may still exist. I should have guessed they might go there."

"Then that's where we'll go."

Siniva looked at her then, his gaze cold and distant. At first, she thought he meant to deny her, to tell her *they* would not be going anywhere. After a few seconds, he only nodded and walked away. The rain picked up then, the water that soon ran down from her hair masking the tears flowing down her cheeks.

Raine felt along the dragon web one more time, hoping to find some trace of Vanuthan, some sign that she might still live. When she found nothing, she let go of that unfamiliar power connected to creatures that denied her and dove back into the veins of daenox flowing through the ground deeper down. The daemon power calmed her. It did not stop the flow of tears, but it eased some of the pain and fear.

Imperious was taken. Vanuthan was dead. Kyouin appeared unstoppable. But was he really? If they could convince the dragons to come and fight, Kyouin's army would not seem so powerful. And she was not useless against him. She could break his control of the daemons and turn them against him. Not in the numbers necessary to make a big enough impact yet, but if she practiced, perhaps she could do more.

She shuddered at the memory of her contact with the undead warrior. There were no answers there. She could not bear that kind of contact again. Daemons and daenox infected animals were something else. The bearlike daemon she and Rakas had faced in the woods had an intricate weaving of daenox controlling it, but the beasts in the army were different. It stood to reason that Kyouin, even as powerful as he was, could not manage a weaving that complex spread among that many creatures, which meant his daemons could become her daemons. She just needed to figure out how to turn more of them at once.

Raine let her awareness sweep through the flows of daenox, touching upon numerous daemons spread out over miles in the direction they would be going. There would be plentiful opportunities to practice controlling them along the journey, though that was not the same as breaking someone else's control. She swept out further still, spreading her awareness through the many veins of daenox pulsing through the ground.

They would go to find the dragons, and she would experiment with controls like those she had encountered in the minds of Kyouin's daemons. She would figure out how to counter them and take control in greater numbers. Somehow, she would learn how to thwart him and, by the time she met Kyouin and Theruses again, she would be the one to fear.

"Daemon's blood."

The exclamation pulled her back into herself. Darkin was standing in front of her, and for just an instant, he was almost as clear as if they stood in the light of an overcast day. Then the darkness swept back in, and he was little better than a shadow in the rainy night.

"What's wrong?"

"When I walked up to you just now, there was a glowing violet ring around the iris in your eyes. It was..." He stepped closer, and she braced for him to tell her how freakish she was or how frightening it had been. "...extraordinary," he finally finished, and she could hear the breathy awe in his voice.

She stared at the shadowy figure in the darkness, quite at a loss for how to respond. What made him so willing to accept what she was? He had seen her lure and kill animals in the woods with daenox to feed Vanuthan. He figured out she was the one making the daemons switch sides in their flight from Elysium. Yet here he was, having seen her eyes apparently glowing with daemon power, and he still found no reason to reject her.

One of her father's memories came to her then. A day he fled into the woods after the daemon-seed drove him to injure another Legion soldier in training. Darkin had followed him, and Dephithus had wondered then at the other young man's composure.

"What do you want?" Dephithus demanded, his temper high.

"I was walking by when you pulled your little move in the arena. I thought maybe you could use a better sparring partner to burn off some of that destructive energy."

Dephithus glanced at him. "You would put yourself in my path after what I just did."

"Life is full of risks. I never learned anything from avoiding them."

Dephithus grudgingly cracked a grin. "You don't learn much if you get killed in the process either."

"I'd rather die young with a life full of experiences than grow old never having tried anything." Darkin said, grinning back.

Dephithus shook his head, chuckling softly. "One might argue that some risks aren't worth taking."

Darkin shrugged. "I've always been terrible at telling the difference."

Even with the distance of time, the grudging admiration her father felt back then was strong enough that she could barely differentiate it from her own emotions.

Darkin placed a hand on her forearm, perhaps reassuring himself that she was still there in the dark. "I don't understand how you are who you are. I don't understand your power or why being near you makes me feel so alive. I only know you are someone extraordinary, Raine, and I hope you know I will always welcome you. I believe Suva and Kovial feel the same."

Raine's pulse raced. She remembered the light kiss she had given him. That had not been intended to mean anything beyond expressing her gratitude. Even so, she found herself leaning closer to him, wanting to try again, but not entirely sure why. Among the things she still did not understand, not even with the aid of her parents' memories, relationships were at the top of the list. Was this just curiosity or were the butterflies fluttering madly in her chest a sign of something else?

"I will always welcome you."

Those words played back in her mind. Maybe it was gratitude that compelled her to want to lean into him.

Darkin's hand tightened on her arm suddenly. He turned away from her, peering into the dark, and she became aware of rustling sounds in the brush not far away. Then a flow of daenox swirled around her. She put a hand on Darkin's shoulder.

"Don't worry. They're friends."

He glanced down at her. "You're sure?"

"Yes." She stepped up next to him and called out, "Rakas?"

Shadowy figures moved through the trees, some riding, some leading their mounts. The rider in the lead hopped down from their mount. A raspy laugh told Raine who it was instantly.

"Little dragonkin," Nakia greeted. "I feared we had lost you for good. Lucky for us, your moody man-priest seems to have a compass tuned to you."

Alarm spiked in her chest. Was Rakas tracking her somehow? She looked around and spotted a Rakas shaped shadow coming up along Nakia's left.

"How did you find me?" The words came out more accusing than she intended. She did not want the others to know how much the idea of him being able to track her frightened her. Before anyone could question her tone, she turned to Darkin. "Please, lead Nakia and the others to the camp. I need to talk to Rakas."

Darkin hesitated a moment, then she made out his nod in the darkness.

"Come with me. I'll get you settled with the others."

As he guided them away, Raine could hear him asking if anyone was injured and a swell of gratitude lifted her. Whether or not he ever had been a bad person, she did not feel that he was one now. Still, she needed to think harder about what she wanted from him before she did something foolish. Her lack of experience in the world made it much too easy for someone to take advantage of her, even if they did not mean to.

There were other problems to address right now, however.

"How did you find me?"

"That's not something you can do anything about." The dark shadow of his hand gestured toward the camp as if to suggest following the others.

Raine shook her head. "I want to know," she insisted, standing her ground.

Rakas relented. "Your presence is unusual. When you're reaching out through the flows of daenox, it feels like the dragon web and the daemon power are weaving around each other, but not in a hostile way. It's different. I'm not sure you can do anything about that, but I'm fairly certain it's how Kyouin found you the first time."

Raine shivered and peered into the darkness. There was always some new challenge to deal with, and it seemed like the last one rarely got resolved first. At least, with Rakas here, she might have help figuring some of the daenox powers out instead of flailing in the dark hoping to get something right.

"I'm glad you're back," she said softly, turning toward the camp. "But don't read too much into that."

He chuckled dryly. "Don't worry. I won't."

CHAPTER TWENTY SIX

Before dawn, they were up and riding again. It had not rained long the night before. Even so, occasional drops of water from damp trees reminded them that this was not the ideal time of year for traveling. Especially given that their hasty escape left little time for packing supplies. The troubadours were the best prepared, but not to provide for all thirty-one of them.

For now, the group stuck together. Raine suspected she and Siniva would branch off on their own before long. The Legion soldiers probably had some destination in mind other than the Illtide Coast to search for dragons, but they were angling in the right direction for now. Siniva had made no effort to speak to her since their brief encounter in the night. He had gone back to not looking at her again, which made her feel like the prior night's encounter had been a dream. It was disconcerting.

The young king was at least as noncommunicative as Siniva. His soldiers looked after him dutifully, doing what they could to see to his needs. He remained silent through it all, staring at nothing so hard she worried his eyes might burst. His clothes were already showing some dirt and wear from their harried escape and a night in the woods. There was dried blood on the hem of his fancy cloak that she did not think he knew was there. No one seemed of a mind to point it out to him.

The soldiers were still deferring to Darkin, who had selected their path based on the ability to keep in the cover of the trees. The appearance of dragons, especially one fighting for the enemy, had shaken the soldiers. Keeping to the trees helped maintain a sense of safety from that airborne threat. They were all on edge as it was, casting nervous glances at Raine and Siniva with some frequency. Since Siniva stayed as far from Raine as possible, that meant there was a lot of twisting back and forth in the saddle going on, which made those wary looks more obvious.

The troubadours, however, were more than happy to ride with the two dragonkin, though Siniva managed to drive away everyone who attempted to join him until Nakia, who had either been accepted or simply ignored his attempts to drive her off. Knowing Nakia, Raine suspected the latter.

Darkin primarily stayed at the head of the group while Suva moved around more, often trailing behind to make sure everyone was accounted for and no one was flagging from injuries. Kovial, restricted by his own injury, rode beside Raine much of the time, ignoring the strange looks his fellow Legion soldiers gave him for it.

When she caught Rakas looking her way, she motioned him over.

"What can I do?" he asked when he had worked his way over to her side, apparently recalling that he had asked to be there to watch her back.

"Darkin's arm. I noticed this morning that his sleeve is covered in dried blood. He must have opened the wounds yesterday. He's trying not to favor it, but…"

Rakas was already nodding. "I'll do what I can to help him out for now. Perhaps, when we stop this evening, I can walk you through a more thorough healing."

"I would like that. Thank you."

An unbidden smile of gratitude turned her lips and her father's memories of the night Rakas and Amahna put the daemon-seed in him crashed in on her. She reeled, and her stomach turned. She bent over the saddle, grabbing a handful of Hydra's mane to steady herself. Fortunately, Rakas had already started working his way up to where Darkin rode at the front before the thank you was entirely clear of her lips so had not noticed her sudden affliction.

Someone's hand touched her arm. "Are you all right?"

Raine wiped away a tear, swallowing back against nausea, and made herself sit up. She composed herself and looked at Myrza. Those eyes, full of concern and affection, grounded her and helped her push away her father's memories.

"I... Yes. Thank you." Raine glanced after Rakas. He was up beside Darkin now. They exchanged a few words and Darkin pulled up his sleeve. As he did so, he glanced over his shoulder, giving her a smile and a nod of appreciation. Raine found herself smiling back. Her cheeks growing warm.

"You like him."

Suddenly, Raine's entire face went hot. "I don't know," she blurted.

"It wasn't a question." Myrza gave a light laugh, though there was something sad about her smile. "I had hoped to be the one to win that smile from you."

Raine looked at her, suffering from a dizzying rush of pleasure at the way the woman was regarding her. "You did. You do. I mean..." Her tongue felt like it could not make articulate sense of anything she was thinking or feeling.

Myrza only smiled, offering no assistance.

Raine suddenly yearned to disappear into the trees

and play with the daemons. That made sense. These emotions made absolutely none. Physical maturity was coming on much too fast for her to wrap her head around. There was something she liked about it though, if only she did not feel so out of control. How did dragons handle maturing this quickly?

"That's my horse!"

For a few seconds, Raine was not sure what had happened, but the group came to a sudden stop. Several soldiers were drawing their weapons and turning toward her. Hydra had also stopped, and his muscles were bunched, ready for action. The young king was pointing at her, his staring eyes now alive and blazing with accusation as he kicked his horse toward her. The soldiers opened a path for him. More of them turned their weapons on her now.

Rage and fear swept in, drowning out the emotional confusion of moments ago. She reached down, drawing on daenox. No one was taking Hydra away from her.

King Allondis was almost to her when Darkin charged in from the periphery, driving his horse between them and cutting off the king. He did not draw a weapon, but he faced Allondis, sitting tall in the saddle. She could not see his face. The look of outrage on the king's face said a great deal, however.

"That is my horse. She stole it," Allondis accused.

The soldiers around them were lowering their weapons. They looked confused and uncomfortable. Suva and Kovial moved up in between as well, making a more formidable barrier between the king and Raine. Several of the troubadours had their hands close to what weapons they wore, ready to face off against seasoned troops in her defense. Rakas was also watching with a focused intensity. She could feel him drawing on the same veins of daenox beneath the ground. Whatever she felt toward him on behalf of her father, she could not help being grateful for his support now. His, and that of her new companions.

"We all have our mounts, and the one you're on is a fine one. Leave it be, my lord," Darkin urged. There was a faint edge of warning in his tone. "I can promise you she did not steal that horse."

The other soldiers were standing down now, many sheathing their swords.

Allondis glanced around at them. "Don't listen to this traitor. He led the enemy to us."

"Your Highness," one of the other soldiers spoke up now. "If he hadn't signaled us, we would not have known to come to your aid. We wouldn't have even known the enemy was in our midst. He's the reason we're all alive right now."

"And I am the king," Allondis declared.

"That horse belonged to Dephithus," Darkin stated, keeping his tone level. "She is his kin. There is no wrong being done here."

"Dephithus is a criminal," Allondis countered.

"Dephithus," Raine began, feeling a spike of fear when everyone looked at her. She swallowed and forced herself to continue. "Dephithus was killed fighting the same gold dragon that attacked Elysium yesterday. Before he died, he gave Hydra to me." It was not precisely true. Dephithus was already dead when she found Hydra outside the cave, but the stallion had defended her from Theruses. She considered that a clear enough choice on his part to justify a little fabrication.

"How is she his kin?" one of the soldiers asked.

Raine's gut clenched. The truth would only make them more suspicious of her. She had seen enough reactions from others to be confident of that. She glanced at Darkin, not sure where else to look, and he gave a discreet nod before facing the soldier who had spoken.

"She is his half-sister. A child of his blood-father, Lornin," Darkin lied smoothly.

"How do you know her?" the soldier persisted.

Allondis sat silently glaring at Darkin, nodding in support of the soldier's questioning.

Kovial spoke then. "When I was too injured to ride home with my troop, I stayed in Corbent Calid to heal. The troubadours she travels with escorted me to Imperious when I was well enough. I had the opportunity to get to know her then. Raine is a kind young woman, and I assure you she would not steal from anyone. Hydra was given to her by Dephithus, to whom he was given as a Dawning Day gift by the late Lady Avaline." Kovial inclined his head and softened his voice when he spoke her name. "Darkin speaks truly. No wrong is being done here."

"My personal guard would not have allowed this," Allondis stated, glancing around at them as if he expected that to rally someone.

"My lord," Darkin began, his tone staying calm even when Allondis turned a furious glare on him. "We should move on and find a safe place to set up camp where we can devise a plan. We have lost a great deal and have very few resources with which to get it back. There are more important things at stake than the future of a horse."

No one said anything. After several tense seconds, Darkin picked out Suva and another soldier with his gaze. "You two. Take the lead. Keep us on this heading within the cover of the trees."

Suva and the other woman nodded before moving up through the soldiers to the front. The rest began to turn, following them. Darkin held his ground. Allondis stared past him at Raine for a little longer.

Raine watched him. She could see the hurt and anger at war behind his gaze. He did not have the devotion of his soldiers. That spoke poorly for his actions as king.

Now, with Imperious lost to Kyouin's army, that lack of loyalty had turned him into a figurehead. With the threat to Hydra ended for now, her defensive fury faded away, and she found herself feeling sorry for Allondis. She knew because her father had known, that Allondis was never groomed to be a king the way Dephithus had been. That fate was thrust upon him when Dephithus succumbed to the daemon-seed. Now he was little more than a lonely young man in fine clothes that were good for nothing out here.

Allondis met her eyes, seeming to really see her for the first time. Whatever he saw did not seem to please him. He jerked his horse's reins, steering the animal roughly around and kicking it after the others. When a few more soldiers had passed, Darkin turned his mount so he was facing the right direction alongside her.

"Shall we?"

Myrza and Kovial moved out, adding a few more riders between her and the king. She urged Hydra to a walk alongside Darkin's mount.

"Thank you."

He chuckled, steering his mount so that they ended up riding a short distance off to one side of the main group. "I had to save the king."

She looked over at him, her brows pinching together in confusion.

"Do you really think a king's flesh is any tougher than that of a deer?"

Raine suddenly felt a bit sick. She had not even considered that she might do to a man what she had done to those animals to feed Vanuthan. Just doing it to them had been horrible enough.

Darkin shifted his mount closer and placed a hand on her shoulder. There was something in his soft smile that eased her distress. "You never even thought of that, did you?"

She shook her head, afraid to speak past lingering nausea.

He squeezed her shoulder and took his hand away. "I don't think it would have mattered. I don't know if you noticed, but you had a lot of support outside of me, Suva, and Kovial. Siniva, Rakas, and most of Nakia's band all looked ready to come to your defense. You inspire loyalty far better than Allondis ever has."

"Even Siniva?"

Darkin nodded.

Something swelled in Raine. It was a good something. It made her feel stronger and less alone. Maybe she was wrong. Perhaps she could belong somewhere after all.

She glanced over at Allondis, feeling another pang of sympathy for him. "Don't be too hard on Allondis. I don't think he was ready to be king. I don't know if he will ever be ready to be king. I doubt this is where he expected his life to take him."

Darkin's smile made her skin tingle in a way that was both pleasant and unnerving. "You are far more forgiving than I."

Her gaze sank to his lips, and she faced forward, trying hard not to think of their lips touching. He faced forward as well, taking away the pressure of his gaze.

"If you want, I could show you how to use that sword."

She had almost forgotten the weapon. It was like an article of clothing, only with a deeper meaning to it. She wore it, like the serpent dagger and Avaline's ring, to connect herself to family that was gone and to what their deeds had brought, both good and bad.

"Suva would probably help you out with that dagger as well," he added. "That is her specialty."

Her father's memory of when he and Suva had coupled with the ferocity of wildcats trying to kill one another jumped into her mind. She stared hard ahead, her face growing warm. Would she ever be able to practice daggers with Suva without thinking of that?

"Perhaps the sword, if it wouldn't be too much trouble," she answered.

"It would be my pleasure."

Darkin stepped outside the big barn. Inside, Suva and another soldier were making rounds to deal with those who still had injuries to tend. A few of the healthier soldiers had gone in search of game to supplement the food stores they found in the house. Kovial and Raine were talking in one corner when he left, their smiles telling him the conversation was a casual one. They settled Allondis into the nearby house with a small group of guards to keep an eye on him. He retreated into his silent, staring state after the confrontation about Hydra. For now, at least, he did not seem inclined to cause any more trouble.

The homestead they were borrowing appeared to be abandoned. Since there were no bodies, it seemed more than likely that the family had taken themselves to one of the cities for safety when the daemons became too numerous. As such, he doubted they would mind the Imperious Legion soldiers using it as a safe house for a short time.

"Darkin."

Darkin's hackles went up. He did not appreciate his name being growled in that manner. Then again, if this man's vocal cords were as dragonlike as the rest of him, perhaps he could not help growling. Darkin had certainly never heard him do anything else. For the sake of diplomacy, he was willing to assume that for now.

"It's Siniva, right?" He offered a hand in greeting. Siniva glanced at the hand and made no move to reciprocate the gesture, so Darkin withdrew it. "How can I help you?"

"You can stay away from Raine."

Darkin breathed a bitter laugh and gave a shake of his head, his desire for diplomacy vanishing. "You're welcome."

Siniva's eyes narrowed. "What do you mean by that?"

"I mean, I didn't see you stepping in to defend her against Allondis."

"It wasn't necessary."

"Because someone else did it for you," Darkin snapped.

The soft patter of rain starting to fall on the trees reached his ears. He was surprised he could even hear it past the blood pounding in them. Siniva was an easy hand taller than him and more musclebound than most of the soldiers there. He did not fancy a fight, but he was not going to let this man, or whatever he was, tell him how to act around Raine when he had been the one to come to her aid not a few hours past.

Siniva stared at him, his strange eyes burning with some inner fire. Then that faded, and he took a deep breath, releasing it slowly. "Thank you for helping her. I just ask that you remember, she's not even six years old. She's only a child."

That made Darkin exceptionally uncomfortable. He shifted his feet, trying to think of something to say to that. If she was who they said she was, then what Siniva was saying was not untrue. Yet, physically, she looked no less than perhaps seventeen. How was he supposed to reconcile that? He would never be attracted to a child the way he was attracted to Raine? Everything about her was confusing. At least he could honestly say he had not kissed her in the woods. That had been entirely her doing. He could not deny, however, that he wanted it to happen again with an almost desperate yearning.

"Come now, Siniva," Rakas interjected, "you know that isn't entirely accurate."

The big man bristled, his lip lifting in a silent snarl as Rakas joined them. The slender man with his black on black eyes took no notice of the expression. Darkin would not dare disregard Siniva's anger quite so blatantly. Perhaps Rakas had a death wish. Of course, he did control daenox. He might depend on that to save him if the hulking dragonkin attacked him. At least the dragon-man's anger now had a new target, though Darkin had the uncomfortable feeling that he was in danger of being pulled into the middle of some long-standing animosity between the two if he was not careful.

Knowing that, he still could not quite help wanting to hear what Rakas had to say. If it helped him balance out his feelings for Raine, he was all for learning more.

"This doesn't concern you," Siniva stated, his tone a clear warning.

Rakas gave him a wary look, but it did not stop him from going on. "If Raine were all human, she would be only a child. However, dragons mature at a much faster rate than humans do, and Raine's physical development is mimicking that of a dragon."

"She's still mentally a child."

Rakas smirked. "Is she? What makes a dragon's mental maturity the equal of their physical maturity?"

Siniva's expression hardened. Whatever Rakas was getting at, he knew the answer, but he was not going to give in.

Rakas shrugged. "You, of all… *people*, should know this. It's their ancestral memories. The memories passed down from their parents and grandparents and so on."

"Raine only has her parent's memories to draw from," Siniva said, his flat tone making it clear he did not like the direction this was taking. His eyes were on fire again, and Darkin had the strong sense that Rakas was about to get burned.

"Yes, but that's far in advance of what a child of six would know, is it not?"

Darkin wanted to thank Rakas. What the man said made sense and made him feel a lot less awkward about his attraction to Raine. However, since literal flames were dancing around Siniva's fingertips now, he was not sure he would ever get that chance. He certainly was not about to get in the way of someone who could do that. He took a step back. A raindrop hit one of Siniva's fingertips and sizzled, a tiny plume of steam rising. Rakas held Siniva's gaze, his black eyes staring into the other man's burning red-bronze ones.

"There you are." Raine came trotting toward them.

They all faced her. Her gaze flicked quickly from Siniva's flaming fingertips to his rage-filled eyes and over to Rakas who wore the hint of a smug smile. She mustered an innocent smile as if she had not noticed any of those things.

"Rakas, Kovial thought you might be able to help with one of the injured soldiers in the barn. Come on, I'll take you to him."

As soon as she arrived, she was off again with Rakas in tow. Quite aware, Darkin suspected, that she had interrupted something that might have turned bad quickly.

Darkin glanced down at Siniva's hands. "That's a fascinating trick."

"I'm a dragon," he answered. "She's a little too clever for her own good."

"Hm." Darkin glanced after Rakas and Raine. "Almost like she's wise beyond her years."

Siniva was glowering down at him now. "Did you miss the part where I said I'm a dragon."

"No, Sir." Darkin shook his head emphatically, a burst of alarm bringing a metallic taste to his mouth. "I just have a problem keeping my mouth shut sometimes."

"Obviously." The fire vanished from around Siniva's fingertips.

"Do they all know that you're a dragon?"

The rain was coming faster now, dampening down their hair, and he could feel the cold starting to nip at him. They needed to get inside, but there was more to say here.

He wanted to get Siniva to warm to him, if only a little.

"Raine and Rakas know. And Nakia."

Darkin nodded. "I want to teach her how to use that sword."

"She knows how. Her parents were both Legion soldiers," Siniva argued.

"She may have the basic knowledge from their memories, but she doesn't have the experience or the physical training."

Siniva glanced sideways at him. "True. I would like to see her learn some defense that doesn't rely on daenox. However, we'll be heading toward the Illtide Coast soon so there won't be much of a chance for you to work with her."

Darkin looked up at him, recognizing that the sinking sensation in his gut was dread at the idea of parting ways with Raine. He needed to ignore that. He needed to be a leader first, not a lovesick boy. "The Illtide Coast? Why?"

"I believe the rest of the dragons are there."

"Joining the dragons makes sense for you, but Raine's not really a dragon. Why would she go there?"

"The dragons are meant to balance the daemon power. They can't go on letting it run rampant like this. If they don't intervene soon, the daemon forces will become too strong and make regaining the balance too costly. I hope to convince them to help, but I fear they are punishing humanity for the betrayal that left us all trapped as stone statues for centuries. That kind of thing is not easily forgiven."

"I imagine not," Darkin replied.

The dragons would be the kind of allies that could take back Imperious if they could be convinced to do so after what humanity had done to them. Who better to convince them than the king of Imperious himself, come to see them in person to make right the wrongs and rebuild the old alliance? Of course, Allondis would require considerable coaching before he would be someone a dragon would pay any heed to. It was worth a shot, however. They had very few other viable options. Most of the Legion was either back in Imperious, dead or surrendered to the enemy, or out in troops strewn all over the land fighting daemons. With daemons harrying people everywhere, few other lords would be willing to leave their own lands unguarded to help retake Imperious.

Do we really have so few options, or am I trying to convince myself so I can justify following her?

Darkin shook himself. "We should get out of the rain. I need to speak with the king anyhow." As an afterthought, he added, "Please don't kill Rakas. His skills are useful."

"I'll try to restrain myself," Siniva answered. He started walking toward the barn.

Darkin made his way over to the house. Inside, it was warm and smelled of cooking stew. The fire was stoked in the hearth, crackling and warm. The furnishings were simple. Everything was roughly made and probably appalling to a young king used to living in the palace. To Darkin, it looked glorious. He wished he could bring Raine in from the barn to enjoy a bit of relative comfort. With Allondis there—currently wrapped in blankets on a chair staring into the fire—he did not dare bring her in.

He walked over to one of the soldiers. "How is he?" he asked in a low voice.

"He hasn't said a thing since he made the stink about that horse," the other man whispered.

Darkin nodded. Allondis was not entirely stable. He would have argued that the young king was not sound before all of this, but now he was balanced on the edge ready to dive down into madness. Keeping him together would require some delicate handling. Getting him to go along with what Darkin wanted, however, might not be all that hard.

Darkin walked over to the chair, noting that the king pressed himself into the back of it at his approach. Trying to be sensitive to the king's discomfort, he sank down to his knees next to the chair, making himself less threatening. They had not exactly had the best of relationships up to this point. He needed the king to feel like he had some control of the situation.

"Your majesty." He bowed his head in a show of deference. "I learned that the young woman, Raine, and her companion, Siniva, are planning to go in search of the dragons."

"They must be mad," Allondis muttered, glancing past Darkin into the fire. "The dragons will eat them."

That was not at all the direction he wanted this to go.

"I don't know," Darkin said thoughtfully. "According to the histories, the dragons were once our allies. If they could be talked into such an alliance again, they would have the power we need to fight the daemon army. If the dragons came to help, Raine and Siniva would be hailed as the heroes who saved Imperious."

At that, Allondis focused in on him. "Heroes?"

"Well yes. If they got the dragons to defeat the daemon army, what else would they be? Their physical differences would no longer matter. They would be loved by the people. It might really help them find a place in society. I hope they succeed."

Allondis looked back at the fire, silently repeating the words "heroes" and "loved" as he stared into the blaze. The flames reflected in his eyes.

Darkin waited, letting him mull over those things for a few minutes then added, "If we find a place to hide for a time, we can probably just wait this out."

"Hide," Allondis repeated. He focused on Darkin again. "We would hide. They would be hailed as heroes, and we would be the cowards who hid?"

Darkin shifted back on his heels, making a show of looking troubled. "I hadn't thought of it that way, but what else are we to do. We have no way to call upon troops, and very few troops we could expect to join us if we did.

To go back to Imperious with less than an army would be suicide."

A new light, separate from the reflected fire, lit the king's eyes. "We could go to the dragons," Allondis said. "We could be the ones to save Imperious."

"That's true." Darkin lifted himself up a bit, pretending a tentative excitement. It was not all pretend. Raine would not be leaving, not without him. "In fact, it makes more sense that the king of Imperious should negotiate the alliance. Why should two dragonkin be the ones to arrange a new alliance between humankind and dragons?"

"Precisely," Allondis stated, warming to the idea.

"A wise decision, my lord. I will leave you to your meal and let the others know we'll be heading toward the Illtide Coast on the morrow."

Allondis said nothing. He turned his attention back to the fire, his eyes bright with his heroic future. Darkin backed silently away, letting those thoughts become rooted in the king's mind. He had accomplished what he came for, now he would leave the minding of the king to these soldiers and return to the barn where the people he cared about were waiting.

CHAPTER TWENTY EIGHT

The next morning, the drizzle that had lasted all night let up again. Raine watched from her seat on a stack of wood outside the barn while five sets of two soldiers each prepared to split off from the main group. Darkin was sending them out in different directions to search for more Legion soldiers and other allies who might rally to their side in the effort to defeat Kyouin's army and reclaim Imperious. He and the other soldiers worked on a plan late into the night, taking note of, but largely ignoring, Siniva's objections to the idea of any of them coming along to find the dragons.

Raine thought it was a sensible idea. She and Siniva could travel faster alone, but the soldiers could help deal with danger, and it did make sense to have someone from Imperious along when requesting the aid of the dragons. She was somewhat less enthusiastic about Allondis being part of that contingent. He did not strike her as an individual the dragons would be impressed by. She had also seen him watching Hydra again and did not appreciate his continued interest in her horse. At least she knew there were several in the group who would defend her right to the animal. That included three of the remaining ten Legion soldiers—Darkin, Suva, and Kovial—who had already gone so far as to defy their king in her defense.

Her gaze drifted over to the troubadours who were currently grouped by a small animal pen having an intense discussion about where they were going from this point. The route to the Illtide Coast was not an easy one, and there were only a few villages along the way that were big enough to perform in. Raine could not decide what she wanted for them. Nakia was quite skilled at dealing with Siniva's moods, and since Vanuthan's death, he was moodier than ever. On the other hand, as much as she liked having them around, Myrza and Darkin both left her feeling flustered and confused. With only one of them there, it might be less stressful.

No. She wanted them to stay. For all that she tried to convince herself that it was better if they left, and it probably was for them, she would miss them terribly. Even Siniva had warmed to some of them. Nakia mostly. Enough so that she almost wondered if the two shared an attraction. If the troubadours left, she would never know.

Rakas still kept mostly apart from all of them except for her. That was his nature. He was trying to atone for sins he could never atone for. She did not envy him.

She glanced around for Siniva.

The Fire Dragon had come into the barn the previous evening glaring death at Rakas. Whatever had him hating Rakas more than normal lost his interest after Darkin came in and announced to the soldiers that they would be going to the Illtide Coast in search of the dragons. Since then, Siniva had been watching Darkin with uncomfortable intensity, willing him to slip and fall on his own sword, she suspected. It only stopped when Siniva wandered off in the morning, saying he would be back before they left. Since she knew where both Rakas and Darkin were, she was willing to give the dragon his space for now.

Raine took a few minutes to dive into the dragon web and make a brief, futile search for any sign of Vanuthan. When that failed, disappointment and sorrow tying knots in her gut, she probed around for any dragon that might not be closed off to her to no avail. She soon abandoned the web and sank her awareness into the daenox, searching out a daemon nearby to manipulate. She used the daemon power to compel it, manipulating her influence to send it in different directions for a short time simply to get a feel for what kind of weaving of daenox was most effective.

When she drew herself back from the daenox, she spotted Myrza walking her direction. Even walking, the woman's movements were uncannily fluid and graceful. The lack of a woman's physique and her androgynous features made her no less feminine and beautiful. There was a hint of sorrow in her greeting smile that told Raine all she needed to know. They would not be coming.

Raine stood.

"Walk with me?" Myrza invited.

Raine nodded and fell into step with her, finding that her throat had gotten a bit tight. They walked out away from the others, moving into the trees still within sight of the barn.

"You know what I'm going to say."

Raine nodded, staring down at the ground, sudden tears stinging her eyes. Odd as it was, some of the troubadours really had become a bit like family to her. More of one than she had ever had before at least. It would hurt to see them go their own way.

"We can take care of ourselves well enough, but we aren't soldiers. There's nothing for us where you're going. We live off our audiences. Off the coin they share and the energy they give us. We aren't going to find much of that along the route to the Illtide Coast."

Raine nodded again. There was no arguing with the truth.

"We would much rather keep you with us, you know. Marisa and I were all for trying to convince you to come with us or perhaps kidnap you, but Nakia said no. She said she would miss you and Siniva, but you have your own journey to go on now. I kind of hate her when she is right."

Myrza's voice sounded tight and Raine wanted to say something supportive, but nothing came to her. All she could do was nod again and roughly brush away a tear.

Myrza jumped a few steps ahead suddenly and turned to put herself in front of Raine. She stopped there, forcing Raine to stop as well.

Raine glanced to one side, certain she would be a blubbering mess the moment she met Myrza's eyes.

"Please look at me, Raine. I can't leave without looking into those amazing eyes one more time. I want to be able to remember your face when I can't sleep at night. I want to hold your memory close to my heart until we meet again."

It seemed like a special kind of honor to be the memory someone held so dear, so Raine made herself look at Myrza. Tears broke from her eyes. They were big, silent tears. Myrza smiled at her then, and tears began to creep down her own cheeks. Her gaze sank to Raine's lips.

"This isn't how I hoped it would happen, but... Might I? Just once?"

Raine knew what she meant. She felt it through her entire body, a spark of anticipation as Myrza leaned in and their lips touched in a soft kiss. It was different than the kiss she had given Darkin. It was not a kiss of gratitude. Nor was it a kiss of passion. The time for that had passed without realization. This was a kiss of goodbye. When they parted, Raine tasted salt on her lips and wondered if it was from Myrza's tears or her own. Not that it mattered.

"Thank you," Myrza pulled her into a hug. "I hope we cross paths again."

"Me too." It sounded inadequate but was all she could think to say.

Myrza's focus shifted to something behind Raine. She smiled before ducking away and jogging back to where the troubadours were now readying for their departure. Raine turned to find Suva walking toward her. She dabbed at her tears with the sleeve of her shirt and waited, deliberately not watching Myrza leave. Soon, Suva was standing before her. She placed a hand on Raine's shoulder.

"You really are his daughter, aren't you?"

Raine could tell by her tone that she was not doubting the answer, only needing to have it reconfirmed for some reason. "Yes."

"I can't decide if I should be protecting you like a child or trying to help you navigate the world as a woman."

Raine did not respond to that immediately. She listened to a breeze rustling through the trees and the sound of people and horses moving around near the house and barn. So many people and creatures that knew their place. They had learned it over time. She had no place. Her parents were dead. Vanuthan was dead. Siniva was only barely speaking to her. Rakas interacted with her readily enough, but he was a large part of the reason she was in this situation, willing participant or not in the events that led them all here.

The troubadours had been a brief family. They had not coddled her though. For all that she sometimes wanted to be coddled like a child, she appreciated the way she had been treated among them as more of an equal. Still, she had been somewhat sheltered among them in their strange world of performance and travel.

It was going to be different, traveling with soldiers. At least she had Suva, Darkin, and Kovial to bridge the gap, but there were problems there as well. Those three knew things about her parents that gave them a more profound understanding than most of her unique situation. They did not know the truth about why Dephithus had gone bad though. Perhaps she should tell them. Whether she did or not, Suva had the potential to be precisely the ally she needed to help her figure things out. Things like her longing for a place to belong and her confusing emotions around Darkin.

"I think the latter would be most helpful. I'll never look any younger than this, so I need to be able to interact with a world that will always treat me like I'm older than I am."

Suva's smile had such fondness in it that it almost brought Raine's tears back. She moved alongside her and slid her arm around Raine's shoulders. "A very mature answer."

Raine put her arm around Suva's waist, and they turned toward the homestead together. "Do you think taking Allondis to the dragons is the right thing to do?"

"Hm." Suva slowed her steps, forcing them to a snail's pace. "If you had asked me if I thought we should try to get the help of the dragons, I would have said yes. Taking Allondis there is a different matter. I'm not sure our young king has the diplomatic skills to manage such a critical encounter. I'm also not sure Darkin is pushing this agenda for the right reasons."

"What reasons is he doing it for?"

Suva chuckled. "Perhaps I should have said *reason*. And if you don't already know the answer to that, we really need to work on your relationship skills."

"You think it's because of me." Raine felt that it was true even as she said it. Part of her thrilled that he should be so taken with her that he would let it drive such an important decision. Another part of her shivered in terror of the things she did not understand about human emotions and how powerful they could be.

"I've never seen him take an interest in anyone the way he has in you."

"What about you? He cares about you a great deal," Raine countered.

Suva chuckled. She kicked a stick out of their path. "Darkin and I have a substantial history together. We have been lovers now and then when it suited us, but we fit together more like siblings."

"Like you and Kovial?"

Suva's brow crinkled. "Not exactly. Kovial is my brother, but he's too nice. When I'm being a brat, he never has the decency to fight back and put me in my place the way Darkin does. He just gives me that insufferable patience. Kovial's dear to me. Darkin helps me keep my perspective."

"You're lucky," Raine stated.

Suva gave her a sour look.

"You are. I mean, I know your father wasn't good to you, but you're lucky to have Darkin and Kovial."

Suva stopped them and gave Raine a guarded look. "What do you know about how my father treated me?"

Dephithus's memories flooded in. Uncomfortable memories of him and Suva coupling violently. It was their words afterward that mattered though.

Suva barked a bitter laugh. "I don't believe in making love. This is the only way I do it."

"Why? Because this is how your father does it to you?"

"I know what my father said to hurt you after you two… coupled."

Suva chewed at her lip and looked away for a few seconds before blowing out a heavy exhale and facing her again. "It's really uncomfortable having you know about any of that."

"I don't know about it. I remember it."

Suva lost what little color she had. "That's even worse."

"Can I tell you something? About my father." Raine's gut turned to mush then. Maybe she should not tell. It felt like betraying Dephithus somehow, but few people knew why he had gone bad the way he had. If Suva was to be her ally and confidant, maybe she should know. Maybe she should know everything. It might help her understand things better.

Suva gave her a long look and took a deep breath before answering. "Is this something Kovial and Darkin should know? If not, don't tell me. If so, perhaps we can all find a time to talk about it together. I keep very few secrets from them, Raine, and the ones I do keep eat away at me. I don't want to add to that list."

Something dropped in Raine's chest. She might be an ally to them. She might even be a friend at some point, but she was still an outsider. She was not part of their group. It was the three of them and her. It might never be any different. They had years and years of history together. She had not been alive for even half of those years.

Raine drew daenox up into herself, letting it calm and comfort her. She made herself smile. "Maybe you're right. Let's get back."

CHAPTER TWENTY NINE

The five groups of soldiers and the troubadours departed shortly after Raine and Suva returned to the camp. Siniva reappeared as soon as the others were gone and Raine passed along Nakia's goodbye to him. He only nodded brusquely and set about readying his mount for the day's travel. Perhaps she had read more into his relationship with Nakia than was there. Or maybe he was lying with his body the way people seemed fond of doing. Hiding his real emotions behind a cold exterior.

Or maybe it was just her. Maybe he did not want to share his emotions with her in particular. She had caused Vanuthan's death, after all.

Raine drew in a little more daenox. When she turned around to go get Hydra ready, she saw Rakas watching her. He knew she was holding onto the daenox. She could see it in his eyes, in the warning there. She looked away.

For the rest of the day, they rode in relative silence. Some of the Legion soldiers talked amongst themselves. Darkin and Suva alternated riding lead and tail. Kovial rode near Raine, but she made no attempt to engage him and kept responses to anything he said mostly monosyllabic. Siniva rode on the opposite side of the group of soldiers. Rakas stayed near the back in his own shroud of silence.

Raine was not sure if it was intentional, but the other soldiers always kept at least two riders between her and Allondis. With only seven of them remaining, it was not as easy as it had been before, so it certainly had the appearance of a deliberate maneuver.

Raine ignored them all. She rode through the veins of daenox beneath the ground and sought out one daemon after another, reaching into them and figuring out how to control them. They were quite malleable creatures. With no way to distinguish her compulsion from their own desires, it took little daenox to move them around. It did get a little trickier trying to control more than one at a time. Kyouin must have found a way to control them without maintaining a constant awareness of each individual creature.

She thought back on what she encountered in the brain of the bearlike beast that had attacked the troubadour camp. For a few minutes, that line of thought sent her feelings spiraling over the kiss Myrza had given her and the companions she had lost today. She pulled herself back from those thoughts, her chest aching and hollow, and considered the daemon-bear again. Somehow, the daenox in its brain was functioning, without Kyouin's continued input, to compel the beast to come after her. What she ran into in the beasts in Elysium had been different.

Now that she thought about it, the bear-beast had not come after her at all until she attacked it with the thrust of daemon-power.

Raine pulled Hydra back, waiting for Rakas to catch up before letting the stallion fall into step again.

"How can I be of service?"

"You remember the night the daemons attacked our camp..." she gave him a second to nod recognition before going on. "They passed you and me by in the woods. They weren't sent to attack us."

Rakas looked thoughtful. He absently brushed away a fly that landed on one hand and shook his head. "No. I would guess that they were sent to attack the troubadours you were traveling with. Kyouin didn't want to hurt you physically. He wanted to torment you by attacking your companions and sending the dagger."

"That's what I think too. You don't think..." Her chest tightened then, making it harder to breathe.

Rakas looked at her, his gentle half-smile tinged with sorrow. "You can't do anything for them, Raine. They were watching out for themselves and making their own decisions long before you came along. All you can do is hope that they won't be a target without you there. I would venture that the people with you now are in more danger than the ones who have parted ways."

Raine swept through the daenox for as far as she could reach. There were daemons within that range. Plenty of them. None seemed to have any particular interest in coming their way, however. For the moment, it was safe enough. How long would that last?

She glanced around at their group. Everyone here wore a weapon except Rakas, who had already proven he could take care of himself without one. She was probably the least prepared in the event of some attack. What she had done to kill the animals for Vanuthan could be used to kill any beast or man, but using it in an emergency was different than having the time to think through the process while luring innocent creatures to their deaths.

Rakas was right about Fools Errant. They were on their own and probably safer for it. Here, their greatest vulnerability was the same thing that put everyone in danger. Herself.

They came upon a stand of massive, old trees by the side of the wagon track they were following, where chunks of wood had been cut to seat size, and several fire pits were neatly ringed with stone. Many a traveler had camped here, so they decided to take advantage of the site and stop early.

Allondis looked weary and unwell. He grumbled some about the lack of accommodations, but he was soon silently staring into a fire from his perch on the choicest of stumps from the selection available.

There were still a few hours of daylight left. Raine waited while Darkin sent a couple of soldiers out to see if they could catch some small game. As soon as they turned to leave, she walked over to him.

"Darkin."

When he turned, his smile and the delight in his eyes at seeing her there was almost enough to make her forget how apart she felt with Suva that morning. She longed to believe she could be as important to him as Suva and Kovial were. She could not though. No matter how she looked at it, she was a new entity in their lives. There was no way they could ever feel for her as strongly in such a short time as they did for one another after a lifetime of friendship.

The ache in her chest made her return smile falter.

His smile faded in response. "Are you all right?"

"Will you show me how to use my mother's sword?"

He glanced down at the weapon hanging useless at her waist and shook his head. Her chest tightened. The urge to flee into the woods and find sanctuary among the daemons almost took her, but then he smiled again. There was a fondness in that smile that sparked hope in her no matter how much she tried not to let it.

"First, you will acknowledge that the weapon you carry is no longer your mother's sword. It's yours. Then we'll find some suitable substitutes so that neither of us loses a limb teaching you how to wield it."

Raine found herself smiling tentatively. The wanting surged as well. A yearning to be held by him. Touched by him. Kissed by him. She stomped it down fiercely. She needed to be realistic and practical.

"Suva."

Suva, who was talking to another soldier a short distance away, glanced over their direction. Her eyes took them both in and narrowed ever-so-slightly. "What?"

"Keep an eye on things for me. I'm going to show Raine some sword basics."

Suva smirked. "With her sword or yours?"

There were barks of laughter from several soldiers. Raine felt her face growing warm.

"Funny." Darkin shook his head at Suva. "Come on. Let's find some suitable weapons."

"Captain."

Darkin turned toward a soldier who was piling wood in one of the fire rings. He was a young man with dusty blond hair and striking light blue eyes. He nodded toward one of the horse lines.

"There are a couple of practice swords in my sleeping roll. You're welcome to use them."

Darkin stared at him for several seconds, looking perplexed. "It's Jaxon, right?"

The young man nodded.

"You carry practice swords around with you? You just happened to have them on your saddle when we fled Imperious?"

Jaxon looked around at everyone who was staring at him. He shrugged. "My sister and I were about to ride out with a troop. We always take a couple practice weapons with us for something to do and to keep ourselves sharp on the road."

"Where's your sister now?"

Jaxon stared at the fire he was building. "She was riding next to you, Sir, when we left Elysium."

He did not have to say more. Raine had seen the soldier and horse next to Darkin go down when the daemon attacked them. The other soldiers turned solemnly back to their activities.

Darkin walked over to Jaxon and placed a hand on his shoulder. "I'm sorry."

Jaxon gave a small nod. "The swords are still on my horse. The bay there with the white nose. I'd like to see someone using them."

Darkin said nothing more. He walked over and retrieved the practice weapons from where they were stuffed in the sleeping roll, then led Raine away from the camp. They did not go far. Darkin found a reasonable clearing a little bit out beyond the big trees. Raine appreciated that she would not have to feel the eyes of the others on her here as he handed her the hilt of one practice sword.

"Remember, we don't have any of the normal practice gear to help protect us from injury. My armor will help, so you don't need to be as careful, but I'd rather not have either of us come away hurt."

They both set aside the real weapons they carried, and he stepped up next to her, reaching one arm around her to show her how to properly hold the sword. Raine tried to focus on what he was saying, but his nearness distracted.

What would it be like to kiss him for real? To be kissed by him? She liked his strong yet slender hands. He was tall and lean and handsome, and she wanted to do more than show him gratitude with her kiss. She might be young in human years, but her body was maturing fast, and the memories of her parents were not all those of children. The combination left her confused and full of longing. Still, they were little more than strangers in truth.

Darkin stepped away, looking her over with a thoughtful expression. "It's a little unnerving how much your stance and the way you hold your sword reminds me of Dephithus. You might be a quick study," he added with an encouraging smile.

She was not though. A full hour later, she was hot, sweaty, and frustrated half out of her mind. When she engaged with Darkin in battle, all too aware of how careful he was being not to hurt her, she felt like an uncoordinated toddler. Her parents' memories barged in with flashes of battle, of practice combat, of running through the fields together, of the Mother Tree, of Dephithus striking the fatal blow on Larina in the tourney. She struggled to push them away and focus on the present.

Darkin remained patient and consistent. She wanted to scream at him for it.

"Ready to try again?"

Raine stared at him for a few seconds, fighting the urge to yell at him for his insufferable patience. Then movement to one side of the clearing caught her attention. Siniva stepped away from a tree he had been leaning on. She flushed at the thought of how long he might have been watching.

"No, she's not." He walked over to them and stopped, staring judgment down on Raine that did not sit well with her current temper. "Until you stop fighting your parent's memories, you will remain a child in a woman's body."

Pent up frustration burst inside her, a flash of white-hot anger briefly obscuring her vision. She turned it on Siniva. "Until you confront the guilt you're running away from, you will remain a dragon in a man's body."

His eyes blazed to life with that inner fire. "I did it to save you!" He lunged toward her then, one hand up as if to strike or grab her.

Before she could react, she found herself staring at Darkin's back.

"Back off!"

For a tense moment no one moved or spoke, then Siniva turned and stormed away. Raine placed a hand on Darkin's arm, feeling the muscles there trembling as hard as her own were with the charge of confrontation.

"I'm sorry."

"For what?" Darkin turned to face her. "He should learn to control his temper."

"He's the Fire Dragon," she defended.

"Don't make excuses for him." He touched her face with gentle fingers then. She could still feel the tremble in him through that light contact. "He should never have come at you in anger. Are you all right?"

She looked into his eyes, thrown off balance by the depth of the concern in them. Behind that concern was something more carnal. Desire. A desire he was keeping tightly leashed.

Her pulse raced, and she was trembling still, but it was no longer just from the alarm of Siniva coming at her. She wanted to be desired. She liked the way Darkin looked at her. She liked the careful way he touched her. She liked that he had stepped in, placing himself between them to protect her.

"Kiss me," she invited.

Darkin hesitated, his eyes searching hers.

Panic twisted in her gut and she fought the urge to run again. Had something changed, or had she read him wrong from the beginning? She had no experience with these things. Maybe she had mistaken his looks.

She started to turn away. "I'm sorry. I thought you wanted…"

His hand caught her arm, and he turned her gently back to face him. "Raine," he breathed her name, his voice tight, "there's nothing I want more. I just don't want to feel like I'm taking advantage of you."

She met his eyes again. Her gaze drifted down to his lips. She wanted to feel them on hers. Not in a kiss of gratitude or goodbye. She wanted to feel all the wanting and passion that had been in her parents' first kiss.

Before she could put voice to her thoughts, Darkin leaned down to her. She met the kiss with her lips and all the rest of her, moving her body closer to his. Darkin responded by sliding his arms around her and pulling her against him.

There was hunger in the kiss, but not just from him. Her body sparked to life in places and ways she had not known were possible. Sensations and emotions she never experienced before threatened to drown her. At least she was in his arms. She would not drown alone. He continued to taste of her lips and she of his again and again, the passion between them rising. She slid one hand up between them and touched her fingers to his neck, feeling the solid reality of him as she surrendered to the moment, her eyes closed so she could spiral away from the rest of the world.

He was the one who finally disengaged, stepping back from her. He moved her out to arm's length and looked down at the ground between them, his dark hair falling into his face. He was breathing hard. Raine was still spiraling.

After what might have been an eternity listening to him breathe and feeling the pounding of her heart in her chest, Darkin stepped close again. He looked at her with eyes full of wonder, as if she were some new and glorious thing he had only just discovered. He cupped her cheek gently and gave her one more soft, brief kiss.

"It's starting to get dark," he murmured, his breath warm on her lips. "We should get back to camp."

Raine said nothing. She followed him to get their things and wondered what came after this.

Darkin led the way back to camp. He longed to reach back and take Raine's hand. To reassure himself that she was there, vibrant and real. He had no idea what to do with this. His emotions were running at a fever pitch. It was not that he was inexperienced in the realm of intimacy. He had plenty of lovers over time. He and Suva had even found release with one another many times, but this was not the same. This was not an urge for sexual release. He wanted to know her: her body, her heart, her hopes and dreams. He wanted to be the one fighting at her side and the one holding her close when she needed it. This was a tempest of uncontrolled emotion that had no place in a time of war.

There was no time to think about it when they got back. Two women came riding down the road and were turning in to their camp. One wore Legion attire and the other a drab brown dress that did little to mask a simple beauty accented by blazing emerald eyes. Several of the soldiers were standing, though none had drawn weapons. Most of them recognized and greeted Kayd. She was a respected warrior and remained a fixture around the Elysium palace and grounds after her injury forced her out of active duty.

King Allondis did not stir from where he sat staring into the fire. Darkin felt a sinking in his gut. This man was not in any condition to negotiate with dragons. They had to figure out how to deal with that before they got to the Illtide Coast.

He almost jumped when Raine grabbed his arm. She took a step past him, staring at Kayd. "My mother's aunt," she breathed.

Before he could stop her, she ran over to where the two women had stopped and were dismounting. Kayd looked more than a little surprised at Raine's approach. The woman with her eyed Raine with an unnerving intensity while placing a hand protectively over her own belly.

"You're my mother's aunt," Raine declared.

Kayd took a step back, using her horse to balance herself as she reached to pull her crutch down from behind the saddle. "I suspect you have me confused with someone else."

"You are Myara's aunt," Raine countered with the utmost confidence.

Leaning heavily on the crutch, Kayd stared into Raine's slit-pupiled eyes. After a few seconds, she looked from Raine to Suva, Rakas, and Siniva, the three of whom had managed to create a semicircle of support behind Raine in the short time she had been there. Darkin felt a little like he had missed some cue. Each of the three met Kayd's gaze in turn and nodded in response to her unspoken question. Raine glanced around at them and flushed, frustration darkening her expression as she apparently realized the problem. As far as Kayd was concerned, she was much too old to be Myara's daughter. Darkin's heart ached for her, creating a tightness in his chest.

"Perhaps we should talk," Siniva offered helpfully.

Kayd nodded. "I think that's a good idea. If someone could assist Jadean in getting the horses settled."

Several soldiers stepped up to provide assistance at

her request. Siniva offered an arm to Kayd to help her along. Raine turned to follow, giving Suva a meaningful look that she responded to with a quick nod. In turn, Suva turned to him and gestured him to join them, doing the same for Kovial. Whatever was about to happen, Suva had some insight into it that made Darkin a little jealous. At the same time, he appreciated that Suva and Raine had connected enough to earn them inclusion in this exclusive conversation.

They all started to follow Siniva and Kayd, but Raine stopped, letting the others go ahead, and turned to Rakas, who was hanging back. Darkin slowed, falling behind to watch as Raine leaned close and whispered something to Rakas. The man swallowed hard and nodded. Darkin would have sworn he saw the gleam of moisture in those black eyes. When Raine turned to follow the others again, Rakas did not join them.

When she and Darkin caught up with them, he heard Kayd telling Siniva how she had managed to sneak out of Elysium in the aftermath of the battle and came upon Jadean on the road. She spoke a little about the carnage she left behind and how the remaining troops had surrendered. At the back of the group, Raine took Darkin's hand, just for a moment, and his chest ached with the longing to pull her into his arms and hold her close. He squeezed her hand once, hoping to convey support before she let go.

Siniva made short work of lighting a fire, making no effort to hide his nature from this intimate group. He stacked a bit of wood and snapped his fingers next to it. Flame jumped from his fingers to the wood, and it was instantly burning. It turned out to be a proper way to set expectations.

It was Raine who did most of the telling, with some assistance from Siniva when she stalled on occasion, becoming lost in memories that were not her own. It was strange to see the Fire Dragon working so supportively with her after their earlier confrontation.

The story Raine told began with her father, Dephithus, before his birth, and how the dragons had placed power in him from within their stone prisons to start a process that would eventually set them free. The story turned dark quickly on her father's Dawning Day when two individuals who were working to free the daenox placed a seed of daemon power in him to undermine the dragons' plans and begin freeing the daenox.

Raine did not say how that deed was done, but the haunted look in her eyes and the way she drifted off in the telling, requiring several gentle prompts from Siniva to get started again, told Darkin more than he ever wanted to know. She also did not give names to those who did the deed, but the uneasy look that passed between her and Siniva at that moment made him uncomfortably suspicious of one person who had been excluded from their gathering.

As the telling progressed—Raine painfully reliving her father's torment and sharing an abbreviated version of events with them—Darkin began to regret the ways he had manipulated Dephithus. He had not known what was going on with the young heir to the throne, and if he were to be honest, he had not really cared. He had only cared about what he could gain from the situation. Now it made him feel like he was almost as bad as those who had put the seed in Dephithus in the first place. Suva and Kovial looked troubled as well.

Raine continued to her part in the tale, telling how a greater dragon power had been placed in her to combine with the power passed down from Dephithus. She also told them briefly about her life as a captive in the Dunues Mountain cave. Kayd openly wept then. He suspected those tears were for Myara's tragic death as much as for what Raine had suffered. Suva and, to his surprise, Siniva, both shed some silent tears as well. Darkin wanted to weep, though he did not let himself. He wanted to cry for what she had gone through and for what her father and mother had gone through that she had to suffer anew through their memories. He wanted more than anything in the world to hold her close, but she was not done yet.

She finished, with Siniva's help, by telling how the Fire Dragon and Dephithus had freed her from the cave, an act that led to her father's death and freed the dragons.

Darkin would have gone to her then. He would have taken her in his arms and held her and told her he would do anything to keep her safe even with the others watching. Kayd was closer though, and she pulled Raine to her, clinging to her as they both cried. That seemed right. They were blood family. The others moved away, leaving them to their moment. Darkin found it hard to walk away from her, but Suva took his hand and Kovial's and walked silently back to the camp with them that way.

Late that night, when the camp had fallen quiet aside from a few lookouts posted on the outskirts, Darkin woke to Raine coming to lay down next to him. He made as much room as he could for her on the small bedroll. She curled up against him without a word. He put his arms around her and held her for a long time. It was Suva who eventually woke them that way before the rest of the camp woke. There were few others awake when Raine left his side, including the strange woman, Jadean, who sat on a nearby log, her hand on her belly again as she watched Raine depart.

*

Kyouin watched Theruses and wondered if he had ever seen the man… dragon… when his tail was not lashing.

The dragon needed to relax a bit. He did not think he had ever seen that tail lashing quite this hard before.

"You can't do this," Theruses stated, a growl adding weight to his words.

Kyouin gave a laugh. "I already have."

Vanuthan stood before them, little more than skin and bones with the fatal wounds at her throat from Theruses's teeth hanging open. She was still magnificent in her way, though he did not think the matte grey of her undead eyes was as flattering as the blazing red had been. She feasted on several cattle he had appropriated from a nearby farmer. He was not sure if she could gain much from the meat in her undead state, but it seemed to appease her for the time being.

"How much of her remains in that husk?" Theruses said, his tone more musing now, as though he were merely wondering aloud and not especially interested in the answer.

Kyouin's thoughts wandered to Avaline and Vaneye. Was it the daenox in them both that drew them to each other or was there something else there? Perhaps something more maternal?

"It's merely the husk you call it," Kyouin stated, forcing confidence into his tone. He could not stop a nervous glance at Ryche, who watched them from near one of the stables, his jaw moving as it always did. If he were closer, they would hear that constant clicking of teeth, as unnerving as the endless dripping of water from a leaky roof.

Kyouin knew how irritating and insidious that sound was. He had lived with a leaky roof in his bedroom for years. It made damp and mold in his bedding and left him feeling ill off and on for most of that time. Until the daenox found him. Until he felt it moving through him one night and, through sheer frustration, managed to use it to seal all the leaks in his room. That was the beginning.

Theruses turned to him, his black eyes narrowing with keen insight. "You're a child, Kyouin, playing with toys you don't understand. I will make you one last offer. I will stay here and help you manage this army, but you will share its command with me."

Kyouin's hackles went up. "I will not share *my* army with you. It's mine. I need and want no help from you." The dragon-man's slow nod said he had expected nothing different, which only irritated Kyouin more.

"If you change your mind, you can use the daemon power to call upon me. I may or may not choose to answer." With that, he gave one last disgusted glance at Vanuthan and strode away, turning into his dragon form the moment he had enough space to do so and flying off into the greying sky.

"My lord."

Kyouin turned to face an aged warrior. The man, along with three others, stood around a woman and her three clinging, crying children. The woman's hair was in disarray, and her dress sleeve was torn. Her eyes were puffy as if she had been crying, but she faced him now, her head high and her eyes filled with hatred and defiance. A wolf protecting its brood.

None of them had the pallor of illness about them.

"Very good." Kyouin ignored the woman and her children for a moment, making it clear how little affect her defiance had on him. "I have another task for you."

The man nodded.

"Send some men out to find a group of troubadours. They go by the name Fools Errant. Find them and bring them back here." There was a chance Raine might still be traveling with them. If not, they might give him more leverage when she finally came to him.

The man gave a nod and strode away.

Kyouin took a few steps closer to the woman and

her children and sank down on one knee, putting himself closer to the childrens' height. There were two girls
and a boy. The eldest, one of the girls, was too old, but
the other two were around the right size. The young
boy and his older sister hid their faces in their mother's
skirts. The young girl stared wide-eyed at Vanuthan
with a mix of terror and fascination. Kyouin focused his
attention on her.

"What's your name?"

The woman pulled the girl closer, but he had already gotten her attention. Her gaze bounced from him
to Vanuthan and back, perhaps to make sure the dragon
remained occupied with the cattle.

"Vinya," she answered, her narrowed eyes telling
him she wisely did not trust him.

"Vinya," he repeated. "How would you like to live
in the palace?"

She perked up at that, her gaze darting up toward
the palace. "Mother says it must be nice there."

"It is. It's very nice."

She smiled. Kyouin gave a satisfied nod before
standing up to face her mother.

Vaneye was a disappointment, but he was not willing to give up on finding himself an apprentice of sorts.
Someone would have to rule his army and Imperious
when he was gone. He could try to breed his own suc-
cessor, but infants were a hassle, and it would be years
before the child was old enough for him to find out if
it could handle the power of the daenox or would succumb to it in the same way Vaneye had.

He met the mother's eyes. "I'll make you an offer."

The woman shook her head, keeping her children in
close to her.

"Hear me out," Kyouin said, keeping his tone reasonable. "I will take your daughter Vinya to live with me
in the palace. In return, you will have one less mouth to

feed, and I won't feed your other two children to that dragon."

The woman's eyes went wide, her mouth falling open slightly as if she could not quite believe she heard him right. He gave a slight nod to two of the warriors. They grabbed the other two children, wrenching them away from her. The children screamed. She reached after them until the third warrior brought his sword point to bear on young Vinya, who cowered back. Kyouin gave a slight shake of his head. The warrior corrected, raising the point up to threaten the woman directly instead.

Kyouin smiled. "Two for one. It's a fair offer."

For the next several days, Darkin drove the group hard. Somehow, knowing the truth about how all of this had come to pass and how significant a part of it Raine was—by no fault of her own—made him more determined to see it through. They stopped in a village to stock up on supplies, bartering for food and warmer attire for the trek ahead. Raine and Siniva stayed out of town to avoid conflict, so Darkin took on the task of gathering things for them. It turned out that he was a little too good at finding things to fit Raine. She was delighted, but Siniva made a sour comment about him memorizing her shape overly well as he shrugged into a cloak that was a few sizes too big.

Through the long days of travel, Darkin caught Raine looking his way often. It was not hard to catch those glances, given how often he was looking her way. What had happened between them seemed like something they should keep to themselves for now. Unfortunately, that meant they had little opportunity for another such encounter. She did come and sleep beside him a few more times but seemed only to want silence and the comfort of his presence. As much as he loved having her close, the lack of time to talk left him frustrated.

He yearned to keep working with her with the sword, both for the time alone and to see her better able to defend herself, but Suva encouraged Kayd to take over that training. The former Legion soldier's injury put limits on how far she could take things, but, for the moment, Raine was in her hands. Both he and Suva sometimes joined in if there was time, working with Raine while Kayd looked on and offered feedback. It was not the same, however, and he fancied he could see his frustration mirrored in Raine's eyes.

Jadean, the daenox priestess, had taken to spending much of her time with Siniva. That surprised him some since he had expected her to find more in common with Rakas. Rakas, however, kept his distance from both newcomers. He did steal more of Raine's time, taking her around with him when he performed healing for those with injuries that still needed attention, teaching her how to use the daenox in that way. Darkin's wound was mostly healed now, so he did not get any of that time either. Raine and Kayd spoke for long hours during the day while they were trekking through rugged terrain up into the mountains standing between them and the Illtide Coast. When Kayd was not riding with Raine, Rakas was, and Siniva scowled at the two during those rides, even though he was often riding with Jadean, who struck Darkin as no more trustworthy than Rakas.

For all that he envied the time Kayd got to spend with Raine, it did make him happy to see the way bonding with her mother's aunt made her shine. It was as if she had found a part of herself she was missing in that relationship. For her, there was something important in connecting to her parents through those who knew them. The belonging he and his companions had tried to offer her could not compare to what Kayd had to offer. He knew that and tried not to let himself resent the woman's arrival. He did resent it though. His emotions when it came to Raine were something south of rational.

"She's as happy as I've seen her," Suva stated, riding up on his left. "Still pensive and unsure but smiling a bit more. If Siniva would stop holding her at arm's length, I suspect she'd be even better."

Darkin cast a glance toward the back.

Suva followed his gaze. "Kovial took tail. He says his arm is feeling a lot stronger, and he wants to be more help."

Darkin nodded. "Good. We can use another reliable soldier." Even he heard how distracted and irritable he sounded despite his efforts to be diplomatic.

"Give it a little time, Darkin," Suva remarked a little too insightfully. "She's not a child, but she is very inexperienced in many ways. She's only been out of those caves for a matter of months. That's not a lot of time to figure out all the complexities of life even with the help of someone else's memories."

He let her words hit him in that irrational place that wanted to steal Raine and run away from all this. "I know," he answered, because a part of him did know.

"I've never seen you lose your head over a girl before." Suva chastised. "We've got much bigger problems to deal with right now than your feelings of jealousy and abandonment."

Jealousy and abandonment?

Darkin met her eyes, ready to deny any such thing, and found he could not. Leave it to Suva to be blunt and frustratingly accurate. "Like what?" He lowered his voice. "Perhaps you refer to a king who's completely unfit for his station and a coming parlay with a bunch of enormous lizards who could eat us all as a snack if we step wrong."

Suva grimaced. "With juvenile king catatonia leading those negotiations, how could it go wrong?"

Darkin could not stop a wry smile. "Maybe it wouldn't be so bad if they ate him."

Suva chuckled and said nothing for a time. She pulled the hood of her fur-lined cloak up against the cold. There was deep snow covering the ground off the road now, and it was getting much colder. It was even starting to cover the road, which would require more careful navigation to make sure they did not get off route.

Darkin caught himself glancing at Raine to see if she looked warm enough. She did have the hood of her black cloak pulled up. He had covertly traded one of the king's jeweled rings for a fine black woman's cloak with subtle black embroidery down the sides that was lined in soft black fur. It looked exquisite on her. The king's jewels had all been entrusted to him in a small pouch so they could travel more discreetly. He did not think the man would notice one missing ring when he finally got them back.

Raine was focused on a conversation with Rakas now, her lips pursed together in the sweetest look of intense concentration. A bit of her bronze-black hair fell free of the hood. She brushed it back under with one perfect hand covered in a matching fur-lined glove.

Suva cleared her throat, and Darkin scanned the rest of the group as if that had been his intention all along. Everyone was wrapped against the growing cold. Everyone except Siniva who rode with his oversized cloak hanging open and no gloves. Being the Fire Dragon appeared to have its advantages.

"We do need to figure out how we're going to handle this." Suva's tone was serious now. "Have you talked to Siniva about dealing with the dragons? Maybe he could help coach Allondis in how to approach it."

Darkin's chest tightened in the way it always did when he knew he was shirking something very important. Or rather, when he knew he had been caught doing so. She was not going to have much patience with him if he admitted that he had not done so because he was still holding onto resentment toward the dragon-man over the incident with Raine.

"That's the loudest no I've never heard," Suva answered for him.

"What does it matter?" Darkin growled in frustration. "Allondis won't do anything unless he thinks it's his idea. How are we going to convince him to take Siniva's advice?" He was being defeatist, and he knew it was not productive, but Suva was one person he could let his frustration show around without fear of judgment. She would let it wash over her and say something blunt and forceful to shove him back on track. That was what he wanted right now. It was what he needed.

The whistle of a projectile flying through the air only gave a second of warning before the solid thunk of the arrow hitting its target. One of the soldiers jerked, twisting in his saddle so hard that he and his horse went down. There was movement in the trees. A band of people in heavy, roughly fashioned furs charged on them from both sides. Another Legion soldier went down almost before any of them could get their weapons out.

Darkin held his hands aloft and backed his horse a few steps with his legs. It was all he could do. There was no point going for his sword. They were surrounded. A good thirty or more armed individuals had emerged from the trees. He could see at least four with crossbows lingering further back. If they retaliated, more people would die. Two of their number might already be dead. He had to hope the attackers did not want to risk their people any more than he did. A small exhale of relief slipped between his lips when the rest of the party heeded his quick surrender and followed suit, raising their hands up away from their weapons. The ambushing party let no more bolts fly, and no one else attacked.

The big man who appeared to be their leader said

something in a language Darkin had never heard. Uncomfortable silence extended, then the man repeated whatever he said again.

"He said," Rakas began, moving his mount very slowly closer to Darkin with his hands up, "if we give them our horses and supplies, they'll let us go."

"That's not much of a bargain," Darkin answered. "We might freeze out here before we get to another town again without horses or supplies."

"Do you want me to tell him that?" Rakas asked, his tone cynical.

"Of course not. Tell him to give us a moment if he would. He has the upper hand here."

Rakas relayed the information. The big man gave a sharp nod. Darkin began to wrack his mind for some better option.

The attackers tensed. Darkin turned to the sounds of another horse moving up behind him. It was Allondis, kicking his mount up to a trot, outrage turning his face red.

"Tell them to let us pass or face the judgment of the King of Imperious," he shouted, grabbing at his sword hilt.

Darkin was not the only one who tried to shout a warning at the young king. It did not matter. As he stared back at Allondis, he heard a crossbow release. The bolt tore through the king's throat, blood spraying up on the bottom of his chin and down over the heavy brown cloak he wore. More blood sputtered between his lips as he tried to say something else. Darkin watched the life fade from his eyes a few seconds before his body fell from the horse.

Anger and frustration tempted him to do something stupid. Knowing he was no different than any other soldier, he quickly glanced around at the remaining riders to make sure they were still in control of themselves.

Most looked ready to tear someone apart with their teeth, but they held their ground, their martial discipline holding them back. Then he met Raine's eyes, his stomach doing a flip when he noticed the subtle glow of violet in them.

"Tell him that we'll let the rest of them live if they leave now," Raine declared.

Before anyone could say anything, strangled cries from the four holding crossbows drew their attention. Numerous daemons emerged from the woods around them, bringing the four in the back down quickly with the element of surprise in their favor. The daemons took out their initial prey with disturbing efficiency before turning their attention on the others. More joined the first then, including a pack of daemon-wolves and some mutated creature that might have once been a mountain cat. A fire of hunger and madness blazed in the eyes of those creatures. That they were not attacking anyone else yet said volumes about the person controlling them.

The circle of warriors around them began to falter, many of them turning sideways, unsure how to react now that they were also surrounded. The daemons stood staring at them, low growls enhancing their menace. Further back, Darkin thought he spotted something else moving in the trees. Something larger than the beasts in closer.

He glanced toward Rakas and gave a slight nod.

Rakas relayed Raine's message.

It took only a few seconds, during which the daemons began inching closer, for the enemy leader to answer with a gruff nod. As soon as he did so, some of the daemons backed off, stepping to the sides to offer a path by which they could depart. The warrior gestured to his party, and they began to file warily out between the snarling beasts. As soon as the rest were clear, he followed them. Despite the growling and the drool of hunger dripping from their jaws, the daemons held their position as the men gathered their fallen and dragged them off into the trees.

Darkin and several others were already on the ground, rushing to check on the fallen. The woman, Jadean, was kneeling in the snow beside Allondis who had a thick arrow shaft protruding from his neck. She glanced up at Darkin, the shake of her head confirming what he already knew.

"Daemon's blood," Suva cursed under her breath where she now stood next to him.

"This one's still alive," Kayd shouted from where she was kneeling awkwardly down beside one of the other soldiers.

There was a rush of activity then. Darkin took advantage of the distraction to look around for Raine. He spotted Hydra off to one side with no rider, and his heart started to race. When he spun around, he almost ran into Suva who pointed out to their left. Looking in that direction, he saw Siniva in the trees near some bloodstained snow, holding Raine tight against him. Her shoulders shook as she wept. Siniva stood silent, his eyes closed, his face drawn with some unspoken sorrow. Beyond them, a few daemons lingered, skulking in the trees.

Kayd started to limp past him toward the two. Darkin caught her arm gently. "Give them a minute. I think he's the one she needs right now." And how it stung to say that.

"Did she do this?" Kayd asked in little more than a whisper.

Darkin did not answer. He did not think it was necessary. Right now, he had other issues to deal with.

He turned back to the troop. The cold felt harsher and crueler now. He felt it in his fingers, his face, his toes, and very deep in the center of his chest. One soldier lay dead. Another soldier lay bleeding in the snow, two of his fellows working with his injury using traditional methods while Rakas did what he could with daenox. A few feet away, the king lay dead. Someone had already covered his face with a cloth and crossed his hands on his chest.

Darkin's comment about Allondis getting eaten by dragons did not seem as humorous now. Then again, given how the king had handled this conflict, perhaps it was for the best. The dragons would have certainly eaten him the first time he opened his mouth.

He fought back a somewhat hysterical giggle that threatened to slip out at this most inappropriate time and sobered himself by looking over the few soldiers that remained.

"Now what?" he asked of no one in particular.

"Now you have to lead them," Suva answered.

Darkin glanced at Kayd standing on her other side. Her nod made his gut twist in knots.

I didn't want to kill anyone." Raine tried to stem the tide of tears, but something felt irretrievably broken inside her. There was a hollowness in her chest as if all that was good had been drained away and would never return. She was trembling too, like a frightened pup. Trembling so hard she thought she might fall if Siniva were not there holding her, his strong arms tight around her.

Since she decided she would find a way to turn Kyouin's daemons against him, every spare moment that she was not training the sword with Kayd and the others or learning healing from Rakas, was invested in manipulating daemons. The more creatures she could influence at once, the more effectively she could upset Kyouin's control and wreak havoc upon his army.

When the ambush happened, she already had some twenty or more daemons moving through the area under her influence. It was easy enough to draw them into the attack. The fear and outrage she felt at seeing members of their party go down so suddenly was more than enough to stoke the blood lust in the daemons.

It hit her especially hard seeing Allondis go down. She had been watching him when the arrow hit. She had seen the spray of blood and the instant of shock in his eyes. At that moment, as in many others, she was thinking about possibly approaching him. He might have the title of king, but he was alone among them, feeling out of place and lost. Not so different from her. If she could connect to him, perhaps she could help him find his place and start becoming the man they needed to convince the dragons. She had considered trying to talk to him many times, but the memory of his accusations regarding Hydra held her back. Now he was dead. She did not need anyone to confirm that. The life had been gone from his face before he hit the ground.

Riding on that rage, it had been easy to send the daemons after their attackers. Then she discovered the real horror of what she was doing. Because she remained connected to them while they were killing this time, not letting go when they attacked as she had in the fight at Elysium, she felt their killing frenzy and the satisfaction when their prey fell. That prey consisted of other people. Humans who probably had lives and families waiting for them. She killed them as surely as if she used her own two hands to do it. The wave of hunger from the daemons desiring to consume their victims left her reeling with a sense of nausea, but she managed to hold the connection to keep them from indulging.

Once their attackers were gone and the daemons sufficiently banished from the area, she withdrew from them and from the daenox. The very thought of touching it again made her trembling worse. She had partaken of a different side of the daemons that had long been her companions. Would she ever be able to see the innocence in them again? Whatever innocence she still had felt ripped away, leaving a raw, open wound in its place.

How did Kyouin stand it?

Or perhaps that was the real difference between them. Perhaps he did not care or even liked it. Unfortunately, that made him stronger than her when it came to using daemons as weapons.

"You saved the rest of us, Raine," Siniva murmured,

his lips close to her ear, keeping the words he offered her private to them. "If we had given them what they wanted, more of us would have died in these mountains. The loathing and guilt you feel will consume you if you let it. You have to focus on those you saved."

There was such pain in his voice that she listened to him, hearing the words he did not say. The pain did not ease, but she managed to control her tears and trembling enough to draw back from him. The moist tracks of tears running down his face brought understanding. She now knew why she could not reconnect him to the dragon web.

"Siniva, how did you free yourself from the statue and break from the dragon web?"

He lowered his gaze. "The original dragons of the web, the web-builders, figured it out for me. They needed someone to save you so they could go free, and they didn't trust Dephithus to succeed. I was the closest to the caves, but it would take a great deal of power to break from the web. To avoid ending up in a new stationary prison as Vanuthan had, I needed to change into human form and make that my prison, which would require even more power. The web-builders used most of the power stored in the web to imbue you with enough to free us. There wasn't much left for me to use, so they told me to use that trickle to power my natural skill with fire and burn the village my statue resided near. I was to burn the village and all the people in it, then use the power of their deaths to free myself into a human form."

His voice caught. He held his silence for a few seconds during which the distraught voices of those trying to save the other wounded soldier traveled to them. She could smell the blood in the snow and feel the cold air around her, except in front where Siniva's warmth kept it at bay.

"I did what they asked. An entire village of men, women, and children. Simple shepherds who lived a peaceful life there. They weren't even strangers to me. I had seen many of them when they visited the grave-yard. They didn't deserve it. I wanted to die with them, but I was too much of a coward. I did what the web-builders required of me. I burned the villagers alive so the dragons could go free. I'm not even sure it mattered. Dephithus might have freed you without my help."

Raine pushed aside her own pain and placed a gloved hand on his cheek. She waited for him to meet her eyes. When he did, she said, "You are wrong, Siniva. When my father stayed to fight Theruses, I might have found my way to the entrance of the cave, but I would not have stepped out into the light. I was terrified. I had never seen the natural light of day with my own eyes before, and it hurt. I couldn't have left that cave without you driving me on."

A raised voice caught her attention. Darkin was standing before the remaining members of their group, Kayd and Suva on either side of him. All eyes were on them. The third soldier lay unnaturally still. The efforts to save him had failed.

"Imperious has lost her king, but I will not stand by and let that daemon lord rule her," Darkin declared. "Our ancestors had an alliance with the dragons once, but they betrayed them. We need to convince the drag-ons that we are not going to do the same and that we want to rebuild that alliance. We may not have a ruler, but people will suffer if we don't find a way to stop this. I'm not giving up on our people."

"What about her?" One of the few remaining sol-diers asked, pointing in Raine's direction.

Darkin did not turn, though many of the others glanced over at her, open suspicion in their eyes.

"Her? You mean the young woman who just saved our lives?"

"By controlling daemons," another soldier pointed out.

"As I see it, there is nothing at all wrong with having someone on our side who can turn Kyouin's daemons against him," Darkin countered.

The soldiers glanced around at one another, less confident now until the one who had first spoken raised his voice again. "She's been working her powers over you," the soldier argued. "We've all seen it."

There were a few nods of agreement.

"Horse farts," Suva barked. "Raine's probably one of the most trustworthy people here."

"I'd second that," Kovial added from the back.

Darkin did glance back at her now. "The only thing she's done to me is win my heart with her remarkable courage."

Raine held his gaze until he looked away, wishing she could see in herself what he seemed to see in her.

The soldiers glanced at their comrades. There were some shrugs and shifting feet.

"We can't hang around here," Darkin said when no one else spoke. "Let's tend our fallen and find some-place away from here to camp and plan."

There were murmurs of assent then. Darkin turned around. Raine caught his gaze again. There was power-ful longing in those dark eyes. He wanted to come to her, but he knew better. Right now, he needed to be a leader and not do something that would encourage the idea she had undue influence over him.

She gave him a slight nod. Understanding his situa-tion even if she did not like it.

Siniva put his hand on her shoulder, expressing his own understanding at that moment, even though they all knew he did not approve of her relationship with

Darkin. Now that he had unburdened himself of the truth behind his breaking from the web, she suspected she might be able to reconnect him to it as she had Vanuthan. If she did, would he stay, or would he go to the rejoin the dragons? Perhaps now was not the best time to try it. Besides, she wanted to get away from the metallic stench of the bloodstained snow.

A few hours later, they had moved on and found a place to set camp. Siniva and Darkin had a brief conversation off to one side. Afterward, they came back and revealed Siniva's nature to the remaining soldiers. There were some objections until Siniva stood in the center of the place they chose to camp. Heat swept off him in waves, melting the snow and drying the exposed ground. The soldiers accepted him a bit more quickly then, though they still looked wary.

Once they were settled, the Legion soldiers gathered to confer about how to proceed now that the king was dead and what to do with the bodies. They brought the dead with them strapped on their horses. It was not practical to consider carrying the bodies with them all the way to the dragons and back if that was to be their goal, but many of them were firmly against the idea of leaving the fallen soldiers and the king here in the woods to be consumed by predators. The cold at least offered some preservation and helped mute the scent of death that would draw those predators to them, giving them a little time to deliberate over the matter.

Kayd was included in the discussion, and Siniva joined in, offering his opinion whether they wanted it or not. Rakas had wandered off alone somewhere as he was sometimes inclined to do. That left Raine and Jadean sitting alone together next to a second fire. Jadean watched her intently whenever Raine pretended not to be looking, but if she faced the woman directly, Jadean instantly looked away, her hand moving to her belly. Finally, wearying of the odd game, Raine got up and moved to sit next to her.

"Are you expecting a child?"

Jadean put her hands under her as if to help herself up, looking for a moment as though she meant to move away. Then she met Raine's eyes for perhaps the first time and slowly settled back down. Her manner struck Raine as defensive and reluctant, as if she carried secrets she wanted to be proud of but was ultimately ashamed to share.

She glanced down at her belly. "I met a man on the road one dark night. He and I were traveling in opposite directions, and we offered one another comfort for that night. I carry his child now."

That seemed innocent enough, but it did not explain why the woman was so interested in and yet avoidant of her. Nor why she was so protective of her unborn child in Raine's presence. "Have you seen the father since?"

"No. He's dead now, or so I have been told. He died freeing his daughter from a cave in the Dunues Mountains." She looked hard at Raine now, her gaze shrewd and expectant.

Raine's gut lurched. The sound of an icy wind blowing through the tops of the tall, snow-blanketed evergreens became louder in her ears. She pulled the hood of her cloak forward.

The implication that Dephithus had lain with this woman on his way to save Myara and Raine was not all that upsetting. What left her shaken was the idea that this woman carried a child that was her half-brother or sister and had said nothing about it until now.

"Then this child and I are kin. Why didn't you tell me before?"

Jadean glanced warily toward Kayd where she sat at the bigger campfire, focused on that conversation. "I promised Kayd I would not tell you of these things."

Raine latched on to her choice of words, recognizing that the child was only one of the secrets this woman was keeping. The icy wind seemed to bite through her cloak now. "These things?"

Jadean hesitated, glancing from Kayd to the fire and back to Kayd again. Finally, she shook her head. "Kayd will have my hide for this, but you have a right to know."

Raine felt impatience like an itch in that hard to reach place between her shoulder blades, accompanied by a thick dread that built at the back of her throat, making it hard to swallow. "Know what?"

Jadean shifted closer, both hands resting on her belly now. "Kayd and I did not escape Elysium. We were sent to find you. Kyouin wanted us to let you know that he has Lord Mythan and Myara's parents in his custody. Your grandparents."

Jadean was silent for a few minutes, letting those words sink in. The wind was definitely colder now. It felt to Raine as if her cloak and gloves had vanished. She shivered as she stared at Jadean, waiting for the rest.

"He wanted us to tell you that their fates are in your hands. If you go and meet with him, he will spare their lives."

Raine wanted to scream and run and hit something, all at the same time. Her chest tightened with fear even as her vision reddened with rage. Kayd was her mother's aunt. They were connected by blood. So why was Jadean the one sitting here telling her these things? Why was Kayd not the one telling her this and helping her figure out how to protect the people Kyouin had taken from them.

And what was she supposed to do now? Now that she knew, how could she ignore it? By not telling her when they first arrived, they had already risked the lives of Mythan and Myara's parents.

On the other hand, Kyouin might not let her go again if she came to him, not willingly at least.

"Why didn't Kayd want to tell me?"

Jadean lowered her gaze to the fire, the flickering of the flame reflecting in her emerald eyes. "She was afraid you would try to help them."

Raine could only stare at her in confusion. Of course, she would try to help them. It was the right thing to do. Was her life worth so much more than theirs that they should be left to die so she could stay safe? All she had done so far was destroy things. Perhaps this was her chance to make something better. Besides, if she went to Kyouin, maybe she could keep him distracted long enough for Siniva and the others to secure the help of the dragons.

She shook her head slightly. "I know better than to think I could face Kyouin alone."

Jadean smiled at her and reached out to squeeze her hand. "That's what I told Kayd. We'll go to the dragons. If the daenox is not controlled, it will only continue to grow stronger and more people will die from it."

Raine only nodded, as if in agreement. A gust of chill wind howled through the branches above them.

CHAPTER THIRTY THREE

Raine curled up on her sleeping roll after her conversation with Jadean, taking the opportunity to get some sleep while the others debated their future and that of the bodies they had carried here with them. She asked Jadean to wake her when the others concluded their business or sooner if Siniva happened to leave the group. The fact that the woman was carrying Raine's half-sibling did not make her immediately trustworthy, but something told her she could rely on Jadean for this small task. After reluctantly reaching through the daenox to ensure there were no threats nearby, she slipped off into a restless sleep.

Jadean proved Raine right, shaking her gently awake sometime later.

"They are done talking," Jadean murmured.

Raine nodded and sat up. She drew back the hood of her cloak, letting the icy air drive away lingering grogginess. A glance around the camp found Siniva settling off to one side, the furthest from the fires. He was the one she needed to talk to first. Without his agreement, her plan would not work.

She stood, muttering a thank you to Jadean, and walked over to where the dragon-man was kneeling to lay out his bedroll. His bronze-red eyes looked up into hers and concern furrowed his brow. He stood.

"Is something wrong?"

She shook her head, though she knew he had already seen through her. It would not matter if she could make him believe her concerns only involved where they were going from here, which they did, in a way. "Are they going to continue to the dragons?"

Siniva's eyes narrowed as though he meant to see into her mind. After several seconds, during which she did her best to meet his eyes, he nodded. "We will all continue to the dragons. It would be foolish to turn back after coming this far."

"Is that what you said to convince them, or did you remind them that they would have to clear their own snow from the next campsite without you?"

Siniva smirked and said nothing.

"I'm glad. Promise me something, Siniva."

Resistance hardened his features. She could not blame him. Even with all they had been through together, it was hard to learn to trust, especially given some of the conflicts that had come up between them. When it came down to it, she could not honestly say he was wrong to be wary.

"Please."

He gave her a hard look. "I don't like your tone. You sound like someone who's planning something."

She silently cursed his perceptiveness. "Just promise me that, no matter what happens, you will reach the dragons and get them to help push back the daenox."

He looked puzzled now. "An odd ask, since that was my plan regardless."

"I know. I just..." What could she say that would not rouse more suspicion? Her gaze drifted to the bodies lying in the snow. The answer came to her then. "It hasn't been an easy journey. If anything happens, I want to know our efforts won't be wasted."

Siniva's shoulders relaxed. His smile was full of gentle sympathy. "We've had our differences, but I won't let anything happen to you, Raine. If it will put your mind at ease, I promise."

"Thank you." She breathed a sigh of relief and stepped into him, putting her arms around him in a brief embrace that he returned, if somewhat uncertainly. She bid him goodnight, feeling his gaze on her as she returned to her own sleeping roll. When she turned around, however, he had gone back to settling in for the night.

After that, it was merely a matter of waiting some more. She did her best to pretend sleep for a time, making sure not to really doze off. It was not too hard. Her nerves crackled like lightning through her entire body. She listened for the breathing of others in the camp to slow. When it seemed calm and quiet, she did as she had done many nights before and got up, padding softly over to where Darkin lay.

When she started to kneel next to him, his eyes opened, black in the darkness, and he lifted his blanket so she could snuggle in next to him. "I hoped you would come."

Tonight, she did not put her back to him as she had before. Instead, she lay on her side, facing him. Once she was settled, he sought out one of her hands with his own and softly asked, "Is everything all right?"

"Darkin?"

"Yes?"

She chewed at her lip for a few seconds. Would he be as easy as Siniva had been? "Will you promise me something?"

She could feel him tense, pulling his hand as if he meant to take it away. She tightened her hand on his, keeping the contact.

"Promise what?"

"No matter what happens, promise me you will continue to the dragons and convince them to come fight the daenox."

His hand relaxed into hers, his tone softening. "That's still our plan, Raine. You'll be there to help us see it through. I won't let anything happen to you."

Apparently, all men are that arrogant.

She squeezed his hand, feeling a surge of warm affection for him and for Siniva. "Just promise me. A lot has happened, and I want to be sure all that we have lost won't be for nothing."

"Will my promise make you happy?"

She knew he would not see how shaky her smile was in the darkness. It was hard enough to keep her hand from shaking in his. "Yes."

"Then I promise."

Raine kissed him then. She kissed him as though she meant to make him a part of her, pressing her body close. He slid an arm around her and pulled her in tight, returning the passion in that kiss. Suddenly the cold was gone, and she could feel the physical manifestation of his desire pressing against her. Her body ached in response, yearning to give him what he craved. She thought it was what she wanted too, though she had few references to go by. Only her parents' memories. Her father's encounter with Suva had been more like a cat fight than lovemaking, and the coupling between her parents that led to her conception was bittersweet at best.

Regardless, now was not the time. She was sure she did not want that here and now, where they would have to be rushed and secretive. Despite his apparent interest, he did not push for more than to taste her mouth and feel her against him. Perhaps he shared her feelings on the matter, or perhaps he was letting her set the pace. Either way, she appreciated his restraint.

In time, she pulled away. They were both breathing hard, their breath mingling in the small space between them now. She gave him one more kiss, this one more chaste. A goodbye kiss.

"I should go."

"You don't have to," Darkin murmured, his voice deepened with the hunger that still lingered hot between them.

"It's better if I do."

He did not argue.

Raine got up, instantly mourning the warmth of his body next to her. She crept back to her bedroll, clinging to her resolve, and waited there for a time, listening to the others and keeping tabs on the one soldier who sat up on watch. With the group reduced as it was, they were taking shifts one at a time.

When all seemed calm and the watch had moved to the farthest corner of his circuit around the perimeter of the camp, she gathered her bedroll quickly and carried it, along with her things which she had prepared earlier, over to where the horses waited. She drew on daenox to mask herself from sight and to mute any noise she might make while she put all her equipment on Hydra. The stallion seemed to sense the gravity of the situation, standing still as a statue even as his muscles trembled in response to her nerves.

As soon as she was ready, she pulled Hydra away from the horse line and walked him a short distance from the camp, continuing the flow of daenox to mute the sound of their crunching through the snow. She glanced back once. In the dark, she could still make out the shapes on their sleeping rolls gathered close to the fires in the dry area Siniva had made. Siniva lay with his back almost against the snow, his inner fire warming him more than enough.

A chill of fear swept through her. The idea of striking

out on her own terrified her. This was the right choice, however. She needed to do what she could to protect those whose lives were now in her hands. The ones she was leaving behind here could finish their journey without her.

Hydra stomped next to her, and she turned, barely holding back a cry of surprise when she found a hooded figure standing there in their path. The other figure also had a horse in tow.

"You didn't make me promise," Rakas said softly.

She stared at him for a few seconds, wondering how he knew about the promises. Ultimately, it did not matter. She was not going to let him get in the way. "Don't make this harder," Raine stated, keeping her tone firm to convey her resolve. "I need to do this."

"You don't need to do it alone."

She looked at him there in the dark, his horse packed and ready to go. Had she been connected to the daenox earlier, she might have caught him eavesdropping, as he most clearly had been. There was no way she could deny that she did not really want to go alone, and the others would probably prefer not to have Rakas with them anyhow.

"Fine. Let's get moving."

Without further discussion, they mounted their horses and started away from the camp, back the way they had come. A few lazy snowflakes swirled down through the sky, lit by the moonlight that streamed through an opening in the clouds. If they were lucky, the heavier snow would hold off for a while. It would be hard enough to stay on track in the dark without fresh snow obscuring the path.

Raine stopped them again once they were far enough away that they could not see the light of the campfires any longer.

"What is it?"

"Give me a few minutes. There's one more thing I need to do," she answered, reaching into the dragon web.

She closed her eyes and focused, drawing the power with her as she sought out Siniva's presence with a little extra help from a tendril of daenox. She approached carefully this time, pleased to feel the web reaching toward the Fire Dragon at the same time something in him reached for it. She was right in thinking he would be open to the dragon power now that he had unburdened himself of what he had done to get free of his stone prison. She held the web back, keeping it at the edge of the range that seemed to draw Siniva's innate power to it. Little by little, she allowed the two powers to get closer, struggling to maintain her tenuous control of the power of the web. Finally, the two touched, wrapping around one another like lovers, and warmth swept through her. If she had done it gently enough, it probably would not wake him.

Let him dream of spreading his magnificent wings again only to find that he can really do so when he awakens.

Opening her eyes, she faced forward, a smile on her lips and a tear quickly growing cold on her cheek.

"Let's get moving."

They had only gone a few feet when crunching sounds in the snow to the left of the trail caught their attention. Another rider was coming out of the trees toward them. Raine placed a hand on her sword hilt. Somewhere in the back of her mind, a little voice rejoiced in the fact that it had been an automatic reaction.

"Lead on," Kovial's voice said in a firm tone that told her he meant to come if she liked the idea or not.

Raine grimaced. "Am I really that bad at sneaking away?"

Kovial chuckled under his breath. "I couldn't sleep. I almost woke Darkin and Suva when I saw you leaving, but you were obviously trying to go unnoticed. I wanted to respect your right to choose your path but thought you might need a little help.”

Raine peered into the dark, drawing on daenox to enhance her vision. As best she could see, no more riders were waiting to join them. Perhaps a few companions was not such a bad thing, but they needed to go before they drew anyone else out into the night.

“All right. It would be foolish to bicker over it. You can both come, but you need to respect that this is my choice and understand that I won’t let you interfere in my decisions.”

Rakas moved his head slightly in what she chose to assume was a nod, though it was hard to tell with his hood up.

Kovial grinned. “Since I don’t even know where we are going, I’m not really equipped to argue.”

“We’re going back to Elysium,” Raine said.

The declaration was met with silence. Whether either of them disagreed with her plan. They chose not to voice their opinions for now.

Raine stared ahead into the darkness. The snow seemed to glow in the moonlight that streamed between the clouds. She did not really need to enhance her vision to find the way forward. The snow brought a cold with it that she could live without, but she loved the way it made the world sparkle, hiding the dirt and darker things in a blanket of shimmering white. It also seemed quieter in the snow, as if the dense layers of white insulated the world.

She was stalling now, and she knew it. Squeezing her legs, she urged Hydra onward.

It was only a matter of seconds before two more horses were crunching through the snow after Hydra. She allowed herself a tiny, relieved exhale. The idea of going back alone had been terrifying. Now she did not have to rely solely upon herself. It might get harder toward the end when she had to convince them to stay out of the city and let her face Kyouin one her own, but for now, she appreciated their company.

CHAPTER THIRTY FOUR

Darkin snapped awake, his heart pounding. His ears still rang with the ground shaking roar that had woken him. He was on his feet in seconds, staring at the massive red-bronze dragon standing in the road alongside the camp. It took him a few seconds, and a quick scan of the camp, to process what he was looking at. Siniva had changed into his dragon form.

For some reason, it had not occurred to him to question why Siniva had never changed into a dragon before this. He rather assumed it was because there were still a few Legion soldiers who were not aware of the truth, not until now at least. The fact that he changed now in front of everyone led Darkin to wonder what was different. He had not heard many dragon roars in his time, but something about this one struck him as distressed.

The one other thing he noticed in his scan of the camp was that several others were missing from their places. Raine, Kovial, and Rakas were all gone. He might have believed they had wandered off to relieve themselves, except it was not only that their bedrolls were empty. Their bedrolls were not there at all. Nor, now that he glanced at the horse lines, were their horses. Suddenly, the dragon's distress made a lot of sense, as did the promise Raine had made him make last night.

Pressing down the surge of panic and a growing sense of betrayal, Darkin ordered the few remaining soldiers who were grabbing their weapons to stand down and walked toward the massive beast. Even knowing who it was, approaching the enormous predator with his huge clawed feet and a jaw full of teeth as long as Darkin's forearm took some willpower.

The snow around Siniva had already melted away, and there was a noticeable increase in temperature when Darkin got close to him, the heat far more intense than usual. He suspected that might be as much because of Siniva's upset over Raine's departure as because of his altered form.

"She made you promise too, didn't she?"

Siniva's head dropped low, his flame-colored eye coming level with Darkin's head. "She did it to both of us?" His eye closed for a second, his mouth twisting in what Darkin suspected was the dragon equivalent of a grimace. "I thought she was asking because she was shaken by the ambush."

"Me too." Darkin gave himself a mental kick. He should have known better. They both should have.

"Did she give you any idea where she might have gone?"

"No, but she didn't go alone." Now Darkin was sure the expression was a grimace.

"Rakas is not the companion I would have chosen for her."

Given what he now suspected about Rakas's involvement in Dephithus's downfall, Darkin could not disagree on that point, however. "I would trust Kovial with my life. He'll keep her safe."

But why didn't he say anything to Suva or me? Why didn't he wake one of us?

Suva was storming toward them now, giving the dragon a defiant scowl that dared the beast to try anything, as though she could do something about it if he did. Kayd was right behind her, her gaze sweeping the camp until she spotted Jadean. She motioned the woman over with a sharp gesture of one hand and continued toward them. Jadean placed her gloved hands over her belly and started toward them, her steps slow and reluctant.

"Where's Kovial?" Suva demanded.

"Where's Raine?" Kayd demanded as well, arriving almost on Suva's heels despite her injury.

There were definite downsides to being the one in charge. Although, his biggest problem seemed to be that he had never been in charge of Raine in the first place. "I don't—"

"I think I do," Kayd interrupted. She grabbed Jadean's arm when the woman slunk up behind her and jerked her forward into the middle of the small group. "You told her, didn't you?"

Jadean's eyes went wide, but the set of her jaw was defiant. "The girl had a right to know."

Darkin felt a burning, dangerous anger rising in him. "Know what?" He growled.

A much more intimidating growl emanated from somewhere deep in the dragon's chest as he lowered his snout to look down it at Jadean. Heavy snowflakes started to fall around them, melting in the air when they got too close to Siniva's heat.

Jadean cast an anxious glance at the dragon and sidestepped a few feet away from him. "We didn't escape Elysium. Kyouin sent us to find Raine. He's holding her grandparents as *guests* in the palace. He wanted us to invite her back to Elysium to meet with him and let her know that their fates are in her hands."

Darkin's anger expanded to encompass Kayd. He pinned her with his gaze. "You both lied to us."

"I didn't know what else to do," Kayd defended. "That man is mad. You can see it in his eyes. He had

Lady Avaline there. She was an animated corpse." Kayd's voice cracked as she said those words. She swiped at a rogue tear that crept down one cheek.

Darkin managed not to look at Suva in the few seconds it took for Kayd to control her emotions, though it took some effort. They both had known what Kyouin planned to do with Avaline, but they had not been in much of a position to do anything about it. There was no point in bringing that up now.

"If Raine goes back there," Kayd continued, "who knows what he'll do to her. All I know is that I believe he will kill them if he gets the notion whether or not Raine meets with him."

Darkin's chest twisted with fear. He loved Raine. He had never felt this kind of love for anyone, and it was currently shredding him inside. He promised her they would continue to the dragons. He promised. And yet, they did not know what would happen to her if Kyouin got his hands on her. All he knew was that he agreed emphatically with Kayd's assessment of the man. On the other hand, they also did not know how much of a head start Raine had or how fast she was moving. They did have a dragon. That gave them some advantage when it came to speed. But it was a dragon who had made her the same promise Darkin had made.

"Kyouin won't hurt them or her," Jadean blurted.

There was a flash of almost scalding heat next to Darkin. Suddenly Siniva was standing there in his more human form. His eyes were narrowed at Jadean. Kayd was also giving the woman a suspicious look.

"How can you know that?" Siniva demanded.

Jadean shifted her feet, wrapping her arms protectively around her belly. "He's obsessed with her. With her power and her exotic appearance, but mostly her power." Her gaze turned distant then. "Together, they could conquer this world with their powers. That future is bleak, but it's up to the dragon-child to decide which future will come. She will fight him, or she will give in to him to protect those she loves. I cannot see what she will choose, only that it will determine all of our futures."

"You can see the future?" Darkin asked.

"Sometimes. I can't really control it, and my pregnancy seems to interfere with it. Mostly I can see the future of those I touch, but the dragon-child has distorted many of those visions. What happens between Raine and Kyouin will have a profound impact on all of our futures."

"I'd rather you never say their names in the same sentence again," Siniva growled.

Darkin bristled and caught himself before snapping at Siniva for focusing on something so inane, though he did get an unpleasant feeling himself when she said their names together. He needed to understand what was going on. One thing, in particular, did not make sense. "How well do you know Kyouin, Jadean, because you seem to know a fair bit about his motivations, and I don't buy that you figured it all out through your daemonic foresight."

Jadean scowled at him then. "Don't judge so. We both know your beloved gets most of her power through the daenox as well."

Siniva gave Darkin a cross look, and he felt an odd heat under his collar.

Did she have to say beloved?

Not that it was not an inaccurate choice of words, but his relationship with Siniva was tumultuous, and they needed to be allies right now. He did his best to shrug the statement off.

Kayd stepped up to his rescue. "Just answer his question, Jadean. You were already there when I was taken to the throne room with Mythan. How well do you know Kyouin?"

Jadean shifted her feet. "Out paths crossed soon after the daenox started working free. We found a common bond in the way the daenox seemed to have chosen each of us and in the powers it gave us that made us outcast from most people. I didn't understand his thirst for chaos and the hatred he carried with him until we coupled, and I saw some of the suffering and horror he would bring. I wanted to stop him then, but what I saw paralyzed me with fear. I let him finish. I pretended to enjoy it so he wouldn't turn his consuming hatred on me."

Jadean stopped speaking and stood staring through them for a minute or more. A visible shudder swept through her. Darkin felt a touch of pity rising up in him. The others appeared to share his feelings. They gave her a moment, letting her gather herself before continuing.

"I tried to get as far away from him as I could, but something tied me to him after that. The daenox in him was far more powerful than what flowed through me, and he had far more control of it. From that moment on, whenever he wants me there, I cannot refuse him. No matter how far I go, I can't resist his need. The longer it takes me to return to him, the more painful it is for me, so I have learned not to wander too far."

Something else occurred to Darkin then, sparking a flame of dread in his gut. "Does he know where you are?"

"You mean, can he sense me?" She frowned. "I'm not sure."

"That's comforting," Suva grumbled. "Why did Kovial go with them?"

"You know your brother. He believed Raine needed him more than we did," Darkin answered.

Suva met his gaze. The answer felt right to Darkin. Kovial was fond of Raine, and he had no reason to fear Rakas. The man had healed him, after all. Given

Kovial's desire to be useful and do good, it made sense that he might have decided to help Raine. Why he did so without consulting them was something of a mystery, but perhaps he had not felt like he had time. Who knew, really? He was an adult and did not have to come to them to get approval for his decisions.

Suva finally gave a small nod. There was a hint of hurt in her eyes and Darkin sympathized. He felt somewhat betrayed by Kovial and Raine both, but dwelling on it was going to accomplish nothing. They had to come up with a plan to move forward.

"What now?" Kayd asked. "Do we go after them, or do we try to find the dragons?"

"We don't need to find the dragons," Siniva stated. "Raine figured out where they are, and I can feel them now. We are close, but I don't see how we can get there and back to Imperious before Raine does."

Darkin glanced at the man, the dragon, next to him and smiled, faintly amused that he should be the one to point out their advantage. "Maybe we could. If we could fly at the speed of a dragon."

Siniva glanced down at his hands and, for a few seconds, Darkin would have sworn the imposing man was going to break into tears. Then he took a deep breath and nodded. "In dragon form, I might be able to do it."

"Excellent," Darkin nodded. It felt good to have a plan, especially one that would allow him to keep his promise to Raine and still be there to help her face Kyouin. "Then we'll fly to the dragons. The rest of you can go after Raine and the others, and we'll meet up outside of Imperious."

"Exactly," Siniva started, his expression brightening with, Darkin suspected, the same revelation, "we can..." He trailed off and gave Darkin a shrewd look, the brightness in his expression quickly clouding over. "Wait. We?"

"Yes." The snow was starting to fall harder now. In the back of his mind, he hoped Raine and the other two were out of the area enough that they might not get hit by this heavier snow. On the other hand, it might slow them down some, which could be a good thing so long as they did not get lost. "I can ride on your back, or you can carry me."

Siniva was shaking his head. "No. Dragons don't carry people. Not ever. I'll go to the dragons alone."

Darkin felt his temper burning higher again. He needed to be calm and rational. He was the leader here. Besides, he was dealing with a dragon. There was little doubt about who would win that fight. Still, it was not until he thought of Raine and how she would feel if she saw him yelling at Siniva that he managed to tamp down the rising rage.

"We need someone from Imperious there if we are to convince the dragons to come to our aid," Darkin suggested. "Or can you say with certainty that they will respect your council and travel to Imperious to face the daemon army on your request alone."

Siniva's defiant stare stayed steady for a few seconds before faltering. He looked down, shifting his feet. There was some deeper conflict here that Darkin almost felt guilty for stumbling upon, but he had been trying to be diplomatic about this. Now he wished he had at least pulled the dragon aside before pressing the issue.

"Dragon's don't—" he started to say without conviction.

"For Raine," Darkin interrupted gently.

Siniva drew in a deep breath and let it out slowly. Then he met Darkin's eyes and nodded.

CHAPTER THIRTY FIVE

Riding a dragon was nowhere near as glorious as Darkin had imagined. The massive beast had hard ridges going down his neck and spine, and his scales were no softer. He had fashioned a padded saddle with a horse blanket, some bedrolls, and rope. Siniva almost called off the whole idea when Darkin first tried to put it on him. Fortunately, the dragon cared about Raine enough that he relented after a brief discussion. The result was still uncomfortable, but the biting cold wind up that high in the air was enough to make him forget about other discomforts.

Another problem, not one Darkin had expected, was that, though he typically had no fear of heights, that fearlessness had an upper limit. When Siniva reached a comfortable soaring altitude, Darkin glanced over the side. His head took a violent spin, his stomach threatening to bring up breakfast. At least he had thought to secure himself to the dragon along with the saddle, so he did not have to find out the hard way how far it was to the ground, but he started to question his earlier enthusiasm for this idea.

The first night, when they settled down to get some rest, Darkin could not remember another day in his life when he felt so sore and drained after a day of riding. It was in that state, at the end of a long day soaring through the clouds in the makeshift dragon saddle, that he realized he and Siniva now had only each other for company. It seemed likely that their evenings were going to be less than pleasant.

The great dragon returned to his mostly human form with a much-subdued manner. He lit the firewood Darkin had gathered and slumped silently down against a log. There had been no opportunity to talk while flying, so Darkin could not know what thoughts drove him to his current state. He found himself stepping lightly around the camp they made, trying not to draw attention to himself any more than necessary. When they had settled to eating, curiosity finally overrode caution.

"So…" Darkin hesitated, put off by the dour look Siniva gave him as soon as he made a sound, but he had the dragon-man's attention now, so he might as well continue. "Why did you wait until Raine was gone to turn into your natural form? Obviously, she knows you're a dragon."

"It's none of your affair," Siniva grumbled.

Darkin shrugged off the temperamental response, turning his focus on some tough meat he was attempting to chew to a soft enough state that he could at least swallow it. Siniva ripped off another bit of his own dried meat with a grimace. He looked no more satisfied with the meal than Darkin was. They had flown too long to have any light left for hunting, however, so travel rations had to suffice. In fact, given how long they had flown, it made sense that the dragon-man might be weary and disinclined to chat.

"You care about her. I realize that," Siniva stated.

Darkin's skin prickled with unease at the choice of subjects. Talking about Raine was safe enough if they did not go into his relationship with her. "Enough to want to keep my promise, but too much to let her face that bastard alone." There was no need to elaborate on who 'that bastard' was.

"In these things we agree," Siniva answered. A few minutes passed, and it seemed like that might be the end of it, but then Siniva drew in a deep breath and spoke again. "I couldn't turn into my dragon form before. I was trapped in this form until Raine figured out how to reconnect me to the dragon web. She did it right before she left, while I was sleeping, freeing me from the human prison I had created for myself." His head came up, his eyes burning with a fierce light. "I can never repay her for that… and yet."

Darkin waited for several minutes, trying to be respectful and give the other time to gather his thoughts. Eventually, he relented to his burning curiosity again. "And yet?"

Siniva's hard gaze bored into him. "If Raine had not gone to help you three escape Elysium, Vanuthan would still be alive."

Some of the conflict between Raine and Siniva made more sense when he heard the heartache in those words. He could not argue that Siniva was wrong either, no matter how much he wanted to be able to. If Raine had not come when she did, turning daemons to their side to help them escape, he and the others might not have survived. Vanuthan also helped secure that escape, breaking the last line of warriors that stood in their path. If she had not been there, they also would have had to deal with the gold dragon by themselves, which would have been a losing battle no matter how he looked at it. Now seemed the wrong time to mention any of that.

"It's cold up there," Darkin muttered.

Siniva glanced up toward the night sky. A wistful smile curved his lips. "It's good to be able to fly again."

Darkin nodded, staring into the fire. "I imagine it is."

After a few minutes of silence, he looked at Siniva again. The dragon-man was still staring up at the sky. When he realized he was being watched, he lowered his gaze to meet Darkin's eyes. "That, at least, is a problem I can solve."

"What is?"

"The cold. I am the Fire Dragon."

Siniva's grin then said volumes about how much he loved being what he was. Darkin wished he could take that much pride and pleasure in some part of what he was. Maybe, if he could help bring the dragons to Imperious and protect Raine, perhaps then he might know what that felt like.

*

Kyouin began to draw daenox up through the floor around the chair Vinya sat in. The young girl's eyes went wide, and she tried to recoil. The ropes binding her to the chair kept her from getting far.

No matter how much time he put in trying to spoil her and make her comfortable, the girl refused to trust him when it came to the daemon power. She ran from it every time he tried to bring it into her.

"You forced my hand, Vinya. I was trying to do this nicely."

Vinya screamed something, but he could not make it out past the gag. She had quite the screech when she was angry or frightened. He had not wanted to gag her, but he could not tolerate that noise.

Tears were running down her cheeks from her light hazel eyes now, and a glistening stream of snot ran toward the cloth gag. It would soak in, which was a bit gross, but it was not going to hurt her any in the long run. She squeezed her eyes shut as violet tendrils moved up around her, weaving like serpents.

Kyouin paused the tendrils of daenox, letting them hover in the air around her without touching her. "It isn't too late to do this the nice way. Wouldn't you rather welcome the power rather than have it forced into you like this?"

Vinya opened her eyes. Her nose and cheeks were turning red with her distress. After a few seconds staring at him, she refocused on the violet tendrils. Her expression calmed, the flow of tears slowing, and Kyouin used a bit of daenox to cut through the gag. A new one could be manufactured quickly enough. To his pleasure, she did not scream.

"I'm scared."

Kyouin let the daenox drop away and walked over to sit on the floor next to the chair. He looked up at her, placing a hand on her knee. Perhaps what she needed was honesty. It had seemed foolish to waste explanations on such a young creature. Now that he thought about it, however, he might need a child who could handle the truth if he were to get what he wanted out of this.

"Vinya, this world is changing. The powers that are taking over will destroy the weak and embrace the strong. Do you think that you're weak?"

She shook her head with conviction.

Kyouin smiled to himself.

"I'm merely trying to advance the process so that you can begin to become the formidable woman you are meant to be. This power, the daenox, will embrace you and help you become stronger, but you must accept it. If you accept it willingly, you will be that much stronger. Do you understand?" Since conversation appeared to be having a positive effect, he used more daenox to cut the bonds holding her wrists.

Vinya immediately used one sleeve of the pretty purple dress he had given her to wipe her nose. "Won't it hurt me?"

"Do you believe you are weak?"

She shook her head again. The conviction was not as firm this time, but he thought it might be enough.

"Then, you'll be fine."

When he cut the bonds holding her legs in place, she met his eyes and nodded.

"You can close your eyes if it helps," he offered.

"Will you hold my hand?"

Kyouin took her hand.

Vinya met his eyes. She kept staring hard into them as he drew tendrils of daenox up around her. Then he plunged the tips of those tendrils into her and pumped daenox into her little body, forcing more and more into her until her eyes rolled back and she began to convulse. Even then, he did not stop. He filled her with the daemon power until she slumped over in the chair, unconscious. Then he lifted her and carried her to her bedroom, leaving the daenox to do as it would with her. They would find out soon enough if she could tolerate it.

When he came out of her room, a young man was waiting for him between two guards, knelt there on one knee, staring at the floor. He was a lovely youth, his skin uncommonly flawless for one his age. Rare desire stirred in Kyouin.

"What is this?"

"My lord," the young man started, still staring at the floor, "the troubadours calling themselves Fools Errant have arrived and await you in the main hall."

Kyouin hated the main hall. It was too big, but he could tolerate the mistake given that they had found him the troop.

"Stand up," he ordered.

The young man stood, still staring at the floor.

"Look at me."

The young man looked up, his blue eyes not quite meeting Kyouin's gaze. There was no sign of illness in his healthy skin tone and bright eyes. He could make a fine distraction.

"How long have you been in Elysium?"

"Only a few days, my lord."

Kyouin's chest grew heavy with disappointment. A few days was not long enough to know if the daenox would break him. He turned to one of the guards, both of whom had visible sores and unhealthy pallor from their inundation in the daemon power that now surged through every part of Elysium.

"In a week, if he is still healthy, bring him to see me."

The guard nodded.

The young man kept his expression neutral.

"You may go."

He watched the trio walk away before heading to the main hall.

Leaves and other detritus tracked in on people's shoes littered the halls of the palace. The beautiful floors were streaked with smears of mud in many places. Most of the cleaning staff had fallen ill from the dense concentration of daenox he and his army brought to the area. Eventually, he would have to bring more people in to manage the mundane tasks. For now, the remaining servants were reassigned to more important duties such as cooking, disposing of waste, and maintaining his private quarters. There were always growing pains with significant changes.

Along the way, he summoned some undead warriors and daemons to attend him. Things tended to go more smoothly if he brought reminders of his power to his audiences. People were less inclined to disagree or show their tempers with his daemons and undead lurking about the room. Disagreements were tedious. He much preferred to avoid such things.

Fools Errant had arrived at the perfect time. Raine would return any day now. Kayd, he could not trust, but Jadean believed everyone should have a chance at all possible futures. She would feel the girl had a right to hear his message. He suspected Raine would have separated from the group she escaped Elysium with by now to avoid putting them in danger. So, he sent danger to find them in the form of an undead dragon.

The group waiting in the main hall were a motley bunch of misfits. Even so, there was a cohesiveness to them in the fitted attire they wore that showed off physical assets. One man displayed flame tattoos and several scars over a muscular torso. The women openly displayed feminine curves beneath snug leather and cloth outfits that were designed for both protection and freedom of movement. All wore weapons, though for some that equated to no more than a dagger. He was not worried about their weapons. The daemon power was his shield.

There were eight of them with Siniva and Raine gone. *Eight?*

He recalled there being seven in the troop aside from Raine and Siniva in Corbent Calid. Had they recruited another member? He recognized all but one from the previous encounter. The man looked vaguely familiar in the sense that he looked like someone Kyouin had seen before, though he could not quite place who or when. The man met his gaze, his blue-green eyes steady and unwelcoming. There was confidence in his bearing that bore watching.

"Welcome to my humble palace." Kyouin spread his arms wide as he strode toward them to encompass the vast main hall, grand and elegant even in its unclean state. "You may bow or curtsy if you wish, but I require no such gestures of obeisance."

None of them made any such gestures.

The woman in front spoke. He remembered her for the pink in her hair and the no-nonsense severity in her gaze that she gave him a full dose of now. "Why are we here?"

Kyouin offered a warm smile to her scowl. "I invited you here—"

"Under armed guard," she interrupted.

"To ensure your safety." He did not let his smile falter. "I invited you here to perform for my troops and me. They could use a morale boost."

She glanced around at the daemons and undead lurking in the room. It was clear their company made her uneasy, but it did not surprise him when she shook her head. "While we appreciate the opportunity, I've noticed much sickness here. I would prefer not to jeopardize the health of my group."

Kyouin resisted the urge to threaten them... for now. "I can provide accommodations in the palace. You'll be fine here."

"That's a generous offer, but we also have engagements elsewhere. We'll have to decline."

Kyouin's smile grew. The daemons and undead who had been at ease now came to attention, the warriors drawing their weapons and the beasts baring their teeth. Some of the troubadours shifted into a tighter group.

The leader's smile grew to match his own. "There now. I knew if we tried hard enough, we could be honest with each other." She cocked her head to the side and narrowed her eyes. "Why do you want us here so badly?"

Kyouin offered a nod of respect and signaled his warriors and daemons to relax again. He almost hoped this woman did not succumb to the daenox. "Might I have your name?"

"Nakia."

"And your fellows?"

She hesitated a moment, then did a quick pass, pointing at each member of the troop in turn. "Cadovan, Marisa, Myrza, Kelcy, Idrin, Florin, and Ahric."

Most gave a small nod in response, though Cadovan and Ahric did not.

"I brought you here because a special guest is coming to the palace soon. I thought she might be more comfortable with friends around."

Nakia caught on quickly. "Raine."

Her expression gave away none of how that information made her feel. A few of the others were less stoic. The woman introduced as Myrza paled and gripped Marisa's arm when Raine's name came up. She cared about Raine. He hoped the feeling was mutual.

"I told you we shouldn't have gotten involved with that girl," Florin grumbled from the back.

Kyouin found it distantly humorous that the man did not get a warning look just from him, but also from all of the women and two of the men in the group. The man took a step back and held his silence.

"If you agree to not cause trouble, I'll give you freedom within the palace and the Elysium grounds."

"But we won't be allowed to leave," Nakia stated.

Kyouin shook his head slowly to make sure the message was clear to everyone.

"Do we have a choice?"

"I think you know the answer to that."

Her tightly pressed lips and sharp nod said she did.

They made good time heading back down the mountainside. Raine kept them on course even in heavy snow by using the power in the dragon web or the daenox to follow traces left by the hundreds of living creatures that had used those worn paths before them. Neither Kovial nor Rakas asked how she kept them on track with the limited visibility and fresh snowpack. She suspected Rakas already knew. Kovial seemed content not to know too much.

By the same methods, she could tell they were being followed. Among their followers, however, there was no trace of the very familiar presences of Darkin and Siniva. Through the dragon web, she could tell that Siniva was getting closer to the other dragons. The two who had promised her were going to keep their promises. Whenever she thought of it that way, her eyes stung with tears, and her throat tightened. She wished them well on their journey, hoping earnestly that Siniva did not lose patience with Darkin along the way and eat him.

Now that she was delving into the dragon web more, she noticed that it had been stronger when they were closer to the dragons. Now that they were moving away, the dragon web was losing potency, and the daenox was becoming more powerful again. For the moment, the dragon web was still the stronger of the two, but it would be the other way around soon.

They did not talk much the first several days or sleep any more than necessary. Was the silence because the others regretted their decision to come with her or were they, like her, pondering the seriousness of what they might face back in Elysium? They did not know yet that she had no intention of allowing them to accompany her past the gates into Elysium. She also did not tell them that they were being followed out of fear that they would want to wait for the others to catch up. For now, they were pulling ahead, increasing the distance between themselves and their followers. Those who followed were moving at a slower pace. They were probably carrying the bodies of the king and their fallen comrades, and they did have pregnant Jadean with them.

What will I do when I get to Elysium?

Raine stared into their small fire now, chewing at whatever tasteless bit of dried food Kovial had handed her when she sat down.

She could not hope to defeat Kyouin in combat. No matter how many daemons she turned to her cause, he still had human and undead warriors to fight for him. If she met with him, however, maybe she could talk him out of his current path of destruction. She did not believe that though, no matter how much she wanted to. Kyouin was mad. Whether he was simply mad with power, mad with the hurt of past wrongs, or mad because the daemon power had driven him over the edge, did not really matter. Chances of negotiation having desirable results were so slim it barely made sense to try.

"We seem to be making good time," Kovial commented, giving the strip of dried meat in his hand a long stare. "What will you do when we get to Elysium?"

Raine found herself looking to Rakas. Her father's rapist, willing or otherwise, was not the one she ever expected to be turning to for advice, but Kovial was the one asking the question so that only left her one option.

Rakas avoided her, turning to gaze into the fire the moment she looked his direction.

For a few seconds, she struggled with a surge of anger, then she realized he was right to turn away. They were here to support her. This journey was her idea, and it was a journey she had expected to make alone. If she did not know what her plan was, she could not expect the men following her to know.

"I'll meet with Kyouin."

Now Rakas looked up at her. "Because you expect him to come around. To disband his army and relinquish control of Elysium."

He was deliberately digging at her. Forcing her to acknowledge how little thought she had put into this. She was not going to let him get to her.

"No. To see if I can get him to release the people he's holding, and to look for weaknesses that can be exploited."

"Be careful," Rakas cautioned, "he seems to already know some of your weaknesses."

"It seems to me that she is one of his weaknesses," Kovial suggested around a mouthful of dried meat. "What kind of meat is this?"

Rakas grimaced. "Whatever they couldn't get the dogs to eat, I suspect."

There was wry laughter around the fire and a few minutes of silence as Kovial passed around some nuts and cheese that were more palatable. Raine accepted her portion and found herself staring at her gloved hand, wondering how long it had been since she had held food in it without a glove on. The days were blending together. The strange white silence of heavy snowpack created a sort of timelessness. It had gotten warmer as they worked their way back toward Imperious. The snowpack was diminishing, and it was almost warm enough to go without gloves, but she had gotten used to them, and, if she were to be honest with herself, she liked wearing them because Darkin had selected them for her.

"It has occurred to you, hasn't it," Rakas began, "that you might be his weakness, and if you walk into his hands, he might not let you walk out again."

A violent shudder made Raine drop her handful of nuts. She leaned over to pick them up. Eating a little dirt was better than wasting the scarce rations they carried. They could hunt, but preparing fresh meat took time away from travel and increased the risk of the others catching up with them before Imperious.

"It has occurred to me." She used her cleanup task as an excuse not to look at either of them.

"That's a good point. What if Rakas is right?"

Raine could feel their eyes on her. She collected the last of the nuts and sat up. "It doesn't matter. I need to do something to help the people he's holding. I can't wait and hope he'll keep them alive long enough for the dragons to save them. They're in danger because of me."

There was another stretch of silence, and she dared to hope the conversation was over. Rakas, now tossing evergreen needles in the fire to watch them burn, spoke into the stretching silence.

"You're wrong, you know."

Raine was inclined to agree with him regardless of what it was he thought she was wrong about. She had no experience with things like this. How could she hope to have any clue as to how to go about it?

"About what?"

Rakas smirked. She would have sworn he mouthed the word 'everything,' but that was not what he said. "It isn't your fault that they're in danger. Kyouin's obsession with you is entirely outside of your control. You're making a choice to try and protect the people he's holding in

Elysium because you have a great capacity for love and caring. That's why you aren't sitting here alone, and it's why your future has the potential to be so much greater than his. Don't squander that."

Raine could not swallow the cheese in her mouth. Her throat had closed up. "Excuse me," she managed to choke out.

She hurried away toward where she had gone earlier to relieve herself, hoping they would assume that was the reason for her departure. When she was out of sight, she used daenox to silence her footsteps and moved around to the horse line, sneaking up alongside Hydra to bury her hands in his black mane, pressing her face to his neck. The stallion stood there patiently, somehow sensing that she needed him to be still.

"It almost sounds like you intend to let her face Kyouin alone," Kovial said, agitation in the sharp cutoff of his words.

"I do," Rakas answered, softly enough that she barely heard him.

"Well, I don't," Kovial snapped back.

"It's how she wants it," Rakas persisted.

"That doesn't make it a good idea."

"It doesn't make it a bad one either."

Raine leaned away from Hydra's neck, peering toward the campfire under his throat.

Kovial threw up his hands. He was not wearing his gloves, so his pale skin picked up a soft glow in the moonlight. It made her smile to see him moving his arm so well now. He started pacing then. "I thought you just told her not to squander what she has to offer the world."

"Raine cares about the people Kyouin has in Elysium. If she doesn't make an appearance soon, Kyouin might harm them. It will crush her if something happens to them. What Kyouin won't do is hurt her, not if he thinks there is a chance she'll come around to his side. All she has to do is keep him distracted long enough for the dragons to come."

Raine rubbed Hydra's soft nose and watched Kovial pacing. He paced back and forth in front of the fire several times before stopping to face Rakas.

"Don't you think you should tell Raine all of this?"

"I just did."

Rakas chuckled. Raine felt her cheeks growing hot. She should have known better than to sneak around using daenox when he was there. He was too well tuned to the daenox and to her in particular. Since there was no point pretending, she walked out from the horse line and returned to the campfire. She sat down in her previous spot. Kovial followed her example after a few seconds.

"What if they don't come?" They were hard words to say. It was her greatest fear, and she did not want to acknowledge it.

"The dragons?" Kovial turned to Rakas. "Yes. What if..." He trailed off when Rakas held up a hand.

"That's why we're here. If the dragons don't come, we will have to find a way to get Raine out of Elysium."

"No." When they looked at her, she stared back, more than willing to fight over this part. "I don't want anyone else coming in there if the dragons don't come." She turned her attention fully on Rakas then. "You said yourself, he won't hurt me."

Rakas gave her a stern look. She could feel the argument slipping out of her control even before he even opened his mouth. "Only as long as he thinks you might side with him. How far are you willing to go to convince him of that?" His words began gaining volume and intensity as he spoke. "Will you let him use your power? Will you let him see how strong you're becoming? Will you raise the dead for him? What if he wants you to hurt someone? To torture someone? Could you kill an innocent person just to save yourself?"

Raine flinched back from him. "Stop it!"

But Rakas did not. He stood and moved closer to her. "Stop what? Pointing out the flaws in your reasoning? Questioning your strategies?"

"Yes!" The scream choked off, turning into a sob. She put her hands over her ears, trying not to hear him. She should not have let him come. She should have known he could not be trusted.

"I won't stop. I owe your father that much at least." His voice cracked. When she looked up, tears were running down his cheeks, sparkling in the cold moonlight. "I will let you go in there only because I believe you can help the people who matter to you and mattered to him. But I won't leave you to die in there or, worse yet, be broken by that bastard."

She could only stare at Rakas then. What was she supposed to say to that? She could not forgive him for what he had done to Dephithus. For all that he had tried to back out at the last minute, he had come to her father's Dawning Day with a purpose. An evil purpose. There was no value in punishing him for it though. He punished himself for it, berating himself mentally every moment of every day. She could see it in his perpetually haunted gaze, and if she let herself, she could feel it through the daenox.

"For what it's worth," Kovial said into the awkward silence, "I agree with Rakas on this."

The words broke through their locked gazes, and Rakas turned away. He busied himself setting up his bedroll near the fire. The only thing he said for the rest of the evening was a curt goodnight before pulling his blanket over the cloak he had wrapped snuggly around himself.

Raine and Kovial followed his example. Raine summoned a daemon-wolf to the camp and bound her influence over it so that it would keep watch and wake her if anyone or anything threatening approached. That would allow them all to get a reasonable rest before heading out again.

For a long time, she lay awake staring up at the stars. She loved the stars, gleaming overhead like gems of water on the ceiling of the cave, glittering in daenox light. Seeing the stars like this meant the night was clear and therefore colder, but she was willing to suffer a little for the tradeoff.

Rakas was not wrong. She knew that. There would be limits to how far she could go to pretend to side with Kyouin. She only had to look at the destruction he had wrought and the diseased warriors and undead who followed him to know that. He destroyed life, making a mockery of it without any hint of remorse. It was not just Kyouin either. Theruses appeared to be working with him, and she knew that Theruses had no qualms about making others suffer for his desires.

If the dragons did not come, she could foresee no good outcome. The world would suffer until the daenox reached the dragons. By then, it might be too late for them to turn things around. She hoped they would be smart enough to realize that.

Siniva had spoken truthfully. As they soared high above the landscape, he radiated heat out from his body that kept Darkin warmer than when he was sitting by the campfire in his heavy cloak. The only downside was that this comfort meant Darkin noticed the discomfort of his seat more. He was willing to make the trade to keep his fingers and toes from freezing off. Raine had not expressly said that she preferred him with all his parts attached, but he did not care to risk it.

According to Siniva, they would reach the coast to-day. Darkin could see the ocean now. At least he thought that slightly darker line of grey-blue meeting up against the dark clouds on the horizon was the ocean. It was hard to tell with the wind from their speed creating a constant stream of tears from his eyes. Around the campfire last night, Siniva said they would also find the dragons to-day. He told Darkin he knew that because he could feel them through the web. He made a point of emphasizing his connection to the dragon web several times through-out the conversation. His pleasure at being able to be a dragon again and connected to the dragon web had be-come almost palpable. Soaring through the sky all day appeared to lift his spirits considerably.

Perhaps, now that he was a much happier Fire Drag-on, he would not mind Darkin's interest in Raine so much, though Darkin thought he might wait until after they had a hopefully successful meeting with the dragons to test that theory.

One second, they were soaring through the sky, the next there was a violent, jarring impact, and they were tumbling in a spinning freefall that had his stomach instantly lodged somewhere around his back teeth. The roar Siniva let loose then was full of rage and something else. Something that sounded to Darkin distinctly like despair.

Darkin could do nothing to help himself or Siniva. He was tied to the Fire Dragon's back, so he at least did not fall off, but what he could make out in the chaos of their falling was that another dragon, an emaciated red one that looked disturbingly familiar, had latched on to Siniva from below and was trying to get in a lethal strike. The most unsettling thing was that the other red dragon did not make a sound as Siniva roared and struggled to break free of it. His thrashing confused Darkin as well. It seemed more like he was trying to extract himself rather than fight back while the other dragon bit and clawed at him.

Then Darkin caught a glimpse of the other beast's neck as they continued to spiral downward, and he noticed the gaping open wounds there. Another fleeting glimpse of the dragon's face revealed matte grey eyes. It was then that he understood. This was Vanuthan. This was Siniva's companion brought back from the dead by the bastard they all wanted to send to his death. Siniva clearly did not want to hurt her, but he had to know she was beyond being hurt.

"Siniva!" He screamed as loud as he could, knowing the sound was going to get lost in the rushing of air and the racket Siniva was making. "It's not Vanuthan! Not anymore! Siniva!"

If the Fire Dragon did not fight back, they were both going to die. The undead dragon's claws and teeth had opened wounds on Siniva's shoulders, much too close to where Darkin was sitting, and along his neck. None were deep enough yet to kill, but only because Siniva's twisting about had prevented her from getting a good strike in so far. Siniva was going to fall to his death because he could not bring himself to hurt the dragon he remembered her to be, and he was going to take Darkin with him.

And Raine will be left to face Kyouin without us. Without the dragons.

"Siniva! Raine needs us!" Darkin screamed again, so hard this time that his throat and chest hurt from the effort. He punched at the base of the Fire Dragon's neck, bloodying his knuckles against unyielding scales. "I won't let you fail her!"

Siniva's roar then was full of so much anguish that it brought tears to Darkin's eyes, tears that were whipped away from his face by the force of the wind. Somehow, he must have heard Darkin's screams for he began to fight back, ripping and tearing at the undead dragon. Intense heat began to rise off him, becoming almost painfully hot, before a billow of flame erupted from his mouth, setting one of the other dragon's wings on fire. The undead Vanuthan began flailing, unable to keep herself aloft on her own with the damaged wing, but she kept hold of Siniva, her claws dug deep into his sides, dragging him down with her.

The Fire Dragon fought harder. Vanuthan lost her grip on one side, twisting in the air. Her long tail swept around and struck Darkin a glancing blow to the head that plummeted him into darkness.

*

If there was one thing Darkin was sure of when he struggled up from the inky blackness that clung to him, it was that never, in the entire history of headaches, had there been such a potent headache as this. He knew full well that the pathetic moans he heard were coming from his own mouth. He wanted to stop them because the noise made the headache worse, but he could not seem to control it.

"Will he live?"

The deep voice was agony to his pounding skull, but the melodic voice that answered was as soothing as the other was painful.

"If you will move aside, Colvan, and allow us to work, he will. Let Kalphana put him back to sleep. Then I can do more for him."

Darkin tried to open his eyes but letting in even the tiniest bit of light made it feel like someone was trying to split his head in two with a dull hatchet.

Something rested over him like a heavy blanket. It was warm. That deep yet melodic voice began humming softly next to his head. The sound eased the pain, not only in his head but other pains he had not noticed until they started to fade. He felt the blanket growing heavier. Or was he growing heavier? It did not matter. He let the weight draw him down, sinking him into darkness again, but this time it was a peaceful, welcoming darkness.

*

When Darkin awoke again, the voices were back, or perhaps they had never left.

"You saw the other... beast. Who would do such a thing?"

"That was Vanuthan, Colvan, not some beast. One of our own defiled with daemon power."

Darkin opened his eyes. Not much could compare to the disorientation he felt when he found himself looking up at the heads of five dragons that stood conversing over him. It was unsetting, and yet, even feeling as small and vulnerable as he did, a rush of childlike wonder swept the fear from him.

"That thing might have been Vanuthan once," the biggest of the five dragons, his hide a gleaming silvery-charcoal color, emphasized his words with a growl. "Whatever she was in life, she was dead long before Siniva took her down."

"Fortunate for him," this one was a slightly smaller bronze dragon, perhaps the second largest in the group. "I imagine we won't need to punish him for turning on his own kind under these circumstances."

A dragon with brilliant blue scales tilted its head down, stunning pearlescent eyes gazing down on him for a moment. Its mouth curved in what Darkin hoped was a smile before it looked around at the others again.

"The man is awake now. Perhaps he can help explain what happened."

The dragons moved back so they could look at him. Darkin started to sit up and another dragon, this one with scales the same beautiful pearlescent white as the blue one's eyes, lowered its head down next to him.

"Slowly now," the feminine voice advised, "you were badly injured."

"Don't mother him, Rythis."

This voice, though tight with pain, was very familiar, and relief flooded Darkin. He turned toward the speaker and saw Siniva, in his dragon form, limping gingerly toward them. The Fire Dragon's bronze-red hide was riddled with deep gashes that were still raw and in need of much healing. He looked awful.

"You shouldn't be moving around," the white dragon, Rythis, snapped at him. "Your wounds are deep and will break open."

"I won't be excluded," Siniva snapped back.

"Back off, Siniva," a booming voice demanded from somewhere behind Darkin.

Turning he saw yet another dragon, this one scaled in violet and blue, with massive horns curved down on either side of its head. Its eyes were the same vibrant color as its scales. The others moved aside to clear a path for the magnificent creature. Even the larger charcoal dragon stepped back and inclined its head deferentially.

"R'Gos," Siniva also inclined his head, grimacing as the movement pulled on raw wounds.

"What happened to Vanuthan?" R'Gos asked, his gaze on Darkin now. "We felt her rejoin the web and then felt her torn away from it again a few hours later. Now she attacks you with intent to kill not far from our sanctuary, and I'm told she was dead long before she did so. Killing one of our own kind is a vile offense that requires decisive action. However, this is an unusual case."

Siniva kept his head slightly inclined as he started to speak. "Vanuthan—"

"Not you," R'Gos interrupted. "I want the man to speak."

Darkin's head was starting to hurt again. He finished sitting up and faced the impressive dragon, determined not to show his weakness when it mattered this much. He had to be strong, for Raine.

"Vanuthan was killed by another dragon in Imperious. A gold dragon."

"Theruses," Rythis hissed.

There were soft growls from several of the other dragons.

"Perhaps she was, but even the Death Dragon doesn't have the power to animate the dead," R'Gos stated. "How did she come to be here?"

Darkin was not sure he believed that Theruses could not raise the dead. The Death Dragon, from Raine's account, had considerable abilities with the daenox, which was what Kyouin used to raise his undead. For now, however, it did not matter. He was confident Kyouin was behind this particular raising of the dead.

"A man took over Imperious leading an army of warriors, daemons, and undead. He animated her corpse after Theruses took her down and sent her after us." To be fair, he did not know that for certain. The pieces of the puzzle fit together well enough that he was willing to stand behind the supposition even under the scrutiny of a ring of dragons.

The other dragons made sounds of anger and outrage, but none spoke. They deferred respectfully to R'Gos who turned and walked away from them, his violet and blue scales rippling hypnotically in the grey light of a bright but overcast sky. He stopped a short distance away, staring off toward the ocean.

Darkin looked beyond the big dragon and noticed the wall of sheer cliffs that dropped off into the raging waters below. Waves crashed against those cliffs, creating a constant barrage of rumblings in the distance. They weren't far from the edge of the cliffs, in a large green meadow surrounded on three sides by rocky crags. Even more dragons filled that meadow and perched upon those crags. A massive cave entrance opened in the side of the crags opposite the cliffs, perhaps six dragons high and half as wide. There were carvings of dragons chiseled out of the rock around the meadow, most of them worked into the stone around the entrance of the cave.

R'Gos lashed his massive tail then, the movement so fast and fierce that Darkin startled. The dragon spun around and flared out his wings, stretching them wide. He let out an earsplitting sound then, somewhere between a roar and a deafening bark. He repeated that sound three times. Darkin covered his ears, desperate to spare his recovering head the torture.

As R'Gos strode back to them, more dragons appeared, emerging from the cave and flying in from outside of the meadow.

R'Gos looked from Darkin to Siniva, then back again. "Why have you come here, human?"

As wobbly as he felt, Darkin forced himself to stand and face the dragon. This was for Raine and for himself and for all the people of their lands. "I came because the man who did this is wreaking havoc upon our lands and killing our people with his daemon army. The daenox he wields is spreading sickness throughout Imperious and the surrounding regions. Right now, Raine, the dragon-child you created, is heading back to Elysium to face him alone, to try and stop the destruction you are allowing to spread through our lands."

R'Gos started to growl then, and Darkin held up a hand.

"I know humankind committed an unforgivable act of betrayal against the dragons, but that happened a long time ago. Letting the daenox kill so many of us now will only convince us we were right to do so. And when it is done devastating our population, it will come for the dragons. Now is the time to make a new alliance and heal the wounds between humankind and dragons."

"The daenox will be exceptionally strong when it comes," Siniva spoke into Darkin's brief pause. "With nothing to keep it in check, it is spreading and thriving and gaining power. The army Kyouin leads will grow stronger as well. If it is to be stopped without significant losses, it needs to be stopped now."

R'Gos tilted his head slightly, focusing in on Siniva.

Another dragon moved up next to Siniva then, his hide a shimmering turquoise green. He was longer and more sinuous than most of the other dragons, with webbing between his toes and behind his forelegs. He almost looked like a creature that would be more at home in the water.

"Siniva is young, R'Gos, but he has suffered for our freedom. He has earned the right to be heard."

R'Gos inclined his head slightly to the newcomer. "Cyrsyth speaks truly." His gaze swept the gathering then. "Regardless of what we decide to do, Theruses must be punished for Vanuthan's death, and this man you speak of," his gaze came back to Darkin, his eyes lighting with a menacing gleam, "must be punished for desecrating her corpse."

Hope lifted Darkin, easing the throb in his skull.

R'Gos started to turn toward the cave. "The Council must meet."

That hope dropped out from under him so fast he almost fell over. "No! We can't waste time."

The other dragons ignored him, but Rythis lowered her head in front of him. "You must be patient."

He met her eye. "How long have we been here already?"

"A few days. It took time to heal you both, and Siniva will need more healing before he can fly."

"But we…" Darkin trailed off when a hand came to rest on his shoulder. He glanced over to see Siniva there in his human form. His fiery eyes were glazed with pain.

"The dragons won't act without the Council's decision. If we want their help, we have to abide by their rules."

Darkin turned to watch several of the dragons disappear into the darkness of the cave. He wanted to run after them, to tell them Raine needed them now, but he was no dragon. He would have to follow their rules if he wanted their help. He did not have to like it though.

CHAPTER THIRTY EIGHT

For Raine, riding into Elysium alone was as hard, if not harder, than stepping into the daylight for the first time after years living as a prisoner in the darkness of the cave. For a full two days after they arrived and set camp in the forest outside the city, she managed to put off going in, using daenox to cautiously observe Kyouin through his daemons in a way he was unlikely to notice. By noon of the third day, she could feel the group following behind them closing in. Once Suva and Kayd arrived, she would have an even harder time getting away, so she struck out for Elysium.

It might have been easier with Hydra as her companion, but she would not risk the stallion, so she had taken Kovial's mount and left Hydra with him. Kovial would treat him well if she never came back. When she came within sight of the outer gate, she spotted four daemon-dogs and four warriors stationed there. By the time she stopped before the warriors, the daemon-dogs had come to her, two on each side, baring their teeth in warning at the warriors. The daemons were easy to turn, and the warriors were wary but quick to acknowledge her.

"You're the one he's expecting, aren't you? Storm or River or something like that," one of the warriors ventured.

She took a deep breath and made herself scowl down at the man, trying not to see the sores that oozed on his face. "Raine."

"That's it!" He stepped aside, gesturing for the others to do the same. "I'll escort you to the palace."

The idea of going anywhere with him repulsed her. "That won't be necessary. The beasts will escort me."

The man started to step toward her, "I think…"

He trailed off when the daemon-dogs stepped to intercept him, all four growling and baring their teeth at him.

"I think that's reasonable," he stated, stepping back away from her, his eyes on the daemons.

The encounter at the inner gate went much the same. Soon she was heading up the road toward the palace with an escort of four daemon-dogs, three daemon-wolves, and a massive catlike creature with a set of spikes running down its spine that ended in a macelike ball at the end of its tail. She made her way at a casual pace up the road, trying not to let any of the warriors, undead, and beasts along the way see how terrified she was riding through their domain. In her mind, memories of the battle she had witnessed here, of the blood and carnage, warred with her parents' memories of this place.

For once, her parents' memories were the ones she chose to focus on. Myara and Dephithus racing each other to the stable for practice or tumbling down a grassy hill and laughing together. Practicing in the various arenas. Growing up in a happy place where peace had reigned for their entire lives. There were less pleasant memories from after the daemon-seed was placed in her father, but she managed to hold those back, even when she rode past the place Amahna and Rakas had taken Dephithus to commit the vile act.

Her escort acquired another member, this one much less welcome. The undead warrior on his undead horse rode over from beside one of the stables. He made no move to interfere, only followed along, his teeth constantly clicking as if he would speak, but could no longer manage it. There was no way to discourage him without engaging directly with him, so Raine made a point of not looking at him and, more importantly, not feeling him with the daenox.

What would happen when she reached the palace? Would she have to ask to see Kyouin? There was something unsavory about the idea of requesting to see him when seeing him was really the last thing she wanted to do.

When they got up near the entrance to the gardens in front of the palace, Raine dismounted. She sent most of her escort away, intending to keep only two of the daemon-wolves to take with her beyond that point. She considered bringing the cat-beast as well, but it was so large it seemed inappropriate to take it indoors.

The cat-beast yawned when she turned to it, displaying massive upper canines that still jutted out around its lips when it shut its mouth again. Then it hissed and snapped at a fly that dared to try to land on Raine's arm. She placed a hand on the black daemon-cat's head and stroked her fingers along the short black fur there. The daemon pressed into her hand, making a deep rumble in its throat that she was reasonably certain was a purr.

Raine smiled faintly. It was the best she could muster under the circumstances. "Certainly, a palace has halls big enough to accommodate you, my friend."

Decided, she walked into the front garden with the daemon-cat and two daemon-wolves as her escort. It was not much, considering all Kyouin had here, but it made her feel a bit less out of control. The undead warrior did not follow, which also helped her maintain at least an outward appearance of calm.

When she walked up to the front entrance, the guards there inclined their heads and opened the doors, making no effort to stop her or her companions. That they were expecting and welcoming her only served to fray her nerves even more. Undoubtedly that was what Kyouin was hoping for. Even knowing that, she could not stop the expanding knot of fear in her gut.

The halls of the palace, so magnificent in her parents' memories, were dingy and dark. Only perhaps half of the sconces were lit, and dirt tracked in from outside had been left to accumulate. There was even a musty smell that reminded her of well-trod soil. This had never been her home, but it had been her father's. A refreshing swell of outrage rose in her, taking away some of the power of her fear.

A smaller, almost normal looking hunting dog entered the hall from a side corridor. When it looked at her, she noted the matte grey eyes. It might look normal, but it was daenox infected. It whined softly and took a few steps down the hall, then turned back and looked at her expectantly.

Kyouin had sent her an escort.

Raine wanted to turn the creature, to free it from Kyouin's influence, but she needed to confront the man eventually. Dragging it out would only make her more nervous. Placing a hand on the comforting shoulder of the cat-beast next to her, she started after the dog. As soon as she moved that direction, the dog turned to lead them down the hall.

They turned several more times until they came to a hall that was cleaner than the rest. Partway down was a set of guarded double doors. The dog stopped here, and the two guards offered Raine a slight bow. These two looked healthy. They were perhaps resistant to the daenox. She nodded back, and they opened the doors for her.

The room she walked into was large with almost no furnishings. It was an indoor training room for teaching the courtly art of ballroom dancing. Both of her parents had learned to dance here, and the joy of those memories clashed with the way she felt at seeing Kyouin standing in the center. Several of his undead warriors stood at attention along the walls.

Raine entered with her small escort of daemons. She could not stop a flinch when the door slammed shut behind them.

Kyouin was dressed in much finer attire now, though his color choices remained rather drab ivory and shades of brown with some very subtle gold embroidered accents on the jacket lapels and cuffs.

He came forward with a smile, not even glancing at the creatures she brought with her. "Raine, I'm so glad you could come."

Tendrils of daenox bearing his presence wove up into her daemons.

She met his eyes, giving a small shake of her head. "Don't."

The daenox retreated.

She acknowledged this with a curt nod. "Where are they?"

"They're fine. I have some other people here I think you'll be happy to see." He turned away and nodded to one of the undead near a door in the left wall of the room.

When the door opened, another guard came through with Nakia walking behind him. Raine felt like someone had punched her in the gut as she watched the rest of Fools Errant filing in behind her. She was not happy to see them. She could hardly be less happy. Kyouin had managed to acquire so many of the few people that meant something to her. He had the upper hand here, and there was not much she could do about it.

The last man to file through the door was not a member of Fools Errant, but Raine knew him. Only from memory, of course. It was Lornin, Dephithus's blood father. Her grandfather. He looked healthy, strong, and angry. She could not ask how he came to be with them under the circumstances, but he appeared to know something about the situation from the intense scrutinizing look he gave her.

None of them said anything.

Kyouin turned to Raine, his smile broad and open as if he genuinely believed this would make her happy.

"Send them away," Raine demanded, "I don't want them here."

Kyouin's smile faltered. "They're your friends."

"Exactly."

A shadow dropped over his features then. His gift to her had been a disappointment, and it broke his pleasant façade. "I can't. Not yet. Perhaps, once we have talked a bit and come to an agreement."

Raine clenched her teeth to fight back tears. She could not appear weak before him, but the situation felt hopeless. "I want to see Mythan and my grandparents."

"Soon."

"Now."

Kyouin nodded, but he looked angry now. Raine wondered if she had pushed too far. Diplomacy was apparently not her strong suit. Nothing was, if she thought about it. Nothing but amusing daemons with light shows of daenox.

Kyouin motioned one of the guards over and murmured something to him. The guard nodded and left the room.

"What do you want from me?" Raine asked.

How was she going to get all these people out of his hands? How was she supposed to deny him anything he wanted while he had them?

Kyouin brought his smile back, though it seemed less genuine now. "The world is changing, Raine. Those who can't handle the daenox will die off. Those of us who can, will become the new custodians of this world. You and I, together, could help this change along. We can control it and build a world of people who are like us. People who understand us and don't fear us."

Raine stared at him, trying to figure out if he was serious. Did he really think this was a good idea that others would flock to? "I don't have a lot of experience, but if you're doing all of this to make friends, I think you're going about it wrong."

Kyouin scowled at her, not appreciating the humor. "I'm talking about building a world where we are no longer the freaks and monsters. I'm offering to make you a part of that."

Fresh anger flooded her, making her face hot. "Have you looked at me? I will always be a freak and a monster." She could feel the eyes of the troop members on her. Some of them would agree with the statement, though Nakia, who was the only one currently visible in her periphery, scowled and shook her head in firm disagreement.

Kyouin took several quick steps toward her. The daemon-cat hissed at him. He only gave the beast a passing glance before fixing her in his gaze. "You are magnificent, Raine. You are beautiful and powerful and unique," he emphasized each word with a squeezing of his fist. "There is no one else like you in all the world. You are truly special. You deserve to be appreciated for all that you are and all that you could be. Anyone who thinks otherwise doesn't deserve to be in your presence."

Raine could only stare at him for a few seconds, taken aback by the admiration in his gaze and the passion behind his words. Did he honestly think so much of her? Why would he torment her the way he had if those words were true?

"Do you believe all that?"

"With every fiber of my being, yes. Everyone should yearn to be what you are."

He took another step closer, and she placed a hand on the daemon-cat's shoulder to quiet the beast, setting the daemon-wolves at ease with a soothing touch of daenox.

"But you killed Vanuthan," she stated, grasping at something to put between them.

His jaw clenched. Smoldering hatred made his expression hard. "No. Theruses did that on his own to try to turn you against me. I swear I had no part in her death."

She searched his eyes, looking for the lie in them, but he seemed sincere. "If you truly think so much of me, let the others go. You and I can work this out together."

Kyouin looked, at that moment, like a puppy that thought it had found a home. She could almost imagine him wagging his tail. He glanced over his shoulder at the troubadours, and hope blossomed in her chest. He heard her request and was considering it. Maybe this would work.

Then the door in the side opened. The guard he had sent for her grandparents stepped in alone. His uneasy glance at her made her stomach drop like a stone. Kyouin met him halfway and they began to speak in hushed voices. Raine drew on a tiny fragment of daenox to pull their voices to her.

"Where are they?"

"My lord, there's a problem."

Raine felt a spike of cold fear stabbing painfully through the bloom of hope in her chest. It was suddenly harder to breathe.

"What problem?" Kyouin demanded, his voice rising enough that she could almost hear him without the daenox.

"Well, we thought the palace servants were taking care of them. You know, bringing them food and water, but... well, it turns out they weren't."

Raine was starting to feel like she might be sick.

"And?" Kyouin prompted.

"Well, they're dead. All three of them."

"Imbeciles," Kyouin shouted, and a thrust of daenox sent the guard flying across the room. He slammed into a wall and slid lifeless to the floor.

Raine did not look at the guard. Her eyes burned with hot tears. She pulled daenox into her, letting it ride through her on the storm of rage and sorrow. Her daemons charged and she threw the power at Kyouin, meaning to break his body with force the way he had broken the guard, but he was quick to react, drawing a sturdy, semitransparent barrier of daenox up between them. One of the daemon-wolves hit the barrier and fell to the floor with a cry. The animal convulsed there for several seconds, whimpering as blood ran out its nose and ears. Then it was still. Her other two daemons cowered back from it.

Raine started frantically testing the barrier with daenox, looking for a way to dissipate it, until cries of alarm and outrage drew her attention to the troubadours. Kyouin stood with one arm outstretched, the hand cupped as if holding something. In a direct line from his hand, Myrza was hanging suspended in the air, making small choking noises. Her face was already starting to turn red. The barrier Kyouin erected now blocked Raine and the others off from him and Myrza.

Raine drew back the daenox she had been using against the barrier and took a step closer to it. "Let her go."

Kyouin shook his head. "I'm sorry. It's clear that you're going to need more convincing. For now, I'll take her with me. We'll talk again when you've had time to calm down and realize this wasn't my fault."

Kyouin started rotating the barrier so that it forced the others away from the door they had entered through. He lowered Myrza and took her through the door ahead of him.

"No!"

Raine's shout was ignored. The door slammed shut behind him. The barrier rotated the rest of the way, blocking them all from the door. Then it spread around the room, cutting them off from the other door as well and trapping them in with his undead warriors.

Raine sank to her knees. She was a fool to come here. The people she had come to save were dead, and now others were at risk because of her. Nakia started to walk over to her, but the daemon-cat stepped between them and the surviving daemon-wolf growled. Raine put an arm around the neck of the cat-beast and wept into its soft black fur.

CHAPTER THIRTY NINE

No matter how he tried to look at it, things had not gone well with Raine. There had to be a way to fix it.

Kyouin dropped Myrza in a corner of his private rooms. She crumpled there, holding her throat, making wretched choking noises as she struggled for air. He waited, watching her.

This woman cared about Raine. He had figured that out by her response when he mentioned Raine the day they were brought here. She was also someone Raine cared about given her reaction a moment ago. Perhaps she would have some insight into how to fix this fiasco. He was not ready to let Theruses prove him wrong yet, especially not because some incompetent fools failed to consider that his prisoners might need to eat and drink. He needed to find the guards he had ordered to lock them up and make an example of them. As their leader, it did not seem unreasonable to expect that they could handle the relatively simple process of keeping prisoners alive without him having to guide them through it. If they had been undead, the oversight might have been understandable. It was a good thing he had given Fools Errant some freedom to wander Elysium, or they might be wasting away in a room somewhere too.

Myrza had stopped choking and was now breathing more normally. He leaned out the door and sent someone to bring wine and glasses. If he wanted her to help him, he needed to try to smooth this mess over first. Or he could just force the issue, but that was risky. If Raine learned that he had treated her any worse than he already had, she was not going to come around anytime soon.

He needed to figure something out quickly. Right now, he was using Vinya's body as a source of power to keep the shield up around the room. Vinya had not woken yet. The stress of the power he forced into her had placed her in a coma, though she appeared otherwise healthy, which was encouraging. He had someone caring for her around the clock, which was apparently what he should have done for Raine's grandparents. As long as Vinya remained unconscious, the shield could draw off the daenox in her, but if she woke up, things could get messy.

Myrza was sitting up with her head against the wall, her eyes closed. An occasional tear slipped out to run down the side of her face into her hair.

"I'm sorry about that."

Myrza choked a laugh. A few more tears ran down her cheeks. She did not open her eyes. Kyouin took advantage of the moment to look her over. There was something slightly off about her that caught his attention. She had a surreal beauty that was almost more boyish than womanish. She did not really have pronounced feminine curves, and he rather liked that about her. Now that he really looked at her, he found himself becoming aroused, which was not going to help his current situation.

There was a light knock on the door. The wine arriving at the perfect time. He left her there for a few minutes while he collected the wine and poured from the decanter. Carrying one glass with him, he walked over to crouch down in front of her.

"This might help."

Myrza opened her eyes. Her gaze touched on the wine glass then moved up to his eyes. "I hope your daemon army rips you apart one little piece at a time while you scream and beg for your life."

He drew in a calming breath. She was not very receptive to his efforts. Begging was not in his repertoire. He had begged on the streets for his mother for almost a year. He would never beg for anything again.

Calm.

"I deserve that." He held the wine glass a little closer. "Things went very wrong back there. Raine is powerful. I didn't know what she might do, so I panicked. I didn't intend to hurt anyone."

Myrza scowled at him, but she reached out and took the wine this time.

"I need to fix this. You know her. What can I do to make this better?"

Myrza sipped the wine. then she smiled at him. It was not a friendly smile. "You know what I said about your daemons ripping you apart. I bet she'd like to watch that."

Kyouin felt his hold on his temper slipping away. If he went back in that room without this woman, he would never win Raine over.

"Is there anything I can do to make this up to you?"

"You don't get to make up almost choking someone to death," Myrza snapped. "I would rather die than help you win Raine over."

There was loathing in her eyes. Judgment and disgust. She was no different than anyone else. She would never understand.

She's just like Father.

Daenox rushed through him, welcoming and warm. He lifted her by the throat again, this time with his hand. He used the daenox to give him strength and slammed her head back, cracking it hard against the wall. The wine glass fell from her hand, breaking with the delicate crack of fine glass and spraying red across the marble floor. Her eyes rolled back. Her body twitched a few times in futile protest, but she was unconscious from the blow to the head long before she stopped breathing. He threw her down in the puddle of spilled wine and broken glass and stared at her, watching her face for any signs of life. Blood from the back of her head mingled with the wine. There was blood on the wall too, a rivulet of it running down toward the floor.

This day really was not going his way.

Raine needed to understand that Myrza and the others were not like them. It was better this way. Better that they die rather than suffer in the world he was creating. She was not going to understand that though. She was too young. Too naive. Perhaps the answer was not to win her over, but to keep her here until she saw the truth for herself. Sometimes, teaching required a firm hand.

Kyouin leaned out the door and sent for someone to clean up the mess he had made. Then he poured himself a glass of wine and settled down into one of the luxurious beige chairs that sat around the table. He took a long drink.

For the moment, he would leave Raine with the others behind his barrier. He needed to think.

*

Raine did not indulge her rage and sorrow for long. The voices of others in the room reminded her that there were people here who needed her help. Although her help had not proved to be that useful for her grandparents or Myrza. Most of Fools Errant was in this room and very much alive along with her blood grandfather. She was not sure if she dared to acknowledge Lornin in any way, however, with the undead warriors looking on. She did not know how much they understood or how much they could relate back to Kyouin.

She made herself stand up, calming the remaining two daemons and getting them to settle on the floor so the remaining members of Fools Errant and Lornin could approach.

"You do have his defiance… and perhaps some of his features," Lornin stated, looking her over.

Raine only stared at him. She did not dare say anything to prove their kinship. Mythan and Myara's parents were dead. Dead because someone forgot to provide them with basic needs. They had been neglected to death. Just thinking about it made her feel sick again. Rakas was right. She could not go far at all to convince Kyouin she was on his side. Not now.

Nakia stepped forward then. "I see you didn't bring my other fire dancer back with you."

"He's…" Raine glanced around at the undead warriors again and amended her response. "We parted ways a while back."

Nakia inclined her head, her gaze flickering to one of the undead to show that she understood the problem. "That's a shame." She gestured to Lornin. "This is our newest member, Ahric."

Raine nodded to him, appreciating that she had a name to call him by now. "A pleasure." She turned to the door she had entered through. "I'll find Myrza." she stated, reaching into the barrier with careful tendrils of daemon power. "My daemons will help you if you get in trouble."

"How will you get out?" Lornin asked. "You saw what happened to the beast."

Raine made a point of not looking at the poor dead daemon-wolf. She began to pull from daenox in the barrier, drawing that power into herself and replacing what she took with daemon power of her own. If the power in her and that in the barrier matched closely enough, she should be able to move through it. At least she hoped so.

Raine started toward the door.

Nakia grabbed her arm. "Whatever you're trying, perhaps you could use the other daemon-wolf to test it first?"

Raine did look at the dead wolf now. It had died quickly but in great pain. She met Nakia's eyes, knowing her own eyes would be glowing with that ring of violet now that she had drawn so much of the daenox into herself. Nakia withdrew her hand and stepped back. Raine started toward the door again. Her hand shook as she brought it up to the barrier, her stomach clenching with fear. The undead warriors did not move. Whatever orders Kyouin had given to allow her to enter Elysium unhindered were apparently still working in her favor. She reached through the barrier to the door. Pain sparked along her skin as her hand and arm passed through. She clenched her teeth against it.

Opening the door, she rushed through the barrier. The pain took her breath away, but it did not seem to do any lasting damage. Once she was through, she glanced back into the room, seeing the others through the blurry violet haze of the barrier. The guards outside the room looked a bit surprised to see her there, but they still did nothing to impede her passage.

Now that she was outside of it, she could feel the power maintaining the barrier coming from the next room down. That mean Kyouin must be there and Myrza might be with him, though the door they had exited the room from was on the opposite side.

I can't attack him.

She reminded herself of that several times. Her initial attack had been born of pure rage. If she followed through and he retaliated, she and the others here would most likely die for it. Somehow, she had to set aside her hatred until she could get the others out of here or at least distract him until the dragons could get here… if they were really coming. She had to trust Darkin and Siniva to succeed or she would lose hope and do something reckless.

Raine walked to the door of the next room. How was she supposed to be civil after what he had done? This man had allowed her grandparents to die. She focused on the people in the next room; Fools Errant and her grandfather. Myrza also needed her to be calm and rational. If he had killed Myrza, however, how could she hope to contain the hatred and rage?

The answer was all around and in her. The daenox and the dragon web. Raine let the power she had drawn from the barrier flow out of her and pulled on power from deep in the ground. Dragon power and daenox that did not taste of Kyouin's influence. She let it flow through her. The two powers were like an electrical storm inside her at first, but she wove it together, making it into something new. Some peaceful balance of the powers that calmed her, giving her the strength to go forward.

She faced the door. It was her responsibility to protect the people in the next room and Myrza. That was important. That was why she had to keep things under control until the dragons arrived. Remembering that she was needed kept her focused. With the confidence the powers gave her, Raine stepped up to the door and opened it.

What she found in the room, however, was nothing like what she had expected. Kyouin was not there. Nor was Myrza. It was a large bedroom with a fancy canopied bed in the center, maroon curtains tied to the posts. In the middle of the bed lay a young girl in a purple dress, her long, dark hair smoothed down around her. She did not stir when Raine entered, and the power flowing out to the barrier was coming from her. The child was overflowing with daemon-power, but not power she controlled. The power reeked of Kyouin.

Raine walked up to the bed to stare at the young girl, trying to make sense of what she was seeing. The girl's face was streaked with the dry salt of her tears. She twitched and moaned softly now and then, as though trapped in a nightmare.

After a few minutes, Raine turned to face Kyouin where he stood in the doorway now, his presence betrayed by the power that flowed through him.

"What is this?"

His eyes narrowed a touch, as though suspicious of her calm.

Raine patiently waited for his answer.

After perhaps a minute of uncertainty, he moved into the room, walking up alongside the bed. He gazed down at the girl as a parent might look upon their sleeping newborn. "Her name's Vinya, I'm helping her become like us. She's the first to show any promise."

"How long has she been like this?"

He set his jaw and looked up at Raine. "A while, but she shows no sign of the sickness. She could be the first of many to join us."

"If this is the future, it will certainly be quiet."

Kyouin's chuckle faltered when she did not smile. He gave her another wary look. She could feel him reaching into her with daenox. She shoved the power away, giving him a hard glare.

"Where's Myrza?"

At this question, Kyouin appeared to relax, his shoulders sinking down away from his ears. "She's returning to the others as we speak. I didn't mean to hurt her. If you hadn't…"

A slight narrowing of her eyes was apparently enough to convince him he should not finish that sentence. "Show me that she's safe and we can talk. That is what you want, isn't it?"

He nodded, but his expression hardened. "We talk first. Then I'll let the others out, and you can spend as much time with them as you like."

She breathed in, glancing at the girl on the bed. This girl was another of the people she needed to save. Right now, however, she needed to buy them time. The brilliant light of the blended powers inside her was not enough. Her parents laughing as they raced down the hall outside this room in her memories, gave her what she needed to move forward.

"All right. We'll talk first."

Kyouin gave her another of those worried looks, his shoulders tightening up again. "Follow me." His steps faltered when he moved to walk away from her. He glanced over his shoulder, his gaze straying briefly to the sword at her hip as though worried she might come at him from behind.

It was not really a bad idea, but now was not the time. If such an attack failed, there would be no one to stop him from taking his rage out on the others. Now was the time to be calculating and patient.

There were a lot of things Raine did not have much experience with, even given the advantage of her parents' memories. Wine was one of those things. When she woke the next morning with a roiling gut and a hammer pounding its way out of her head, she thought, for a few minutes, that she might have been poisoned. A little creative application of power from the dragon web, using something she had learned from watching Rakas heal with daenox, allowed her to calm things down enough that she realized her condition likely had more to do with an abundance of wine than any deliberate attempt at poisoning.

That was not to say there was nothing deliberate in Kyouin's generous refilling of her wine glass throughout the evening, but he had not held her mouth open and forced her to drink it. She had done that on her own to help calm her nerves. Typically, she would have used daenox for that, but she limited her connection to the daemon power while in his presence because, while it did allow her to keep tabs on his activities, it also connected them in a way that felt much too intimate.

Maintaining a minimal daenox connection and using the dragon web to help her keep her wits about her, she was able to imbibe far more than she might have otherwise without feeling the full effect until now.

Now she stared at an unfamiliar ceiling trying to recall precisely how she had ended up here... wherever here was. She had a vague recollection of someone—not Kyouin—escorting her to a room at the end of the evening. If she remembered correctly, he had sent one of his guards to escort her. That was preferable to having him anywhere near where she was going to sleep, and she seemed to remember saying something to that effect.

Though some things were a little fuzzy in her memory, she thought she had managed to get through the evening without really agreeing to anything, but without outright disagreeing either. Mostly, she discovered that encouraging him to talk about himself and his grand dreams of weeding humanity out to create a daenox compatible race, one that would be loving and accepting of him, allowed her to avoid saying much at all. Kyouin had not been conservative with his own wine consumption either. Now she knew many awful things about him. Even given how cruelly his father had treated him, the things he had done to his family were abhorrent, but she could not let him know she felt that way. Not yet.

For herself, all she had to do to get through the evening and make him feel like she was his ally was to nod and make sounds of assent mixed in with the occasional targeted question to keep him talking. She got the strong sense that he had not talked that openly to another living human in some time.

A deep thrumming sound drew her attention. She rolled up on her side to peak over the edge of the bed. The daemon-cat she had brought in with her the previous day was resting there, purring in its sleep. The other thing she noticed as she rolled over was that this room was familiar. This was her father's old room. Nothing had been moved from the last time he had been in here. Everything from some clothes he had discarded on the floor to a worn leather armguard he used in archery practice that was laying on the long chest at the foot of the bed remained as he had left it.

Her boots, with the serpent dagger still sheathed in one, were sitting next to the chest. Her sword was laying on the far lower corner of the bed on top of the fitted leather jacket she had been wearing. She had climbed into the bed without taking anything else off. They were not the most comfortable clothes to sleep in, but she had slept in them on the road enough times that she was used to it.

Raine rested a hand on the cat-beast's head. It shifted, and the purring grew louder. With her hand on its soft fur, she closed her eyes, pillowing her head on her arm, and breathed in the memories of her father in this room. The earlier ones. The happy ones. She could almost hear Myara knocking on the door in the night. The secret knock they had made up for when they wanted to sneak out and have nocturnal adventures around the palace. Two taps. A scratch. Three taps. The silence of finely wrought hinges opening followed by hushed voices and giggles.

There was a gentle knock on the door. The cat-beast was up on its feet in a second, growling. Raine hushed it with a touch of daenox and got up. The woman at the door, one of the palace servants, was one of the few she had seen who looked healthy, unaffected by daenox. She was carrying a platter that smelled safe, which was the best she could hope for after her wine intake the previous night.

"Lady Raine." The servant inclined her head.

Raine could not stop a small giggle at the address. Still, she was the daughter of the former heir to the throne of Imperious. She had some right to the formal address.

"Yes?"

"My Lord thought you might wish for a little something to settle your stomach before you face the day."

She started to smile her appreciation, but the smile faltered. She glanced at the cat-beast next to her. If the cat was here, then it was no longer guarding Fools Errant.

"Where are my friends? The troubadours?"

The woman stepped in, eyeing the daemon-cat warily, and set the platter on a side table. "He said you might ask. My Lord requested that they perform tonight and allowed them to go into town to gather some things Lady Nakia requested."

A small snort of a laugh escaped Raine then, imagining Nakia's face if she heard someone refer to her as *Lady*. Hope sparked like a deep breath of fresh air in her chest. "He let them leave?"

"Some of them stayed behind, most of the men I believe, and your daemon-wolf is with them. This creature," she gave the cat a cross look, "came to you on its own. It walked up and down the hall yowling until someone let it in here."

The huge cat beast opened its jaws in large yawn, displaying teeth that made the serving woman's face go white.

Raine nodded, swallowing disappointment. "Thank you. If you see Kyouin, tell him I will join him in Vinya's room when I'm done here."

The woman nodded and left her.

That was one thing she had gotten out of their long evening together, other than too much wine and a rather excellent meal. Kyouin had agreed to let her try and bring Vinya up from her coma.

She sat next to the table and pulled the cover off the platter. The cat-beast settled next to her. After a few seconds to gauge her stomach's reaction to the shocking assortment of foods there, she set a platter of seared fish that did not strike her as all that stomach settling on the floor. The daemon cleaned it up with surprising neatness.

"You should have a name if you're going to serenade me in the palace halls at night."

The daemon-cat glanced up and made a small chirping sound in its throat.

Her father had spent time with a daenox infected cat when he was reading in the archives. That cat he had come to calling Prophet because of how many of the books there had been written by prophets. He had been fond of the animal.

"Shall we call you Prophet, after my father's cat?"

The daemon-cat gazed at her with its matte grey eyes and made another chirping sound. She always had a calming effect on the daemons, just as they did for her. It was nice to have one around again, no matter how poorly she might be judged for keeping such a creature close.

She scratched behind its ears, eliciting a purr robust enough that it vibrated through her fingers. "Prophet it is."

When she had her fill of bread and other mild foods and drink, she pulled on her boots, jacket, and weapons and left the room with Prophet at her side. Without Kyouin next to her, she felt more at ease using daenox to search through the palace. She located Lornin and some of the members of Fools Errant in some well-guarded servants' quarters. For the moment, it would gain her nothing to go after them. If she tried to get them out and failed to intercept the others before they came back, it would only put them in danger.

It was easy to find Vinya's room again. The amount of daenox packed into her little body lit her up like a beacon when Raine reached out with the daemon power. Kyouin entered the room a few seconds after she did, likely keeping track of her location in the palace through her use of daenox. When he stepped into the room, Prophet, who took up nearly half as much space as the bed itself, snapped to his feet and snarled. Raine placed a hand on the beast's shoulder, wary of the bony spikes that grew up off the creature's shoulder blades. She did not encourage Prophet to settle back down, though she did discourage him from attacking for now. Two guards followed Kyouin carrying a large, plush chair between them.

"I thought you might like someplace more comfortable to sit," Kyouin stated, wringing his hands with awkward anxiety.

He's looking for my approval.

The realization was somewhat disconcerting.

"Thank you. That was thoughtful." She reminded herself of what he had done to his sister before she could start to appreciate the gesture too much. To avoid looking at him, she turned to move Prophet and herself out of the way so the men could place the chair beside the head of the bed.

"Can I help?"

To undo what he had done, she would have to use the power of the dragon web. Daenox would only compound the problem. Besides, she did not want him here watching her.

"I think this is a solitary job. Tend to your affairs. I'll seek you out when I'm done." She delighted inwardly at how adult that sounded.

Kyouin said nothing. He lingered in the doorway, stepping aside enough for the guards to exit. His awkwardness after spilling his soul to her the previous evening was starting to fill the room. Trying to ignore him, Raine settled in the comfy chair and turned her attention to the little girl. Prophet growled once then dropped to the floor with a grunt next to the chair. After a few minutes, during which she simply stared at the girl, unable to do anything with him staring at her, he finally turned and started to leave.

"Oh."

Kyouin turned back too eagerly.

"Could you send someone with some meat for Prophet?"

His gaze dropped to the daemon-cat, and his eyes narrowed, his face coloring slightly. "You named it?"

She stared back now, sending his incredulity back at him. "Not all creatures are here merely to be used. I would not have this one neglected to death the way you would allow others in your care to be."

He winced at those words. She doubted he felt bad about what had happened to her grandparents, but he probably regretted reminding her of it. He nodded and left the room.

It took several minutes for her to calm her own anger enough to start working on Vinya. The girl was as healthy as could be expected. A few of the remaining serving women had managed to get fluids into her with some care. The daenox did not seem to be making the girl ill, so Kyouin was right in that much. The girl was more like them in that one little way. How he could put so much weight in merely being able to tolerate the daenox was beyond her, but there was a certain madness to his method that went outside of any logical understanding.

At first, it was awkward, drawing daenox out of the child and forcing it back into the saturated ground using the dragon power. Eventually, it got easier and faster. And Raine relaxed into the work. Prophet slept and groomed and slept some more. Sometime later, when a large chunk of raw meat arrived, Raine used her power to inspect it only to find it laced with poison. She sent it back with a message for Kyouin that such an excellent cut should be his to eat. Prophet would be content with a less quality cut. The meat that came back after that was untainted and accompanied by some tea and pastries for her. These she ate a few of and saved the rest for Vinya, who, by late afternoon, was awake and famished.

The girl was remarkably accepting of her situation. Raine, who was rather exhausted by the time the child woke, introduced the girl to Prophet. She watched the girl eat to keep her from overdoing it while struggling not to fall asleep in the comfy chair. It was strange to think that, in standard human years, this little girl was older than her.

The girl licked some crumbs from her fingers then yawned. She gazed at Raine with tired eyes. "If I sleep, will I wake up again?"

Raine nodded. "I'll make sure of it."

"Will you stay with me?"

"How about if I lay down with you?"

Vinya nodded, and Raine settled next to her on the bed. The girl pressed up against her and was asleep in seconds, only a few seconds before Raine.

*

Raine woke to a strange tugging sensation. At first, she thought it was Vinya but, as she woke more, she realized it was something within her. Before she could focus enough to figure out what it was, she realized voices were coming from outside the room. She was trapped between Vinya's small form on the edge of the bed and the massive daemon-cat who had stretched over the remainder of the bed behind her. The fine bed linens might never be the same.

"They've been asleep for hours." That was Kyouin's voice outside the door. He sounded as if finding her here this way vexed him.

Raine strained her ears, listening carefully. She did not dare use daenox to enhance their voices with Kyouin there.

"Kill her now."

Rage burst through her. That was Theruses. The one who destroyed her father and mother and killed Vanuthan.

"Something is wrong with the daenox," Kyouin declared, his voice rising with agitation.

"Yes. The dragons are in Imperious. They are trying to balance it."

Hope lifted Raine, and she dove into the dragon web. She had been so focused on Vinya, she had not taken time to reach out for the dragons. Now that she did, she could feel that they were very close. It was as Theruses said, they were drawing out the daenox from the swollen veins in the earth and dissipating it. That was what caused the tugging sensation that woke her. The process was slow, but there was no doubt about it.

"I need to do something," Kyouin declared.

"By all means, go stop the dragons." There was a chuckle in the Death Dragon's voice. She wondered if Kyouin noticed it or if he was too worked up.

"I will. Stay here and make sure she doesn't leave Elysium."

"You would be wiser to kill her now while she sleeps," Theruses advised.

"Let her sleep in peace," Kyouin hissed. "I'll be back soon."

Raine held her breath, listening to Kyouin's hasty footsteps retreating. A few seconds later, she could hear another set of heavier footsteps sauntering away. Now, while the dragons had their attention, was the time to act. Theruses would be a problem, but he was a problem she would have to deal with eventually.

When she looked at the child, hoping to extract herself without waking her, Vinya was already staring up at her.

"I'm coming with you."

CHAPTER FORTY ONE

The dragons were right about their readiness to travel. Darkin and Siniva convinced them to leave despite the warnings Rythis gave them that the journey would be hard on them in their current states of injury. It was hardest for Siniva. The Fire Dragon lagged behind the others, slowing their pace with his labored flying. Kalphana, the Dream Dragon, carried Darkin to relieve Siniva of that burden, though it did not seem to make much difference. Even with Siniva's sluggish pace and need for breaks, they made much better time on their return trip.

Darkin mostly struggled with a dreadful headache, though he had other aches through his body that grew worse with the flying. There was the added problem that the Dream Dragon did not have Siniva's heating ability, so he was constantly shivering, which only worsened his pain. To ease his suffering, however, Kalphana used her unique powers to force him asleep through large portions of the journey.

The white Song Dragon, Rythis, was always nearby, humming her music when he woke. He suspected that had something to do with how fast his injury continued to heal. Siniva flew close as well, offering heat when he felt strong enough to do so. Rythis used her songs to heal Siniva whenever Darkin was awake, allowing him to recover even while he strained the injuries with his flying.

Once, while they were stopped to give Siniva some rest, Darkin asked the Song Dragon why she only healed him while he slept but did not do the same for Siniva. She explained that it was because his human mind would not be able to handle her meddling within him while he was awake. Then Kalphana forced him asleep, and he woke feeling even better. Strangely, he felt more hopeful as well, despite the days they had lost. Raine and the others could not travel nearly as fast on the ground as the dragons could flying a straight line through the sky. They would be there for Raine. They would bring her the dragons.

Even knowing how fast the dragons could fly, he was surprised when he woke on Kalphana's back in the dark of falling night and could see the lights on the outer wall of Elysium shining in the distance. The lingering ache in his head faded before the prospect of seeing Raine again, of showing her that he had kept his promise.

He glanced around, catching sight of Siniva off to the Dream Dragon's left and slightly ahead. The Fire Dragon dipped clumsily with each sweep of his wings, straining against fatigue and the pain of his injuries. His spirits had recovered even less than his body. Having to fight Vanuthan, his dearest friend, even though it had not really been her, had crushed him. Darkin worried that the dragon was in no condition physically or mentally to go into a fight.

Siniva started sinking down. For a few seconds, Darkin thought his strength had finally failed him, but then other dragons began to drop down with him, following him toward the woods. They aimed for a large clearing. Kalphana tried to make her landings soft for Darkin, but the impact was always jarring, sending a little spike of new pain through his skull. This time, he did not care, he was almost back to Raine.

He was nearly free of the ties that kept him on the dragon's back before they touched down, eager to get off and find out why they were stopping here. It became apparent, when he dropped to the ground and saw four figures emerging from the edge of the trees, one leaning heavily on a crutch.

Siniva and two of the other dragons, Rythis and Colvan, changed into human form, going forward to greet them. R'Gos followed though he did not change shape. Dozens of other dragons began landing in the clearing behind them. Darkin hurried forward to greet Suva and Kovial, gripping arms and offering a brief embrace to each.

"It's good to see you both well." He gave Kovial a long look. "Did you keep Raine safe?"

Kovial shrugged and kicked the grass. "As long as I could. She's in Elysium now."

"How long?"

"She rode in yesterday."

Suva nodded. "She went in just before we caught up with them here."

"She's been in there almost two days then." Anxiety twisted Darkin's gut into knots and made his muscles twitchy with the need to act.

"The daenox is uncontrolled," Colvan commented, a scaled-down version of his horns protruding through a mop of charcoal hair.

The Storm Dragon was taller than Siniva by several inches in his human form, more so with Siniva hunched and leaning against a tree from the pain.

Rythis peered around them with catlike eyes that were the same pearlescent white as her long, wavy hair. She was younger than Darkin had expected. A woman in her late twenties or early thirties at most from the look of her. Her stance was that of someone expecting an attack.

"The web is weak even with us here," she stated, rubbing her hands along her arms as though cold in a gesture that seemed almost too human.

"The veins of daenox are swollen like bloated corpses," R'Gos growled, his deep rumble vibrating through them. "The web will get stronger as we force the daemon power to reabsorb and dissipate out through the ground."

Somehow, it did not surprise Darkin that the massive River Dragon chose not to take human form for this meeting. He had a somewhat disdainful sneer for their human allies even now, choosing mostly to avoid looking at them as though they were beneath his notice. Even with some of his allies in human form, he kept his head high above them, relying on his booming voice to bring his words down.

Kayd was staring at the dragons, her mouth slightly open. She had seen Siniva in his dragon form, but this gathering of the magnificent beasts left her speechless. To be fair to her, both Suva and Kovial were also staring unabashedly at the gathering of dragons filling the clearing, their burnished scales glowing in occasional streams of moonlight that broke through the cloud cover.

Rakas alone seemed unfazed by the great beasts. Nor did he bother to direct his voice up for R'Gos, forcing the River Dragon to tilt his ear toward the ground to hear. "I dared a trip into the city yesterday. Many of the people of Imperious who haven't fled the city are dead or dying from the saturation of daenox gathering around Kyouin and his army. Many of those who fled fell on the roads to attacks from daemons drawn in by that same confluence."

R'Gos glanced down at Rakas, open disgust in the curl of his lips. "I did not think it would get so powerful so quickly. With Theruses and this Kyouin both in Elysium, along with that girl, the veins of daemon power here have expanded at an unprecedented speed."

Darkin bristled at the way he said *that girl*. "You mean Raine."

R'Gos did not spare him a glance. "This clearing should do. The council will begin the process of reigning the daenox in. It will be a slow process until the two powers come more into balance. The rest of the dragons will stand guard around us. I do not think this Kyouin will stand idly by while we choke the power that feeds his army." The big dragon started to turn away.

"What about Elysium?" Suva asked even before Darkin could get the same words out of his mouth. "We need to get Raine out of there. She's the reason you're free."

R'Gos gave her a dismissive glance. "The girl served her purpose. Now we will serve ours. That is the only reason we came here."

"You took your sweet time about it," Darkin snapped. "While she was here trying to figure out how to stop it, you were off sulking in your sanctuary."

R'Gos whipped around, bringing his head low this time so Darkin could get a good look at the size of his teeth when he snarled. "Your kind don't deserve our help."

"We are not our ancestors. What point is there in punishing us for their deeds?"

R'Gos lifted his head away, which, if Darkin were to be honest with himself, was a huge relief. Eaten by a dragon might sound impressive on his gravestone, but he was not going to be much help to Raine that way.

"I will waste no more words on you. Especially on this subject." R'Gos gave him a stern glower. "The girl is an abomination. One we created only out of necessity. It is better that she die fighting for this cause than live beyond this fight and taint the world with her presence."

Siniva stepped away from the tree. "Vanuthan would have protected her."

"Which is why she's dead."

Siniva growled.

R'Gos chuckled at him. "Don't push your luck, Siniva. You aren't strong enough for a fight right now." He turned and began to walk toward the rest of the dragons waiting in the clearing. "Come Colvan. Rythis. We have an arduous task ahead."

Rythis gave them an apologetic look before turning to follow R'Gos.

Colvan shifted his feet. "This has to be the priority." Then he turned to follow, changing back to his dragon form as he went.

A few strides later, Rythis also changed form.

They all stared after the dragons. Silence hung heavy over them.

"R'Gos is right about one thing," Siniva finally said. "The daemon army will not sit idly by. Once the dragons begin the process of bringing the daenox back into balance, a great deal of Kyouin's army will probably leave Elysium to try to stop them."

Darkin nodded. "Then we go in after they go out."

"Several troops are hiding out around the area who were brought in by some of the soldiers you sent," Suva offered. "Some are already falling ill from the daenox, but many are still healthy enough to fight. We could take them in with us."

Darkin gave her a long look and shook his head. She did not say as much, but her pallor and the shadows under her eyes told him she was one of those falling ill. She would not be going in. Besides, this was a moment that would decide their future relationship with the dragons if they all survived.

"No. We'll put the troops to helping defend the dragons. The confrontation will draw even more daemons in from all around the area. With all that attention out here, I think we would be better off to take a smaller group and sneak into Elysium."

Rakas nodded agreement. "I agree. We have a better chance of getting in and back out again if we don't draw too much attention."

Suva's lips were pressed together in a firm line of disapproval.

Darkin gave her a nod, recognizing that she had something to say and wanting to acknowledge that she was being respectful about it. "What is it, Suva?"

"Maybe you're right. Maybe only a few of us go in at first. But there should be someone out here ready to bring in a troop if we aren't out by a preset time. That way, if we run into trouble, help won't be too far behind."

"Yes. I think that makes sense. Kayd can oversee coordinating troops out here to defend the dragons." Kayd nodded in response to his glance. "You and Kovial can help with that, but one of you needs to be ready to break off and lead a troop into Elysium if we aren't back out on time. You can decide between you who goes in and who stays out here."

This time Kovial was the one who looked displeased. "Suva and I planned to go in with you."

"I need people I can trust out here helping the dragons and available to save our asses if things go wrong inside those walls."

"Who's going with you then?"

While they were talking, fourteen of the dragons had formed up in a circle in the center of the clearing, including R'Gos, Rythis, Colvan, and Cyrsyth. Their heads were bowed to the middle of the circle, ears or horns almost touching. Their wings were outstretched and laying across one another to create a connected ring. Around them, the rest of the dragons were forming a larger circle facing outward, ready to defend the council as they worked.

"I will come with you. I can help turn away daemons and keep them from reacting to us." Rakas shuddered suddenly and cast a glance at the ring of dragons. "My power may be a little unstable with this going on, but I'm better protection than nothing."

Darkin nodded.

"I will also go," Siniva rasped.

Darkin nodded again, extinguishing the ready argument in Siniva's eyes. The Fire Dragon was injured. He could be a liability, but he had earned a right to be part of this. And besides...

"Rakas can use daenox. You can use the dragon web. Between the two of you, we shouldn't have any trouble finding Raine."

Both men nodded and met his eyes, Rakas with his eyes blacker than pools of ink and Siniva with his eyes of fire. They were a strange trio, but he believed they had the best chance of success, and he was not going to risk failure to avoid hurt feelings.

Kayd, who had been silent until now, gave a firm nod and stepped forward to grasp his arm. "Bring her out alive."

Darkin nodded.

Suva stepped forward after Kayd moved. She also grasped his arm. "Be safe."

Darkin pulled her into a hug. He did the same with Kovial. When they stepped back, he looked the three over. "You three, be careful. I have a feeling things may get ugly out here."

Kayd grimaced. "I'm counting on it."

CHAPTER FORTY TWO

They did not have to wait long before Kyouin's forces began pouring out of Elysium headed for the clearing in the woods. The dragons' attack on their source of power worked like a very compelling summons to the daemon army. Watching them flood out through the outer gates—daemons, undead, and human warriors in the thousands—Darkin started to feel guilty for leaving the others behind to deal with it.

It did mean that his little party of three would have a lot less to deal with beyond those gates. Even with the dragons quelling the daenox, Rakas seemed confident that he would be able to turn away any daemons that might notice them. That would not work for the human warriors, and when Darkin asked about the undead, Rakas balked.

"The undead are just daenox creations like the daemons, right?"

Rakas shook his head. Before answering, he swept the area a few times with his gaze, making sure they were out of earshot of anyone. They were creeping along the outer wall now in the darkness. Rakas had cloaked them in an enhanced wedge of shadow with daenox to make sure they would be especially hard to spot by anyone up on the wall.

Rakas motioned them to move forward, whispering

as they went. "Daenox is a part of the natural world, as are the various daemon forms it gives rise to on its own. The undead are not a natural occurrence. Kyouin forced that animation on the dead. Now they are neither alive nor dead. They still feel like death, however. There is something about coming into contact with the daenox in them that feels like I imagine dying would feel, only it's your mind that is dying."

Darkin shuddered with the unnerving sensation that something was crawling over his skin. "All right. We'll just have to be careful about the undead like we are the human warriors."

They were in sight of the main gate, and it was guarded. Kyouin, for all that he came across as out of his mind, was not an idiot. There had been other openings in the walls prior to Dephithus killing Myara's young soldier friend outside the palace on her Dawning Day. Those entrances had been temporarily sealed by Mythan after that. Then more permanently sealed by Alondis who had been unquestionably paranoid, enough so not to leave himself any alternate escape routes, which Darkin always thought a strange choice.

"Rakas?"

"Mmhm," Rakas muttered, his attention on the guards, which included a couple of daemon-dogs.

"It was you, wasn't it, on Dephithus's Dawning—"

"Not the time," Siniva snarled.

The flash in the Fire Dragon's eyes told Darkin that conversation was over.

Rakas was staring at him, and Darkin was grateful for the night that hid the flush in his face. Sometimes he really did have a problem keeping his mouth shut.

"Sorry, my mouth got away without my brain's supervision."

Siniva gave a soft snort.

Rakas turned his attention back to the gate. "There

are only two daemons. I should be able to turn them
to our side. I doubt they can take out all four guards,
however, so we need to be close enough to make good
on our advantage before I do it."

"I could turn into a dragon," Siniva offered.

"That might ruin our stealth approach," Darkin answered.

The Fire Dragon's chuckle turned into a pained
cough, but when Darkin glanced at him, concerned, he
gave a nod and took his ax from his belt.

"I am good enough for this."

"Comforting," Rakas muttered under his breath.

They moved in closer, keeping tight to the wall
so Rakas's wedge of deeper shadow would keep them
hidden.

"There might be more inside the gate," Rakas
warned.

Darkin carefully drew his sword. "Turn the daemons."

There was a snarl by the gate. Two of the guards
were down in seconds under the two daemon-dogs.
Siniva and Darkin were in the fray almost as fast, charging the remaining two guards as they went to the aid
of their companions. Siniva, with his injuries, was not
fast enough. The guard he was after managed to cleave
a blow through the middle of one daemon-dog's back,
taking the beast down with a piercing yelp.

Siniva's ax bit into the guard's neck while the other
threw off the dead dog and started to his feet. Darkin
had planned for his companion's current weaknesses.
He left his sword buried in the fourth guard's chest and
came around with his dagger in time to drive it into the
throat of the man who was getting to his feet.

They were fortunate that no one else had been stationed
inside the gate. Darkin retrieved his sword, wiping the
weapon clean on one warrior's leg. The remaining daemon-
dog sat and stared up at Rakas, its tongue lolling out the

side of its blood-slicked jaws. It could almost pass for a normal dog if he did not look at the strange grey eyes.

The guards lying dead and dying at their feet all looked surprisingly healthy. There was no sign of sickness from the daenox. In all his time fighting the daemon army, he had never seen this many healthy warriors all in one spot.

"He's putting the sick on the front lines against the dragons and holding back the healthy ones. He's weeding out his own army," he stated.

"That means we're up against stronger enemies behind the walls." Rakas patted his leg. The daemon-dog responded like any dog would, trotting to his side and pressing its head up under his hand.

Darkin smiled at his companions. "Stronger, yes, but they also have more to lose. They are up against dragons now. They might be willing to reconsider their alliances."

"Sounds good. You go talk to them," Siniva said with a nod toward the palace. "We'll keep watch here."

"Thank you, Siniva, for your support," Darkin gave the dragon-man a wry look. "It is worth keeping in mind, however."

The region between the two walls was high risk. As far as he could see, there were no troops there, but there were sure to be lookouts on the inner wall. Moving across that open space, it would be hard to remain unseen.

"Can you shroud us enough to get us up there?"

Rakas eyed the space between the two walls. The dark would help, but there were breaks in the cloud cover that let the moonlight through on occasion. He scratched the daemon-dog behind the ears and gave a thoughtful nod.

"I should be able to enhance the shadows enough to get us through unnoticed as long as we don't end up in a direct beam of moonlight."

"Are you bringing the daemon with us?" Darkin asked, slightly disconcerted by how doglike the animal was acting. How much of that was Rakas's influence on it?

Rakas looked at him, his black eyes becoming empty pits in the darkness. "Are you turning down the help?"

"Not at all." Four was better odds than three, even if the fourth was a daemon. He had seen Raine turn them often enough to realize that. It was just disconcerting how quickly his enemies could become his allies in this war. "Let's go."

The trip up to the second gate was mostly uneventful. The one time they got caught in moonlight, they moved out fast, and there was no sign that they were noticed. They curved around so that they were not approaching the gate directly to give themselves a little time to figure out their opposition. Like before, they crept up to the wall itself and made their way along it toward the gate where someone on the wall would be even less likely to notice them.

The stakes were higher at this gate because they would be fighting in sight of some of the inner facilities. According to Rakas, there were perhaps a hundred daemons on the grounds still, though they were well dispersed, indicating that Kyouin was not planning for an assault on the palace. He was not actually getting an assault, only a rescue operation. Rakas and Siniva both sensed Raine inside the palace. She seemed to be moving around freely. Rakas said she had a daemon with her and he and Siniva agreed that it was probably an ally given Raine's skill with daemons.

All of this was encouraging, but it only made him more eager to get to her. What was happening behind those walls? Why had she not left now that the dragons were here?

"I sense five daemons around the gate," Rakas whispered.

"Can you turn them all?"

"I believe so. I'm not as good with daemons as Raine is. Managing six at once will be pressing my limits."

It was not the most reassuring statement, but Darkin tried to be encouraging. He needed his allies to be confident. "Good. Do the best you can. What about undead?"

Rakas swallowed so hard it was audible in the darkness. Darkin made himself put a hand on the man's shoulder for reassurance. There was silence for several seconds, then Rakas shuddered hard.

"There is one."

Darkin gave his shoulder a squeeze before taking his hand away. "Thank you. I can see two warriors from here. If they are the only ones, that puts two human warriors, one undead, and five daemons. With our new friend here," he nodded to the daemon-dog, "that puts us up nine to three, assuming you can turn all of the daemons."

"I have an idea," Siniva rasped.

The tightness in his voice caught Darkin's attention. "Are you good for this?"

"I am," Siniva answered, his voice stronger this time.

"All right. Let's hear it."

"Six daemons should be able to take down the three warriors fairly easily with the element of surprise. We don't know what's beyond that gate, but if we get the daemons to kill the guards and go on a rampage beyond the gate, we might be able to sneak in during the distraction."

Darkin gave Siniva a long, scrutinizing look. There was a dark patch on the side of his fitted jacket. The wound there must have opened in the skirmish at the first gate. Avoiding a fight would be in their best interest at this point. In different circumstances, he might send Siniva back out, but the dragon-man was much more likely to be seen without Rakas to hide him. None of them really needed more combat right now.

He turned to Rakas. "Can you do that?"

Rakas glanced over at Siniva. His gaze set briefly upon the dark patch on Siniva's side. He turned back to Darkin and nodded. The resolve in his expression promised his best effort. That was all Darkin could ask.

Rakas knelt in front of the daemon-dog and scratched the animal's head. "I don't expect you'll survive this, my friend, but I wish you luck."

With that, the animal turned and started toward the gate, moving in the low crouch of a hunting predator. When he was almost there, someone cried out and the daemon-dog charged, joining in a brief, but efficient attack. There was one yelp. Darkin glanced over at Rakas.

"We still have six," the man answered, "though one is injured. They're running for the lower barracks. The archers on the wall will have good targets."

Someone up on the wall hollered, "Rogue daemons!"

Darkin nodded. "That's our cue."

They hurried to the gate and moved through, stepping around the bodies there. He hesitated for a second as he passed the undead warrior. There was something about killing undead that never made sense to him. It seemed they could not function past a certain amount of damage. In this case, one of the daemons had ripped the undead warrior's head off. That was rather decisive damage. It also suggested that at least one of their daemons was a substantial beast.

There was more light within the inner wall, but even here, there was enough space between the buildings that dark shadows were in ready supply. The daemons had the attention of the few warriors on the wall and a small group of warriors up near the lower arena. One of the daemons racing toward the group was about the size of a bear, and Darkin did not doubt it was the one that had ripped the undead warrior's head off.

The whistle of an arrow proceeded a sharp yelp. One of the daemon-dogs went down midstride, hitting the ground with enough momentum to slide several feet. Rakas winced and looked away, focusing his attention on their goal. Darkin followed suit.

They made their way quickly up through the darkest areas, Rakas still enhancing the shadows to keep them hidden. Rakas also kept their most significant threat, the daemons who could undoubtedly smell them, from coming after them. When they got up around the upper stables and training facilities, they had to slow down. There were more enemies here and less darkness.

They skirted wide, avoiding the main road to come at the palace from the side, sneaking past the grounds-keeper's house that was the last building between them and a stretch of garden outside the palace itself. Darkin's flesh was on fire with anxiety. They were so close now, and it was going too well.

They hunched alongside the corner of the house for a few minutes, scanning the area for threats before they made the last sprint to the palace.

"I never doubted you would change sides someday, Rakas."

The deep voice came from the shadows in the now open door of the house. When they turned, a huge man with horns, scaling, and a long tail that wound lazily around his thick ankles, stepped out of the doorway. He was a dragon barely bothering to try to pass as human. As far as Darkin knew, there was only one dragon not on their side.

"Theruses," Rakas answered, his voice tight with fear and something else, something his expression confirmed as loathing.

Siniva growled, and Darkin drew his sword.

CHAPTER FORTY THREE

Try as she might, Raine could not sense Theruses. He had found some way to hide from her, whether she searched with daenox or through the dragon web. His connection to the web was weak, so that part did not come as much of a surprise, but he should have been as much of a beacon in the daenox as Vinya had been before she drew out the daemon power. She was not going to let fear of the Death Dragon keep her locked away.

When she stepped into the hallway, there was no one around. Whatever Kyouin intended when he told Theruses to make sure she did not leave Elysium, she had little doubt the dragon would go about it in his own way.

With Prophet moving ahead of her and Vinya keeping close behind one leg, Raine made her way through the palace, heading directly for where she sensed Lornin and some of the Fools Errant's members to be. She still did not sense Myrza, Nakia, or Cadovan. If she freed the others, perhaps they could help her locate those three.

When she reached the room, only two guards stood outside of it. A significant reduction from when she had sensed it early. The guards were both human, and she did not detect ill effects in either of them from the daenox. It came as little surprise that Kyouin was holding back those who could withstand the daenox. They were the start of his vision for the future.

With Prophet there, it took almost no effort to convince the two guards that they needed to be somewhere else. One even set the key to the door on the floor for her before rushing off. They might get reinforcements and come back, but she had a feeling she had seen the last of them for this night. She unlocked the door. Marisa, Kelcy, Idrin, Florin, and Lornin were all inside, and all of them, even Florin, looked close to tears with relief when she stepped through the door.

"I don't care whose daughter you are," Lornin remarked, getting up from a chair in the corner, "I'd be proud to call you family."

Raine shook her head at him, though a spike of joy shot through her, leaving her feeling more than a little giddy. "We aren't out of here yet."

There was distinctly more apprehension in the room when Prophet came in. The big beast sat next to her, and Vinya crept out from behind him. Raine held a hand out to the girl who came forward and took it, eyeing the others with some uncertainty.

"This is part of my family, Vinya. They'll help take care of you until we find your family."

Vinya nodded, her gaze going to Marisa who apparently looked the least untrustworthy.

"Where are the others?"

"Cadovan and Nakia are in the next room behind some barrier. We can see each other if we open the door, but we can't hear each other." Marisa answered, gesturing to a door in the right wall of the room.

Raine's mouth went dry suddenly. "And Myrza?"

Marisa broke down crying.

"That bastard killed her," Florin explained even though the explanation was no longer necessary.

For several seconds, Raine could only stare at him as

if he had spoken some other language. Then the room seemed to wobble around her, and she wanted to scream or break down crying like Marisa. Or kill someone... someone in particular.

It was Lornin's steady gaze that centered her. She still had people to protect. The time for revenge and mourning would come later.

Now that she knew the barrier was there, she could sense it with daenox, but only faintly. Kyouin had designed it to be invisible to her. He had designed it to hide the truth from her. Nakia and Cadovan had never gone to Imperious. He had hidden them away so she would believe that they had gone to town along with Myrza. So she would believe Myrza was alive.

Raine could not focus. Her vision blurred, and red closed in around the edges. Prophet stood and started growling, though the beast seemed unsure about what he should be growling at. Everyone else, except Vinya, backed away from the daemon-cat.

She swept out with daenox and dragon power together, searching for Kyouin. She would kill him. She would tear him apart with the power he claimed as his own. She would...

It was not Kyouin's presence that stopped her. It was the presence of three others. Darkin, Siniva, and Rakas were inside Elysium. They were coming for her. Somewhere else, also inside Elysium, was Theruses.

With a new sense of urgency and purpose, Raine seized the power of the dragon web and used it to start drawing out the daenox from the barrier in the next room, dragging it back into the ground, which was becoming a little less saturated, a sign that the dragons were hard at work balancing the powers. If she had known more, she could have done this to the first barrier he put up and perhaps have saved Myrza. If she had only known.

Quiet tears ran down her cheeks as she pulled down the barrier. Prophet walked over, pressing his face against her shoulder, knocking her a little off balance. She appreciated the comfort. It seemed unlikely that anyone else here would offer it. For all that they knew her, most of them were wary of her. They were not like her. Kyouin was not like her either. There was no one else like her in this world. Kyouin had been right about that much.

As soon as the barrier was down, she pulled open the door. She barely had time to recognize Nakia before the woman stepped out and put her arms around Raine, shoving Prophet's head out of the way as if he were some docile little barn cat.

The gesture shocked Raine so much she almost did not know what to do. After a few seconds, she returned it, but as amazing as the unexpected embrace made her feel, there were others in danger. She eased back. Nakia was quick to let go, not one to overstay any moment.

"I knew you would get us out of here. I never doubted you."

Behind her, Cadovan gave a nod to confirm her words.

"I didn't get..." Raine trailed off when Nakia put a finger to her lips.

"There will be time for that later. We need to get out of this mess."

Raine nodded, gratitude for the other woman's understanding almost bringing more tears. She was right, though. There would be time for that later, if they lived that long.

Prophet stood to one side, looking slightly incensed, his macelike tail lashing back and forth. It caught the leg of a table and smashed right through it, toppling a rather expensive looking vase that shattered on the floor. The massive cat jumped, staring back at the table in surprise.

Raine patted his head. "We'll have to work on your spatial awareness later." She faced the others. "The dragons are outside Elysium working to balance the daemon power. Most of Kyouin's army has gone to stop them, but there are still dangers inside the walls. Rakas, Darkin, and Siniva are also here somewhere, coming to help. We need to find them and get everyone to safety."

All eyes were on her. Several of them nodded and watched her, waiting for her direction. It was a strange sensation to be the one in charge. She wondered how Darkin could stand it. All that responsibility. The weight of so many lives on his shoulders.

"Follow us," she indicated Prophet. "Vinya, I want you to stay back with Marisa, understand?"

The girl nodded. She walked over to Marisa who wiped at her tears with one hand and held the other out to Vinya. When they clasped hands, Raine nodded and turned away. Having Vinya to watch would keep Marisa going for now.

It was uncomfortably easy to get out of the palace. Every serving person scurried out of the way, and the guards stepped aside, bowing their heads and making no move to impede either her or her followers. It made her skin crawl with unease. Either they were still deferring to her due to Kyouin's old orders, or, and she suspected this was the case, Theruses had instructed them not to interfere. If it were the latter, then he would be waiting outside where he had room to shift into his dragon form. Knowing the other three were getting close to the palace only made that possibility less pleasant.

When the guards at the front doors went so far as to open them for her and her party, Raine's stomach felt as if it fell into her shoes. Theruses wanted her dead. He would not care what Kyouin had told him. He was no one's ally.

Taking a deep breath, she began to draw on dragon and daemon power, filling herself with both as she walked outside.

The timing could not have been better... or worse. If she had come out a little sooner, she might have found Theruses before the others did. She might have kept them out of it. He was waiting, and he was not alone. Darkin, Rakas, and Siniva were all there, facing him.

He looked past them and smiled. "Welcome, Raine."

They could not help it, the three glanced back at her, and Theruses changed form so quickly it was hard to follow. One second, he was mostly human, the next he was a massive gold dragon towering over them. With a swipe of his clawed foot, he sent all three men flying. Darkin hit the ground hard, but he was struggling to his feet within a few seconds, gazing around unsteadily, perhaps searching for his sword. Rakas got lucky, landing in some bushes that broke his fall, though he got caught up in the thorny branches and likely had more than a few nasty cuts. Siniva landed closest to the Death Dragon. He lay there holding his side and coughing, spitting up something dark in the dim light from the garden lanterns.

The Death Dragon chuckled, looking past Raine at those who followed her. She could hear them drawing their weapons, weapons Kyouin had not felt it necessary to take from them, and Prophet's hackles went up as the daemon-cat snarled at the dragon.

"Is this the army you bring to face me, Dragon-Child? Will you watch as I pick them apart one at a time?" He lowered his head, his gaze homing in on Siniva. "Shall I start with your savior?"

Darkin staggered over beside Raine. She did not look at him. She continued to pull the powers into herself, drawing them in until she could not bear anymore, then drawing more. She handed Darkin her sword and the serpent dagger from her boot.

"Raine," he paused, shaking his head a little as if he were having trouble focusing on her, "What are you doing?"

She turned and kissed him once. Then she stepped toward Theruses. "Don't touch him."

Theruses looked at her, his eyes narrowing. "You can't stop me, Dragon-Child."

He started to reach one clawed foot toward Siniva and Raine took a few more steps toward him. There was so much power in her now that it began to spill out, the wavering violet light of the daenox lapping out from her along with the invisible dragon power that poured out with it. She wove the two powers together, letting the daenox, still the stronger of the two, for now, change her, and letting the dragon power decide her form.

She screamed then. There was pain like nothing she had ever felt. Like nothing Dephithus or Myara had ever felt. It lit her blood and bones on fire, breaking her body apart and reforming it into something new. What felt like an eternity later, she was remade, and she was powerful. More powerful than she had ever been.

Raine spread her wings and opened her long jaws, letting a ground shaking roar of challenge blast between rows of deadly, tapered teeth.

The Death Dragon faced her and answered the challenge. Together, they lunged into the air, rising above the palace. She could feel Theruses inside her, trying to use his unique power to sap the very life from within her. Holding to her hatred, holding to the memories of what he had put her family through, she rose high and dove down at him, slamming her new weight into him and grabbing hold of him in a deadly embrace that he returned. They dug their claws into one another, cutting through hide and scales that most weapons found hard to penetrate. They struggled to keep their wings clear of one another and remain airborne while fighting to get a deadly strike in on the other.

For now, the pain of his claws and teeth cutting through her flesh only fueled her rage. It was his power over death that weakened her, making her falter. He lashed around with his tail, catching one wing. The tear was small, but it was enough to make her side of the fight harder, forcing her to put more energy into staying airborne. She wanted the battle away from her companions, so she drew on the powers of daemon and dragon to help her carry on.

They pulled apart, tearing away pieces of each other's flesh as they separated. For a few seconds, they flew up, rising higher. Theruses, unhindered by the wing injury she suffered, surged up past her and flipped in the air, diving back down at her. Raine did her best to brace for the impact, but it was too powerful. She fell a long way beneath him, her torn wing tearing more with the effort of arresting her fall with his weight behind it. With her focus on trying not to be smashed into the ground, his strikes got past her guard, his teeth ripping into her flesh.

Her only goal was to protect her friends, and she was going to fail. If only she had something. If only she had power over death, or fire, or something to give her an advantage the way he did.

But perhaps she did. Perhaps she had something even better. The real dragons each had some unique power, but she was not a real dragon. She had the power of daenox and the dragon web. She could be whatever kind of dragon she wanted to be.

Remembering the light shows she put on for the daemons, Raine drew on more daenox, keeping the dragon power focused on maintaining her strength and her form. She drew spears of daenox light from her jaws, from the lines of her wings, and from her chest. Spears of light that were as deadly as they were beautiful. The light shot through Theruses. Hundreds of spears of daenox light, the daenox he tried to rule, stabbing through his wings, his legs, his chest, and his neck. A few spears shot into his head, one penetrating his eye. He threw back his head, convulsing in agony as the spears tore through him, unable to even cry out in his pain.

Raine let out a roar of rage and struggled to break free of him as they both plummeted toward the ground. In his pain, he only gripped tighter. She could not arrest the fall for both. She let out another cry. A long sorrowful cry this time. One meant to say goodbye.

CHAPTER FORTY FOUR

Normally, Kyouin would have ridden out with his army. He liked to watch up close as his warriors and beasts tore apart the enemy, usually from behind a barrier of invisibility. This was different. This was not a troop of soldiers or a band of angry citizens. This was not even a regular army. This was a sizeable gathering of dragons. As much as he wanted to be sure of his superior power, in this case, he was not.

So, instead, he led everyone, even Theruses, to believe he was heading out to the front line. Then he took a small group of his undead warriors and retreated to one of the smaller audience chambers. There he put up an invisible barrier that would block entry, detection, and sound, and settled into the throne. Avaline was among the undead warriors, which meant Vaneye was also there, since his little brother now followed her everywhere. He could trust the undead to remain true whatever happened. They were his creations with no desires of their own.

Once he was settled, he rested back and used daenox to take him to the battle through the minds and eyes of his daemons and undead. It was easy to jump from one to another and manage the action from afar. Some of the management he left to his undead officers, but he needed to be involved, especially given that he could not, for some reason, ever jump into Ryche's head. Ryche was an effective killer, but his orders could not be managed from a distance like the rest of the undead and daemon troops.

When the first wave entered the clearing, it was a stunning sight. Even despising the dragons as he did for what they were trying to do, he could not deny that the gathering of the giant creatures was impressive. Dragons of all colors and variations stood in a large circle facing outward, prepared to defend a much smaller circle of dragons facing inward in the center. Those on the inside were the dragons he needed to get to. That much was obvious.

To get things rolling, he rushed in using the body of a daemon-dog only to be crushed by a clawed foot larger than his body. Kyouin jumped minds an instant before death. He did not like being present in that moment. After death was something else. Raising them did not bother him. Being there when the life left was something else, and it made him uneasy. It was too hard when that intimately connected to differentiate his life from theirs.

That was one of his advantages, though. If a dragon killed one of his better fighters, he simply raised it from the dead and sent it back into the fray. Dragons were hard to injure though. Their underbelly, which looked like a good target, was covered in a thick hide that only the sharpest blades or spears could penetrate. The scales elsewhere were resistant to all except direct stabbing damage, and even then, the point had to slip up under the scales to be effective.

The wings were different. The wings could be damaged, and once damaged, the dragons were grounded at least and could not perform their devastating air attacks. As soon as he figured that out, he sent his archers and daemon infected birds after the wings. Injuring the wings also appeared to cause a great deal of pain, leaving the dragons' reaction times impaired on the ground.

Kyouin loved it then. He had a whole troop of undead archers, and he rode in one after the other with them, watching their arrows tear through those vulnerable wings. The screams of injured dragons rent the air, far louder than those of his own injured, of which there were plenty.

He dove into the mind of a massive elklike beast with two long spikes atop its head and barreled into the battle. He dodged around several warriors who were harrying a blue dragon. The dragon swiped out and sent one warrior flying along with his mount. He ducked the elk-beast's head to avoid being struck by the helmet, which he thought might still have the head in it. As the blue dragon spun one way to ward off another attacker, Kyouin lunged, lowering the beast's magnificent head and ramming those long sharp horns through the dragon's side. The resulting shriek of pain was glorious. The elk-beast, however, could not get its head free, so Kyouin left it there and moved on.

It was going well. In no time, there were already dragons down, dying or dead, and more daemons were being drawn in from all around by the chaos. He had lost hundreds, but they were replaceable. This battle had to be won, and soon there would be enough of an opening to get in some attacks on the inner circle of dragons.

Kyouin jumped into the head of another undead archer, ready to enjoy another dragon's scream of pain, when a different cry went up. This cry was that of a warhorn. His army did not have a warhorn like that. He jumped to a daemon near the back of the army on the side the cry had come from in time to see warriors surging out of the trees. They were Imperious soldiers. They could not have gathered that many, but with the dragons on one side and Imperious soldiers on the other, this side of the battle was about to turn against him.

Kyouin jumped back to the archer, cursing that he could not get into Ryche's head to turn his attention to this new threat. At that moment, he could not even find the undead Ryche on the battlefield. He signaled the other archers and started to turn them toward the Imperious troops when a burst of daenox much closer to his real body caught his attention.

Kyouin snapped back to himself and reached out with the daenox to find the source of that massive power flux. It was easy to find. Right outside his palace, he could feel Raine, and she had done something to herself. She was changed somehow.

A loud roar rent the air, and another responded in kind. Kyouin went cold with fear.

Theruses.

"No!"

He got up from the throne. Pain burst through his back between his shoulder blades. It took his breath away. He staggered several steps, twisting around as he sank to one knee to see what had hurt him. Behind him Avaline stood, a slightly greyish fluid running from the inner corners of her eyes. Her right hand was in the air, and the sheath that usually carried her dagger was empty. She stared at him for a few seconds, then she lowered her hand and walked back to where Vaneye lay on the floor. He did not appear to be breathing. The daenox had finally finished him.

Kyouin tried to reach around to pull the weapon out, but he could not get a hold of it. Every movement made the blade dig in deeper, making it hard to catch his breath. Avaline sat on the floor and pulled Vaneye's body onto her lap, cradling him there.

Kyouin struggled to his feet. The door of the room was open. The other undead were gone, perhaps ordered out by Avaline. He staggered out, pain blurring his thoughts and making the world swim around him.

Outside, the human guards were also gone. There was no one in the halls.

Several times he staggered into the walls. The wound was bad. He needed help, but they were all gone. His guards and servants were gone. There was no one to help him. The doors were all standing open. Even the main door at the front of the palace was standing open. Outside the front entrance, he saw two dragons leap up into the sky. All his prisoners were standing there as well, staring up at the two dragons locked in combat. With the dagger in his back, Kyouin found he could not look up.

*

Darkin could do nothing. He held Raine's sword and dagger and watched as she, remarkable woman that she was, screamed in apparent agony, then turned into a dragon. She was probably the most beautiful dragon he had ever seen. Black as night with a brassy sheen to her scales and a violet glow around her. Her eyes were the same metallic brassy black that they were in human form, just much bigger now. She was finer boned, more like the delicate Song Dragon, Rythis, and much smaller than the massive gold dragon facing her.

Despite the obvious size disadvantage, she roared out a defiant challenge. Theruses answered it. The two dragons surged into the air, taking their fight to the sky.

The massive daemon-cat she had come out with slunk back in the shadows, cowering and watching them with wide grey eyes now that Raine had left it.

Rakas, still half trapped in the thorns of the bush he had landed in, rivulets of blood running from scratches all over his face and hands, was staring open-mouthed up at the dragons. Siniva had not managed to get up yet. He was still spitting up blood. He was going to be of no help. Nakia, however, had run over to help the Fire Dragon. Without a dragon to help them, the next best thing had to be a daenox priest.

Darkin rushed over to Rakas, helping him free of the bush. "You have to do something."

"What can I do? I have very little experience in the realm of dragon fights."

Darkin looked up. He could remember all too well the way Vanuthan's claws and teeth ripped through Siniva's scaled hide. The dragons above were locked together and appeared to be having a hard time holding altitude. Drips of blood were spattering on the marble walks between the gardens.

He started to turn toward the palace when someone shoved him. He hit the ground again, the wind knocked out of him once more. Rakas was standing where he had been, blood spilling between his lips. He stared at the palace doors, or rather, at the man standing just outside those doors.

Kyouin stood there, his hands still outstretched before him with whatever daenox attack he had thrown at Darkin. An attack that Rakas had taken for him. Rakas fell, slapping down with that gross lack of control that said he was dead before he hit. As Darkin lunged to his feet, Raine's sword in hand, Kyouin changed his focus, preparing to attack Darkin. Then his clothes spontaneously ignited. Darkin did not question good fortune. He lunged, bringing the sword around in a swing that cut deep into Kyouin's neck until it lodged in partway through his spine.

Darkin jerked the sword back, refusing to leave Raine's sword in the detestable man's flesh. His spine cracked the rest of the way through, and the sword broke free. Kyouin's head fell to one side, held on by a flap of flesh. The leader of the daemon army fell.

Flashing light from above drew their attention back up. Bright colored lights were bursting around the dragons, seeming to emanate from Raine's body. There were no roars of pain. No sounds at all, just light, followed by a heavy spattering of blood that sent everyone who could move that fast sprinting for cover. Then the dragons' battle took them out over the field next to the palace. They all watched as Raine and Theruses started to fall, gaining speed as they plummeted toward the ground.

Let go. Let go, Raine.

Even as he chanted it in his head, he knew she would let go if she could. They tumbled through the air. A long mournful cry blasted out seconds before they hit the ground. Darkin felt as though he hit with them. Tears burst into his eyes. A pain that was more than physical sped through his body like wildfire even as he struggled not to be sick.

He started to move toward where the dragons had fallen when the daemon-cat stepped out of the shadows toward him and snarled. For a few seconds, he thought it was growling at him, then a mounted figure rode up beside him. The stench alone was enough to warn him, and he quickly backed away. Everyone else did much the same, though a few of the Fools Errant members were too busy retching to move.

The undead warrior on his undead horse looked down at Darkin. One of his eyes, barely held in by strands of rotten flesh, protruded out a little farther than the socket. The flesh of his cheek hung down on that same side, exposing his teeth. Darkin swallowed bile and backed up several more steps, trying hard not to breathe in the stench, but it seemed to seep through the tissues of his nose.

The monstrosity lifted the spear he was carrying. Darkin raised his sword, trying to convince himself he could win this fight, but Ryche urged his horrifying mount forward and stabbed the spear through one of Kyouin's eye sockets. Then he lifted it, the small bit of remaining flesh ripping away when Kyouin's torso was almost a foot off the ground. High enough that Darkin noted with some distant confusion that there was a dagger between the man's shoulder blades. Then the flesh tore, and Ryche rode off with his grisly prize while Darkin and several others deposited their most recent meals on the garden walks.

A horrible wail drew his attention back to where the dragons had fallen. It was the daemon-cat making some miserable yowling sound as it stood over a small figure. There was only one dragon there. A gold one.

Darkin ran toward the small figure, his chest bound tight with dread.

She lay there, outlined by the moonlit gold of Theruses's wing that she had landed on. There was blood on her lips and numerous gashes over her arms, chest, and one down her cheek bleeding freely. She did not stir when he knelt next to her and spoke her name. The others started gathering around. The little girl that had come out with Raine and the others walked over to the daemon-cat and stroked its leg. The beast quieted some, though it still made a low moaning sound deep in its throat. The girl leaned against it. She stared at Raine, a tear running down her cheek.

Raine was breathing, but a little more red showed up on her lips with each breath. They needed help. They needed Rakas, only he was dead.

"Rythis could help."

He looked up at Siniva who stood behind him, one arm around Nakia who appeared to be holding him up.

"We can't take her down into the battle," Darkin objected, though a tiny glimmer of hope sparked in him.

"I wouldn't risk moving her at all," Nakia stated, her gaze following the shallow rise and fall of Raine's chest.

The thunder of hooves preceded a group of riders with Suva and Kovial at the head. As soon as they got in sight, Suva hurried over and leaped off. Kovial was not far behind.

Suva knelt next to him. "No. Raine," her voice cracked.

"One of the dragons can probably help," Siniva stated, "but she won't leave before they're done balancing the powers. How is the battle down there?"

Kovial looked Siniva over as he spoke. "A lot of dragons are wounded, and many can't fly. A few are dead. The inner circle is still intact though, and when we rode out, the tide seemed to be turning. Some of the daemons are leaving now that that daenox is weakening. They could use a Fire Dragon to help secure a victory."

"Siniva's too injured," Darkin stated, trying to save the Fire Dragon the indignity of admitting his own limitations.

Siniva pushed away from Nakia. "I'll manage. I'll be back soon with Rythis."

With that, he limped away from them and changed into his natural form, rising laboriously up into the night sky.

Darkin glanced around at the small group of soldiers that had joined them. "Where's the rest of the troop?"

"Cleaning up," Suva answered. "We met almost no resistance coming in, but there are some undead still roaming about."

He met her eyes, and she nodded, standing up.

"Come on, Kovial. We're taking the troop back to help Siniva."

Kovial was in the saddle almost before she finished speaking.

The night folded around Siniva. Up here, above the chaos, there was a certain peace, even though every wing beat was agony. Cool air rushing over his always hot hide was soothing, though he could feel it more on places that were damp with fresh blood from his injuries. He needed Rythis too, but Raine needed her more, and he was going to get her there no matter what it took.

Through the dragon web, he could feel the pain of many injured dragons, some direly so. They also would need Rythis. How was he going to convince her to come first to a girl who, despite recent events suggesting otherwise, was not a dragon?

It took only a few minutes to reach the battle. Even from here he could see many daemons retreating now. The undead and human warriors needed more persuading. There were also archers down there. If they had caught on to the vulnerability of the dragons wings, which Suva's comments suggested they had, he would not want to get in their range. He could see them now, arming their bows, but he was still high enough to be safe.

Off to the side, streaming down from Elysium at full speed, he spotted Suva and Kovial with their troop returning to the fray. As he circled, he watched them coming in on the edges of the battle. They appeared to be calling the other Imperious soldiers to them, making a direct line for the archers on the far side. As the soldiers rallied, they left other parts of the battle open. Siniva grinned. He was not in good shape, but he could do a few passes breathing fire down on the bastards they had opened up for him.

Siniva drew on the fire that heated him from within and dove down in the wake of the passing Imperious troop. He blasted fire through the ranks of daemon warriors and undead, listening to them scream. They were already broken. Kyouin was dead. Theruses was dead. The daemons were fleeing. The rest merely needed to admit their defeat, and he was here to encourage them.

For a few passes, he enjoyed watching the daemon army dissolve into chaos so much he almost forgot his pain, then, on the fourth pass, his chest seized up, and he spat more blood than flame. His fun was over. With Suva and Kovial leading the Imperious troops to pick off archers, his last efforts were not in vain. The remainder of Kyouin's army fell apart and began to flee, most getting picked off by enraged and wounded dragons in their retreat.

His attempted landing turned into more of a tumble from the sky. His legs refused to hold him, and he crashed into the ground. The dragons in the outer circle could do nothing but move out of his way as he slid to a stop a few feet from the inner circle. A few riders worked their way to him through the onlooking dragons. Siniva lay there, his breath straining in and out of his lungs. The mere thought of rising from this spot was too exhausting to contemplate with any seriousness.

Suva rode up next to his head. She leaned over from her saddle to place a hand on his brow. "Don't worry, my friend. We'll make sure Raine is cared for if I have to drag a dragon there myself."

Siniva's weak chuckle turned into a bloody cough. When the coughing stopped, he exhaled and closed his eyes. He needed to rest.

*

For the next several days, Darkin oversaw the management of the battle's aftermath. Dragons that were not too injured to fly agreed to help bring in human healers from outside of the area. Those healers stitched and bandaged wounds for humans and dragons both. They also brought with them salves and tinctures to help with pain and healing. Tinctures he appreciated as he ran about with the three broken ribs Theruses had given him. By comparison to many, he had gotten off lucky.

Those wounds beyond the scope of the healers were tended by the Song Dragon, Rythis, and Shelith, the Life Dragon who had flown in with another group of dragons after the fighting ended.

Management also meant overseeing the hunting and destroying of undead still lingering in the area spreading illness with their corruption. That process was mostly successful, though they never found Ryche and his grizzly trophy.

It also meant finding people to help clean up the mess and begin the process of restoring Elysium and the city of Imperious. Raine's grandfather, Lornin, was by his side through most everything. The man was confident, sensible, and silent most of the time unless he had something truly constructive to offer. He had disappeared for a while after they found Avaline in the throne room. His once wife begged for an end to her undeath, and he insisted on striking the blow that ended her misery. Then he had gone away somewhere for the rest of that day.

Darkin appreciated the unspoken pact they seemed to have over the first several days not to speak of those they had lost or those who still danced on the edge of death. There was too much to be done to dwell on those things. Suva and Kovial had entered into that unspoken pact as well, and they threw themselves into the work of cleaning up with an intensity that bordered on madness.

Darkin did the same.

They could not find Vinya's family, so the girl stayed in Elysium. She helped where she could. When she could not help, she followed Darkin around and mimicked his every move. He rather enjoyed his little shadow. She gave him hope where he might have had none. When she got tired, she would wander off. He would often find her taking Prophet for a walk. A young girl and a deadly daemon. A most unlikely pair.

Most daemons had dispersed. The concentration of daenox that had drawn them here and made them as strong as they were had been forced out. The big daemon-cat Raine called Prophet stayed. Outside of his walks with Vinya, the beast never left Raine's side. He even slept in her room, often with Vinya curled up against him. Darkin hoped the beast knew something the rest of them did not.

Like Siniva, Raine hung in the balance. Healers and dragons had done everything they could for the two. The rest was up to time and the strength in them. For Siniva, he could barely imagine the mighty dragon not pulling through, especially with Nakia nursing over him like she had been. Every time he checked on them, Nakia was at his side, tending to his needs and regaling him with the mishaps and adventures of Fools Errant. Darkin did not know if Siniva could hear her, but he was probably having some unusual dreams if he could.

Raine, however, looked so frail and delicate lying in the bed they had placed her in. She looked like someone who could not possibly fight her way back from the injuries she had sustained. Darkin hated seeing her like that, so he kept himself very busy. When she woke, because he refused to believe that she would not, it would be to something better than the chaos they had found when they got here.

aine woke alone. Alone and in the palace, which terrified her for a few seconds, until she noticed how subdued the daenox was. The dragon web, by comparison, was quite strong, suggesting that the dragons were still in the area. For now, she was too weak to delve too deeply into the powers, so she pulled back and took inventory of herself.

That was a mistake. The pain that seemed to radiate to every extremity of her body only intensified when she focused on it. Her entire right arm and shoulder were bound in some sort of immobilizing device that fastened around her neck and chest. There were bandages wrapped around much of her torso as well, and her lower right leg was also immobilized. There were stitched wounds in her other arm and one she could feel running down from her ear to the corner of her mouth. They were wounds she had sustained fighting Theruses. A fight that felt more like a distant nightmare and dream wrapped in one.

Was I really a dragon?

In this state, just sitting up proved a daunting and painful experience. She was carefully wiping tears from her cheeks with her usable hand when the door opened. Prophet and Vinya sprinted in.

"She's awake," Vinya squealed with glee, flouncing

in place with more energy than Raine could fathom at that moment.

Much more dignified, Prophet walked up to Raine and sat, then inclined his head in what almost seemed a bow. She touched the crown of the beast's head with one hand, and he started to purr. For reasons she could not quite understand, Raine started to cry.

That was how she was when Darkin walked in.

In a gesture that was strangely similar to the daemon-cat's, Darkin sank down to his knees next to her. He opened his mouth, staring up at her with eyes that spilled over. Raine moved her hand to his cheek. He took it gently in his hand, kissing her palm as if the nectar of life were in it. She found the tears coming faster now. They stung as they ran over the stitched wound in her face.

"How do you feel about women with scars?" She managed to get the words out, though the movement of her mouth pulled at the stitches.

His smile made her heart ache.

"Nothing could make you less beautiful to me. Besides," he managed a tremulous smile, "you earned every scar you wear, and you should wear them with pride. No other warrior or dragon could have fought that battle so well."

She grinned. It hurt a lot. "You really are a soldier, aren't you?"

His smile was stronger this time. "You shouldn't be moving around."

Raine's pain level agreed with him, but she could feel a tugging through the dragon web now. The dragons knew she was awake, and they were summoning her. There were a few things she needed to know before she faced them.

"What of Theruses?"

"Dead."

She gave a slight nod, wary of unnecessary movements. She had thought the Death Dragon was dead before they hit the ground, but it was comforting to hear it confirmed. "And Kyouin?"

"Also, dead."

There was some guilt in the relief she felt then. It was wrong to be so comforted by the death of another, but she could not help it. "What of our... allies?" She said allies because she could not get the word friends out without her throat constricting.

Darkin lowered his gaze. "Some dragons died. Siniva has not woken yet. His injuries were severe."

The pain in her chest and neck then had nothing to do with her injuries. "Anyone else?"

"Rakas died to save me. I don't..." his voice cracked, and he paused to swallow hard. "I don't understand why he did it. It doesn't..."

Her finger on his lips stopped him. His tears ran quietly down his cheeks. More tears stung the wound in her cheek.

"I understand," Raine said softly. "He knew how much I care about you. He did it for me. He did it for my father."

Darkin hung his head, and she let him be there for a time. The tug through the dragon web was becoming more insistent though, so she touched his face again, getting him to look up at her.

"The dragons want to see me."

Darkin's expression hardened. "They can wait. You're in no condition to be walking around."

"I need to go."

He stood, perhaps hoping to assume a position of authority. "Your right side is in pieces. Your arm is broken. Your leg is broken. You have a broken collarbone and several broken ribs. That's just the big stuff. Rythis healed your internal injuries as best she could. You're a mess."

That explained why she hurt so much. "Then I'm going to need your help."

Darkin stared at her, his mouth slightly open as if he could not quite fathom her obstinance. Prophet stood up and edged in between him and Raine. The daemon-cat positioned itself next to her. Raine took hold of the spines on its shoulder to try to help herself up.

"Horse farts," Darkin grumbled. He pushed the daemon-cat aside, earning himself a growl, and moved in to help Raine stand. "Do you remember the part about the broken leg?"

He was right. She was in no condition to be trying to move around. Prophet placed himself on her injured side, perhaps to add support if she should need it. She suspected she would be more likely to put her eye out on one of his boney spikes if she fell, but she could not bring herself to shoo him away.

Vinya grinned up at them. "Are we going to see the dragons?"

Raine nodded.

Darkin made a somewhat disgusted noise that seemed to emanate from his throat and sinuses at the same time.

The dragons of the council, along with a few others, were kind enough to meet them in the meadow behind the palace. Even with that courtesy, getting there was a special kind of torture. About halfway there, Lornin appeared. He and Darkin hunted down a chair and a few more guards to lift it. They carried Raine the rest of the way to the back of the palace in this somewhat undignified fashion. She insisted, despite the agony, on walking through the door with their help to go face the dragons.

The magnificent dragon she knew from the web was R'Gos, stood at the center of a half circle of dragons waiting for her. His expression was not one of sympathy or benevolence.

"Dragon-Child," he inclined his head slightly in acknowledgment.

"R'Gos," she answered with a similar gesture. If he wanted her to bow, he would have to wait for several weeks more healing.

"The council—"

"Wait!"

The shout came from beyond a line of dragons. R'Gos glanced that way with an irritable flick of his tail.

A pale blue dragon with gold tips on her wings and ears moved slowly through the line. When she stopped, she lifted one wing, and Siniva came forward in his human form, leaning heavily on Nakia.

Raine smiled so big that she feared her stitches might pull free. Despite the pain, she could not stop smiling while Siniva and Nakia made their slow way inside the ring of dragons where the council members waited. She wanted to run to him and throw her arms around him, but now was not the time, and she was confident she could neither run nor throw her arms around anyone at the moment. For a few seconds, she wondered why he arrived at a council of dragons in human form, then Nakia smiled at him, a smile with none of the usual sarcasm in it, and she understood.

When they stopped, the two inclined their heads briefly to R'Gos.

R'Gos narrowed his eyes at them before turning back to Raine. "The council must make a judgment. You took the form of a dragon and killed Theruses. It is forbidden for a dragon to kill another of its kind. You must face suitable punishment for your crime."

Cold panic burst through Raine's chest, making her dizzy for a few seconds. Before anyone else could speak, a clarifying rage burned through that panic. "A dragon you would have had to put to the same trial for Vanuthan's death," she countered.

"His punishment was ours to decide," R'Gos deflected.

The rage burned hot and pure, helping her think past her pain. "And now you will decide mine as if I were a dragon. Under any other circumstances, I doubt you would afford me such honor."

"She has a point." Siniva's statement was punctuated by a weak cough.

"With her spirit, perhaps she deserves to be tried as a dragon." This came from one of the other council members. A big charcoal dragon the web identified as Colvan.

R'Gos gave the two dragons withering stares, but he hesitated a few minutes before speaking again. A few minutes that Raine spent desperately missing the chair they had left inside. Darkin was there, however, a strong presence supporting her by her good arm. Even with that, she was not sure how much longer she could stand here like this. Hopefully, Darkin would catch her before Prophet did.

"You are right. Under no other circumstances would I afford you the honor of recognizing you as a dragon." He inclined his head slightly, pausing for a few more thoughtful seconds. "Theruses committed many crimes beyond killing Vanuthan. His punishment would have been death. A punishment he would not have submitted to willingly. With as many wounded and dead as we have already suffered in this, I should perhaps thank you for taking his life."

Perhaps you should.

Raine bit her tongue, trying hard not to say what she was thinking. If R'Gos was waxing benevolent, she needed to let it happen.

"The best I can do is forgive your crime. I have other responsibilities to attend. When you are ready, we will meet again to discuss alliances and decide on a new leader for this kingdom." R'Gos inclined his head again. As he turned away, he leaned close to the pearlescent white dragon. "Rythis, ease her pain."

Then he started walking away, but he paused once more and looked back, his long head a massive shadow profiled in the bright light of the setting sun. "Rest, Dragon-Child. You will need your strength."

The Song Dragon was heading their direction, as were Siniva and Nakia.

"I'll get the chair for you," Lornin stated before walking away.

Darkin leaned close to her. "I think I just fell in love with you a bit more, watching you tell off the leader of the dragons."

Raine smiled at him. Blast it if smiling did not hurt the worst.

"Kiss me, gently, please."

Darkin obliged, leaning in to place a gentle kiss on her lips and lingering there for a few seconds. "I thought I lost you."

"Me too," she answered.

"That's enough," Siniva grumbled.

Darkin moved back. Prophet growled at the dragon-man until Raine shushed him.

Siniva gave the beast a sour look. "I don't understand why that thing insists on following you still, even into a meadow full of dragons."

Nakia chuckled. "Is it such a mystery. You're still following her." She turned to Raine then. "Hydra was getting restless in the stall, so we put him out in one of the pastures. He seems to be enjoying racing around with Thorn."

Raine gave a reserved smile of gratitude. Her face had taken about all the smiling it could for now. Lornin set the chair behind her, making sure it was stable before nodding for her to sit. He was a man of few words in all her parents' memories. It was good to see that some things never changed. She sank into the chair with Darkin's help. Prophet curled next to it, and

Vinya sat down in the grass with the daemon-cat.

Rythis settled herself on the opposite side from them.

"We will have to figure out what to do about the lack of a ruler in Imperious," Darkin stated.

Rythis shushed him. "Those are the tasks for the healthy. Raine is not ready yet. Go tend your troops, little warrior, and I will tend to your love."

Darkin stared at her. Raine could almost see him trying to decide if 'little warrior' was an insult or a compliment.

"Don't call her his love," Siniva objected.

"Off with you too," Rythis ordered, turning her calming gaze on the Fire Dragon. "You have healing to do and your own love to tend you."

As the others turned away, Raine settled painfully back into the chair. "Do you think we should finish building the sanctuary in the forest? We could do it in Vanuthan's honor."

"Hush," Rythis soothed. "There will be time for such things later."

Raine closed her eyes, feeling the daenox and the dragon web falling into balance as most of the dragons left the clearing. The lingering warmth of the fading sun eased her to the edge of sleep as Rythis sang softly next to her. Her good hand slipped down off the arm of the chair to rest on Prophet's head. Vinya's fingers touched hers as she rested her hand on his head as well. There was still much to be done, but Rythis was right, that was work for after she had healed some more.

*

Raine settled on one of the branches of the Mother Tree, letting her parents' memories flood her. She could see her father through Myara's eyes and her through his. They were both smiling, their happiness simple and pure. Raine smiled too.

Those who hurt you both are gone now, and I will see Elysium restored.

It would not be the same as it was when they lived here. There were daemons in the world now, and dragons, along with the powers that sustained them. The dragons had made her a tool to be used and forgotten. But she had proven herself to be more than that.

"How is my little Dragonkin?"

Darkin climbed agilely up into the tree, his injuries healed now. He stood on one branch and leaned into her, stealing a warm kiss that kindled a fire through her.

"I'm much better. Rythis said my body heals like that of a dragon."

He sank down on a nearby branch. "Are you ready to deal with the council?"

They would meet soon with a council of dragons and human leaders to discuss who would sit on the Elysium throne and how they would deal with the few bands of undead still roaming the region. Some said there was a band of undead gathering behind an undead warrior on an undead horse who carried around a rotting head on a spear. She was not worried about Ryche. R'Gos was harder to handle than any undead, but she had surprised the dragons before, and she meant to go on doing so.

She closed her eyes, remembering for a moment what it was like to spread her wings and leap into the sky. After a few seconds, she opened them again and smiled at him. It was getting less painful to do so now that the stitches were out.

"I am."

THE END

ACKNOWLEDGEMENTS

As always, there are many people in my life I'm leaving out here for brevity sake. All of you are still very important to me and I am always thankful for you.

There have been a lot of changes in my life over the last few years and some of you have stuck beside me through this in ways I will never forget. This list includes my dearest friends and family to my heart, Rick and Ann, my most ardent supporter, my mom, Linda, and my incredibly devoted and patient partner, Kai.

I want to thank Missy and Marla, who took a chance and joined my group of beta readers for this project. Your input was truly appreciated.

Lastly, I want to acknowledge Robert, my excellent cover artist, and Brian, my editor and formatter. I value the work you do and the people you are. Thank you for working with me and being a part of this process.

AUTHOR BIO

Nikki started writing her first novel at the age of 12, which she still has tucked in a briefcase in her home office. She now lives in the magnificent Pacific Northwest tending to her sweet old horse and a wondrous cat-god. She feeds her imagination by sitting on the ocean in her kayak gazing out across the never-ending water or hanging from a rope in a cave, embraced by darkness and the sound of dripping water. She finds peace through practicing iaido or shooting her longbow.

•

Thank you for taking time to read this novel.
Please leave a review if you enjoyed it.

•

For more about me and my work visit me at
http://elysiumpalace.com.

OTHER NOVELS by NIKKI McCORMACK

CLOCKWORK ENTERPRISES
The Girl and the Clockwork Cat
The Girl and the Clockwork Conspiracy
The Girl and the Clockwork Crossfire

FORBIDDEN THINGS
Dissident
Exile
Apostate

THE ENDLESS CHRONICLES
The Keeper

ELYSIUM'S FALL
Dark Hope of the Dragons

STANDALONE WORK
Golden Eyes

www.ingramcontent.com/pod-product-compliance
Lightning Source LLC
Chambersburg PA
CBHW070744120726
47910CB00001B/164